FIRST CONTACT

It was about the size of a man, but bluish. It had a streamlined shape and a fluked tail. And jointed arms that ended in . . . hands. But Zeke knew of no seagoing creature with hands.

Then he saw Natalie. One arm was immobilized and she was trying to fight off the monster with the other. Even using legs against a creature without them, she wasn't having much luck getting free. It tried to hit her, but the water slowed its swing and robbed it of force. Somehow the thing detected Zeke's approach. It quickly turned its attention away from Natalie . . . and Zeke saw its face.

It was like nothing Zeke had ever seen on a human. This was the face of an alien who lived and moved in the sea.

The creature produced a device, a device that was obviously a weapon, and pointed it at Zeke. . . .

If you and/or a friend would like to receive the *ROC Advance*, a bimonthly newsletter featuring all the newest and hottest ROC books and authors, on a complimentary basis, please fill out this form and return it to:

ROC Books/Penguin USA
375 Hudson Street
New York, NY 10014

Your Address
Name _____
Street _____ Apt. # _____
City _____ State _____ Zip _____

Friend's Address
Name _____
Street _____ Apt. # _____
City _____ State _____ Zip _____

STARSEA INVADERS:
FIRST
ACTION

by

G. Harry Stine

A ROC BOOK

ROC
Published by the Penguin Group
Penguin Books USA Inc., 375 Hudson Street,
New York, New York 10014, U.S.A.
Penguin Books Ltd, 27 Wrights Lane,
London W8 5TZ, England
Penguin Books Australia Ltd, Ringwood,
Victoria, Australia
Penguin Books Canada Ltd, 10 Alcorn Avenue,
Toronto, Ontario, Canada M4V 3B2
Penguin Books (N.Z.) Ltd, 182–190 Wairau Road,
Auckland 10, New Zealand

Penguin Books Ltd, Registered Offices:
Harmondsworth, Middlesex, England

First published by Roc, an imprint of New American Library,
a division of Penguin Books USA Inc.

First Printing, August, 1993
10 9 8 7 6 5 4 3 2 1

To:
Cindy and Paul

No defects to be afraid of, for the double shell is as firm as iron; no rigging to attend to; no sails for the wind to carry away; no boilers to burst; no fire to fear, for the vessel is made of iron, not of wood; no coal to run short, for electricity is the only mechanical agent; no collision to fear, for it alone swims in deep water; no tempest to brave, for when it dives below the water it reaches absolute tranquility. There, sir! that is the perfection of vessels!

—Captain Nemo,
Twenty Thousand Leagues Under the Sea
Jules Verne, 1874

The submarine has been the subject of considerable research and development by the major powers ever since World War II. Major breakthroughs in hull design and methods of propulsion have revolutionized naval warfare . . . New technology continually upsets the delicate balance of power . . . The submarine seems destined to be the most influential and versatile warship of future navies.

—*The Encyclopedia of Sea Warfare*
Oliver Warner et al., 1975

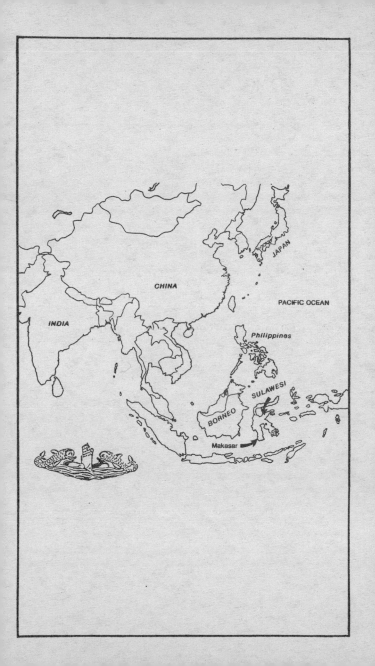

1

"Captain, this is the OOD. We have a masdet contact. A big target, sir."

Captain William M. Corry reacted immediately in his usual cool, collected manner. He'd been engrossed in studying the action options available to him when the U.S.S. *Shenandoah* reached Makasar. This was a typical power projection mission for a carrier submarine such as the *Shanna*. However, the matter of the missing American businessmen, factory supervisors, and their families put a different spin on it. The American embassy in the Sulawesi capital had been unable to get the local government of the island republic to act. So Corry knew it wasn't going to be a straightforward mission.

He fingered his terminal and saw that LCDR Natalie Chase, the boat's Navigation Officer, was the OOD on this watch.

Then he activated his intercom, composed himself in a fraction of a second, and replied, "This is the Captain. Do you have any specifics on the target, Commander?"

No one would guess that William M. Corry had always had a speech impediment. He was a stutterer. But he always had it under control. The boat's Medical Officer, CDR Laura Raye Moore, knew it, and the fact was part of his naval medical record. But everyone else believed that Corry's habit of pausing before speaking was merely the Commanding Officer's way of carefully considering what he was going to say before he said it. This was truly the case, of course.

Corry wasn't upset at being interrupted for a mere masdet contact report. Every one of the crew knew that Chinese Han class boats might be in these waters. The East Indies had become one of the twenty-first-century's hot spots because of conflicting interests. West World's investment in the resources of the Indies was hotly contested by the growing interests of China. And the equally growing sea power capabilities of the People's Republic of China could mean that the huge Asian nation was involved in whatever was going on in Makasar.

"No, sir," Chase replied. "Only that it's big. And it's extremely quiet. Present course looks like zero-two-five toward Bone Bay. The target will cross our bow in approximately thirty-two minutes at its present vector. Range unknown. The only other data I have on it are somewhat unbelievable. Its apparent displacement is on the order of fifty thousand tons."

Corry decided the contact was no Chinese Han boat.

"Is it closing, Commander?" the CO of the *Shenandoah* asked with some anxiety. An unknown IX that large running silently submerged could be a threat, given the international political situation in the Orient.

"Not at the present time, sir," the nominal Navigation Officer of the SSCV (see Glossary) replied, then went on to explain, "I wouldn't bother you except we've never seen any submersible this large on the mass detector before."

"You were quite correct in notifying me, Commander. I'll be right there. Carry on. Steady as she goes. Come to Condition Two," Corry told her.

"Come to Condition Two. Aye, aye, sir!" Chase repeated the order back to him.

The Flores Sea wasn't a nominal operational area for the United States Navy's Rivers class aircraft carrier submarines. And it was the first time one of the

390-meter ships, the only ones large enough to mount the new underwater mass detector, had been in these waters. The OOD had properly notified the Commanding Officer of unusual data from a new underwater sensing system.

Fifty thousand tons submerged put the target in the same displacement class as the SSCV-26 U.S.S. *Shenandoah*. Yet, none of the other four Rivers class ships were in this region. That's why Corry had received orders from CINCPAC to divert from air exercises at the Kwajalein Naval Air Training Area.

Whatever the target was, it merited Corry's immediate attention.

Bringing the ship to Condition Two was a prudent move. It wouldn't awaken the one-third of the ship's crew who were asleep, and it wouldn't put the Air Division or the Marine Battalion on alert, only on notification. But it would double the on-deck complement.

The intercom came alive with a quiet female voice repeating, "Hear this! Hear this! Come to Condition Two! Condition Two!" Back in the twentieth century, the United States Air Force had learned that people paid more attention to a female voice. The U.S. Navy had been late in accepting this finding, along with others like it.

Corry slipped his wireless neurophone over his left ear and "heard" the same voice repeating the message in his head. Its electronic signals interfaced in a noninvasive manner with Corry's nervous system.

Unlike many other members of his crew, Corry was a traditionalist in dress. He never wore the blue poopie suit affected by submarine crews. He buttoned the collar on his khaki shirt and tightened his black tie. When he left his cabin, he was only a few steps from the control room.

The ten-meter-by-ten-meter control room or bridge was only one reason the crew's nickname for the *Shenandoah* was "the starship." Even Corry believed it

would make a better starship bridge set than those
appearing on some of the television space operas.

"Good morning, Captain," the small, slender, dark-
haired woman officer greeted him as she arose from
the command chair.

"Good morning, Commander," Corry replied. Protocol required this exchange, but Corry didn't greet
the other officers and crew members on duty. "I have
the con."

"You have the con, sir," she repeated back to him
but only stepped aside. He hadn't relieved her as OOD.

"Please give me a status report, Commander."
Corry knew what it was, but he asked anyway.

"Sir, the ship is at one hundred meters, course
three-one-zero true, speed forty knots. Position zero-
seven-slash-four-niner-slash-two-five south, one-two-
zero-slash-five-zero-slash-zero-three east. Mister Leighton will update the nav computer on the hour, sir."
Chase confirmed the reading on the digital telltale
above the helm position.

Corry could see it. To an outsider, this procedure
might seem redundant. However, on a submarine
nothing is done without purpose. No one assumes anything. The digital readout could be in-op.

In the twenty-first-century world of automation, artificial intelligence, nanotechnology, neuroelectronics,
and robotics, the United States Navy continued to rely
on people. Naval technology was a tool to help people
to do what the CNO wanted them to do.

Corry was joined almost at once by three other officers—a full Commander, a pretty naval aviatrix wearing the pips of a Commander on her flight suit, and
a stiff Marine Major.

"Good morning, Captain!" The spare, trim CDR
with black hair and piercing blue eyes was dressed as
Corry in khaki shirt and slacks with a properly knotted
black tie.

"Good morning, XO," Corry replied to CDR Arthur E. "Zeke" Braxton.

"A big target, sir. Could the Chinese have something bigger than the Han boats?" Braxton asked, looking at the masdet remote display.

"I'm reluctant to assume anything at this point, XO. Or to do anything right now. Let's see if we can get some more data on this IX masdet contact first," Corry advised his Number Two officer and paused.

"Good morning, Captain," said the attractive young woman who had accompanied the Executive Officer. "Sir, I can launch two Sea Dragons within a minute of surfacing if you need to have a look," she said.

"Good morning, Commander. Yes, you might ready those planes, Terri," Correy told her, addressing CDR Teresa Ellison by her nickname. As the ship's Air Officer and CAG, she was an aggressive, shit-hot pilot in her own right. She was not known for being hesitant to initiate action of any kind. Her air combat experience confirmed that. Corry often had to temper her tiger juice with a bit of caution. He was glad she was aggressive. However, sometimes that trait had to be channeled properly. "Right now, I want to find out if the masdet has spotted a humping big whale or something we should be worried about."

"Good morning, Captain," Marine Major Bart Clinch spoke up. "Sir, it could be a Chinese submersible landing craft. Intel has been hinting at it."

"Good morning, Major. I appreciate your input. I've seen the OPNAV reports, too."

"Nothing to get your water hot about, Bart," Zeke remarked to him.

"You'd better hope my water's hot if it's something we have to force to the surface and board," Clinch growled.

"And it could be a false target, Bart," Braxton reminded him, trying to maintain the friendly, cooperative nature of interchange between officers in an SSCV. This was tough to do. The boat's people were different from the "brown shoe" aviation department. Both were different from the gung-ho Marine battalion.

It made for interesting times. And it either created outstanding diplomats among the officers of the *Shenandoah* or they were gracefully reassigned elsewhere in the Navy on the recommendation of the Captain.

"Zeke's right," Corry added, also trying to play the diplomat. He would rather be a diplomat than a martinet. Although the captain of a naval vessel was still the last of the absolute monarchs, Corry preferred leadership by example to command by terror. "The masdet is so new that we could be getting an anomalous reading from it."

"Why not ping the target and see what it does?" Terri suggested. That remark was typical of her aggressive approach to life.

"I may do so after it crosses our bow. And I'll let it do that without changing our course or depth. If the target is indeed another ship, we're the burdened vessel here," Corry observed thoughtfully. To him, any unidentified underwater object that moved was a "target." The old submariner's adage said that a ship is either a submarine or a target.

However, Corry was concerned about this "anomalous" reading from the newly installed mass detector. For the first time, a submarine had "underwater eyes" other than active or passive sonar. The new mass detector sensor somehow made use of the arcane principles of modern physics. For fifty years, the science johnnies at White Oak Laboratories had dreamed of it and tried to figure out how to make it work. Now the tech-weenies had brought it to reality. The "masdet" could detect the presence of an object having a density different from its surroundings. How it accomplished this was still more classified than even the Captain of the *Shenandoah* was privileged to know. Only the "Special Sensors Officer," LT Charles Ames, knew anything about the masdet.

So the Commanding Officer of the carrier submarine—itself an impossibility a hundred years before—said to his XO, "Zeke, you might want to stick your head into the masdet compartment and monitor this firsthand for me, please. I'll listen for you on N-fone channel Tango."

Braxton unclipped the N-fone from his ear and adjusted it. "Aye, aye, sir." And he was gone.

"Stick around, Terri," Corry told his CAG. "You might as well watch this develop here."

"Yes, sir!" Ellison really wanted to jump up to PRIFLY and get two of the Black Panthers ready to launch when and if the *Shenandoah* surfaced. But she was in contact with her Flight Deck Officer, LT Paul Peyton, by N-fone channel. That would have to do for now.

So Corry and two of his division officers sat in the control room and watched.

Most naval operations—especially those that involved SSCVs—meant a lot of waiting. Even on the attack boats engaged in interdiction or defensive/offensive actions, people had to wait while ships and targets moved. Sometimes it was a matter of watching and waiting to see what the other vessel was doing.

The masdet made it easier. It would have been the best of all worlds if the masdet could provide range data on targets whose mass was unknown. In this instance, mass had to be inferred from gravitational effects on the environment. That made ranging problematical based on secondary effects.

Masdet signal has changed, sir, was the quiet N-fone report to Corry from his XO in the masdet compartment.

Corry touched his ear lobe and activated his N-fone transmitter. *What's happening, Number Two?*

He heard Zeke's "voice" in his head. *Mister Ames says the target has surfaced. The target's situation at the air-water interface has changed the signal.*

Number Two, has it detected us?

I don't know, Captain. It hasn't pinged us.

Any other acoustic signals?

Mister Goff says negative, just the usual organic noises out there, sir.

Terri Ellison also heard the exchange on the N-fone channel. "Captain, if it's on the surface, let my chickens go take a look at it!" she insisted verbally.

When Corry didn't answer immediately, she urged, "Sir?"

He shook his head. "No, Terri, not if it hasn't spotted us. And I don't think it has."

"But, sir!" Her hands were clenched into fists.

Terri Ellison revealed again the aggressive side of her personality in an environment that left Corry no alternative but to deal with it at once. He didn't like to do that on the bridge. He would rather have talked to her privately afterward.

Corry had never regretted the Navy's decision to allow women in combat leadership roles. He knew that the sort of warrior woman who was good enough to perform well under combat conditions was far more aggressive than most men. Rudyard Kipling had been right about the female of the species.

So he gently laid a hand on Terri's shoulder, as a father would calm an agitated daughter, and gave her a firm but gentle reprimand. "Commander, our orders are to proceed to Makasar and carry out a power projection mission. Our presence must convince the Sulawesi government to take some action concerning the continual disappearances of American citizens on the island. I don't intend to chase unidentified masdet contacts. We'll continue to monitor the contact as long as we can. However, we'll not deviate from our mission unless that target takes aggressive action against us. Understood?"

Ellison relaxed, but the fire didn't leave her eyes. She paused before replying in a crisp manner, "Yes, sir!"

Captain, the contact is gone! came the report from Zeke Braxton in Corry's ear. *Like it took off and went airborne!*

Sure enough, the masdet monitor screen showed no mass anomaly out there any longer.

Corry rose to his feet. "Order stand down from Condition Two, Commander," he told the OOD. "Resume the watch. You have the con. Steady as she goes."

"Aye, sir. Stand down from Condition Two. Steady as she goes. I have the con," the petite officer repeated. The Chief of the Watch responded the same way when she passed the order on to him.

"What's the ETA for Makasar?" Corry then asked her.

Natalie Chase stepped over to the navigational displays where the Assistant Navigation Officer, LT Bruce Leighton, was on watch. It didn't take her more than fifteen seconds to respond, "Fourteen hours and ten minutes, sir. I expect we'll be able to surface inside the harbor mole at sunrise as planned."

Corry touched his ear again. *Zeke, I want to see the division officers and chiefs in the main wardroom at ten hundred hours for a final scrub of the operation tomorrow.*

Aye, sir! I'll plan to close the Dolphin Club at fourteen hundred hours then.

Corry turned to the Air Officer. "Terri, you're on edge today. Take an hour before the Oscar briefing and work off some steam. Find someone to take some lumps with you in the gym."

"Is that an order, sir?" Ellison snapped back deferentially.

"No, just a bit of advice. The time for aggression may come tomorrow."

Ellison wasn't a bit offended or even set back by that remark from the Commanding Officer. She had pre-combat jitters, and she knew it. The crazy masdet contact hadn't helped, coming some fourteen hours before surfacing at Makasar. She also knew what would take the sharp edge off her jitters if either Bart or Zeke was available. And if the Dolphin Club stayed open long enough after the Papa briefing.

Commander Teresa Ellison was a twenty-first-century Amazon.

2

The wardroom was too small to contain all the officers of the U.S.S. *Shenandoah*. The various divisions aboard the carrier submarine—ship, air, and Marine—included ninety-eight officers. An auditorium would have been needed for all of them to participate directly in the Oscar briefing. Even a carrier submarine didn't have that much space.

So Zeke Braxton had arranged for only the department heads to be in the wardroom. The other officers convened in their respective division wardrooms and were present by means of the ship's interactive closed-circuit television system.

Thus, the twelve department heads had plenty of room. The main wardroom was their nominal mess and recreational facility in any event.

All twelve came to their feet as Captain Corry walked in.

"Please be seated," Corry told them easily. Life in a carrier submarine was in many respects like that in the previous counterparts of the SSCVs: the nuclear submarines and the aircraft carriers. The officers and crew were a team. They served aboard the *Shenandoah* with pride because they'd been carefully selected from volunteers. Each person was an individual, of course, and personal differences often surfaced. But the social lubricant of manners and protocol kept friction at a minimum.

Discipline was tight, but morale was high. It had

been a long time since Corry had taken serious disciplinary action at a Captain's Mast.

However, he knew that all wasn't sweetness and light in the ship. Unofficial reports got to him. Most minor infractions of naval or ship's regulations by members of the crew were handled by the CPOs. The officers, especially the department heads, usually took care of the few that occurred among them.

Troublemakers or misfits somehow were transferred out early. Captain Corry had never denied a request for transfer. He and the others sincerely believed that if a person didn't want to serve in the *Shenandoah*, that person shouldn't be in the ship, period. CINC-PAC and DCNO(PERS) agreed, operating with the philosophy that they could find the proper place for everyone in the Navy.

The U.S.S. *Shenandoah* wasn't always a happy ship. But she was a good ship, a taut ship, and a ship in which people wanted to serve.

"Let's keep this short," Corry suggested as he took his seat. "We've got to make an eight-hour time shift from Zulu to Sulawesi time, which is Zulu-plus-eight. Everyone should try to get some rack time tonight and be up in time to get a good breakfast before we surface. Zeke, please proceed."

Braxton stood up and moved to the display. As he touched the keypad, a three-dimensional image of the Makasar harbor and environs appeared in the holo tank on the wall. He faced the officers and the pick-ups, stating what everyone knew: "American citizens and diplomatic personnel have been reported missing in the Republic of Sulawesi. The government of Sulawesi has shown reluctance to take measures that would improve the security of American citizens who are in the country for diplomatic, business, or recreational purposes. The number of missing Americans has increased in the past three months. The Captain of the U.S.S. *Shenandoah* SSCV-Twenty-six received Execute Order Five-Three-Alpha-Zero-Four from the

Secretary of Defense through CNO and CINCPAC. This Execute Order directs the Captain to proceed to Makasar, surface the ship within sight of the city, launch air cover or search aircraft if necessary, airlift a contingent of ship's Marines to the United States embassy, assist embassy personnel in their efforts to locate the missing American citizens, and take whatever steps are necessary to ensure that American citizens wishing to leave Sulawesi are evacuated by ship or by air."

Braxton looked around, then turned to the image of Makasar in the holo tank. With his laser pointer, he emphasized his statements as he went on, "The real purpose of this mission is power projection. Its objective is to prod the government of Sulawesi to establish measures that henceforth will protect the lives of Americans and other nationals in that country. The secondary objective is to assist our legation in Makasar in obtaining information, if possible, concerning the disappearance of over a hundred Americans. As is nominal on a power projection mission, the unstated objectives resemble those of the policeman on the beat. Although we have excellent communications with CINCPAC and CNO, the Captain has broad authority to modify the objectives and take action as conditions warrant."

Everyone knew what the XO meant. The United States didn't throw its weight around on the international scene. Nor did the politicians and high brass micromanage a mission such as this. The naval establishment had confidence in Captain William M. Corry. Otherwise he wouldn't be in command of the *Shenandoah*.

The unsuspected was always a factor in a mission such as this.

The officers and the crew knew it. That's what added spice to otherwise boring exercises and port visits.

Once the ship had surfaced, they could be called upon to perform a wide variety of missions.

Braxton looked at LCDR Mark Walton, the First Lieutenant of the ship and therefore head of the Ship Division. "Commander, your input, please." Zeke sat down.

Walton was all business. He was a serious man intent upon progressing up the line of command. He wanted his own SSCV command some day. So he took care not to make mistakes, if possible. However, when he did make mistakes—as everyone did—they were little ones and he owned up to them promptly. He used his own laser pointer to illuminate locations in the holo tank display.

"Sir, the ship will proceed at suitable clearance depth to this point one thousand meters off the south end of the Makasar harbor," Walton briefed them. The department heads had thrashed out the overall ops plan and then done the detail staff work required for their area of responsibility. This Oscar or Orders briefing was the final scrub of the plan. Each division chief presented part of the overall. If any officer had any question or saw any inconsistency in the ops plan, this was the final opportunity to speak up. Once the Oscar brief was finished, the ops plan was firm, subject only to opportunistic changes authorized at the moment by the Captain. "The ship will then be surfaced at twenty-two-twenty Zulu time, which is sunrise at Makasar. All hands will be mustered to Condition One, General Quarters, Battle Stations. Deck guns and missile launchers will be at immediate standby in the event of incoming fire. We do not anticipate incoming because of the element of surprise. We will not drop anchor initially. The ship will immediately be configured for flying off. Questions?"

Walton looked around, but it was apparent he didn't expect questions. He was right. He usually was.

"Thank you," Zeke told him and looked at the Air

Group officer. "Commander Ellison? The air operation, please."

CDR Teresa Ellison bounced to her feet. She didn't use a laser pointer. She didn't have to. And Terri Ellison paid little attention to formal protocol. That was typical of the "brown shoe" aviation part of the Navy, anyway.

Another Air Group trait was extensive use of jargon:

"Victor Alpha Six Five will have a flight of four Tigers over the ship by twenty-two-thirty Zulu. They will be configured for Fox Four. They will maintain CAP until bingo fuel. They will be replaced then by the standby flight of four Tigers and return to trap. If necessary, we are prepared to fly off the entire attack squadron for any air assault mission that becomes necessary. If that occurs, Victor Papa Three Five will assume the close-in CAP mission configured for Fox Three. Victor Charlie Five Zero will fly off the Marine contingent no later than twenty-two-forty-five Zulu. Escort for Victor Charlie will be provided by a flight of four Tigers from Victor Alpha. We will maintain active air ops until ordered to recover and stand down. We will establish and maintain airborne communications with Makasar TRACON in order to preserve airspace safety. I don't want our hardware to tangle with any hypersonics or commuters. We do not anticipate any operations involving Makasar International Airport except possible emergencies where my hardware can't make it back to trap. A Victor Charlie COD ship will be available as a Sucker, and Marine will provide a security detail to accompany the R-and-R crew. Any questions?"

There was one. Gunnery Officer CWO Joseph Weaver raised his hand. "Commander, you sound like you expect to get shot at."

"Guns, I always expect to get shot at when we surface and fly off unannounced in a new harbor," Ellison snapped.

"Well, Commander, if you get shot at, we'll get shot at, too. And we'll shoot back just like you will," Joe Weaver reminded her. He was a stocky, pugnacious-looking little man, one who had come up through the scuppers and now wore the shoulder boards of a Chief Warrant Officer. "Somehow in the planning, ma'am, we neglected to coordinate freaks."

"You have our transponder squawks, Guns."

"Yes, ma'am, I do. But I've seen transponders go toes-up by being shot out, too. We need to be able to talk to your airplane drivers JIC," Weaver pointed out deferentially. He had no problem with women in the Navy or in ships such as the *Shenandoah*. But regardless of their rank, he always treated them as ladies; that was part of his upbringing. He also had the polite approach of a swabby who has become a warrant the hard way.

"Guns, check with me after the Oscar brief," Communications Officer LT Ed Atwater told him. "In this environment, the aircraft drivers will be using standard UHF. No need for the security of SWC."

"Thank you, sir."

"Any others?" Ellison wanted to know.

There weren't.

Braxton pointed a finger at the Marine battalion commander. "Major Clinch, please give us the Marine operational overview."

Bart Clinch stood up and walked to the holo tank display. He picked up the laser pointer. There was a no-nonsense aura about him. When he spoke, it was in a loud voice of command. "Company Alpha under Captain O'Bannon will board a Sea Dragon at twenty-two-hundred Zulu. Company Alpha is armed and configured for a FIG mission. When the ship is surfaced, Victor Charlie squadron will transport Alpha to the American embassy." He aimed the pointer beam at the image of the embassy in Makasar. "Although command of the unit remains with me, Captain O'Bannon will report to the commander of the Marine guard detail at the embassy and stand by there for further orders. However, Sergeant Major McIvers and I will be with Alpha. Company Bravo under Captain Gamble will stand by in full readiness to board the Sucker aircraft in FIG configuration and provide security for any R-and-R operation. Company Charlie under the command of Captain Miller will stand ready in reserve with FIG configuration. Semper Fi, sir!"

Clinch didn't expect any questions. That was obvious from his stance and the way he snapped off the laser pointer and set it down firmly and noisily on the low lectern.

But he got a question.

Zeke Braxton phrased his remark as a question, but it was apparent that the XO didn't like what he'd heard. One element of the Marine plan had changed since the Papa briefing. Apparently, it had been changed unilaterally by Clinch. "Major, may I ask why you now intend to accompany the embassy unit rather than remaining in the CIC?"

Braxton was a challenge to Clinch in many areas. And vice versa. The Marine officer believed the XO was a "systems warrior," a man who never came face to face with the enemy but fought from the cockpit of a Sea Devil attack plane or the control room of a submarine. Clinch liked to be out in front, leading men. As a Marine, he knew he was in many ways subservient to the naval officers under whom he served. He tried to compensate for that. He wasn't always successful. It was more difficult to do this with Braxton who not only outranked him but also competed with him for the off-duty attention of Terri Ellison.

"Because I lead from the front, Commander!" Clinch told him forcefully.

"In this mission plan, Major, your battalion is spread among three tasks. Unity of command takes precedence, as you agreed in the Papa brief," Zeke reminded him.

"Which I do not exactly like. I am a strong believer in concentration of mass." Bart Clinch was a pugnacious and stubborn man, even when he found himself caught trying to do something he thought he could get away with because he was the Marine battalion commander.

Corry acted at once to halt any further confrontation between two of his division chiefs. He would have a word with Clinch when this mission was over. At that moment, however, he behaved in the manner consistent with his position as the master of a vessel. "Major Clinch, until such time as it becomes necessary to alter the operational plan, please conform to that plan. I want you here in CIC with me."

Clinch knew better than to pursue the matter any farther. It was his own fault that he'd been caught, and he knew it. He privately cursed his penchant to be somewhat of a braggart. Try as he might, the blood lust of pending combat, albeit a low probability in this mission, had triggered his deep-seated fears and he'd responded with a bit of bravado and machismo. Bart Clinch was outwardly a brave man; deep inside he harbored the fear of death that's in any person, even a warrior. But warriors aren't supposed to reveal they're afraid of dying.

"Yes, sir!" was all that Clinch could say. However, he said it stiffly and with no hint of resentment in his voice. Regaining his composure, he shot a quick glance around the wardroom and at the video pickup. "Any other questions? No? Very well." And he sat down.

Braxton stood up. "Are there further reports or status briefings?"

Silence from a hundred officers.

Braxton then gave some orders of his own. "The watch lists will not be changed. But we will time-shift eight hours ahead at fourteen-hundred hours Zulu. Lunch will become midrats and breakfast will be available at surfacing-minus-three hours. Don't let your people skip breakfast. The Dolphin Club will be closed at fourteen-hundred hours until further notice."

He then addressed Captain Corry. "Sir, we are ready in all respects to carry out Execute Order Five-Three-Alpha-Zero-Four." And he sat down.

That was Corry's signal to rise. An Oscar briefing was just that: brief. It was the final scrub of an operational plan. It was brief because it had been thoroughly worked through beforehand. In many ways, it was a formality. And thus it was done in a formal setting.

Not all of the activities in the *Shenandoah* were formal.

"This mission," Corry told his officers, "doesn't appear to be hazardous. But be forewarned. Everything we do has some hazard associated with it. And it could become hazardous. So don't get complacent. We're not planning to get into a shooting fracas, but you're authorized to shoot if shot at. In short, we're here in a typical naval action of this century: power projection and protection of lives and property. So let's do our usual outstanding job of doing what we're paid to do. XO, dismiss the officers!"

He turned and walked out.

"Dismissed!" Zeke repeated to the attendees.

Terri Ellison grabbed Bart Clinch by the shoulder and led him aside.

"Dammit, Bart, did you take idiot pills today or something?" she snapped at him.

Had a man said that to Clinch in that manner, that man would have been dog meat at some future date, especially if Clinch outranked him. But Terri Ellison was a lady, in spite of her aggressive approach to life. Clinch had been raised by a male chauvinist father in a Marine family; thus, he treated women differently. Besides, he had a thing going with Ellison and he wanted that relationship to improve with time. And he knew what she was referring to. So he replied, "A proper briefing always includes the planned location of the unit commander, Terri."

"Maybe. But, hell, if you wanted to go ashore with the first wave, you should have just done it," she admonished him. "You know the drill: Forgiveness is easier to get than permission."

"Yeah, you taught me that."

"Why didn't you apply it to something beyond the two of us?"

"Never occurred to me."

"A hell of a lot of things don't occur to you, Bart. If you'd been a pilot, someone would have hit your minus-x in your first furball." Terri Ellison was a sierra hotel pilot. Although her squadron command had been the famous VAW-113 "Black Hawks," Ellison had given the patrol tactics of the aerial Navy a new meaning. She'd used her defensive missiles in a highly offensive manner during naval exercises. Her unorthodoxy had paid off when her plane had been jumped by two Burmese fighters off Rangoon. She had a confirmed kill on her record.

Clinch shrugged. "So I'll keep a cool stool and a hot pot. You busy? I can order us up midrats."

"I've got work to do," Ellison told him bluntly but didn't specify.

"See you in action, then," he told her, turned, and left the wardroom.

Terri knew her Air Group was ready. She didn't have to mother-hen it. So instead of leaving the wardroom for her quarters, she poured herself a tumbler of bug juice rather than the usual strong, black, traditional Navy coffee. Then she sat down at a table where Zeke Braxton was talking with CDR Ray Stocker, the Engineer Officer.

She wanted the companionship of men right then. She always did just before a mission. It helped her calm her own anxiety.

"Other than that, XO, we're in good shape," Stocker was telling Braxton.

"Well, your trouble sounds minor," Braxton agreed. "As quickly as I can, I'll let you know when you can put your froggies in the water to defoul that steam slot. Do you also want to look at the one on the starboard aquajet?"

Stocker shook his balding head. "None of the diagnostics show anything wrong to starboard. So if it ain't broke, I'm not going to waste time fixing it. I want to be able to move the ship, even at half thrust."

"Make it so, Ray," Zeke told him.

"Ray, did Benedetti get that portside cat working right?" Terri asked as the engineer officer stood up to go.

"I saw the squawk sheet, Terri. I also saw the fix sheet. If it isn't fixed by now, let me know," Stocker remarked.

"Don't worry. I will."

"I don't worry." He left the wardroom.

"Two hours," she said briefly to Braxton.

Zeke knew what she meant. If the Dolphin Club was to close for all hands, it meant all hands indeed. Neither Terri nor Zeke needed a special place, however.

"Terri, even though we're not in Condition One yet, I'm officially on duty. In fact, as XO, I'm supposed to be on duty all the time," he reminded her. Then he added gently, "And so are you."

Terri Ellison sighed. "Oh, Navy, my Navy, what we sacrifice for you so we can be the world's freedom police! Later?"

"Of course. But we've both got work to do now. And it could get rough before it's finished."

She paused before asking rhetorically, "Why do we risk a multi-billion dollar ship just because of some missing Americans?"

"Have you forgotten, Terri?" Braxton said. "The native people of the East Indies were cannibals until the Europeans moved in on them. And they may have reverted to their ancient ways. Not that it will make you sleep any easier, but . . . Excuse me, I do indeed have work to do."

3

When viewed from the sea, the city of Makasar was picturesque. The first rays of the rising sun shone down the streets that ran eastward from the harbor through the old city with its rows of seventeenth-century houses built by the Portuguese. Old Fort Rotterdam, erected by the Dutch to guard the chief port and largest city on the island of Sulawesi, faced a large green square surrounded by other government buildings.

The city was once called Ujung Padang by the Indonesians. The Sulawesi began using its original name, Makasar, when the island broke away from Indonesia several decades before.

Because of its location off the major sea lanes of the twenty-first century and the natural beauty of the Maros hills to the east, Makasar had become a minor tourist center earlier in the century. However, it had now slipped into genteel decadence with a few old hotels along the pristine beaches north and south of the city. Some people still came here to get away from the vibrant world of the market economies. But not many. Makasar was really a city a century in the past, a place that progress had bypassed for more profitable venues.

Makasar's harbor facilities were artificial. They'd been built up over the centuries by the various European nations that had controlled the island and the East Indies. The most recent additions had been put in by various Chinese companies operating out of Singapore. A way point was needed in the Indies, a place to serve as a hub for both inbound and outbound materials and commodities.

As a result, Makasar had a harbor mole to protect its anchorage, wharves, and slips. The largest freighters could safely enter its harbor. Indeed, on that bright, new morning, its harbor and piers were occupied by ships. They had been loading coffee, copper ore, some iron ore from the southern part of Sulawesi, and the ancient export of the Indies, gums and spices. Or unloading LTSL modules of imports for transshipment to other smaller ports on Sulawesi and other islands.

The port of Makasar hadn't come awake and active yet. Not a breath of air disturbed the mirrorlike surface of the harbor.

Without warning, the mirror was shattered as a hulking black shape surfaced, water running off its curved upper surfaces.

Within a minute, the Stars and Stripes ran up the flagstaff at the stern, identifying the nationality of the visitor.

Side hull hatches opened to reveal the ship's gun armament—radar-directed multibarrel close-in defense guns and multibarrel air defense missile tubes. The planar array radar antennas on the hull were uncovered as other hatches opened. At once, the radars began to probe the skies with their electronically scanned beams of energy. They looked carefully in those sectors from which kinetic-kill weapons might come. Those orbital weapons, particularly ones belonging to China and India, were the only real threat to the surfaced vessel in that part of the world at that moment.

The flight deck hatches fore and aft opened. Even in the light of dawn, it wasn't possible to see into the black spaces beyond.

The forward topside flight deck lift disappeared into the hull. Three minutes later, it arose, carrying with it four F/A-48 Sea Devil single-seat VTOLs. Each carried the brightly colored Navy air insignia and the distinctive black-edged orange stripes of the VA-85 "Tigers" squadron on their sides.

Some sailors and docksiders in the sleepy harbor woke up when the U.S.S. *Shenandoah* surfaced. Everyone came awake when the four attack planes lifted off.

In the electromagnetic spectrum, the local air traffic control frequencies came alive.

"Makasar Approach, this is United States Navy Tiger One, flight of four, departing the submarine carrier *Shenandoah* in the harbor. We intend to orbit over the ship in a racetrack pattern at a thousand meters. Over."

"Uh, United States Navy Tiger One, Makasar Approach. Uh, flight in racetrack pattern over the harbor at one thousand meters approved. Uh, please have your flight commander squawk four-one-zero-one."
Only two people were on duty at Makasar International Airport's Terminal Radar Approach Control and the airport control tower. Traffic was zero at this time of day. It wouldn't pick up until later in the morning when the packet delivery aircraft landed and smaller planes took off to make deliveries around Sulawesi. The two subsonic passenger/cargo flights from Jakarta and Darwin weren't due in until noon.

The ship-to-shore frequencies were also busy.

"Makasar portmaster, this is Captain William Corry, commander of the U.S.S. *Shenandoah*."

The message had to be repeated twice more before an answer came. Apparently, as planned, the arrival of the *Shenandoah* in the harbor had caught everyone by surprise.

"American submarine in the harbor, this is the Makasar portmaster. Please give me your official designation again. And please tell me your intentions."

"Makasar portmaster, this is Captain William Corry, United States Navy. The United States Navy carrier submarine U.S.S. *Shenandoah* is presently surfaced in your harbor. This is the Commanding Officer speaking. We are here on a friendly port call."

"Then why have you launched aircraft?"

"Don't you enjoy an air show now and then, sir? Our pilots are in contact with Makasar Approach Control. They do not intend to land in Sulawesi. They have made your local air authorities aware of their intentions. This is standard international protocol, sir."

"Captain, uh, do you intend to allow your sailors to come ashore?"

"Affirmative, and they will be on peaceful liberty. Will you please inform your customs and immigration personnel? Before I allow my personnel to go ashore on liberty, however, we will be airlifting a contingent of United States Marines in to our embassy. This is in response to a request from our ambassador for additional security protection, sir."

The portmaster was looking out the window of his apartment-office. He couldn't help seeing the black hull of the *Shenandoah* dominating the harbor. So he decided he couldn't and wouldn't stand in the way of the United States Navy making a port call. If the Sulawesi government authorities objected to this sudden and unannounced visit, he'd let them handle the situation. His job was to run the harbor in a smooth, efficient, and safe manner. And to collect the various taxes imposed on incoming and outbound ships.

Abdul Haras Subandrio was a prudent man. His ancestors had lived in Makasar for generations. His forebears had worked with Portuguese, Dutch, Japanese, British, and Indonesian officials and military men. He had a good civil service job. He intended to keep it.

Also, it was the first time Subandrio had seen an American carrier submarine. It was the biggest naval vessel he had ever seen. Every other ship in the harbor seemed only a skiff or a junk alongside this huge, high-tech monster.

He picked up binoculars and looked over the ship. He easily saw its gun tubs uncovered, its missile tubes ready, and the activity on the topside flight deck. Eight F/A-48 Sea Devils were being raised from below and positioned topside, ready to take off once their pilots had boarded them. In the air over the ship, four F/A-48s circled in slow hover. He couldn't see what was happening on the secondary lower flight deck. In fact, he didn't know it was there until he saw a large four-engined C-26 Sea Dragon transport emerge from the forward opening. As he watched, it skimmed the harbor at less than fifty meters altitude and headed toward the American embassy ashore.

"Better part of valor and all that . . ." Abdul Subandrio muttered to himself, unconsciously echoing a British merchant captain he'd met years ago when he was new on the job. And he sent a silent prayer of thanks to Allah that he was in a position where this didn't threaten him directly. He was current on all his payoffs to various government officials. And they didn't have an excuse to fire him for following international protocol.

"Welcome to Makasar, Captain!" he therefore said to the Commanding Officer of the *Shenandoah*. As he quickly checked the harbor chart on the wall, he went on, "You may land your liberty boats at Pier Ten. Do you need a pilot?"

"No, thank you, sir. We're preparing to drop anchor if this location is suitable to you."

Subandrio wasn't going to suggest that Captain Corry move the carrier submarine. It was out in mid-harbor. There it was so large and prominent that no other ship could help but see it. And plenty of room existed around it for even the biggest ship to pass it. "Oh, that's just fine where you are, Captain!"

"Thank you, sir. I'll send my Executive Officer by

to see you later today. He'll take care of any harbor fees and the like."

"Oh, no problems there, Captain! You are a visiting warship and you represent the United States of America. I will make no harbor fee charge for such a diplomatic visit."

Captain William Corry knew that. But he'd made the offer anyway. As he cut the connection, he remarked quietly and deliberately to Zeke, "So far, so good. When the Marines reach the embassy, Phase One will be complete. That lowers the anxiety level."

"Captain, I've made contact on the STS with the Chargé d'affaires at the embassy," Zeke Braxton told Corry. "He's getting the Ambassador out of bed to talk to you."

Corry had to smile. "So we got the diplomats out of bed again, eh? Let me talk to the chargé," he said as he reached for the handset held by Braxton. "Who is it?"

"Lowden Manwaring," Zeke said.

Corry took the handset and spoke into it, "Good morning, Mister Manwaring. Sorry to get you up so early, but we've learned that the best time to initiate a power projection mission is to surface in the harbor at dawn."

A cultured voice came through the receiver to Corry. "Yes, Captain, I realize that. We knew you were coming, of course. But we didn't know precisely when you'd get here."

"A company of United States Marines is on the way, Mister Manwaring. They should be over you shortly," Corry reported. "How soon can I speak with the Ambassador?"

"This is Ambassador Abbott," a new voice dripping with Deep South drawl suddenly came over the ship-to-shore radiotelephone circuit. "Glory be, son, you sure picked a right early time of day to drop in for a visit!"

Zeke was listening on a separate handset and suppressed a chuckle. He'd checked out Abbott's background. The man was a mid-aged South Carolina judge who'd helped deliver the state to the President in the last election. It amused Zeke to hear the Ambassador refer to Corry as "son." Corry was two years older than the Ambassador, who obviously hadn't done his homework.

"Good morning, sir!" Corry said brightly, carefully controlling his breathing to eliminate any tendency to stutter. "That's the way we conduct power projection missions. Intimidation of the local government officials by means of surprise. Makes them start to wonder what other magic tricks we have up our sleeves. As for the populace, most of them indeed look on us as wizards who control powerful magic. Which we do. Now, Mister Ambassador, can I have an hour of your time today so we can discuss in private the details of this mission?"

"Of course, suh! I am at your disposal! But why don't you come ashore for lunch at the embassy and bring your leading officers with you?"

Corry had the man's image in his mind. Abbott was a rotund man who enjoyed good food and warm weather. The reports were that he and his family hated the Washington area. They'd had to spend several months there during the winter following the election. Abbott had called in a lot of presidential IOUs to get an assignment to a tropical embassy because he was more comfortable in such a climate. Abbott sweated a lot but preferred that to cold weather.

"I'll fly you, Captain!" Terri Ellison immediately offered.

"Anything to log some time, Terri?" Zeke ventured to ask in a light manner with a smile.

"After weeks in this ship, you're damned right!"

"Captain, I'd like to go with you, sir," Bart Clinch snapped. "I want to check the disposition of Alpha Company around the embassy grounds and inspect their bivouac."

Corry held up his hand without looking at any of them. He went on, speaking into the handset, "Thank you, Mister Ambassador. We'll fly in, of course. I'll have my XO inform you as to who will be accompanying me. Does noon sound like a good hour?"

"When the noon balloon goes up around here, Captain, the sippin' whiskey comes out," Abbott's voice told him. "Sounds fine. You-all come on over about then, and we'll have the red carpet out for you!"

William Corry was a stickler for manners and protocol. Inwardly, he wondered what sort of image Ambassador Robertson Earl Abbott III was giving the United States of America here in Sulawesi with his Good Ol' Boy Down Home approach.

Maybe it didn't matter in this out of the way new nation.

On the other hand, maybe America's image was at the heart of the problem of missing American citizens. Maybe Abbott's laid-back attitude gave the impression that Americans wouldn't bother to investigate nearly a hundred disappearances, including those involving children of tourist families.

A few disappearances were expected here and there around the world. The Department of State expressed regrets to American families in most cases. But it was too expensive and also nearly impossible to chase down Americans abroad who got themselves into trouble and thus disappeared. Or those who disappeared on their own volition for personal reasons.

But Sulawesi had been the site of nearly a hundred disappearances. That was a number State couldn't ignore. It was hard enough keeping it out of the news media, but media attention would have exacerbated the problem right then.

If this power projection mission didn't produce results, then State and Defense had no compunction about unleashing the world press phalanx on Sulawesi. It was the final move in the non-war game. Only big countries with repressive totalitarian governments and massive military machines would withstand a news media onslaught on top of a military and diplomatic power projection push.

When Abbott and Corry had finished speaking, the Captain turned to his officers at the CIC console in the control room. "Zeke, the luncheon meeting at the embassy will be our next Papa briefing. I want you there. But it's also more than that. So see to it that I have all the boatswains and side boys allowed by custom. We'll be watched by the Sulawesis. Terri, you can log your time. Get your Double Coconuts Sea Dragon COD ship ready to depart at eleven-forty-five local. And I want the airborne section of your CAP to fly escort for us. Power projection and image. And, yes, Major, you and Sergeant Major McIvers can join us. Bring along a platoon from Charlie Company as a security guard. We won't carry small arms, but your Marines will."

"Uniform, sir?" Zeke asked.

"What we're wearing is suitable. It's an understatement as well as working gear," Corry decided. "We should appear businesslike. When we visit any Sulawesi personnel on their turf, then we'll pop for dress whites, swords, and gold braid with medals."

SCPO Carl Armstrong, the Chief of the Boat, was listening quietly where he sat next to Braxton. He spoke up when the Captain paused. "Sir, I know this is a power projection mission. But as soon as you feel it possible, I think shore leave would be a good thing to authorize. The crew hasn't been ashore since we left Pearl three weeks ago."

"None of us have, Chief," Corry pointed out. "And a lot of us have families we'd like to call when we get ashore. But business first."

"Aye, sir. Just thought I'd bring it up."

"It's your job, Chief."

Submarine duty, even on a carrier submarine, wasn't much different than it had always been—long cruises, out of touch with the world for weeks or months, confined to the interior of a ship without being able to walk the decks for a breath of fresh air, long separation from families and loved ones, and seeing the same faces and places day after day. However, unlike the SSBNs of the previous century, the SSCVs had to surface to launch and recover their aircraft, their primary defensive and offensive weapons. And once surfaced, the SSCV was as vulnerable as any other ship to the sophisticated weaponry of the twenty-first century.

But apparently not as vulnerable as nearly a hundred Americans who fate was yet unknown.

Insofar as Corry was concerned, learning what had happened to them, getting them back if possible, and repatriating any other Americans were his top priorities beyond his unstated ones: the protection of his ship and crew.

The mission had gotten off to a good start. He hoped it would continue that way. But he didn't count on it.

4

"A most delightful meal, Mister Ambassador," Corry remarked as he finished the ice cream from the silver goblet.

"Yes, it's much appreciated, sir," Terri added. "A welcome break from shipboard food."

The luncheon at the American embassy took place on a covered veranda overlooking a broad sweep of neatly trimmed green lawn. Two groves of trees at the far end framed a view of the Makasar harbor. The lawn was almost as large as the park that fronted Fort Rotterdam on the left. Ellison's C-26 CAG Sea Dragon was parked off to the right on another sweep of lawn. And the U.S.S. *Shenandoah* dominated the harbor view.

"Well, I suspected as much," Ambassador Abbott replied expansively, touching his lips with the linen napkin. "I served as Stores Officer in the old SSN *Spokane,* so I know something about submarine food. We used to walk around on top of the canned goods until we ate them. Didn't have room to store them except on deck. Made it tough for tall men."

"We eat well in the *Shenandoah,* sir," Braxton corrected him gently. "But we're always delighted to dine ashore."

"I figured that the fresh air alone would delight any submariner," was the observation of LCDR Herbert K. Hewitt who served as both the military and naval attaché at the embassy. Braxton knew Hewitt, and so did Ellison. The lanky officer had been one of Zeke's

41

plebes at the Naval Academy, and he and Terri Ellison were classmates. The twenty-first-century Navy was probably much like that of the late nineteenth century: a few thousand officers who couldn't help knowing each other. However, the stigma of the Navy as a "country club" wasn't part of the current image.

"The Marines are happy anywhere," Bart Clinch observed. "That's part of what it takes to be a Marine."

"Why, Bart, I thought your Marines were happiest when they're on liberty in a place like Saigon right after payday," Terri replied with a twinkle in her eyes and a smile on her lips.

Clinch looked sharply at her. "Marines are men through and through," he reminded her, perhaps unnecessarily. He liked Terri. She was aggressive. He liked aggressive people, especially women. "But that doesn't mean they're going to be happy if they end up with AIDS or any form of the Back World crud . . . especially when I get through with them! The Marines are strong advocates of the Dolphin Club."

This talk was about internal ship affairs insofar as Corry was concerned. It had no place at a legation luncheon. But Corry didn't reprimand his subordinates in public. Instead, he changed the subject by placing his napkin alongside his empty dessert dish and remarking in serious tones, "Let's get down to business, Mister Ambassador. You know why we're here."

Abbott nodded, his heavy jowls shaking as he moved his head. The weather was warm and Abbott was sweating. He didn't seem to mind it. The man was exactly as Corry had pictured him from descriptions and photos in the data base and the previous STS phone conversation.

The Ambassador was suddenly serious. "Damned right! Maybe with your help we can get these Sulawesi bureaucrats to do something."

"I understand they haven't been helpful at all," Braxton put in.

"Sorta like hitting the wall at Talledega, son. We just can't get through it."

"It's terribly frustrating to handle tourists whose children have disappeared," remarked Lowden Manwaring, the chargé d'affaires. "Even worse when a young couple has one of them disappear."

"Any change in the count lately?" Zeke asked.

Hewitt shook his head. "One-oh-four. Sixty-eight of them less than twenty-one years of age."

"Mister Ambassador, what is your evaluation of what's going on here?" Corry asked, fishing for any additional information that might provide another piece to this puzzle. "Is it slavery? Or cannibalism?"

"We sure don't know, Captain," Abbott told him directly.

"Certainly you've speculated."

"We have," Manwaring put in with a bit of pique in his voice. The man was a pedant. He lectured. After all, he'd been in Makasar ever since the embassy had opened more than a decade ago when the island split from the Republic of Indonesia to become Republik Sulawesi. He believed he knew what he was talking about. To a large extent, he did.

Corry let him lecture because the Captain of the *Shenandoah* was a listener.

The chargé went on, "Back in the hills, some natives live the same way their forefathers did. They've eschewed progress and refuse to come into the twenty-first century. When the Muslims from India brought Islam to Sulawesi, the tradition of cannibalism declined but didn't disappear. The Portuguese and Dutch eventually managed to stop the slave trade in the nineteenth century but they didn't eradicate cannibalism."

"At least, they made slavery unlawful and prosecuted those they caught perpetrating the custom," Hewitt put in.

Manwaring used the interruption to take a breath. It was apparent to Corry that Manwaring and Hewitt didn't like one another very much. Hewitt was obviously serving his time, waiting for a naval diplomatic slot to open up in Washington. He was on that career path.

The chargé went on, "Both of these detestable human institutions had diminished by the end of the nineteenth century. However, the traditions lingered on among those people still out in the hills. The Indonesians were just as strict as the Dutch. But since Sulawesi split from Jakarta's rule, the local authorities don't seem to have the ability to stem what I consider a rising tide of both slavery and cannibalism."

When the long-winded Manwaring stopped for breath, Braxton said, "Let's take those one at a time. Slaves mean a slave trade, a slave market, and transportation of slaves. Are there any reports of any of these?"

Abbott shook his head. "None. I haven't been here as long as Lowden, but I haven't gotten any reports of these things."

"And my contacts have been instructed to look," Manwaring added.

"I have some pretty deep contacts in the Sulawesi defense establishment, and I haven't found anything even when I went looking," Hewitt admitted.

"So that leaves cannibalism," Corry mused.

"Not a pleasant subject to consider right after lunch," Terri told them.

"A most detestable alternative," Abbott added.

"It's not necessarily cannibalism that's at the core here," Manwaring put in quickly. "Could also be a resurgence of head-hunting. Most Americans equate head hunting with the island of Borneo to our northwest. But the same sorts of people existed on Sulawesi, too. So I haven't eliminated that from my consideration."

Corry believed differently. The captain of the U.S.S.

Shenandoah was a well-read man. Sometimes he didn't have much else to do in a submarine. The same was true of CDR Zeke Braxton. The two men exchanged many books during a cruise. So Corry asked, "Any tribal warfare going on back in the hills?"

Hewitt shook his head. "General Helamahera is pretty gung-ho on keeping the lid on the hill tribes. It's his only excuse for maintaining a defense establishment."

"Is he afraid the Indonesians might try to take back the island?" Clinch said.

"Not at all, Major. The people in Jakarta figured that trying to keep Sulawesi in the Indonesian empire wasn't worth the cost," Hewitt explained. "No oil here. And Jakarta doesn't know how to handle the iron and copper that was discovered after the split. I'm sure that if a situation arose where it would be cheap, fast, and easy to take back Sulawesi, Jakarta might try it. But right now, those three factors don't converge."

"My estimate, then, is that it's unlikely we're confronted with head-hunting," Braxton put in. "That's a warrior trait."

"Head-hunting tribes don't go searching for victims," Corry explained. "They kill strangers who stumble into their midst, or they do their ritual with opponents they've killed in a fight."

"Mister Manwaring, I think we can rule out head-hunting," Zeke concluded.

"No, I wouldn't. I'd keep it as a low-probability cause." Manwaring was wary. In addition, he didn't like being contradicted. "It could be a factor."

"So we'll revisit that possibility if we have to, Low," his boss told him. "The preponderance of vanished children and young people suggests we're looking at something else. Could be due either to cannibalism or to slavery, perhaps in that order of priority."

"Precisely what I was thinking," Corry said in agreement.

"So the nasty question we have to ask is this: Who's hungry out there?" Clinch ventured to say.

"No one," Manwaring told him firmly. "No one starves here. In the interior it's easy to live off the land."

"Cannibalism could be a real driver if the result is considered a delicacy," Clinch continued to pursue this. Of all the top officers of the *Shenandoah,* he would be the most likely to do so. It didn't turn his stomach. He looked on it as just another distasteful custom of inferior types of human beings. An egalitarian Clinch wasn't.

"Yes, but on the other hand I've read that it tastes very much like pork. How's the pig supply on Sulawesi?" Zeke wanted to know.

"As I said earlier, no problem, Commander," Lowden Manwaring reminded him. "Food is plentiful in Sulawesi. And the Sulawesi people have a varied diet. Basically, Sulawesi is a Muslim country except for the few tribes back in the hills who practice the old religions. Muslims have no proscription against specific foods. And we have a very large Chinese minority here who are not Muslim; they're Taoists or Buddhists."

"Captain," Zeke spoke up as an idea struck him, "if the food is as good and varied as it was at lunch, I'll ask Lieutenant Allen and the Supply Department to do a little reprovisioning while we're here."

Corry nodded but held up his hand in a gesture of caution. "Make certain that Doctor Moore and her Medical Department people are along when they do."

"Yes, sir. That's SOP," Zeke said. Cholera, shigella, and other nasty mutated organisms often infested local foodstuffs. An epidemic of any disease in a submarine is a serious problem.

Corry sighed, composed himself, then went on, "You received a copy of the DOD Execute Order that brought us here. We're tasked with helping you learn the reasons behind these disappearances, providing additional security for the embassy if necessary, and helping Americans leave Sulawesi."

"But that really isn't why you're here, of course," Hewitt remarked knowingly. "Basically, it's power projection."

"Current slang for good old gunboat diplomacy," the Ambassador corrected his naval attaché. "And I'm a real believer in that. I need something to shake the hell out of the politicians and bureaucrats here."

"What's your basic problem with the bureaucracy in this matter, Mister Ambassador?" Corry asked.

"Right down at the roots, it's the fact that life is cheap here. It always has been. The birth rate exceeds the death rate. Someday, the Sulawesi are going to run up against the Malthusian Limit," Manwaring said pedantically.

"So no one in Makasar gives a damn about a hundred foreigners who've disappeared over a period of six months," Abbott went on and then began to unload on these fellow Americans. "They've probably had ten times that many Sulawesis drop out of sight. If they know how many are missing. And I don't think they do. They're so damned laid-back that they hardly keep track of anything. At least, that's the case with our foreign aid funds. No one can tell me where that money's been spent or for what. Hell of a situation. And Congress just keeps insisting that it be sent. I'd rather see it spent in parts of South Carolina where it sure as hell would do some good!"

Manwaring looked pained. It was obvious to him that the former federal judge and campaign contributor wasn't really following the official line from the State Department. However, Manwaring had served many ambassadors in his career. He knew that few of them really understood what State was trying to do. The belief still persisted in Old Foggy Bottom that a Back World nation like Sulawesi could be yanked through the industrial phase into the market/service era of the twenty-first century by the continual infusion of money for building infrastructure. The fact that it hadn't worked for over a hundred years didn't count. It *should* work, so those who believed in the principle continued to support it because they hoped it *would* some day.

State hadn't been one of those government bureaucracies that had caught it in the chops by the big changes at the turn of the century. State, the oldest of the cabinet departments, was deeply steeped in tradition and old ideologies.

So was the United States Navy, of course.

But in a different way. In the Navy, tradition was retained because it worked; it made life safer and jobs easier. The State Department never had to worry about having an embassy sink.

"Keeping in mind that I'm restricted by naval regulations as well as rules of engagement, precisely what would you like me to do?" Corry asked, knowing what the answer probably would be.

He wasn't wrong. "I was hoping you could tell me, Captain," the Ambassador admitted. "I've got pressure from Washington to do something because my superiors are getting hassled by members of Congress, who are being bothered by their constituents. State is worried that this will somehow break open in the news media during an otherwise slow period. That's when the news-hawks start picking up little stories like this they've ignored because of more interesting stories."

"We're used to handling the mundane tasks of an embassy," Manwaring put in. "Visas to visit the United States. Emigration permits in cooperation with the Immigration and Naturalization people. An occasional bit of work getting an American visitor out of some sort of trouble with the Sulawesi authorities. And the usual trade tasks involving pro forma invoices and letters of credit and such. Those are rather straightforward. We can go right to our procedures manuals. The same holds true of official visits . . .

although it's been a long time since any high-ranking American has visited here. A very long time indeed."

"And keeping track of the Sulawesi defense situation involves some spook work occasionally. But it's nothing that a naval attaché doesn't know how to handle," Hewitt added.

Corry knew the embassy also carried out tasks that hadn't been mentioned. One did not speak about intelligence work.

It didn't seem to Corry that much intelligence work had been done in this matter.

In addition to power projection, that was one of the reasons the *Shenandoah* was in Makasar harbor.

Plus the fact that Corry had been covertly asked by Naval Intelligence to check into the "spook side." Something wasn't right, and the intel community didn't know why. Naval Intelligence wanted to get the answer before DIA and CIA did. Corry didn't like to become involved in the Washington spook scene. But when Naval Intelligence comes forward with a request, a prudent Commanding Officer will gladly comply.

Captain William M. Corry knew he was going to have to take over the leadership of this mission. The luncheon meeting had confirmed this suspicion. Neither the Ambassador, the chargé, nor the attaché was capable of dealing with it. The Navy had suspected this. So had the NSC. So they'd put a man on the scene who could. And he was backed up by military power if necessary.

But Corry wasn't being permitted to sail into Makasar harbor with guns blazing. Dewey at Manila he wasn't supposed to be.

And he had to do it without tipping off the three embassy people. He didn't know how much of what was going on would be leaked to others. If it was just an internal turf foray in the American government, that was one thing. But Corry was worried that something was going on between someone in the embassy and the Sulawesi government officials. If that was the case, treasonable behavior was involved.

The puzzle didn't make sense yet. If it was cannibalism, who was doing it? Were any Sulawesi officials involved? Embassy personnel? American businessmen? Or were Americans being somehow paid off to look the other way while the Sulawesis or some of the Chinese did things that should not be done in the civilized world?

Because he'd received a carefully worded request for help from Abbott just then, Corry took command easily and gracefully. "Very well, Mister Ambassador. Here's our initial plan. My request to you is to do nothing differently. We'll set in motion some traps to garner either information or people. Or both."

"Good! You have my full cooperation! Keep me informed! What do you intend to do?" Abbott asked.

Corry didn't dare let Abbott know that the Commanding Officer of the *Shenandoah* would be playing by ear until he got more information. It was a matter of "when in ignorance, try anything and you'll be less ignorant." So Corry covered.

"Our activities will not affect your day-to-day operations, Mister Ambassador. We'll maintain the fiction that we're here on an ordinary port call. I'll certainly accept your offer of assistance and I'll keep you informed." That was sort of an open-ended promise on Corry's part. He actually hadn't promised anything. He hoped it didn't sound that way. There were times when he had to be stealthy. This was one of them.

"First off, I need to establish security ashore for our liberty parties. Major Clinch, please move your operational headquarters to the embassy here and arrange for suitable communications with the command center in the ship."

"Yes, sir!" Clinch snapped.

"I'd like to meet with top officials of the Sulawesi defense establishment at their earliest convenience," Corry went on. "I want to propose some joint air-ground exercises in cooperation with their ground and air forces."

"I believe that's a reasonable request within the bounds of the SEATO protocols," Manwaring murmured.

"Herb, contact General Helamahera and set up a meeting," Abbott instructed his military attaché.

"Yes, sir!"

"Let it be known that we intend to spend several weeks here," Corry went on. "We'll conduct some joint exercises, give our crew some well-earned liberty, and reprovision."

"The local merchants will like that!" Abbott observed. The infusion of some American money into the economy of Sulawesi was always welcome. It helped Abbott, too.

On the short flight back to the *Shenandoah*, Zeke Braxton admitted, "Captain, I've seen you manipulate the shore establishment before. First time I've watched you handle diplomats, however. Judging from my experience, I'd venture a guess that there's more to this mission than has been revealed to the officers and crew thus far."

Corry just looked him straight in the eye and replied, "There is. And it's time I let the three of you in on it. See me in my quarters thirty minutes after we trap."

5

In a submarine, day and night don't exist. Deck watches keep their own day-night cycles. The ship itself runs on Universal Time, also known as Zulu Time, just like international airlines and most space habitats. This time-cycling is broken, however, when the ship surfaces and remains in port for more than a daily cycle. This disrupts the circadian rhythm of two-thirds of the crew and affects in a lesser way those of the remaining crew on watch.

And that was the first matter CDR Zeke Braxton had to take care of when the embassy party returned to the U.S.S. *Shenandoah*.

It was then 1400 hours in Makasar.

In the ship, it was 0600 Zulu.

Zeke was used to having his circadian jerked around. As XO, he was always on duty. But right then his body told him it was oh-dark-thirty in the morning, not mid-afternoon.

He felt awake, but irritable with some moments of mild, momentary confusion. Circadian asynchronization had other symptoms, but these two were what Zeke felt right then. This was no condition for the Number Two officer of a carrier submarine to be in.

So he went down to sick bay.

CDR Laura Raye Moore was off duty, but CPO Nat Post, the Chief Pharmacist Mate, was standing watch.

"Posty, I have a request."

"Don't even bother to ask, Commander," Post told

52

the XO as he looked the officer over carefully. The pharmacist's mate didn't need to examine the XO any more closely. "I've got just the stuff for you."

"You usually do, but how could you diagnose my condition visually?" Zeke asked.

"I've seen you strung out by CA before, sir."

Zeke shook his head as if to clear his mind. "Dammit, the dietary change should have short-stopped this!"

"Sometimes it does. Sometimes it doesn't," the Chief said. He opened a cabinet and took out two bottles of pills. "And you aren't the first today, Commander. Most of the midwatch have been to see me. And the morning watch. And the forenoon watch." He counted out four pills from each bottle, slipped them into a plastic baggy, and handed it to Braxton. "One of each every four hours, Commander."

"The usual?"

Post nodded. "And then some. *Wu lin san.* The other reddish tablets are Siberian ginseng. It's pretty good at combatting fatigue."

"Thought you'd have some synthetics for these by now."

Post shook his head. "They exist. But the herbs are cheaper. And since I pick them up out of the ship's general fund at herbalist shops in Pearl and San Diego, I don't have to account for them as closely. I have to account for the synthetics as pharmaceuticals."

"That figures. Thanks." Braxton popped two of the tablets into his mouth and swallowed them. Then, as an aside before he left, he remarked, "By the way, when the Medical Officer comes back on duty, tell her that we will be reprovisioning here at Makasar. So she should have a shore inspection party ready to accompany the stores officer to a chandler."

"Aye, sir! I'd like that assignment myself."

"Yeah, I know. It gets you off the ship."

"That it does, sir!"

Up in PRIFLY, Terri Ellison checked the ops display and told her Flight Deck Officer, "Mister Peyton, trap Tiger Bravo now. Put Tiger Delta on five-minute scramble alert. And strike down the aircraft on the upper flight deck. We're going to be here for a while."

"Tiger Bravo to trap, Tiger Delta on alert five, strike AC on the top deck. Roger that, Commander!" LT Paul "Duke" Peyton responded. "And the starboard cat is working fine."

"I expected it would," she told her subordinate. She slid into her chair and touched the comm controls. "Panther Leader, Alley Cat here!"

"I'm right here, Commander," came a voice from behind her, and LCDR Meryl Delano stepped forward from the aft displays.

"Sorry. Didn't see you. Forgot to check six. That's what we get for making an eight-hour time shift," Ellison muttered. Then she snapped to and looked directly at the commander of VP-35. "Del, the Captain intends to sit here at Makasar for a couple of days. This so-called harbor bares the boat to the Makasar Straits."

Meryl Delano nodded. "Looks more like a beach than a harbor, doesn't it? Except for the piers and that miserable mole out there. Well, I guess they don't get too many typhoons through here."

"We could get it in the chops from any Chinese or Indian boat that happened to come booming through the Straits and saw us sitting here," Terri observed, checking the video displays of the harbor surface. "Do your airplane drivers want to log a little time?"

"Do you have to ask?"

"I should ask, even though I know the answer in advance. Protocol. Look, I want you to put two aircraft out there. One to the north. The other to the south. Data-link their sensors back to CIC. Anything bigger than a dolphin that comes down the Straits, I want to know about it. Same for anything bigger than a junk on the surface or a pelican in the wild blue."

"That's why they put a patrol squadron on this boat," Delano said as he nodded again. "Can do, of course. I'll have two airborne within thirty minutes."

"Make it fifteen."

"We can do that."

"I'll tell Lovett and his people down in Ops." Ellison touched her N-fone earpiece. *Victor Charlie Leader, this is Alley Cat.*

Alley Cat, this is Victor Charlie Leader, Tikki speaking. GA, Alley Cat, the voice sounded in her head.

You'll be flying other missions into Makasar shortly, the CAG told the transport squadron commander. *And do not—repeat, do not—launch without a Tiger element over you. Got it?*

Affirmative, Alley Cat.

I heard that, too, Alley Cat. This is Tiger Leader, Bells on the horn. Do you want the two ships on five-minute alert to do it, or do you want a separate pair to be ready to go?

You can launch the alert-fives.

Thanks, Alley Cat.

I know it gets cramped sitting in those cockpits after a couple of hours.

Oh, I wouldn't say that. After all these years, my bod has pretty much adapted by conforming to the seat contours.

The protocol between the officers of the Air Group wasn't as strict as that in the ship.

It was different down in the Marine battalion.

"Sam, I'm taking Charlie Company out of reserve," Bart Clinch told Captain Sam Miller. "Kit out for FIG. You're going into the embassy."

"Yessir!" Miller snapped back. He was pleased. Better to sit around on their asses on land than spend their time looking at the same walls they'd seen for weeks on end.

"John, Bravo Company is staying here," Clinch went on, addressing his other company commander. "You're in charge of boat security."

"What did I do wrong lately, Major?" Captain John Gamble replied lightly.

"Nothing. But I also want Bravo company to stay alert for possible airborne deployment in FIG config."

"Well, that does take some of the boredom out of it."

"Why the change, Major?" Gamble asked. It wasn't like Clinch to make sudden reassignments. The Marine battalion commander usually briefed his subordinates.

"Change in plan. And it comes from the Captain. So don't feed anything to Rumor Control Headquarters," Clinch warned him.

Gamble nodded knowingly. "Okay, Major. Just wanted to know the reason in case we take incoming."

"The ROEs still hold, John."

"Yessir. I'll remember that, sir. Well, at least Bravo has one consolation in staying in the ship. No Dolphin Club ashore."

Clinch wasn't lying to his officers. He, Zeke, and Terri had been briefed by Corry upon their return to the ship.

The Captain of the U.S.S. *Shenandoah* had a new plan. He'd formulated it because during the embassy luncheon he'd learned what the situation was in Makasar.

"I believe someone in the embassy is lying to me, Admiral," was all that Corry had to report to Vice Admiral Richard Kane at CINCPAC.

CINCPAC had called him and wanted a report. This bothered Corry. He'd been given orders and allowed considerable latitude in carrying them out. He didn't like micromanagement. He felt that Kane's incoming message amounted to just that.

"Is that all you found out?" Kane asked, his image in the little holo tank showing Pearl Harbor in the background through the window.

"That's enough to cause me to re-plan my mission strategy, Admiral. I don't have all the pieces yet. All that I'm willing to report at the moment is that I don't think we're being told the whole story. I'm on the spot here, and I'm the one who's got to put all these pieces together."

"Bill, I'm not trying to micromanage you, but CNO is on my shoulders about this one," Kane admitted.

"Admiral, I figured as much. I don't know why. Nor will I speculate. That's not my duty, and it isn't in my orders."

"So what are you planning to do now?"

"Sir, when I figure it out, I'll tell you." Corry had indeed figured it out with the help of his top officers. But he didn't want to spread it around yet. "I'm meeting with the Sulawesi officials tonight. It's supposedly a purely diplomatic dinner at our embassy. But you know how those usually go."

Kane did indeed know.

"I intend to force the situation . . . in a diplomatic manner, of course."

"Of course. What can I do to help?" Kane suddenly asked, sensing that Corry wasn't going to stand still for micromanagement. As a naval officer who wore the dolphins and conning tower badge himself, Kane understood that a submarine commander always felt alone, unsupported, and dependent upon his own resources. In a world of instant communication, submarine captains could be out of touch for days or weeks, even with the new scalar wave communications.

"What I really need from CINCPAC is constant sea surveillance," Corry went on. "I'm sitting here in this poor excuse for a harbor with my anchor down and my hull bared to the Makasar Straits. We have aircraft on patrol and our sensors up and running. We're watching the usually commercial surface traffic, and we've been able to identify it by means of data exchange with your traffic monitors. But if intel spots any change in the movement of Oriental submarines within a thousand klicks of me, I need to know ASAP."

"Actually, Bill, you've probably got better close-in data than we do because of your special sensor," the admiral told him.

"And that's up and running. But I don't completely trust it yet." Corry didn't mention the anomalous target that had been picked up as they cruised past Bone Bay.

"The Chinese don't seem to have learned you're in Makasar."

"Oh, they know, Admiral. They know! Makasar has a large Chinese population. I'm almost certain that Beijing knew where we were thirty minutes after we surfaced this morning." Corry paused, then admitted, "Actually, Admiral, I'm more concerned about the Filipinos. Or the Taiwanese."

"We all are."

Both nations were island realms. No Filipino or Taiwanese lived more than fifty klicks from tidewater. And the Filipinos had had the U.S. Navy present in their country for nearly a century. They hadn't forgotten that, nor had they failed to learn a lot as a result. Over the past fifty years, both countries had developed a strong sense of naval power, even more so than China or India which were basically land powers. The Philippines and Taiwan were totally dependent upon the sea for their economic well-being. They had learned much from the British in that regard.

"On the other hand, Bill, we have no indication that any space threats are powered up at the moment," the Commander in Chief of the Pacific naval forces went on. He knew that Corry was operating under the very conservative policy of a submarine commander whose ship is surfaced. Any submarine on the surface is a target for space-launched kinetic-kill weapons. Which means setting Condition Two. Kane was gently advising Corry to back off and take some pressure off the crew of the U.S.S. *Shenandoah*.

Corry recognized the move. He also knew it was impossible to crash dive the boat to a safe depth in this "harbor." So he replied, "Thank you for the space status report, Admiral. That's the sort of thing I need to get a lot of."

After signing off, Corry reflected that Kane might not have objected to what was planned.

Corry intended to force the issue and embarrass a few Sulawesi officials . . . but in private.

Abbott had laid on an embassy dinner that evening to introduce Corry and a few of his officers to various Sulawesi diplomats and politicians. So Corry went through his drill of checking the data base so he'd know something about the people he'd be with, carefully reviewing recent activities in Sulawesi, brushing up on history and customs, and finally attiring himself faultlessly in Navy dress whites.

He didn't ask Terri Ellison to join him. Sulawesi was a Muslim country.

But Major Bart Clinch was specifically invited.

"Zeke, stand down from Condition Two to Condition Three at the start of the second dog watch. I should return before midwatch. You have the ship," Corry told his XO just before he boarded a Sea Dragon for the brief flight to the embassy.

When third mess was piped, Zeke showed up in the wardroom and found the ship's staff and department officers there as usual. He didn't waste time but took his seat at the head of the table. The others found their seats.

One of the wardroom rules was a prohibition against talking shop during meals. That evening, Zeke felt the tension in the air. His shipmates were information-deprived. They wanted news. They wanted to talk shop. They fought valiantly against shop talk. But Zeke didn't relax the rule. He was a rational officer and not one to follow tradition and rules for their own sakes. However, this particular mess rule had reasons behind it.

In a submarine, people have a tendency to lapse into the fantasy that this is the only world, that the

world outside is somehow different and distant, that
the ship and their jobs are the only things that matter.
Corry didn't want this sort of narrow perspective to
become entrenched among his officers. Neither did
Zeke. It forced his officers to keep up on their reading, on their knowledge of world affairs, and on their
manners.

In matters having to do with morale, professionalism, and duty, Zeke was indeed somewhat more of a
martinet than the Captain.

However, this wasn't always so.

After the meal, Zeke rose. This was the signal that
the others could rise and leave the wardroom if desired. Some did. Zeke didn't. The meal over, he used
the opportunity to engage in short discussions with
several officers concerning the ship and the people in
her.

He found Terri Ellison at his side. "XO, do you
have a few minutes this evening?"

That was a signal well known to both of them. He
replied, "Certainly."

"May I speak with you privately?" She was wearing
tropical khakis instead of her usual flight suit. The
way she was wearing them made her look very good
to Zeke. She'd also done up her closely cropped curly
blonde hair in a way that was very feminine. She was
slowly coming down from the hype of potential combat. The possibility was still there, however. And so
were the consequences of an endocrine storm.

"Of course. I'll be in my quarters in fifteen minutes." It would be an excellent way to reset his circadian rhythm. Relaxation and recreation always helped
him do that. An additional factor was the leveling
effect that such activities had on his own physically
induced tensions.

Condition Three was in effect. That meant that the
Dolphin Club was open until morning watch.

Other officers didn't miss this exchange between the
two of them. But no one paid attention. It was done

quite discreetly and totally within current naval regulations. It was no secret that Terri Ellison played Zeke Braxton against Bart Clinch when she could. Tonight she didn't have to. Bart Clinch was ashore.

Terri and Zeke weren't the only ones who were to take advantage of Condition Three and the Dolphin Club that evening. People were people.

In the twenty-first-century world of advanced biotechnology as well as advanced personal relationships, even the stodgy Navy had been forced to bow to the inevitable in the interests of the mental and physical health of its people. Especially those who served in such lonely assignments as a carrier submarine whose cruises allowed it to put into foreign ports from time to time. In spite of biotechnology, mutations of AIDS and other diseases kept cropping up, particularly in the tropics where public hygiene was always behind the power curve.

Naval personnel were healthy individuals. The Navy didn't actively promote promiscuity among these healthy people. It wasn't discouraged, either. The Navy didn't have the medical resources to handle what might otherwise become an impossible task of treating an increasingly expanding list of sexually-transmitted diseases. On the other hand, it didn't want to promote the image among American taxpayers and Congress that a naval career was a tax-supported orgy.

If the Navy was still strongly professional, it was known as the service that treated its personnel well. It trusted its people. And God help the person who betrayed that trust!

Besides, the women of America weren't going to have it any other way than equality with men. And there were far more women than men in the United States.

However, no matter the difference between love and war, the two human activities came very close together that evening.

At 2216 hours, Zeke Braxton's intercom came alive.

"XO, this is OOD! Lieutenant Morse on deck, sir. Special Sensors reports two masdet contacts coming south in the Straits. No confirmation on passive sonar or TMF field vector yet. May I bring the ship to Condition Two, sir?"

6

It wasn't a formal state dinner, just a small embassy get-together. The Ambassador was the host, of course. But Manwaring ran the show while Herb Hewitt was there as the military attaché, the intermediary between Captain William Corry, Major Bart Clinch, and the Sulawesis. And it was strictly stag because Sulawesi was a Muslim nation.

The dinner was well orchestrated. Corry expected as much. He found himself sitting between the Honorable Kertanargara Vijaya, the Foreign Minister, and General Achin Helamahera, the Defense Minister.

And this wasn't the wardroom in the U.S.S. *Shenandoah*. The shop talk that began before the dinner continued into the meal.

"An impressive display this morning, Captain," General Helamahera repeated what he had said several times during the evening.

"I've always believed that we should provide a little entertainment and display for our hosts when we arrive," Corry replied.

The meal was as American as possible with Sulawesi embassy cooks using Sulawesi condiments. Corry didn't know how the Sulawesi chef had managed to come up with chicken-fried steak, but it was passable. Or maybe it had been too long since Corry had eaten it properly prepared.

"If we had been informed in advance of your arrival, my government would have provided a suitable welcome," the Sulawesi Foreign Minister said. The tone of his voice betrayed the fact that he was upset over the sudden surfacing of the *Shenandoah* in the Makasar harbor. But he wasn't upset over the food. He liked the way the Americans ate. It was far richer food than he was used to.

"Your Excellency, we do not risk capital ships and their people to potential surprise attack," Corry tried to explain diplomatically.

"But no one is at war with the United States, Captain," Kertanargara Vijaya reminded the naval officer.

"True, but there are several nations, some of them world powers, who might embark on military adventures if they thought they could destroy a major component of our defense establishment," Corry replied. The wine was domestic Sulawesi, which surprised Corry. Then he remembered that the Portuguese had brought Iberian grapes and wine-making techniques with them when they'd colonized Sulawesi centuries before.

"Ah, you have not forgotten Pearl Harbor!" General Helamahera put in.

"We have not, sir," Corry agreed then went on to explain, "A large surface vessel has always been an easy target for submarines, hypersonic aircraft, and kinetic-kill space weapons. That's one reason why the United States pioneered the carrier submarine earlier in this century. A submerged submarine is exceedingly difficult to locate, even in shallow waters." He didn't mention the new masdet aboard the *Shenandoah,* of course. That system was going to change submarine doctrine and tactics.

"Only one reason, Captain?" Vijaya wanted to know.

"There are others, of course. Our surface aircraft carriers finally became old and had to be replaced at about the same time space KE weapons were deployed. Our rationale has been thoroughly explored and discussed in various papers of the American Naval Institute." Corry knew the Sulawesi officials weren't happy with having the *Shenandoah* in their harbor. But international protocol and the law of the sea permitted Corry to do as he'd done. Under international law, any military vessel is allowed to make peaceful port calls in foreign ports.

"We have not had an American naval vessel pay a visit here for a long time," the Sulawesi Defense Minister recalled, looking with interest at the strawberry sundae that the Sulawesi steward placed before him as dessert. Corry had brought the frozen strawberries from the freezer of the *Shenandoah*. "May I assume that your visit is purely diplomatic?"

"No, General, not entirely," Corry said slowly and clearly. He paused a moment to let his statement be fully heard, if not understood. "American citizens have been placed in jeopardy in Sulawesi. A large number of them have disappeared. My orders direct me to assist Ambassador Abbott in recovering them, if possible. And to assist in the evacuation of any Americans wishing to leave Sulawesi."

"As I've told you on several occasions, Vijaya," Ambassador Abbott broke in with his smooth Carolina accent, "the disappearance without trace of nearly a hundred Americans over the past six months gives us a little heartburn. That's an American expression indicating that we're most uncomfortable about it. It's my job here at the embassy to assist Americans in your country, just as it's the job of your ambassador in Washington to help us protect Sulawesi citizens there. My many requests for information about missing Americans have gone unanswered in the last six months."

"That is because we have no information relating to what happened to those Americans," Vijaya countered quickly.

"Suh, I know your system of keeping track of foreign nationals in Sulawesi," Abbott came back at once. He tried to say it in a kind and gentle fashion. Sulawesi was a young and poor nation. It was surrounded by countries that were, in comparison, large and strong—Sumatra, Malaysia, Brunei, the Philippines, Amman, Taiwan, and Australia. Some of these were overtly backed by India and China, two world powers with whom they had long-standing disputes. The Sulawesis didn't fear Australia; the people of that continent had their hands full exploiting their own country's resources. But they did fear the Chinese as they always had because, unlike the Japanese, the Chinese hadn't yet learned the lesson about taking it instead of making it.

The Sulawesi government had been patterned after that of Indonesia from which it had split. The military played a major role in both the economic and security spheres.

Therefore, Vijaya and Helamahera were the ministers who jointly directed an encompassing system of foreign surveillance carried out by their secret police, known only as Sudomo. They didn't pay too much attention to tourists who were really tourists. But they watched business people closely along with engineers and technicians brought in by foreign companies to help exploit the Sulawesi resources.

"So!" General Helamahera exploded. "The real reason you are here with your impressive submarine, its aircraft, and its marine infantry is to push aside my defense establishment and go looking for your alleged missing people by yourselves!" He didn't mention Abbott's oblique reference to Sudomo, but his actions revealed that he'd caught it. He put both hands on the table and pushed his chair back. His face got red. It looked like he would leave the table in anger.

But he didn't. Both Abbott and Corry knew the Defense Minister had to react that way in front of his colleague, the foreign minister. Neither of them would own up to Sudomo.

The Sulawesi Defense Minister probably controlled Sudomo. And the United States government wasn't really sure that Sudomo hadn't been behind all the disappearances.

This didn't explain the missing children and young people, however.

That was the big hole in that intelligence evaluation.

Corry and Abbott had to force the issue and get some answers. This wasn't totally their choice. Both had received orders to do so from Washington. How they did it was up to them.

"Not at all, General," Lowden Manwaring interjected himself into the conversation for the first time. He'd been in Sulawesi since the embassy opened. He knew these two men far better than Abbott did. The Ambassador was, of course, a relative newcomer. "We're well aware that you may not be able to give us answers concerning all the Americans. In common with our government, you don't have all the personnel and facilities you want."

"We know your defense establishment is small because of the nation's limited tax base," LCDR Herb Hewitt added. "As you've remarked to me several times, General, you're pleased with our joint defense treaty because your ministry is often hard-put to maintain national security."

"I have never said that!"

"Please, Your Excellency, but we can speak frankly here," Manwaring quickly said. "This is not an official meeting but a friendly dinner so you can get to know Captain Corry and Major Clinch. We're seriously concerned about our missing citizens. So much so that we have arranged the visit of the U.S.S. *Shenandoah*. We will force nothing upon you; that isn't the way of the world today. We do, however, offer you our assistance and support in the way of our naval forces to conduct an intensified search for these missing Americans."

Twenty-first-century power projection was a delicate matter. Corry had taken several War College courses with that background. It was a matter of knowing how to gently twist the arm of a foreign government without otherwise disturbing relationships. The Americans were new at this. However, they'd spent a lot of time and effort learning what to do and not to do from studying the history of the British, French, Dutch, and Portuguese.

The Sulawesi Foreign Minister didn't have as short a fuse as the Defense Minister. He knew this friendly dinner was more than a mere diplomatic courtesy that would allow him to meet the American naval commander. He had suspected it before he'd arrived. And he was prepared for it. The canny Dutch part of his mixed heritage came to the fore. He dodged the issue brought up by Abbott and replied, "Just what do you have in mind, Mister Ambassador?"

"We want to provide you with some help, Vijaya."

"And what can you do to help if you have only a battalion of marine infantry and some patrol aircraft?" Helamahera wanted to know.

"May I compliment you on your knowledge of how we crew our carrier submarine?" Corry said rhetorically. That wasn't classified information. The General could have picked it up in any of the naval journals and DOD reports.

The General had learned it only that afternoon, of course, in a cram session for the dinner that evening. Hewitt knew how he'd gotten it. The embassy library held the information, and the outgoing telephone call from one of the embassy's Sulawesi contract workers had been monitored. The contract worker was suspected to have connections with Sudomo.

"Don't underestimate the help my eighty-five men can give you, General!" Bart Clinch broke in for the first time. "We'll be right in there working with your people!"

"How? This is supposing that we do it at all," Helamahera said, slowly moving himself back to the table. Maybe these Americans weren't going to embarrass him after all.

Vijaya nodded in understanding. "Yes, I have the

same question, of course. Your arrival this morning attracted a great deal of attention. Many nations now know you're here. If General Helamahera begins a major sweep throughout the island in a search for missing Americans, it may serve to trigger the responsible parties to hide the evidence or the Americans. It may even trigger other nations as well."

That was another piece of the puzzle! Corry now knew that Americans weren't being singled out for hostage-taking, for example. Other foreign nationals had disappeared, too. The Sulawesis didn't want other nations to come in looking for their *own* missing citizens!

It looked more and more like cannibalism with slavery as a remote second possibility. However, Corry now suspected that Sudomo was indeed involved in some way. The General's reaction had been too sharp and quick.

"Well, Mister Minister, our two countries have a mutual military pact," Bart Clinch reminded them. He was impressive in his Marine dress uniform with his chest full of ribbons and marksmanship awards. "Let's take the opportunity afforded by our visit to hold a joint military exercise. We're both going to learn something from that!"

The Foreign Minister warmed to the idea right away. He was looking for a way out of the embarrassing situation of having a superpower come in to take over a job they believed the Sulawesis had botched. With an SSCV sitting in the harbor, it wasn't something he could ignore. Neither could the Prime Minister who had told him to find out what the Americans really wanted and, if it didn't cost too much, to let them have it. He hated himself for being a citizen of a country that was too small to stand up to a big country, even one as benign as the United States. "Excellent idea, Achin, wouldn't you say?" Vijaya addressed his colleague.

The Defense Minister nodded. It was the easy way

out of the present situation that couldn't otherwise be dodged. And it would put Helamahera in charge. He could arrange delays and misdirections. And the exercise wouldn't last forever. Very quickly the Americans would discover that indeed no information was available to them. Then they'd go away and things could return to normal in Makasar.

General Helamahera pulled his chair back to the table and finished his ice cream sundae as he thought some more about this. Finally, he placed his napkin alongside his empty dessert cup as Abbott had done. He wanted a cigarette, so he withdrew a pack from his tunic, extracted one, and lit it. Vijaya did the same.

The smell of tobacco smoke was foreign to Corry. The Navy had been smoke-free for decades. So had the embassy, but ashtrays had thoughtfully been provided for the two Sulawesi officials.

A young male American embassy aide stepped quietly into the small room and said something to Hewitt. The attaché quickly excused himself and left.

"I think," the General finally said, "that such an exercise could be arranged."

"Excellent!" Abbott bubbled.

"Captain, would you care to come by the defense ministry tomorrow at about noon? Bring your staff if you wish. We shall have lunch and then plan this exercise," Helamahera offered.

Corry smiled. "That would interfere with something I have planned."

"Oh?"

"Yes. General, I had planned to invite you and other Sulawesi officials to visit the U.S.S. *Shenandoah* for an inspection and to view our air operations. And I had hoped we might have you as our guests for lunch aboard ship."

No one in Sulawesi had ever been in an American carrier submarine before. "Oh. Yes. Of course." The General was surprised by the invitation, but he recovered quickly. "Then I shall withdraw my invitation, accept yours, and suggest that our planning meeting be postponed."

"We can certainly hold it aboard the *Shenandoah*," Corry expanded his offer.

Hewitt returned at that point, walked over to Corry, and whispered into his ear, "Captain, I've been asked to relay to you a message from the *Shenandoah*. Sensors and airborne patrols have reported two large submerged vessels proceeding southward toward Makasar through the Makasar Straits. The originator is code-named Zeke."

Even inside the small embassy, the sound of a Sea Dragon transport aircraft could be heard as it approached, went into hover, and began to land on the embassy grounds.

Corry got to his feet immediately. With a brief formal bow to the two Sulawesi officials, he asked Abbott, "Mister Ambassador, may I be excused, please?" Corry was flustered, tried not to show it, and almost stuttered. But he kept himself under rigid control. "Circumstances require that I return to my ship immediately. Mister Vijaya and General Helamahera, my invitation stands, and I shall be in touch with Major Clinch and the embassy personnel here concerning the final arrangements. Mister Ambassador, by your leave, sir . . ."

Abbott knew something had come unbonded somewhere. So he simply told Corry, "Captain, of course you have my permission. The concerns of your command always come first."

In an almost preoccupied manner, Corry quickly shook hands with all and turned to follow Hewitt. Once outside the dining room and walking briskly down the hall to the veranda, he asked the attaché, "Herb, anything else in the message you didn't want to mention in there, even privately?"

"Only that the contacts were big, submerged, and fast-moving, Captain."

"Herb, have you ever had any of the new Chinese Han boats in here?"

The attaché shook his head. "No, but I'd sure like to see one of them. They're supposed to be big."

Corry erupted through the French doors, crossed the veranda, and strode over to where the Sea Dragon transport was sitting at idle on the lawn, its cargo door open and the loadmaster ready to receive him aboard. He turned to Hewitt, returned the attaché's salute, and remarked, "Herb, I don't like to say this, but maybe you're going to get that chance."

7

"Two contacts, Captain," Zeke reported.

The bridge/control room was a quiet bustle of activity. Braxton had brought the U.S.S. *Shenandoah* to Condition Two because of the mass detector contact reported by LT Charlie Ames, Special Sensor Officer.

"And the ship is ready to take whatever action is necessary," the XO went on. "We are still at anchor and the flight decks are hot. We're not rigged for emergency dive because we have only nine fathoms of water here. However, the Tigers are ready to launch on five minutes' notice, and the Black Panthers have two additional Ospreys proceeding to the Straits. I have relieved the OOD because Roger Goff needs to get to work in sonar."

Corry nodded in approval. "Two contacts, you say?" he asked.

"Affirmative, sir."

"Identification?"

Zeke shook his head. "No, sir. Masdet contact only. No magnetic anomaly data yet; the contacts are out of range. We have not gone to active sonar."

"What data from the Osprey in the north Straits?"

"No data yet. Panther North One is in a search pattern now. He's stopping to dip a passive sonobuoy every five minutes."

Corry said nothing. He appeared to be studying the various situation displays and data readouts. Actually, he was trying to put the sparse data together into a coherent picture. It was difficult for him to make a definitive threat analysis on the basis of what he had.

Why two targets? he asked himself.

If the targets were Chinese, why two of them? A Han class attack boat plus one of their reported submarine transports, perhaps? Why? The *Shenandoah* had been on the surface at Makasar for sixteen hours. That hadn't given the Chinese time to react and dispatch two of their biggest boats to the Makasar Straits.

Unless, of course, those two boats had been somewhere around the Philippines earlier today.

Corry touched the N-fone behind his ear. *Communications, this is the Captain,* he spoke verbally at the same time he directed his non-verbal thought to the device.

Captain, this is Communications. Lieutenant Atwater here.

Lieutenant, patch me through to CINCPAC.

Aye aye, sir!

It took Atwater some time to set up the satcom link, contact CINCPAC headquarters and get the Admiral on the line.

While Atwater was doing that, Corry turned to Braxton and asked, "Zeke, what do you think? What do we have here?"

The XO hesitated for a moment. When Corry asked for input, one had better think through the reply before answering. The Captain did not like cerebral popcorn. "I think they're Chinese boats, sir."

"Why? And why two?" Corry came back quickly with his famous response, the "most embarrassing question."

"This is the East World sphere of influence where American interests butt up against theirs," Zeke replied cautiously. "Those two boats could have been six hundred nautical miles away when we surfaced this morning. I'd speculate the Chinese want to blunt our power projection by showing up within a day of our arrival. They might send two boats to show us up.

Two boats even half the size of the *Shanna* are just as impressive."

Corry pursed his lips and thought about his XO's response. Then he looked up at the data readouts and remarked quietly, "Interesting hypothesis, Zeke. I'd considered the power projection scenario, but you took it one step beyond by rationalizing the two boat situation. Good thinking."

"Thank you, sir."

"Now, what would you do about it?" Corry pressed him.

"Let them come, sir. And keep them under surveillance. They must know—or they soon will—that we've spotted them." He paused, then added, "And we stay at Condition Two. At least until they surface and invite exchange visits."

Captain, Admiral Kane is on the line for you, the voice of Ed Atwater reported via N-fone.

Thank you, Mister Atwater. Please put it on verbose, Corry told him. He was not one to keep any secrets from the crew that he didn't have to. But before he toggled the comm mike in front of him, he said to Zeke, "XO, go to active sonar now. Start pinging. Let them know we see them. If they ping us, send the signal that I wish to speak with the task force commander."

"Aye aye, sir!"

"Admiral, this is Corry."

"Go ahead, Bill."

"I have two contacts running submerged southward through the Straits," Corry reported. "I have Ospreys near them. The ship is at Condition Two. I've gone to active sonar. I have requests, sir."

"Two targets?"

"Affirmative."

"Huh!" Kane's voice came back with a grunt of surprise.

"Admiral, what's the latest status report on Chinese boats around here?"

"Bill, the latest contact report I have here is two days old. The Chinese patrol boat *Bei fung* was detected submerged at twenty meters depth running northwest through the Tapaan Passage. SLSAR picked up her wake turbulances in those shallow waters. On the next satellite passage, she wasn't there and wasn't northwest of the last sighting."

"I was not told this, Admiral," Corry put in sharply, looking at Zeke with an expression that revealed his displeasure at not being given all the intelligence data.

"As I recall, Bill, it wasn't considered necessary by my intelligence people because of the *Bei fung's* course. It wasn't evaluated as a factor that would affect your operation. Your report indicates the *Bei fung* did a turnabout, got out of the Tapaan Passage, and went deep in the Sulu Sea southbound. So I now suspect one of the targets is the *Bei fung.* The latest report from my spooks shows no other boat in the vicinity. That's why I'm puzzled at your two contacts."

"Thank you, Admiral. You've given me enough additional data that I can carry on," Corry told him. "My intentions are to attempt contact with the *Bei fung* if it appears headed toward Makasar. I'll keep both targets under close surveillance."

"Let me know when you have more data, Bill."

"I'll do that, Admiral. And please do the same."

When the contact was broken, Corry sat back and rubbed his eyes. "It's been a very long day. Looks like it's going to be a longer night."

"Captain, I think you could use some of this." Chief Staff Petty Officer Al Warren set a cup of steaming coffee in front of the skipper. The CPO had been with Corry in several ships. The two men had a personal contract that extended back to the days when Corry was a shit-hot attack pilot and Warren was his aircraft crew chief. They'd gone through submarine school at New London together when it was obvious that OPNAV had pegged Corry as a potential commanding officer. Corry, in turn, had supported Warren. It wasn't the Old Salts Club at work; most naval officers develop team relationships with a petty officer early on and then do what's possible to maintain the team. The Navy knew this and quietly encouraged it.

"Chief, this is the elixir of the gods right now! I never had the chance to get after-dinner coffee at the embassy tonight."

"I can't say it would have helped you, Captain. Embassy coffee tends to be wimpy," Warren remarked. "XO, how about you? Coffee?"

"Thanks, Chief, it would help. Will you have the orderly bring some sandwiches, please?" Zeke responded. "Ham and cheese for me. The usual for the Captain."

LT Marcella Zar turned from her console in the bank just before the Captain. "Sir, the front target should turn southeastward in the next few minutes. It's cleared the shallow water west of the Mandar Cape. I've put the graphics up on Screen Ten."

One of these days real soon, Marcella's going to give Natty Chase real competition in the Navigation Department, Zeke thought. The dark-haired, doe-eyed Lieutenant wasn't just a typical smart-but-plain Navy type; she was professional, brilliant, and quietly rated a high-value "counter" by the male officers. About ten millihelens was Zeke's evaluation. Of course, in his eyes, Terri Ellison was close to a hundred millihelens.

(A "helen" was the unofficial Navy standard of feminine attractiveness, one helen being the amount of beauty required to launch a thousand ships. No one knew a woman with that capability, so a "millihelen" was the amount of beauty required to launch one ship. The ladies of the boat knew of this rating system and didn't mind. Male-oriented it was, but it was also a compliment. No woman in the Navy was *ever* rated at zero millihelens. One millihelen was nominal.)

"Thank you, Lieutenant," Corry told her and punched up the graphic on his display console.

"Why is that unknown running behind the *Bei*

fung—if that's what the lead target really is?" was the comment from LCDR Bob Lovette, the Operations Officer, from his station on Zeke's right.

"That's an ancient attack boat tactic," LCDR Mark Walton pointed out. The First Lieutenant of the ship was on Corry's left and spoke along the command console to the ops man. "Nuclear boats were sonar blind back there. And running in the turbulent wake of a propeller-driven boat also tended to confuse other third-boat sonars."

"Is that what's happening here, Mister Walton?" Corry suddenly asked.

"That's what I think, sir."

"First active sonar data coming in," Zeke observed.

"First hydrophonic data, too," Lovette added.

Corry sat back, listened on the N-fone tactical net and the verbose chatter that often accompanied it, and let his officers do their jobs.

Ralph, can you get a computer match for the hydrophone data?

Coming up! the Intelligence Officer fired back from the tactical computer console two banks down in the room. *Close match! Early data shows a forty-five percent probability of matching the Chinese Wind class boats.*

Damn Chinese are fifty years behind the power curve as usual! That's a Chinese copy of the old Russian Typhoon boats, Walton "muttered." The First Lieutenant was known in the *Shenandoah* for being a naval history buff. He knew his subject well, and no one had been able to trip him up.

But I have no make on any following target! If it's there at all, it's damned near silent!

Is one of our stealth boats tailing it? Lovette wondered.

Not a chance, Mister Lovette! CINCPAC would have told me, Corry put in. *Mister Goff, do you have an active sonar signature yet?*

Affirmative, Captain! Goff was holed up in the sonar

compartment to the rear, working with his people in an area that was still highly subjective in spite of computers and artificial intelligence. *We confirm the Chinese Wind class boat in the lead. But, Captain, we're getting zero active sonar return on the following target. It is stealthed so thoroughly that any return is down in the noise!*

Mister Ames! Corry called up his Special Sensors Officer. *Do you still have a positive masdet contact on two targets out there?*

Masdet has two targets, sir! Now that the range has closed, we have improving data. Identification of the Chinese Wind class boat has allowed me to calibrate the masdet against its known displacement. The following target is bigger. Best estimate right now is fifty-seven thousand tons submerged!

"Captain, that's in the same league as our anomalous masdet target in the Flores Sea yesterday," Zeke reminded the Commanding Officer verbally.

"Yes," was Corry's only reply. Then he signalled his Special Sensors Officer again via N-fone, *Mister Ames, are you certain that your equipment is operating properly?*

Yes, sir!

Are there any similarities between the following stealthed target and the anomaly we detected in the Flores Sea yesterday?

Yes, sir! Same ballpark for the estimated displacement, except somewhat larger.

Larger?

Yes, sir. I estimated the Flores Sea anomaly at fifty thousand tons. The double contact with a known target has allowed me to calibrate the magnitude of the unknown's return. The Wind class boats displace twenty-five thousand tons. Therefore, my estimate of this unknown target is fifty-seven thousand tons.

Another voice broke in on the N-fone channel. *Sonar Officer reporting. We have airborne active sonar contact but zero magnetic anomaly contact. That's the*

*titanium hull of a Wind class boat. It's changed course
to heading one-two-zero, range seven-nine nautical,
closing speed four-two knots.*

"Lieutenant Zar, you were right!" Zeke told her
verbally.

She smiled.

But she was the only one on the bridge who smiled.

General quarters, Mister Braxton! Corry snapped.

The General Quarters alarm sounded throughout
the *Shenandoah.*

*Special Sensor reporting. The two targets have di-
verged. The following target has continued to hold
course one-eight-zero.*

*Sonar reports no active return from any following
target. It's damned heavily sonar-stealthed!*

Captain, this is Air Boss!

Go ahead, Terri!

*When the two targets diverged, Panther North Three
made a visual contact! I have her on the net. Go ahead,
Panther North Three.*

*Shanna, Panther North Three. When the two targets
were reported separating, we got a momentary thirty-
second visual contact of something following the Chinese boat. Bigger than the Chinese boat. Black as coal.
Looked almost like an enormous whale, but it wasn't.
I've seen whales before. It's running submerged, leaving no wake, and not returning pings from active
buoys. Some minor infrared signature which we've recorded. But negative magnetic anomaly and no alter-
ation of terrestrial fields. Air Boss, it's almost like it
was* a huge living thing!

Corry pursed his lips. Something unknown was out
there. It was big and it was stealthy. But he also had
another target. This wasn't quite as unknown, and his
sonar was on it. And it was closing on Makasar.

"Captain, looks like we've got a Chinese boat heading in on us and an unknown doing God knows what,"
Zeke remarked darkly.

Corry didn't answer his XO. Instead, he took several deep breaths, formulated exactly what he wanted to say so he wouldn't stutter, then said firmly via N-fone, *Mister Ames, maintain masdet contact on the unknown as long as possible. Report any change of course or unusual activity. And stay with the inbound target. Air Boss, have the Ospreys converge on the incoming target and track it. Keep aircraft over it. Scramble the Tigers in ASW mode and put them over it. Mister Goff, continue active sonar. Mister Atwater, please send the following signal from the Commanding Officer, U.S.S.* Shenandoah, *to commander of unidentified inbound submarine: You are under surveillance. We will take no hostile action unless you initiate aggression. Please identify yourself and state your intentions. If this is a peaceful port call to Makasar, I invite you to dine with me tomorrow evening aboard my ship. End message. And inform me of any response.*

Aye, aye, sir. It's on its way by STS in your voice as reconstructed by computer. Uh, Captain, incoming message crossed in transmission with yours. Coming on the verbose net now.

The slight garble caused by seawater attenuation and fluctuation of an STS comm signal didn't disguise the definite Chinese accent. "American submarine *Shenandoah* in Makasar harbor, this is China submarine *Bei fung.* I am Captain Dao Ling Qian. I make peaceful port call at Makasar. Please not to make fight with me. I learn of your visit from China embassy in Makasar. I wish to invite Captain Corry to dinner in *Bei fung* next day and become friends."

Corry looked at Zeke, who looked back at him. Some of the tension was gone from Corry's face and eyes. He smiled, removed the N-fone module from behind his ear, and stood up. In verbose mode, he ordered, "Mister Atwater, send my message again and add that I will communicate with Captain Qian once he has surfaced his ship at Makasar. XO, stand down from Condition One to Condition Two. Let me know when the *Bei fung* has surfaced. If nothing happens, we'll go to Condition Three at that time. It's been a long day."

"Shall we continue to track the unknown, Captain?"

"Yes. I intend to consider it as a threat unless it continues its present course and clears the Straits. If it changes course and begins to close on Makasar, we'll go back to Condition One. However, I suspect this is the second time we've encountered the same strange masdet anomaly." Corry paused, then added, "White Oak doesn't have all the bugs out of that masdet yet. We were probably seeing an echo yesterday or a humping big whale trying to mate with a Chinese submarine tonight. Log the details and we'll give the science johnnies something to keep them really busy when we get back to Pearl."

8

"Mister President, this isn't a conflict crisis situation. Both ships are there on overtly friendly port calls." The Chief of Naval Operations knew the President really didn't understand either international law or the seagoing rules of the road.

The nation's chief executive had been a Texas rancher and oilman who'd accomplished everything possible in business. Then he'd gravitated to politics. He turned out to be a successful politician, too. But he depended heavily on his staff to fill in the gaps of his knowledge.

ADM George L. Street, CNO, thought he knew who had triggered the President on this one. It was Street's opinion that the President's source of information didn't know what he was talking about. The admiral's speculation was confirmed when the National Security Advisor spoke up.

"George, do you mean to tell me that this isn't something we should rethink now?" snapped Rex C. Hill, the retired Aerospace Force two-star general who'd been tapped by the President for the job because they were both Texans. Hill had ended a lackluster career by commanding Dyess Aerospace Force Base. He didn't get command of a wing; he wasn't good enough because he was an administrative type, not a combat leader. But Hill had seen to it that a lot of Hood's supplies had been purchased from the President's companies. "What the hell, here we have a Chinese patrol submarine on its way back to Zhanjiang after five months at sea! You people know where it's been. You track their boats every day. Why should this one suddenly do a one-eighty and head toward Makasar unless it meant trouble?"

"It turned around because the Chinese embassy in Makasar reported to Beijing that an American SSCV had surfaced in the harbor. We intercepted all the communications." The quiet, well-modulated female voice hit the assembled and highly unofficial rump session of the National Security Council like a splash of cold water. RADM Dolores T. McCarthy didn't want the former Aerospace Force general to dominate this informational meeting called by the President. Hill had a tendency to do that. He also had a history of taking intel information and, without carefully evaluating it, using it as a pretext to keep the NSC in an uproar and dependent upon him. Admiral McCarthy had been there before. And she knew what she was talking about when it came to intel work.

"And other factors could be involved." The intense man with beady, piercing little eyes leaned forward, put his tweed-clad elbows on the table, and added his carefully selected bit of data. Alan M. Dekker, head of the CIA, also knew what was going on. Or he thought he did.

Actually no one in the room really knew what was going on in Sulawesi.

"Well, it looks to me like we've put a multi-billion dollar ship at risk," the President said with a worried look on his long face.

"The *Shenandoah* is not at risk, Mister President. Any one of the Rivers class SSCVs is perfectly capable of protecting itself in the crunch." H. W. Gilmore was a rare individual. He was the Secretary of the Navy plus a naval reserve aviator. He was carrier-qualified. Furthermore, he'd spent his reserve tour that year in the new SSCV-30, the U.S.S. *Savannah*, cruising the Carib on shakedown.

"I wasn't advised that this could happen when I

approved sending the *Shenandoah* to Makasar," the President reminded the group. He'd gotten word of the Chinese submarine's arrival in Makasar from Hill shortly after it had happened. He'd canceled a 3:00 P.M. meeting with congressional power players to call this rump NSC session. The story might break on the five o'clock news. He didn't know how it would be slanted. But he wanted to have his ducks in line if he had to react with a news conference this evening. The news media were strong antimilitary. The President wasn't a dove, but he didn't believe in using force unless he couldn't get agreement or consensus through negotiation.

The Honorable John D. Long, Secretary of Defense, leaned his stout form back in his chair and told his boss, "Mister President, I believe I can guarantee that the *Shenandoah* is not at risk. My people ran several dozen scenarios through the war gaming system. This situation was one of them."

"Why wasn't I told about it during the discussions leading up to sending in one of our carrier submarines?"

"It would have taken time none of us had," the Secretary of Defense replied easily. He could get away with being more informal with the President than anyone else in the room. Long had been the Governor of Texas who'd nominated the President at the party convention. "The world's oceans are full of ships. They make port calls all the time. The Navy believed that very low risk was involved. Admiral Street and his people convinced Gil and me. Otherwise, I would never have backed the mission despite the growing number of missing Americans."

"And if we treat this as a special incident, we could indeed project the image to China that something's wrong in Makasar. Do we want to do that right now?" Gilmore added.

Dekker momentarily acted as if he wanted to say something, but he was beaten to it by another participant.

"As you recall, Mister President, this is plainly a power projection mission," the Chairman of the Joint Chiefs tried to explain. Aerospace Force General Tony R. Lundberg thought the President had understood what that meant when the mission had been discussed and approved several days before. "As long as we continue to play it that way, the Chinese won't get upset. Hell, if they try anything down in the Indies, they'll have to pull capability out of Asia. That will leave Russia at their under-defended backside. They won't do that in spite of the Russian situation right now."

"Mister President, think of it more in terms of competitive strategies. It's sort of a market positioning move," the Secretary of the Navy suggested.

That the President did understand. But he didn't see how that concept exactly applied to what was going on. "Okay, we all know that power projection was the overt reason for sending the *Shenandoah*. The real reason is to push the hell out of the Sulawesi government to do something about the continual disappearance of American citizens there! Ambassador Abbott's report of the diplomatic dinner last night, their time, was sent over to me from State. Abbott says things were proceeding well until the *Shenandoah*'s Captain got word of the approach of the Chinese sub. It sort of went to worms after that, according to Abbott. But he says he did some fast damage control with the Sulawesis. They don't like being pushed. And they don't like the fact that the presence of our carrier submarine brought the Chinese in. They don't like the Chinese."

The Secretary of Defense countered easily, "Well, they like the Chinese being there less than having us do a little power bumping. The Chinese presence could make our job a little easier."

"Okay, I've spent enough time on this matter today," the President noted, looking at his watch. He was a schedule-type man. He didn't like disrupting his plans with sudden meetings like this. But he'd felt he needed to call the rump session. A plan had gone awry out there in Makasar. He wanted to be absolutely, positively certain that he was on top of the situation if some reporter happened to pop the surprise question at him. He knew that reporters loved to do that. He saw from his watch that he had a few minutes left in this schedule slot. So he asked openly to all in the room, "Anyone here have any additional thoughts on how and why all those Americans are dropping out of sight over there?"

"I've thought something about it, Mister President," the Secretary of the Navy responded in a tentative manner. "During my active duty career, I served on one of the earlier carrier submarines temporarily operating out of Singapore. I've been in the area."

"So? What's happening? Are Americans on Sulawesi being eaten by monkeys or something?" Rex Hill asked sarcastically.

Gilmore shook his head. "No, the monkeys there don't think we taste very good," he shot back with whimsy designed to put the National Security Advisor off guard. No one in the Pentagon really liked Rex C. Hill, General, USAF (Ret.). Gilmore's remark didn't even cause a snicker. These people had a sense of humor. However, in the White House, the awesome feeling of being in a place of power caused everyone to be extremely serious. In fact, Gilmore might have been considered slightly out of line for making such a facetious remark. Humor was reserved for the Chief Executive, if and when he chose to use it. The current President was humorous with his closest friends, but not in his job.

"The secret police of Indonesia were and still are a covert power in that part of the world," the Secretary of the Navy went on in a serious vein now. "They left their legacy with Sulawesi when the island split from Indonesia."

"Mister Secretary, we have no indication that the

Sudomo is involved in this," Admiral McCarthy reminded him. She'd briefed him earlier on the possibility that the Sulawesi secret police were involved and had assigned a low priority to it. None of the input to naval intelligence implicated Sudomo.

"I agree with Admiral McCarthy," the CIA Director quietly put in.

"Alan, you were going to have your people massage the data thoroughly again," the President reminded his intelligence chief. "Any results yet?"

"Nothing on which I'd want to bet the farm," Dekker said darkly.

"Suppose you didn't have to bet the farm?"

"Then I'd say what I've been saying all along: cannibalism."

"I find that hard to believe in the world of the twenty-first century!" General Hill snapped.

The man would probably find a lot of the world out there hard to believe, the CIA chief told himself. Hill operated with his own incomplete world picture. It was far from reality. Dekker got his nose rubbed in it every morning, and he never got used to the smell. He'd stayed with CIA for decades only because the agency gave him the opportunity occasionally to do something about it. It made him feel a little better when he was able to do that.

The Director of the CIA ignored the National Security Advisor. Looking at the ceiling with his big hands folded in front of him, he carefully composed what he said before he went on. "In a way, Gil may be right. The monkeys may not like our taste, but I think someone over there does. So that's my unsupported, unvarnished, unscientific opinion, Mister President."

He paused, then continued, "It's been reinforced in the last twenty-four hours. Why? Because I don't think the Chinese sent that submarine back to Makasar just to get a close look at one of Gil's Rivers class SSCVs. The Chinese can get all the data they want from their little black spies in Singapore and Pearl. And from the British publishing industry."

"So what's brewing in that dark mind of yours, Al? What's your line of thinking right now?" the President wanted to know. Sometimes, this was the only way to get an opinion out of the man.

"Beijing may see this developing situation in Makasar as a prime international incident, and they don't want to be left out."

"Left out of what?"

"Well," Dekker continued, "the Chinese are sort of sensitive about being perceived as ignoring human rights. Which they do because they have so many people over there. And as long as the rest of the world didn't know, they were willing to look the other way. But then they saw us sending the *Shenandoah* to Makasar. They knew it wasn't on a friendly port call. They knew it was power projection. And they knew there was only one reason why it's power projection: missing American citizens.

"So the Chinese are there alongside us to cover their governmental anatomy in the world news media. They want to be seen as a concerned part of this. This educated guess presupposes that some of my unauthenticated data is really valid, and now I think it is," Dekker paused and concluded, "The Chinese have lost three times as many of their citizens on Sulawesi as we have in the last six months."

9

A flight deck on a carrier submarine is surprisingly quiet in spite of powerful jet engines operating at full thrust during aircraft takeoffs and landings.

Back in the last century, aircraft were noisy. They were propelled by brute force. Their inefficient turbofan engines burned hundreds of liters of hydrocarbon fuel every hour. They had few autocontrols and required pilots to fly them every moment by hand using organic sensors—eyes, ears, and "seat of the pants." They bloomed brightly on radar screens and transmitted strong infrared emissions. In short, they were red meat for smart, self-guided interceptor missiles. Pilots began to demand more than speed and firepower. They wanted "low observable" aircraft. In short, they demanded stealthy ships. Aeronautical engineers bitched and moaned and complained . . . and gave the pilots what they wanted. Twenty-first century aircraft were hard to detect. Stealth includes quiet operation.

The air show for the Chinese commanding officer, Captain Dao Ling Qian, used the upper flight deck where the VTOL aircraft of the U.S.S. *Shenandoah's* Air Group could show off their performance. Captain William Corry was letting Commander Terri Ellison run this air show. And she didn't like to cat launch the F/A-48 Sea Devils with full ordnance loads. She pointed out that they were far more spectacular if flown light. This allowed them to make spritely vertical takeoffs and landings. With thirty minutes' fuel aboard, the Sea Devils of VA-65 literally jumped into the air.

Besides, Corry and Zeke didn't really want to demonstrate the lower flight deck with its water-tight fore and aft doors. It had taken more than a little bit of clever engineering to design doors thirty meters on a side that would seal out water at the dive pressures of a submarine. Nor were the electromagnetic catapults with their superconducting parts the sort of high-tech gadgets they wanted to reveal.

But Captain Qian was no dummy. He spotted what Corry was doing and remarked, "You are not using your lower flight deck today, Captain Corry."

Corry smiled and replied, "You wouldn't see much down there. And we can't conduct vertical operations from that deck."

"So? I see. This is impressive. I understand now how valuable is a carrier submarine for sea control and power projection," Qian remarked. "You have all the operational benefits of a submarine combined with the air search and strike capability of an aircraft carrier. China never built any aircraft carriers. We determined what could happen to them if space weapons were used."

"At least you didn't have to scrap any ships," Zeke remarked.

"Yes, but your U.S.S. *Nimitz* finally wore out before you scrapped it," Qian pointed out.

"It became too expensive to repair and upgrade, Captain," Zeke explained.

"So! China has a different economic system. We keep our equipment working longer."

Corry nodded. He knew the real reason. China, for all its wealth, had trouble keeping up. Even with the technical and industrial help of Japan, China was still operating in the last century. As a nation, China really had only two things going for it: abundant untapped natural resources and people. Because a population of more than a billion people posed a management problem beyond Chinese capabilities, the country couldn't properly exploit its resources. Thus it remained a relatively poor country in comparison to other major nations. The more populous it got, the farther behind it became.

Corry could see this lagging economic phase relationship. The S.49 *Bei fung* Chinese submarine was only twenty years old, if naval intelligence was right. (And it usually was.) However, it was literally a Chinese copy of the ancient Russian Typhoon class without the SLBMs. He didn't expect he'd see much that was new during his dinner visit in her that coming evening.

"Will you parade your Marine battalion?" Qian asked. He was interested in seeing if they were carrying any new equipment. The remark was also intended to inform Corry that Qian had done his homework. The Chinese captain knew the *Shenandoah*'s TO&E.

Corry didn't miss it. "I'm sorry, Captain Qian, but they have been deployed ashore at our embassy in Makasar. As you know, we're here to assist the Sulawesi government. More than a hundred American citizens have disappeared here recently."

Qian said nothing at that point. His attention was diverted. A flight of four Sea Devils made a high-speed pass overhead at fifty meters. When directly over the ship, the formation split. The g-loads must have been high, but the pilots executed a horizontal bomb-burst maneuver. The lead aircraft continued forward. The two wing men broke abruptly right and left in what appeared to the flight deck observers to be a right angle turn. The number four ship went into reverse flight and backed up. At that instant, another F/A-48 came in from behind the splitting formation at an altitude of ten meters above the harbor. It performed a sudden pull-up and went vertical over the bomb-bursting formation.

"Impressive," was the Chinese Captain's remark.

Then he got back on the subject. "I would like to speak with you about your missing Americans."

Zeke's eyebrows went up. Corry remained impassive and asked, "Oh? May I ask why?"

"We are here on a similar mission," Qian admitted.

"Have Chinese citizens disappeared?" Zeke was on top of this new development at once.

Qian nodded. "More than three hundred of them. Mostly tourists. But also some who combined business with a short holiday here. China does have a number of representatives in Makasar, you know."

"I am aware of the large indigenous Chinese population here," Corry said. "I was not aware that Chinese people were disappearing."

"Perhaps we can arrange a cooperative activity in Sulawesi," Qian suggested.

"Perhaps."

The luncheon was over, the ship's tour had been given, and the air demonstration wound down as aircraft from the Tigers made formation landings on the upper flight deck. Corry accompanied Qian to the quarterdeck and the accommodation ladder where the Chinese gig waited.

Before Qian was piped over the side, he remarked to Corry, "I will expect you at seventeen hundred hours for a ship tour followed by dinner. Will you bring your division officers?"

Corry nodded. "Thank you for expanding the invitation to include them, Captain Qian. However, I do not want to leave my ship with all my major officers. Some one must remain aboard to assume command if required. I am sure you follow the same precautions because you came alone today."

This statement didn't faze Qian a bit. Or if it did, he remained inscrutable. "Well understood. Bring who you can."

After Qian's gig had departed, Zeke said to his Captain, "I don't recall the intel reports saying anything about Chinese citizens disappearing here."

"They didn't," the Captain of the *Shenandoah* responded.

"New data?"

"Yes. And a new slant on this mission."

Zeke sighed and slammed his left fist into his right palm. "It's going to be difficult enough getting the Sulawesis to cooperate. If we have to work with these Chinese too, it looks damned near impossible."

Corry slowly shook his head. He had a lot to teach this young man. "Zeke, never treat a problem as a problem. Look at it as an opportunity. If you do that, you'll suddenly discover an interesting new course of action that didn't appear to be there before. Come back to quarters with me. I want you to help me draft a written signal to CINCPAC about this."

"Aye, aye, sir." The two of them left the side and walked together through the ship. The enormity of the U.S.S. *Shenandoah* could be grasped by the fact that two people could walk side by side in a passageway. The Rivers class ships were the first submersibles in which this was possible. "How do we turn potential Chinese cooperation into an opportunity, sir?"

"We don't get to see much of the Chinese, do we?"

Zeke shook his head. "No, sir. They're even more secretive than the Russians."

"Not really. They think differently and they have a totally different world picture. It makes them seem secretive," Corry explained. The Captain had studied China during his most recent tour at the Naval Postgraduate School in Monterey. "Working with them presents us with two opportunities. One is the chance to learn more about them. The second is the leverage such a cooperative effort has on the Sulawesi government. Call it double power projection."

Zeke nodded in understanding. He dropped behind the Captain to allow a seaman to pass them in the opposite direction. Gaining Corry's side again, he observed, "I wouldn't want to be in General Helamahera's position right now."

"Aha! So you've surmised that the man is dragging his heels!"

"Yes, sir. Sort of like a cat that's been disciplined to behave itself. He's cooperating . . . just barely."

"So we'll get some more cooperation from him."

"Soon, I hope."

"Number Two, never be in a hurry to get something done," Corry admonished him gently. "On the bounce in response to orders, yes. But unless a firm deadline faces you squarely ahead, just keep plodding along. Keep pushing on the resistance. Later, it will appear to your superiors that you performed with amazing speed!"

Zeke had gotten used to these polemic lectures from Corry. He didn't ignore his Captain. He knew the man was only trying to help him get ahead in the Navy. If Corry hadn't seen promise in him, Zeke knew the Captain wouldn't be wasting his time. "Yes, sir. I see what you mean about the Chinese cooperation matter. I take it you will use the dinner opportunity tonight to find out more about them? As far as I know, no American has ever been in one of the Chinese Wind class boats."

Corry nodded and turned to look at his XO. "That's why I want Lovett, Walton, and Stocker to come with me tonight. You'll have the ship while I'm gone. Yes, I know you'd like to come, Zeke. And I know that you air types went through submarine school with high marks. However, my operations, deck, and engineering officers have spent their entire careers in submarines. I don't mean to belittle you, Zeke, but they will see things that you won't." He paused for a moment, then added, "And I may miss something. A Commanding Officer has a tendency to ignore small details and leave them to his experienced subordinates."

"I've noticed that, sir," Zeke replied lightly. "That's why a Number Two gets so much experience."

Corry smiled. He knew the tension of the last several days was diminishing. His own sense of humor was beginning to return. And he was pleased to see that Zeke was loosening up, too. "Yes, you have learned how to wrestle all types of alligators, haven't you?"

Zeke nodded. "And lots left to tangle with, I'm sure. Captain, I'd like to authorize liberty beginning tomorrow."

"I see nothing wrong with that at this time. But let's make it tentative. I don't expect anything to happen on the *Bei fung* tonight. But I want to coordinate it with Captain Qian. The last thing I need right now is to have American and Chinese sailors get into a brawl in Makasar."

"Yes, sir, but anything would be better than the present periscope liberty."

"Set it up, Number Two. I'll probably sign off on it tomorrow morning."

They met Major Bart Clinch coming the opposite way down the passageway. "Captain, I've got problems!" the Marine officer growled.

"We all do. Anything that I can help with?" Corry asked.

"Yes, sir!"

"Please join Zeke and me in my quarters."

Once in the captain's cabin, Corry sat down behind his terminal desk. Space in a submarine had increased over the years. The Commanding Officer now had three rooms—an office, a sleep compartment, and a head. Corry's desk was clear. Sometimes, a submarine had to perform steep maneuvers like a crash dive, so everything was stowed or secured. Otherwise, sailing in a submarine was probably the most benign environment any Navy person could expect at sea.

"Sit down, gentlemen. Now, what's your problem, Bart?"

"The goddamned Sulawesi want me to keep my Marine batt on the ship and in the embassy!" Clinch exploded, throwing his garrison cap on the desk. "That fucking idiot Helamahera tells me that the Sulawesi Army will do the searching. He wants to use my batt as a follow-up reserve unit to come in and take charge of Americans they happen to find! Shit, they haven't found any yet! What makes them think they're going to do any better in the next couple of days? Christ on a crutch, my boys will turn the goddamned island upside down. If anything can be found, we'll find it!"

Corry didn't reply to Bart's blow-off. He knew some of the ship's chiefs used language that was far saltier, but Corry took pains to set an example for his officers. He could tell Clinch to clean up his mouth. However, he also knew that the Marine officer was upset right then. So he let the man get it out. But he didn't respond immediately.

Bart waited for the Captain's reply. After about twenty seconds of awkward silence, Clinch finally ventured to say, "Captain, I think we're being screwed by these Sulawesis . . ."

Corry nodded. "Probably, Major. What are you going to do about it?"

"I don't know. My first reaction was to tell Helamahera to go piss up a rope and get out of my way. But that wimp bastard Manwaring cut me off at the knees." Clinch was bitching, pure and simple. He had a tendency to do that when someone tried to stand in the way. Clinch was a man who believed that others should lead, follow, or get the hell out of the way. He had his orders: Find a hundred Americans or learn what had happened to them. As the land-based arm of the carrier submarine, he considered that this operation in Sulawesi fell on his shoulders. Sure as hell the Captain couldn't drive the *Shenandoah* up on land and into the hills.

"So, Major, what do you want me to do for you?" The Captain of the *Shenandoah* asked one of his infamous embarrassing questions.

"I don't know, sir. Maybe tell the Ambassador to lean on the Sulawesis."

"Well, Major, I won't do that."

"Sir?" Clinch was having trouble believing what he was hearing. In the year he'd served under Corry, the man had gone to bat for the Marines on several occasions. But the Marine officer suddenly saw that this wasn't going to be one of those times. "May I ask why, sir? And inquire what your plans are?"

"You may ask and inquire. And I'll tell you I'm not going to do much of anything right now. Maybe tomorrow morning. We'll see how my dinner with the Chinese submarine commander goes this evening."

Clinch had cooled down a little bit, but he couldn't help but mutter almost under his breath, "Goddamned Chinks! Come steaming in here and screw everything up!"

"Not so, Major. General Helamahera now has two foreign submarines sitting in his harbor," Corry pointed out unnecessarily. Or maybe it was necessary, given the Marine officer's anger that had caused the man to miss an important factor in power projection diplomacy. "I suspect that the Honorable Kertanargara Vijaya is more than a little upset. And I'm sure they're both closeted with the Sulawesi Prime Minister this afternoon. In the meantime, Major, I might suggest that your Sergeant Major coordinate with the chief of the boat. Zeke is making up a liberty sked, and we're going to need SPs ashore. And they'll probably need some help from one of your companies in the embassy. Please take care of that as soon as we break up here."

"Uh, yes, sir! Do you want me to bring Bravo Company back to the ship?"

"No, because your batt is in good position right now to become airmobile very quickly."

Clinch suddenly realized that this stiff, formal, unflappable, and imperious naval captain had a better overall situational picture. And he was holding to his course while taking advantage of happenings today.

"Suppose one or more crew members disappears on liberty?"

Corry smiled. "Do you have to ask, Major? They won't disappear, of course. But if something does threaten them, we'll know about it very fast. And we'll be able to move very quickly. Won't we?"

"Yes, sir! And decisively, too. What about the Chinese?"

"Bart, the Chinese Captain just told us that more than three hundred Chinese visitors have disappeared here in the last six months," Zeke put in.

Clinch raised his bushy eyebrows. "Oh ho!"

"Yeah, oh ho!" Zeke echoed. "We'll have liberty parties going ashore by oh-nine-hundred tomorrow. Providing the Captain gives the okay later today."

Corry remarked, "The Captain anticipates approval of the XO's request to grant liberty to the crew. Gentlemen, if the local authorities won't move on this matter under our joint American-Chinese pressure, we'll shag ass and bypass." That was the first time either Zeke or Bart had heard Corry use an old sailor's term like that. "So let's be ready to do just that."

10

"Herb Hewitt says he knows an outstanding beach north of here where the spearfishing is good," Zeke told Terri Ellison at dinner that evening. "He says to get a party together and he'll show us."

"Sounds great! Let's do it!" Terri was always ready for almost anything. She turned to the man next to her. "How about it, Norm? You good for a beach party? Laura Raye, I *know* you are!"

"Anything to get the hell out of this composite bottle for a few hours!" was the comment from LCDR Norm Merrill, the Assistant Engineer Officer.

"The water's nice and warm, too. No need for wet suits. Count me in," the ship's Medical Officer responded with enthusiasm. She and Merrill were known for being a pair. They spent a lot of off-watch hours together when the Dolphin Club was open for business.

"Is Hewitt bringing his wife?" Merrill asked.

"He's a bachelor," Zeke reported.

"A bachelor, you say? I'm inviting myself." LCDR Natalie Chase ran an unusual outfit in the *Shenandoah*. The Navigation Department was predominantly female.

"Okay, sounds like we have a sextet," Zeke remarked. "I know the officer who's granting liberty requests, so I think it can be arranged." Corry had given Zeke that responsibility.

"I'd hope to hell you know him. If you don't, I do," Terri told him.

"Twelve hours, how about that?"

"That's enough time to do some serious diving and partying," the Medical Officer agreed. "Request twelve hundred hours to twenty-four hundred hours local time. I don't know what's out there in the bushes that comes out at night. And I don't want to become an expert on rare and exotic tropical diseases."

"Chief Armstrong and I will be working on liberty lists after dinner. See me first thing in the morning. I'll have leave cards ready," Zeke promised.

And he did.

But when Terri Ellison checked in at his office the following morning, she complained, "What the hell, Zeke? Why do we have to wear overboard tags on liberty?"

"You wear an overboard tag every time you goose one of your chickens off the deck," Zeke reminded her.

"Yes, but that's in case the emergency locator transmitter sinks with the aircraft . . ."

"So? Different reason here. I'm having everyone on liberty wear an overboard tag. If they get into trouble, I want the OOD to know right away." Zeke was taking more than normal precautions here in Makasar, and for good reasons. Nominally, an overboard tag was issued to everyone aboard in any situation where they might need a personal locator beacon. The tiny transmitter chip, powered by body heat, would broadcast a powerful signal that could act as a beacon for rescue parties. "I don't want any of our people to end up among the missing. You included."

She smiled. "Well, thank you for your kind consideration, sir!"

"So why are you complaining?"

"An overboard tag can be cold. And it can get in the way."

"Not if we're careful," he told her.

"Uh, I once triggered one accidentally, you know."

"Yes, when you were out with Bart Clinch. I don't get that wild."

"Depends. And jealousy doesn't befit you, Commander!"

"As you just said. That depends."

"On what?"

"Not what. Who."

Often, their conversation consisted of quick one-liners. A lot passed unspoken between them. They knew one another well. And Terri Ellison knew enough about Zeke Braxton to realize that the man needed some competition. It honed him to a finer edge. As XO, he had no professional competition in the ship. So Terri provided him with social competition instead. Major Bart Clinch was just the man for that.

Besides, Terri enjoyed the differences between the two men.

Zeke had Norm Merrill check out six scuba outfits, three extra tanks, and six spear guns. Several months ago, the officers' mess fund ended up with considerable surplus because of the extended action off Cape Horn. The officers and crew had stayed at General Quarters for several days. With the tension and the mixed-up duty·roster, a lot of people missed a lot of meals. Surplus funds in the officers' mess were often used to purchase recreation equipment. In San Diego on their return from Tierra del Fuego, LT Ken Keyes—who was mess treasurer at the time—found a scuba shop that was going out of business. With the approval of all, he spent some of the surplus mess funds to buy a dozen of the best scuba outfits.

The five officers went ashore at noon and were met at the dock by Hewitt who was driving an embassy van.

"Good! I don't have any scuba gear. And I don't dive anyway," Hewitt remarked as they piled aboard the vehicle. "But I did bring along enough food to help us survive the day."

"We ate lunch before we left the ship," Natalie told him.

"Okay, just that much more for supper tonight, then."

"Embassy food, I hope?" Laura Raye asked.

Hewitt nodded. "I know the Navy's policy about eating local foodstuffs. We get used to the Makasar foods. However, I took the precaution of having our embassy medical team run the usual Navy tests on what I brought. Don't worry, Doctor."

"We're on liberty. Call me Laura Raye."

"Two names?"

"I'm twice the woman."

About thirty minutes' drive north of Makasar put them on one of the most beautiful beaches they'd ever seen. Fifty meters or so offshore were about a dozen rocks. The incoming waves of the Makasar Straits broke first over these rocks, making the water over the beach smooth with small combers. Fifty meters back from the beach where the vegetation began, the ruins of an old colonial style resort hotel lay moldering in the jungle undergrowth. A few badly rusted beach tables and the remains of some abandoned beach umbrellas spotted the sands.

Otherwise, it was an unspoiled paradise.

The submariners quickly shucked their khaki tropical clothing. All of them were wearing swimming gear underneath.

"Can I take this damned overboard tag off?" Terri asked. In a swimsuit, she looked far more womanly than she did in uniform. Although she was physically fit and trim, she had an excellent figure that was well proportioned in twenty-first-century style—broad hips, narrow waist, and normal breasts. However, she had powerful shoulders and no excess fat. Her muscles didn't bulge like a man's, but she was physically strong. She could pull nine gees in an airplane and sustain it for minutes.

To Zeke Braxton, she looked very good at the moment with her short blonde hair curled around her face and head. "No," he told her. "Wear it. We don't know what could be in the water out there."

"No sharks, I guarantee you," Hewitt put in. "But squid and men-of-war and sea anemones. Any of which could get you in trouble."

"Just when I thought it was safe to go into the water," Natalie remarked.

"You're not wearing an overboard tag, Herb," Moore pointed out.

"I'm just a naval attaché. I'm expendable," Hewitt explained lightly.

"How long since you had a physical?" the Medical Officer suddenly asked.

"In Washington before I came here."

"I probably ought to check you over," she suggested. Or it might have been a promise.

"Herb, if you get into trouble, you'll just have to yell pretty damned loud," Zeke told him. "The rest of you, keep those tags on. Especially in the water until we get to know this area better. And in spite of Herb's assurances. Have you been diving here, Herb?"

"Nope. As I said, I don't skindive. But I'll wade in and watch you do it."

"How come you recommended this place, then?"

"Some embassy people have been diving here. That's how I knew about it. And we've had a couple of embassy beach parties here."

The water was clear. And warm—about 30° C. Before donning the scuba gear, they went swimming.

"Wow! Almost like taking a warm bath!" Natalie squealed in glee.

"Yeah, I thought it might be colder! It's colder at depth," Norm Merrill remarked, splashing about in knee-deep surf. As an Engineer Officer, he monitored ambient water temperature because it played a large role in the aquajet propulsion system of the *Shenandoah*. At depth, seawater tended to be cooler than on the surface because of the absence of solar heating. "This is great!"

When they put on their gear, they buddy-checked one another. "Don't forget," Laura Raye warned them, "we haven't been diving since we left Pearl. Don't exceed ten meters. Or five fathoms, depending on the calibration of your wrist gauge. That gives us enough air for about an hour."

"We should have brought a compressor," Terri said.

"And ten kilometers of extension cord so we could plug it in," Merrill added.

"Always the practical man," Natalie kidded him.

"If I wasn't, the *Shanna* would have stopped working long ago and we'd be sitting ashore in San Diego."

"Which might not be such a bad idea after all," Laura Raye put in. "We know what's on the bottom around there."

"And you wouldn't have to deal with the Sulawesi government," Herb added.

This was going to be a good party, Zeke decided. In spite of the fact that Hewitt wasn't a submariner, he was Navy. He'd been accepted into the party group.

"Twenty minutes for the first dive," Zeke told everyone. "Then we surface and rendezvous on the nearest of those offshore rocks. Herb, you'll just have to sit and watch."

"On the contrary, sir! We're all Navy. So every job needs a supervisor! Your plan leaves me alone with the booze . . ."

They swam out to where it was deep enough. Zeke deployed the float with the scuba flag, and they dived.

It was good diving. The water, being warm and clear, contained lots of sea life around the offshore rocks. Terri had strapped her underwater camera around her torso and began photographing both fish and underwater plants.

It was quiet under water except for the sounds of bubbles escaping from the scuba valves. That noise was acceptable. And it didn't scare off many of the fish that swam unhindered around the coral and the urchin-covered rocks.

Zeke and Terri stayed together while the other three went on their own exploration of the rocks and coral.

The only dangerous sea life he saw was a large zebra fish. He motioned Terri to remain clear. Its poison spines might not kill, but they could cause a lot of pain and discomfort if a diver reached out to touch it. Terri took some photos of it.

Zeke fired a spear at a passing fish. It looked like a cod that might be good to eat if fried over a fire later on the beach. He was no fish expert, however, so he couldn't identify it. He missed and recovered his spear. When Terri fired at another fish like it, she nailed it perfectly. He could see her grinning at him behind her mask. Well, it had been a long time since he'd engaged in gunnery practice in an aircraft. In spite of the fact that Terri had commanded only a patrol squadron, she had one aircraft to her credit.

At the end of twenty minutes, Terri and Zeke surfaced on one of the rocks closest to shore. It was large enough to hold all of them, sticking up about three meters above the water with gentle wave-worn slopes and terraces available for them to sit on.

Merrill and Laura Raye came up behind them.

As the Engineer Officer removed his mouthpiece and valve, Zeke asked, "Where's Natalie?"

Merrill looked around. "I don't know. She was with us five minutes ago."

Terri had flier's eyes. She saw that Herb Hewitt on the shore was waving wildly to them. "What's wrong?" she shouted in a voice that was surprisingly loud and strong for a woman her size.

Hewitt raised the portable car phone receiver above his head. He'd removed it from the van so he could have communication with the embassy. The attaché's voice came back through the rushing sound of the waves, "Embassy called! Ship called them! Natalie triggered her overboard tag!"

Zeke didn't get the whole shouted message. But he heard enough of it to know Natalie was somehow in trouble underwater. She could have gotten caught in something, been stung by something, or had her scuba gear fail. Whatever had happened, Zeke knew he had no time to waste. He stood up, took charge, and began to organize the group for action. "Merrill, we're going back down to look for Natalie. Now! Right now! Terri, go ashore and bring back the three spare air tanks and the spare scuba unit."

"The hell you say! I'm going down with you to look for her!"

"The hell I do say. Don't argue with me. Do as you're told! Norm, lead me to where you last saw Natalie. Laura Raye, stand by here because we may need you."

"I brought a medical kit. It's in the van."

"Terri, bring that back, too."

"Dammit, I'm no messenger!"

"Terri, right now you're part of an emergency rescue team. We may need those tanks and the med kit." Laura Raye spoke sharply to the CAG who wasn't used to taking orders from anyone but the Captain and Zeke . . . and sometimes not even them if she didn't believe the orders were correct.

But she listened to the ship's Medical Officer. Pilots always pay attention to what doctors tell them. Sometimes they don't like what they hear, but they listen. If pilots don't stay on excellent terms with doctors, pilots don't fly. So without another word, Terri unbuckled her weight belt, dropped it to the rock, then unfastened and slipped out of her scuba harness.

Zeke didn't wait to see what she did. Turning to the Assistant Engineer Officer, he told him, "Norm, lead off. Take me to where you were when you last saw Natalie."

Norm checked his mouthpiece, and turned around

to let Zeke check his bottles and valves. "Right! Check me, then turn around so I can check you."

"Laura Raye, check me!" Zeke snapped. "We can save some time that way."

The Medical Officer did so and, as she slapped Norm on the shoulder indicating his inspection was completed, Zeke also slapped Norm on the shoulder.

Zeke slipped the breather mouthpiece and regulator in place, checked it, and climbed down the rock into the water.

Norm Merrill followed him.

Just as Zeke went under, he saw Terri swimming rapidly toward the beach.

Now, where was LCDR Natalie Chase? And what had happened to her?

11

The sound of escaping bubbles from Zeke's scuba gear almost drowned out all other noises that he could hear in the sea around him. However, as he descended beneath the surface, he detected something that sounded like sonar pinging. It wasn't sonar. The sound didn't have the sharp attack and onset of a sonar pulse. It was softer with a barely detectable, slow buildup. And it was at a different frequency. In fact, it had many higher frequencies in it in the form of harmonics.

Maybe it's the Bei fung *sounding,* he thought. However, what was the Chinese submarine doing pinging sonar if it was anchored in Makasar harbor alongside the *Shenandoah*? Zeke didn't know and didn't try to answer his own question. It had other things on his mind just then.

He followed Norm Merrill, who was flippering hard ahead of him, moving as fast as possible through the water.

The water itself seemed to be cloudier than it had been when he'd surfaced a few minutes ago. He didn't know whether it was fog on his mask's faceplate or the water. Because this equipment was supposed to be the latest high-tech scuba gear with surface-treated faceplates, he hadn't properly spit and washed the faceplate before donning the mask on the surface.

Besides, he'd been in a hurry.

And he could still see well enough to follow Norm. Communication was otherwise impossible. They hadn't brought along N-fone equipment used by Navy frogmen teams. This party had started out as strictly a sport dive for fun.

Zeke decided that the water *was* a little cloudier.

It was so unusual that he brought his spear gun to the ready and made sure it was cocked.

At a depth of about nine meters, the two men came around a rocky corner.

They both saw it.

It was big, about the size of a man.

It was bluish.

It had a streamlined shape and a fluked tail.

And it was doing something with its jointed arms that ended in fingerlike appendages.

In the sea, Zeke had never encountered anything . . . except a fellow human . . . that possessed two jointed arms and hands.

Then Zeke saw Natalie Chase.

She was trying to fight off the creature with only one arm.

Her other arm was immobilized by something attached to the rock.

The creature tried to hit her with one of its "hands." The viscosity of the water slowed the creature's swing and robbed it of force. When the hand connected with Natalie, the blow only jarred her. It didn't keep her from fighting back.

But she wasn't having much luck resisting the creature. She was fighting in an unnatural environment with only one hand. She was also using her feet, a weapon the monster didn't have.

Whatever the creature was, it didn't appear to be helping Natalie.

Zeke had never seen anything like this undersea creature.

It wasn't any known species of whale, dolphin, or shark. If he hadn't encountered them himself while diving, he'd seen them in the various aquaria around San Diego.

He heard its sound over his bubbling air exhaust. It was the same strange sound he'd heard when he'd entered the water a few moments ago. Now, the sound was louder.

He knew that aquatic mammals often produced sonar and lidar returns that were of interest to submarine officers. At the New London Submarine School, he'd studied their organic sonar sounds to help him discriminate them from real targets.

After hitting Natalie, the creature somehow detected their approach, probably from the sound of their scuba air exhaust. It quickly turned its attention from Natalie to Norm who was closer than Zeke.

It was then that Zeke saw its "face."

It had two large eyes set well apart on a flat but streamlined face. They were obviously stereo-optic eyes good for close three-dimensional vision as well as distant vision. A circular orifice was located between the eyes. And a "mouth" opened and closed below it. It was a humanlike face, but it was like nothing Zeke had seen before. It was the face of a creature who lived and moved in the sea.

The creature produced a strange-looking device from somewhere on its body and started to point it at Norm.

It somehow had the appearance of a weapon.

So Zeke raised his spear gun, aimed as carefully as he could under the circumstances, and fired.

Norm Merrill reacted the same way.

Zeke's spear went right up the creature's nostril.

Norm had aimed for where he thought the heart might be. His missile went into the creature's body about a third of the way along it.

The sound stopped and was replaced with a squalling screech that seemed to be a cry of pain.

Then came a strident series of low-frequency belch-like sounds that also had a lot of high-frequency overtones. Zeke thought it might be a cry for help.

The "weapon" fell from the monster's "hand."

And the huge hulk went into spasmodic jerking movements. It thrashed at the end of Zeke's spear lanyard. The lanyard held.

Zeke hoped the spasms were death throes.

A greenish-black fluid—blood?—spurted from the nostril and around the wound from Norm's spear. It quickly mixed with the surrounding sea water and became a dark cloud.

Zeke cinched the spear's lanyard around his wrist. Whatever happened, he didn't want this beast to be "one that got away." Once they'd freed Natalie, he wanted to tow the creature to the surface where Terri could photograph it and Laura Raye could examine it. Zeke knew it was important that they collect as much information about this beast as possible.

Maybe its species was similar to the Komodo "dragons," the primitive dinosaur-like amphibians that had been discovered in the East Indies in the last century.

Or maybe it was a mutated dolphin.

But it didn't look like a dolphin.

Scenes and icons from twentieth-century science fiction horror movies and stories came to his mind. The first nuclear bomb tests had been carried out at Bikini and Kwajalein about a hundred years ago. The radiation levels had long since dropped into the noise level of the natural background radiation. But maybe those tests and the ones that followed it for several decades had produced some viable mutations in oceangoing flora and fauna. Maybe this creature was indeed a mutated aquatic mammal.

But right then he wanted to get Natalie out of there and all of them back to the surface.

The monster ceased its spasmodic jerkings. Its movements became weaker and weaker until they stopped. Zeke heard something coming from it that sounded like a series of rasping gasps. Then it jerked once more and went flaccid.

Zeke hoped it was dead and hoped that it wasn't, too. He didn't like the idea of reacting to an unknown creature by slaughtering it. But that human reaction had saved his remote ancestors many times, and the instinctual action still resided in his genes as a survival mechanism. It would have been better to have taken the monster alive so it could be studied. Alive, it might have been communicative. At least, Zeke had heard it emitting sounds that might have been information-carrying communications. After all, dolphins and whales had their own language.

But that was academic right then. He and Norm had indeed killed it. They had to go forward from there.

Norm was at Natalie's side. Zeke joined them.

Natalie pointed at her right arm.

Her hand, wrist, and about half the length of her forearm were encased in a woven, weblike cylinder that reminded Zeke of a large Chinese finger trap, the toy where once you insert your finger, it automatically clamps down on it if you try to withdraw.

The trap was attached to the rock with some sort of adhesive.

And it was indeed a trap because it had been baited.

The bait was a large, glistening jewel-like object, a pretty bauble that would cause someone to reach out for it.

Natalie's face was visible through her face mask. She looked scared but relieved.

Norm pulled his knife from his waist.

When he cut through the fibers of the web-like tube near its attachment to the rock, it acted like it was a live organism. The severed portion relaxed its grip on Natalie's hand and forearm. The portion remaining on the rock went into thrashing, jerking, pulsing motions resembling those of the creature now floating motionless at the end of Zeke's spear lanyard. The trap also spurted greenish-black fluid into the water.

Natalie was breathing hard and fast. Zeke could see that from the stream of her exhaust bubbles. She rubbed her forearm, nodded, and pointed upward.

But Norm spun her around and checked her tank valves. Quickly, he shifted her change-over valve to feed her mask air from the stand-by tank that was full. That would give her another seven liters of air at 200 atmospheres pressure. Norm was the Assistant Engineer Officer, a technical type. His duties in the *Shenandoah* put him at the interface between technology and people. So he activated Natalie's emergency reserves. He wasn't taking any chances that she might have used up her active tank in the excitement.

And he didn't let her freely flipper to the surface either. He took her arm and guided her upward.

Zeke followed, towing the dead creature by the spear lanyard. At this point, he didn't take time to stop and think about what all this could mean. He just wanted to get out of the water before the creature's companions, if any, showed up. He didn't know how dangerous they might be.

One thing for certain, Zeke thought: *this creature wasn't benign.* Natalie had been snared by its trap—he presumed it was the creature's trap because it was as strange as the monster. If Natalie had been diving alone or even with friends who were not as action-oriented as four other naval officers, she might have run out of air and drowned before being found and rescued. And any unarmed human rescuer would probably have been killed by whatever weapon the creature had started to point at Norm.

It was only when Zeke broke the surface that he realized he should have tried to recover the remains of the trap. And he should have looked for the weapon that the monster had dropped.

But he wasn't about to go back down there without a squad of armed Navy frogmen with him.

Both Terri and Laura Raye were waiting for them on the rock. The ship's doctor had her medical kit and Ellison had brought back the spare air tanks.

Natalie stripped off her mask and began taking deep breaths of air. She looked frightened but not terrified.

Anyone who goes down to the sea in submarines has conquered terror long ago. And she'd been aboard when the *Shenandoah* had been attacked by Chilean patrol submarines off Cape Horn. In fact, she had been the one who'd done the pinpoint navigation that had caused one of the Chilean boats to run aground. The other had broken off its attack for fear of shoals. Her precise maneuvering recommendations permitted Chief Weaver to put two underwater missiles into it. Natalie Chase was no cowering, simpering maid out of a fairy tale. None of the *Shenandoah*'s ladies were.

Imprints of the trap's woven webbing were still visible on the navigator's right arm. It hadn't broken her skin but had indeed held her snugly.

Laura Raye said only, "Let me look at that arm, Nattie. Anything else hurt?"

"Only my pride," Natalie admitted. "I should never have reached for that jewel. I should have seen the trap spread out around it. My arm hurts, but not badly. I didn't break anything. And the monster didn't hurt me when it hit me." She indicated her shoulder where the blow from the creature's hand had landed.

"My God, Zeke, what the hell is this beast you're towing?" Terri exclaimed as she saw the bulk of the monster. It was semi-floating, half of its hulking body on the slope of the rock and the rest in the water.

It was bluish, but that coloration seemed to come from some sort of clothlike outer skin that covered everything except its "face" and "hands." Its two large eyes now stared blankly ahead without movement.

"It was attacking Natalie," Zeke tried to explain as he took off his scuba mask. "Norm and I shot it. Killed it."

It was only then that Zeke was assaulted by the awful, sickening smell.

"Stick it back in the water! It stinks!" Terri urged him.

"Not before you photograph the hell out of it!"

Terri wrinkled her nose. "Ugh! I'll try! The faster

I do it, the quicker we can stick it back! Can you haul more of it out of the water?"

Zeke pulled on the lanyard. Out of the water, the beast was *heavy*. "Norm, give me a hand!"

Norm Merrill looked up from where he was supporting Natalie. He was still wearing his scuba mask. And he didn't want to leave the navigator until he knew she was all right.

"Go help," Laura Raye told him. "Natalie's okay. I'm here with her. Go do it so Zeke can put it back in the water and get rid of that smell!"

"I'll keep my mask on. I thought you were used to organic stinks, Laura Raye," Norm said.

"I don't like to do abdominal surgery. Never have," she admitted. "But this is worse. A lot worse!"

On the rock in the air, the beast was about two meters long. Zeke estimated that it weighed one hundred fifty kilograms. He and Norm had to get down in the water and wrestle the dead body up on the rock.

It was indeed clad in something resembling cloth.

"This is weird," Terri remarked as she pointed the automatic underwater camera and snapped off frame after frame. "What the hell is it?"

"I don't know," Zeke said. "That's why we've got to document it before something happens. From its stink, it must already be decomposing."

"Spread out one of its 'hands,' Zeke! Terri should get a shot of those 'fingers.' They're multijointed and opposable," Norm observed. "I watched it holding and moving objects down there. And I also saw it grab its weapon . . . a pistol, maybe."

The creature's hand was indeed just that. But it had four digits arranged in pairs. From the way the digits were articulated, each finger could be used in opposition to the other three in the same way that the human thumb can touch every other finger on the human hand.

Zeke discovered Laura Raye and Natalie looking over his shoulder at the creature.

"Natalie is okay for now," the Medical Officer reported. "I want to get a close look at this fish from the biological point of view. Certainly, those hands and fingers are different from any animal I know."

"How about that face?" Natalie added. "It *is* a face, too!"

"Terri, get some shots of that, please," Zeke instructed her.

"Damned right I will!"

"Stereoscopic vision," the doctor observed. "Nictating membrane over the eye, but the eye appears normal. It has an iris and pupil. Look, one is dilated and the other isn't. Typical reaction to the death syndrome."

"That means it could use those eyes guiding its hands to manipulate fine objects close to it," Norm added. "Just the way we do."

"No nostrils. Only one apparent intake right on the center line," Zeke indicated where his spear had entered. "I aimed for that, hoping it was a nostril. I figured it was the easiest way to get a spear into its brain. Looks like I was right."

"Mouth below it," Laura Raye muttered as she inspected it. "Look at that jaw, those teeth! Resemble anything you know?"

"Yeah, my own jaw, which our gentle Dental Officer poked and probed just the other day," the Assistant Engineer Officer replied.

"With those teeth and that jaw architecture, it's an omnivore. It can eat anything—plant life or meat—just like we can," Laura Raye said as she peeled back the skin of the lips to reveal the teeth for Terri's camera.

"Which means it could eat us," Terri muttered.

"Yeah. I think it tried to do just that," Zeke guessed.

"Huh?"

"I think this monster lives underwater. It was using

traps baited for humans. I'll bet it was fishing for us," Zeke ventured to say. He was voicing the speculation that was slowly helping him come to a conclusion that he didn't like to admit. "It sure as hell caught Natalie."

The navigator rubbed her right arm. "That it did. I might have cut myself free if it hadn't come along to hassle me. Since I've never been looked at as dinner before, I couldn't tell you whether or not it was slavering over me. But whatever it intended to do, I didn't want to be any part of it!"

Zeke looked at the dead creature on the rock. "I think we may have a clue to the missing people," he said slowly.

Terri Ellison put the camera down and nodded. "I see what you mean. But why hasn't anything like this monster been encountered before? Do you know of any reports?"

"I haven't heard or read of any," the Medical Officer of the U.S.S. *Shenandoah* agreed, then ventured to express her own thoughts. "I don't know of any animal that's structured like this. The hands alone are strange enough. This is quickly bringing me to a conclusion I don't like . . ."

"Are you thinking what I'm thinking?" Zeke wanted to know.

"Maybe. When I said I don't know of any animal that's like this, I meant any terrestrial animal." Laura Raye Moore paused and then said what everyone else was thinking. "I was taught to work using Occam's Razor—seek the simplest possible explanation. When I do that, I've got to postulate that this beast is truly alien. Its origin is extraterrestrial."

12

"Get it back in the water before I get sick!" Terri urged the two men.

"I want to examine it some more!" Laura Raye insisted. "I can stand the smell!"

"Put on your scuba mask and breathe bottled air," Zeke told the pilot. "In fact, I'm going to do that myself. And I suggest everyone else do the same."

"Aha! A breath of sanity in an otherwise bizarre situation!" Norm said. "Laura Raye, if you're right, we've got to get this monster back to the ship before it decays."

Natalie responded after she'd re-donned her scuba mask, "I think she's right. And so are you, Norm. I'll swim ashore and contact the ship on Herb's cellular."

"The hell you will!" Zeke exploded. "No one—repeat, no one—is going into these waters alone!"

"I didn't see any more of these monsters. Only one," Norm recalled.

"But I heard it give some kind of squalling call before it died," Zeke said, remembering the strange sound the monster had emitted before it went into its form of Cheyne-Stokes breathing. "That call probably alerted others like it. They could be down there now. Or shortly."

"So how the hell are we going to get out of here?" Terri asked.

"Wait for low tide," Natalie suggested. As a navigator, she would think of that. Terri, commander of the Air Group, never paid any attention to tides. "Ebb

tide has started already. In a few hours, we can probably wade ashore."

"I'm glad we have a navigator along," Zeke said
with a grin.

"As I remember, low tide in Makasar harbor occurs
about sunset," Natalie went on. She looked at the sky
and then consulted her wristwatch. "Three hours."

"And we're going to sit here and breathe our scuba
air until then?" Terri asked rhetorically. "How much
have we got?"

"I estimate each of us has about ninety minutes on
our backs right now. And Terri brought back the
spare scuba harness with three extra air bottles. I
think we can hack it," Laura Raye guessed.

"Three hours . . . Well, I hope the sunblock didn't
wash off while I was underwater," Terri mused. "Otherwise, I'll be burned to a crisp by this sun."

Laura Raye made a decision. "Okay, that does it!
I can't take the chance that all of us will end up in
sick bay with sunburns. We're pretty much blanched
out. All submariners are. We're much more suscepti-
ble to sunburn than anyone else. The sunblock isn't
supposed to wash off, but it could have. So we're
going ashore, Commander Zeke!"

Zeke shook his head. "No, I'm going ashore.
Armed. And Norm is going to stand up on this rock
ready to fire away at anything that comes after me in
these shallow waters." He stood up. "I'll get on the
horn with Herb and contact the ship. I'll ask the OOD
to send a boat over . . ."

"Or a Vee-stol," Terri put in. "Ginny Geiger didn't
go on liberty. She can send a 'dyne over from her
transport squadron, Zeke. Ask her to bring a sling for
our alien monster."

"I'll request both a boat and a 'dyne," Zeke promised. "But I'll be damned if I'm going to tell them we
want to recover an extraterrestrial dolphin."

"I agree, Terri. If we tell them we found an alien,
someone is going to think we've been out in the sun

too long without our hats. And they'll take their own sweet time getting here! Tell them instead that we found an interesting new form of sea life that may be the answer to all the missing people," Laura Raye suggested.

Terri stood up and extended her hand toward him. "Norm, give me your spear gun. I'll carry two of them."

"Carry them where?"

"With me when I swim back with Zeke."

"Hell, no! I'm not going to put you at risk!" Zeke exploded.

"The hell you say! I'm not going to let you risk your hide just to be a hero, Zeke!" Terri shot back. "Look, as you damned well know, in air combat the one who gets shot down is Tail End Charlie, the lone target. We fly in groups of two so we can check six for each other. So I'm going along with you, and we'll check six for each other."

"No, dammit!"

"Dammit, yourself! When you get in that water, you'll find me beside you! So court-martial me for disobeying orders! Let's stop arguing and do what has to be done before this beast rots here! Or its buddies come and try to pick us off!"

"Uh, Zeke," Norm Merrill ventured, trying not to raise hackles because he was junior to all of them, "if Terri's right—and I will defer to her expertise as she defers to mine—and two of you is good, then all of us would be better. I wonder if any aliens are going to openly attack five of us swimming armed in shallow tidal waters toward the shore. As a submarine tactical officer, would you do that? Even if you outnumbered the enemy?"

"I sure wouldn't," Natalie remarked.

"You're the one who steered us into shallow waters off Cape Horn," Norm reminded her.

"That was a different tactical situation."

"That it was!" Zeke admitted.

"Add to that the possibility that a large number of sea monsters might be able to pick us off these rocks when they find we've killed one of their buddies," Terri said. "We shouldn't stay here another minute! Let's all head for shore and tow this beast behind us! It shouldn't take more than three minutes to swim to where we can wade in. And I can tell you for sure that if anything comes after me during those three minutes, I'm ready for it. And if it goes for me or any of you, I'll attack it. I don't give a damn how big it is. I'll kill it!"

The others knew Terri probably would. And so would they.

Zeke paused for a moment, then made up his mind. Actually, he didn't have to. The other four had already decided what they were going to do. They were not going to remain on that rock. "Okay, don't ever let it be said that the ship's XO never paid attention to suggestions from others," Zeke told them. "Check your spear guns. If you see something that moves and isn't one of us, shoot it in the nostril. Everyone ready?"

They were.

"Swim with your mask underwater until your feet touch bottom and you can wade ashore," Zeke instructed them. "That way, you can check six on everyone else while we're swimming. Norm, you and I will tow Moby Dick here. If we get into a fight, the first priority is to protect each other. If the aliens want their dead buddy back, saving it for study is second priority. We can come back and trap some of *them* for study if we have to!"

Together, they rolled the dead carcass back into the water. And together they entered the water and went under.

At once, Zeke detected the odd keening, pulsing sound he'd heard when he had gone into the water to rescue Natalie.

Something was underwater with them and was pinging them.

He wished he had a frogman N-fone so he could communicate to the other four. But the goal right then was to get to shore towing the alien carcass behind them—and to watch behind them for possible attack.

He could see various dark fluids now seeping from the alien body in tow. They dispersed quickly in the water, making it extremely cloudy in their wake. Good! Maybe that would confuse whatever was out there sounding them.

They hadn't been under more than a minute before Zeke saw one, then two, then several large, dark shapes swimming through the rocks they'd left. Then he heard the strange dolphinlike sounds of their underwater communication. He guessed that at least four and perhaps six aliens were out there, following at the limits of vision in the water.

He checked his spear gun. It was ready. But he wasn't going to waste a shot at long range. If the creatures came close enough to assure a clear shot, Zeke would fire. He hoped the others would follow the same tactics.

They did. They were submarine officers. And, at this moment, they weren't in a submarine; each of them was an individual submarine under possible attack! They seemed to know it and to behave accordingly.

The swim seemed to take more than three minutes. Maybe Terri had been kidding them. Maybe she had merely been trying to give them positive motivation to make the swim in the first place. Yes, it had been tough to go back into the water knowing that *something* down there might come after everyone!

However, suddenly Zeke saw the bottom below him. As he swam against the outgoing tide, it came closer and closer. Finally, he could reach out with his spear gun and touch it.

Quickly, he put his flippered feet down and stood

up. The water was about a meter deep. He was up to his torso in the rolling waves.

And Herb Hewitt was plunging out through the low surf to help them.

The dead alien scraped the bottom and the strain on the towing lanyard suddenly increased.

Without taking off his mask, he called to Hewitt, "Come here and give Norm and me a hand. This thing's heavy!"

"What the hell is it?" the naval attaché asked. He wrinkled his nose. "It stinks like hell! Christ, I could smell it all the way on shore here!"

"It attacked Natalie. Norm and I killed it. We brought it back to see if we can't find out more about it," Zeke tried to explain as he and Norm pulled on the lanyard to beach the alien. They couldn't get the alien any farther up the beach. It was still in about half a meter of water, and that was as far as they were going to be able to tow it. "Help us roll it up on the beach, Herb!"

Hewitt viewed the hulk with distaste. "My God, it's decaying!"

"Yes, and we've got to get it back to the *Shenandoah* so we can examine it!"

"What the hell is it?"

"We don't know," Terri admitted as she walked up onto the beach. She didn't remove her mask. None of the other four did, either. The masks were some protection against the awful stench. She began taking pictures again while the three men struggled to move the monster.

The body was now soft. It squished as they pushed on it. It was coming apart in a hurry.

"Laura Raye, it's decomposing fast!" Norm called out.

The doctor came over and poked at it. "I'll confirm that. Very fast. Faster than anything I know about. Terri, I hope you're documenting this. We may not have enough left in thirty minutes to take back to the ship!"

"I'm shooting as fast as I can," Terri reassured her.

They finally stopped struggling with the alien after

five minutes. It was getting too soft to manipulate. The tide was going out rapidly now, and the monster was almost totally beached.

And it was almost unrecognizable.

"Forget calling the ship! We can't airlift this thing back! The best we can do is document what's happening here!" Zeke decided. He hadn't called the ship on Herb's cellular yet.

Laura Raye pulled some instruments out of her medical kit. "Give me a hand here, someone! I've got to try to cut some tissue samples from it before it comes completely apart!"

The rotten stench was somehow getting through Zeke's face mask now. Swallowing to keep from throwing up, he steeled himself and stepped over to give her a hand.

As she sliced the outer clothlike layer with a scalpel and peeled it back to reveal what was underneath, she recoiled. "Get the hell away from it! Now! It's already full of something that looks like maggots! They're eating it! They don't look like ordinary maggots, and I don't want any of them to get loose on us! Back off, Zeke!"

"Gladly, Doctor!"

Zeke, Terri, and Laura Raye were the only ones who could brave the foul reek, even through their face masks. They backed off to about three meters and watched. The others retreated to a greater distance. Together, they looked on while an incredible series of events took place.

"Don't even open your mouth and inhale," Zeke suggested. "The smell even *tastes* terrible!"

"A whole different biological process is taking place here," Laura Raye explained, trying to observe it as closely as she could. "I don't know what those maggotlike organisms are or how they're harbored in the living body of the alien. Death must somehow trigger their development from an egg or pupal state. But they develop so fast! Where does the energy come from that would allow them to do that?"

"As you just said, Doctor, we're watching a totally different biological process going on," Zeke said, being careful to inhale only through his scuba gear. "Which makes me an even stronger believer that we've encountered some sort of extraterrestrial life form."

"I'll stake my commission on that." Laura Raye Moore didn't realize that she'd have to. "I'm glad Terri got it all in the camera."

Terri was still photographing the scene. "Yup! Got it in the can."

"Look!" Zeke pointed out. "Some of those 'maggots' are leaving the corpse and crawling back into the water!"

"Got that, too!"

"They must have consumed all of the body that they could," the doctor speculated.

Slowly over the next thirty minutes, the body of the alien on the beach shrank in size. More and more parasites left it and returned to the water. Some of them tore off pieces of the outer covering as they went.

Out in the tidewater, Zeke occasionally saw a surface ripple where something had come close to the surface before diving again.

Then he saw something else.

The head of an alien poked above the surface, looked around, and disappeared again.

"Terri, did you get that?"

"What? Where?"

"One of them poked its head above the water!"

"No! Missed it! Damn!" She swung the camera around so it pointed out to sea. "Maybe one of them will do it again . . ."

"And maybe not! Look, record what happens here in front of us," Laura Raye insisted. "That we *know* is happening!"

But by sundown, it was all over. Absolutely nothing was left on the beach except the slightest suggestion of the awful, rotting, putrid stench.

"Well, shipmates, I'm not so sure that I want to picnic on this beach this evening," Norm Merrill remarked as the six of them looked over the spot where the alien had been. He dug his toe into the sand. "I'm not so sure I'm hungry . . ."

"Hell, I'm not so sure we're *safe!*" Hewitt added. "I don't know whether those damned things can come ashore or not!"

"Nor am I," Laura Raye agreed. "Frankly, Herb, I'd just as soon you took us into Makasar so I could get a stiff drink. Or two. Or three."

"I'll go along with that," Norm agreed.

"Well, if that's what you want," the attaché remarked, digging into the picnic basket he'd brought, "we don't have to go as far as Makasar." He extracted a bottle and held it up.

"Glenlivet! Oh, Herb, you are a prince of a fellow!" Natalie gushed.

"And unopened, too! Herb, I thought you warned us about leaving you alone on shore with all the booze," Terri said.

"Things got too busy," Herb admitted.

"Shipmates, I want to get back to the *Shenandoah* with this information! I want to have a look at the photos," Zeke interrupted them. "This incident goes a hell of a long way toward explaining where the missing people went."

"Zeke, you're a zealot!" Natalie told him.

"Maybe. Maybe not. But do you want to sit on this data for another six hours and then explain to the Captain why? Look, I know the man. The sooner we get back with it, the better!"

"You act as if this is something special to the *Shenandoah*," Herb Hewitt said.

"It is," the Executive Officer of the carrier submarine replied, then explained, "These aliens appear to be underwater creatures. The submarine may be the only weapon we have that can be used to fight them!"

13

Captain William M. Corry shook his head slowly. He'd heard the report from Zeke Braxton—supplemented with additional statements from Terri Ellison, Natalie Chase, Norm Merrill, naval attaché Herb Hewitt, and Laura Raye Moore. It was bizarre and improbable. However, their accounts had a frightening reality. "Your report is very difficult to believe," he told the six officers seated in the wardroom of the U.S.S. *Shenandoah.*

Yet he *did* believe them. He had to. The tale of the encounter with the alienlike underwater being had been related to him by his top officers and an embassy attaché.

These were all people whom he trusted. Five of them were graduates of the Naval Academy. They'd served under his command for a year or more. They were all honorable persons. If they'd had too much to drink on their beach party, his Medical Officer would not have permitted them to brief him. All six of them could not have been hallucinating.

Furthermore, when they related their individual experiences, what they said hung together as an integral story. Corry could sense the fear, frustration, terror, anxiety, and disbelief in their minds. They'd been through a traumatic experience. Their naval professionalism had helped them keep their heads in what might otherwise have been a very tragic situation.

"The photos should be processed shortly, sir. I shot a lot of film," Terri said. "I probably should have taken a videocam, but I opted for good quality color film instead. Besides, I had a good waterproof camera . . ."

"It would have been helpful if you could have brought back the remains of the sea monster," Corry pointed out unnecessarily.

"Yes, Captain, but we couldn't," the ship's Medical Officer stated firmly. "It was operating with a different set of biological processes. When I saw it being decomposed by those parasites, I didn't want them or any strange microorganisms or viruses to get aboard this ship! So we had to stand off and watch it being eaten or decomposed. Frankly, in spite of all my training, I didn't want to get close to those maggotlike parasites myself."

"No one aboard could have withstood the odor. That beast stank to high heaven!" Natalie recalled, wishing she could forget the smell.

"I wanted to take a tissue sample . . . until I saw those parasites." Laura Raye Moore also wanted to forget some of the horror she'd seen.

Corry looked at his XO. "So, Zeke, you believe that this monster you killed was 'fishing' for human beings?"

"I do, sir. If I were a fisherman—and some of my forefathers were Maine lobstermen—I'd do it just the way that beast did. Except that it's a sea creature fishing for land creatures."

"This is beginning to make sense, Captain," Herb Hewitt put in. "The Sulawesi government couldn't possibly know about these creatures operating in their waters."

"It's highly unlikely that they do. If they did, it's improbable that they'd allow these creatures to prey on people," Zeke added.

"And I would have caught some rumors and stories about it circulating through the unofficial gossip channels," Hewitt assured them.

Corry had to agree with them. But he wanted to

make sure that they hadn't seen just one isolated creature. "You saw more of them?"

"I saw one more," Zeke confirmed. "It poked its head above water. But I saw disturbances in the water offshore that could have been caused by as many as six others. So I don't think we saw a lone sea fisher. It was part of a social group. It was dressed in some sort of clothing. It carried what I think was a weapon. And I *heard* underwater sounds that were similar to those used by dolphins to communicate. It was *talking* to others. Or communicating with them. I highly discount the possibility that it's an isolated case of a single sea monster. There's a group of them. And they have technology. That trap was sophisticated."

"I'll say it was!" Natalie broke in, holding up her right forearm where reddish welts and a black-and-blue mark from the trap's woven web tube persisted. "I couldn't tell it was a trap when I first saw it. I was attacked by the bait. It looked like a big jewel. When I touched it, it reacted very fast. That trap closed around my hand and arm almost instantaneously. I could have cut myself free with my diving knife except that it had my right arm. It was awkward to reach my knife with my left. Before I could get to it, the monster was there. Then I had my hands full fighting with it. God, it was ugly!"

"We've speculated among ourselves that these creatures are using the shallow seas around Sulawesi and probably some of the other islands as their 'fishing grounds,' " Herb explained.

"From the looks of that trap," Norm said, "they're interested in catching human beings. It was baited with something that would catch the eye of a human being and cause someone to reach for it out of curiosity. By the way, the trap itself was a living organism, not a mechanical device. It bled when I cut it. I killed it, in fact. If I hadn't been so damned anxious to get Natalie out of there, I would have cut it loose from the rock."

"We should have recovered the monster's weapon, too. But we didn't." Zeke didn't feel good about that. In the panic of the moment underwater there, all his rationality seemed to have gone away. "What the hell am I going to forget the next time the *Shenandoah* gets in a bind?"

Captain William Corry sensed that these were six very upset people. A submarine crew—even one as large as that in the *Shenandoah*—has an intimacy and camaraderie that is missing in surface ships. Submarines have always had crews whose members were friends with one another. Except for Herb Hewitt who had become a de facto crew member as a result of the incident, these people were not only his top officers but his friends. The only barrier that stood between them was a formidable one: he was their Commanding Officer.

Corry held up his hand. "Zeke, don't fret about it. I'm not worried that any of you will come unbonded under pressure in the ship. We train very hard for all the possible contingencies we may be faced with in the *Shenandoah*. All of us react in an almost automatic mode when carrying out our ship duties. You six came up against something you were completely unprepared for. You reacted just as anyone would have." He paused and reflected, "In fact, if you had not been naval officers, you probably would have panicked or hesitated. And one or more of you would have been killed. I believe all of you behaved in an exemplary manner. You should be proud of the outcome."

"Thank you, Captain! I will admit I'm damned glad to be back in the *Shenandoah*!" Natalie remarked, still rubbing her right arm. "But I don't know whether I'm proud of the way I acted. I panicked, whether anyone else thinks so or not. I was the one who was trapped. Zeke and Norm were the ones who behaved bravely and saved me. That should be worth the Life Saving

Medal, and I'll write the commendation for Norm and Zeke."

"I'm sure they deserve it, but we're going to have some trouble with awards and commendations in this situation," Corry told them frankly. "I believe you for many reasons. You're people I know. I trust you. But we don't have anything except your verbal report. Doctor Moore couldn't even get a tissue sample . . . Other people probably aren't going to believe you because they don't know you like I do."

"Captain, we have photos," Terri reminded him. "They'll be here shortly."

"Check on them, will you, Terri?" Corry asked her.

"Roger that, sir! I'm anxious to see them, too. Sometimes I think it was a bad dream." She reached up, pulled a ship's intercom handset off the bulkhead, punched in the photo lab number, and began to speak in low tones into the device.

Corry turned to the embassy naval attaché. "Commander, while we're waiting, let me ask you how this will be received at the embassy and especially by Vijaya and Helamahera."

"If we've got photos, it ought to shake them up considerably," Hewitt guessed. "It will also take some pressure off the Sulawesis. I can understand their behavior. They didn't know about these alien fisher things. They really don't know what to do about the missing Americans . . ."

"And Chinese," Zeke added.

"Yes. So they're acting defensive. I think I would, too. Captain, I think we'll get full cooperation from both the Sulawesis and the Chinese when we release those photos to them."

"I'm not so sure the Sulawesis will be happy about it. Release of those photos will probably kill what little is left of their tourist industry," Zeke remarked, recalling the decaying ruins of the old resort hotel on the beach.

"Not necessarily," Hewitt replied. "It may cause

curious people to flock here in throngs from all over the world trying to see these beasts. The Dutch had a lot of trouble trying to protect the Komodo dragons when they were discovered nearby in the last century. And people are travel-happy these days. They're always looking for something new to do and someplace different to go. The potential danger of this just makes it even more interesting . . ."

"Well, release of the photos is going to be up to the Defense Department . . . or maybe even the White House in this case," Corry decided. "Terri, your photos are likely to set the world on its ear. They're the first photos of something we that believe to be an extraterrestrial life form."

"And it's living in the oceans of our planet," Natalie added.

"And 'fishing' for human beings," Norm Merrill finished.

The seven of them sat there for a moment in silence, looking at one another.

It was beginning to dawn on them what they'd done.

And they began to realize how this incident was going to impact their naval careers.

The United States Navy—in common with the British Royal Navy from which many traditions and procedures had sprung—was and always had been a group of highly dedicated professionals. Commissioned or enlisted, they faced humankind's age-old enemy, the sea. Even when at war with other humans, the sea was still their number one enemy. Far more vessels had gone down because of the perils of the sea than had been sunk by enemy action. Technology had always been a tool for human survival at sea and had led to the partial conquest of the world's oceans. Navy people were technocrats. Basically, they were all no-nonsense people with strong and firmly held personal beliefs.

One of the most cherished beliefs of the naval service was that of personal integrity and honor. One did *not* do *anything* that was out of line. One did *not* espouse fringe beliefs, unusual religions, or weird technologies. Change came to the Navy through the quiet, persistent, dogged determination of believers who were forced to *prove* their contentions. In the history of the United States Navy, thousands of people were responsible for the Navy as it was in the twenty-first century. Only a few mavericks such as Rickover appear in naval annals while there are many Moffets and Raborns. In the world of submarines, only the inventor, Holland, stands out; the naval officers who championed the submarines are lost to history.

If the Commanding Officer of the U.S.S. *Shenandoah* reported the discovery of alien intelligent life living in the oceans and preying on human beings, he and his officers would have to prove conclusively with data and documentation that they were right.

Thus far, the only proof—such as it was—was their own personal recollections.

That wasn't enough.

So they sat quietly, thinking these thoughts, while they waited for the photographs.

Even photographs would be looked upon with suspicion. Photos are easy to fake so that even the expert can't tell. Hollywood special effects experts had developed their art to such a high level that nearly everyone now had a reason to distrust photos.

A photographer's mate showed up with two envelopes of prints. "Four sets of prints, Commander, just like you ordered. The extra prints took us a little bit longer to get this out . . ."

Corry and Zeke quickly took one envelope of prints and began checking them over. The others grabbed prints, too.

Corry looked at Zeke and the XO met his gaze.

A pall of disappointment spread throughout the wardroom.

"Great photos of the undersea life, Terri," Norm remarked.

"Yeah, that's a nice, sharp photo of Zeke's spear missing the fish," Natalie observed.

All of the remaining photos that Terri Ellison had taken of the alien sea monster were out of focus, blurred to the point that only rough shapes could be discerned.

"Goddamned camera must have been broken!" Terri exploded.

"No, your camera was working perfectly. Just like it was designed to do," Laura Raye said. "I'll bet if you check it, you'll find it's in perfect condition."

"They why are all these photos out of focus?"

"Not all of them. The ones you took of the underwater vegetation and flora around the rocks are perfectly sharp. Terri, that's an underwater camera, right?"

"Affirmative! One of the most expensive Batavian cameras I could buy! You know I like to photograph undersea life!" the submarine's CAG reminded the Medical Officer. "When I get back to Pearl, I'm going to fold that camera until it's all corners and tell that dealer to shove it somewhere that will make him feel very uncomfortable . . ." Terri Ellison was angry. She had missed the opportunity of a lifetime. She had screwed up the first photographs of an alien being!

She shook her head in bewilderment. "Why? Why?" she muttered to herself.

Norm Merrill tried to explain, "I'm sure you know why. But in the heat of the moment you forgot. That's an underwater camera. Its lens is corrected for the refractive index of water, not air. It was autofocusing perfectly. But it couldn't overcome the fact that it has a water immersion lens on it."

"Damnation! I did forget about putting on the correction lens I use in air!"

Natalie Chase was shaking her head sadly. She was a computer expert. Most navigators were. "We might try computer enhancement and image reconstruction," she suggested halfheartedly. "I don't know if we could improve them much. Edge and contrast enhancement techniques can help a lot. I could try . . ."

"They'll be spotted at once as having been manipulated in a computer," Laura Raye Moore pointed out. She did a lot of enhancement work in sick bay with the various human internal imaging systems she had. "But believable documentation they won't be."

"Well, the color of the monster is right," Zeke observed.

"So is the color of my red face," Terri added.

Zeke looked at her. "You didn't get sunburned today, Terri."

"No, it's caused by embarrassment. That was a stupid mistake. It was the first time I'd used that camera since I bought it in Pearl," she grumbled darkly. Inwardly, she was kicking herself for not thinking straight in the crunch. That never happened when she was in the air. But, again, she had trained hard to be the best possible naval aviator, anticipating all the emergencies, practicing all the engagements and procedures, and fighting to excel at all of them.

This incident had caught her completely by surprise. And she discovered, much to her chagrin, that she was as human as anyone else.

Terri Ellison didn't like that. She wanted to be better than anyone else. Usually, she was. She forced the world to play by her rules when she could. When she couldn't make that work, she played hard by the existing rules. Occasionally—only occasionally—in her life had she been caught by her own human shortcomings.

"And this was *so* important, too . . ." she finally said with a sigh.

"It's still important," Corry told her. "Natalie, would you and the doctor undertake whatever image enhancement you can with these, please? Other people may not believe them when you're finished. However, we'll have a record that will help us when we run up against these monsters again."

He paused and looked around. Slowly and carefully, trying to keep from stuttering because he felt very strongly about what had happened to his officers, he told them, "Don't feel discouraged. We'll get better data. We're going to run into them again. Because we're going to go looking for them. And we'll find them. And we'll get the answers." He stood up. "Doctor Moore, I want you to make sure that everyone gets a good night's sleep. You have my authorization—if you need it, which you really don't—to prescribe sleepy pills for anyone here who might need them tonight. Sleep may be difficult after all that you've been through today." He thought a moment, then added, "Others may not need such help. Zeke, I want you to make sure the Dolphin Club is open all night."

Sometimes human companionship is the best medicine against the fear of the unknown.

14

The engine spaces of the U.S.S. *Shenandoah* were large enough that Captain William Corry could convene the entire Engineering Department and speak to them all at one time. Furthermore, the propulsion system of the carrier submarine was so quiet that he could talk in a normal voice and be heard throughout the huge compartment.

Granted, the ship was at anchor in Makasar harbor. The Deseret Energy Corporation Type PF9N fusion generators and the Westinghouse steam turbogenerators were operating at low output to provide electrical load. However, even when the ship was under way at its maximum submerged speed of 48 knots, the engine room was nearly silent. Quiet operation was a requirement for underwater stealth. Submarines were still the "silent service" of the United States Navy.

Corry stood on a catwalk overlooking the two dozen officers and petty officers of the Engineering Department. Beside him was chief engineer CDR Ray Stocker and LCDR Norm Merrill.

"I'm going through the ship this morning talking personally to every department," Corry began in his precise and measured tones. He had a powerful voice that carried. In spite of his speech impediment, he'd been a valued member of the dramatics group at the Naval Academy as well as the debating team. He'd learned there how to control his stuttering and project his voice.

"You know why we are here," he went on. "We

received a DOD Execute Order to assist our embassy and the local authorities in finding nearly a hundred Americans who have disappeared recently. We believe we may have discovered the cause of these disappearances. However, it may seem to be so bizarre and unbelievable that I wanted to talk to all of you in person, not by means of the ship's P-A system. Unbelievable as the story may sound, your own Assistant Engineer Officer was involved.

"I'm doing this because I want you to get the straight story. I do not want rumors to start. Scuttlebutt tends toward the frightening in a situation such as this. I assure you that the real story is not frightening. Nor are we presently threatened.

"Furthermore, I want to speak to you in person because what I have to tell you is not for discussion or transmittal by any means beyond this ship. Under the provisions of United States Code Title Eighteen, I cannot find a stated reason for classifying the information I'm about to reveal to you. The Espionage and Sabotage Acts never anticipated this. Since I cannot classify it, I can only request that you maintain confidentiality. You may talk about it all you want to in the ship among shipmates. But forget it if you go on liberty or write home. I can ask you only to do this as a request from your Commanding Officer. However, I believe you will see that, if the story leaks, it could create a lot of trouble for us in this corner of the world."

Corry paused, then turned to indicate the Assistant Engineer Officer. "Yesterday afternoon, Mister Merrill went on liberty with a group of four other officers, including the Executive Officer. Therefore, he was present during this incident. In fact, he played a major role in its outcome. He and the XO have been nominated for a decoration. They saved the life of our Navigation Officer."

In measured tones, he went on to relate the story of the scuba diving group. When he got to the part where LCDR Natalie Chase was discovered missing, he turned to the Assistant Engineer Officer and said, "Commander Merrill, please tell the Department in your own words what happened and what you saw."

Merrill did, using the same calm and cautious tone of voice as the Captain. When he had finished with a description of the alien's decomposition, he remarked, "Captain, that's it."

"Commander, are you certain of what you saw?"

"Sir, I'm not sure I got all the details. Things were pretty tense. But I do know what I saw. And I do know that the creature was menacing Commander Chase. I know that the XO and I killed it."

The people in the ship's engineering department were highly trained engineers and technicians. They were also disciplined. They believed that the safety of the ship was in their hands because they oversaw the devices that provided the energy and the propulsion. They showed zero reaction to the tale told by their Commanding Officer and the Assistant Engineer Officer. They expressed no murmurs of disbelief. Their Commanding Officer and their department head were standing before them, along with one of the engineering crew who was known for veracity and integrity. The Engineering Department of a carrier submarine cannot be run by people who don't tell the truth or can't be counted on.

But it was the Main Propulsion Officer, LT Paula Ives who finally spoke up. "Sir, what do you want us to do?"

"Keep this to yourselves," Corry repeated. "Don't let rumors run wild. If you go on liberty, please stay out of the water."

"Yes, sir, you can damned well bet that I will!" was the comment from the Electrical Officer, LT Richard Fitzsimmons.

That brought laughter from the engineering crew.

"In the meantime, we're going to see what we can do to find some of these creatures," Corry explained.

"We'll try to communicate with them. But my guess is that we're not likely to be successful. We have enough trouble communicating between ourselves. And we all speak the same language! My general standing orders remain: If attacked by anything, including a mosquito, defend yourselves. That includes killing the attacker if necessary. And report to your department head immediately if you see anything or encounter anything that might resemble the creature Commander Merrill described."

He looked around, then asked his usual concluding question, "Are there any questions or observations?"

Silence.

"Commander Stocker, dismiss your department and return to the normal duty cycle."

"Aye, aye, sir!"

Six more times that morning, Corry talked personally to the various departments—Operations, Deck, Navigation, Supply, Medical, and the Air Group. He couldn't talk to the Marine batt because Clinch was still ashore with two Marine companies. He was due back at lunch time for an afternoon Papa brief on the situation.

The reaction of the officers and ratings was strangely subdued. Corry didn't really understand this until he'd finished briefing the Medical Department. Then Chief Pharmacist Mate Nat Post told him, "Sir, I'm neither surprised nor frightened. I've been expecting this for years. My grandfather told me he'd expected ET contact, but it didn't happen during his lifetime. He had quite a data base on ET contact reports. It's impossible that all of it could be wild stories."

"Do you know if your grandfather had ever gotten reports of undersea aliens?" Corry asked.

Post shrugged. "Captain, there have always been stories about sea monsters. Most people thought those were tall yarns spun by old sailors. None of them were ever proved. But now I suspect that some of them might have been real."

Corry took out his pocket memo terminal out and made a note to ask CNO to have the Naval Institute research its files for earlier sightings of these alien sea creatures in other parts of the world. That sort of feedback and additional data were what he expected to get from the crew of the U.S.S. *Shenandoah*.

He'd taken the time to make a personal appearance to the entire crew because this was a highly unusual situation. It could have been disbelieved by some. Corry didn't need doubt in the minds of any of the crew. He wanted every crew member to know what had happened and respond to whatever was likely to come based on the scuba party's discovery. This cruise had evolved into one that was far different than anyone aboard—or in the United States Navy—had ever been involved in before.

Corry had a team. He needed to keep it as a team now more than ever. He was aware that the team also helped him convince himself that he was right in trusting those officers who had witnessed the encounter. It was going to be difficult enough dealing with Ambassador Abbott in spite of Herb Hewitt's presence in the party. Presenting the situation to the Sulawesi officials would be yet another challenge.

Corry didn't even want to think about reporting to CINCPAC or the CNO. If he didn't have extremely good information to back up his report, it could mean the end of his career. And those of the officers who'd encountered the alien.

With these black thoughts in mind, the commander of the U.S.S. *Shenandoah* sat down at lunch with his staff and the ship's department heads.

For the first time, the unspoken wardroom rule about no shop talk during meals was broken. The alien encounter was far too unusual. It was the subject of the entire lunchtime conversation. His officers couldn't keep from discussing it. However, Corry made no move to stop the chatter about the alien because the officers of the *Shenandoah* needed to talk about it. And the five officers who'd been there *had* to talk about it. It was therapy to help them handle an otherwise unbelievable thing that had happened to them.

A lot of the talk also got Major Bart Clinch up to speed.

"Dammit, if I had been called to come with my Alpha Company, we would have had a lot of dead monsters," he growled aggressively. "We'd have blown those damned things right out of the water for attacking Natalie."

"The one we saw was armed, Bart," Zeke reminded him.

"So? A pistol is a pistol, if that's what it was. So it couldn't have been lethal beyond a short range. You can pack only so much energy into a handgun, XO."

"Unless it's a technology we don't have, one that can store energy in less volume and release it faster than a subnuclear explosive," was the comment from Ray Stocker. The Engineer Officer knew something about devices with high energy density. Such energy sources drove the *Shenandoah*.

"And if it released the energy in a shorter period of time, the monster would have to handle the recoil . . . or a very hot pistol." The Gunnery Officer, CWO Joe Weaver, also knew what he was talking about. Guns, missiles, explosives, warheads, nuclear explosives, and subnuclear devices were his profession.

Zeke listened with a grin. Clinch was a hard driving warrior type. Bart Clinch was no space scientist. On the other hand, the ship's crew had to be made up of practical scientists, engineers, and technicians who understood why things worked and how to keep them working. The *Shenandoah* needed a man like Clinch to head up the ship's naval infantry, the Marine batt. He was Terri Ellison's male counterpart, a person who was combative and gladly took on the world when necessary. Zeke didn't know which of the two was closer to being the ultimate twenty-first century warrior.

He understood the relationship between Terri and Bart. That didn't mean he liked it. However, Terri apparently didn't enjoy always being with another basic warrior type. She and Zeke had their own relationship, for which Zeke was thankful. And he tried not to be jealous when Terri played off Clinch against him. The two men were close friends in spite of their mutual interest in Terri Ellison.

No woman, even an Amazon, can really understand the bonding between two men who serve their country, albeit in such widely different professions requiring such different personalities. On the other hand, Zeke also knew that women, especially service women, had their own unique forms of bonding. Those manifold relationships between men and women made life in the *Shenandoah* far more interesting than if the relationships had been based purely on sexual differences.

After the stewards had cleared the lunch dishes, Corry rapped on the table with his knuckles. As the wardroom became quiet, he stated, "I called this informal meeting at lunchtime in order to discuss ideas and suggestions concerning what we do next and how we do it."

Corry knew what he wanted to do: Find out more about these underwater aliens. However, it was a totally new wrinkle in this cruise. The discovery of the aliens was so bizarre that none of his naval education, training, or experience had prepared him to plan the next step. However, the officers of the boat were smart, thoughtful people. He knew that if he got a discussion started, they'd use their expertise and background to develop a workable plan. It was therefore up to him to stimulate their thought processes. And that's what he did.

"We've discovered what we believe to be a cause of the multiple disappearances of American and Chinese citizens on Sulawesi. And probably the disappearances of unnumbered Sulawesi citizens as well. We must get the American embassy involved because we're supposedly here to support their effort in this regard. Then we must work with the Sulawesi government. That's going to be more difficult. I'm sure you all realize that I can't simply tell Ambassador Abbott or the Sulawesi defense minister that we've discovered extraterrestrial underwater cannibals fishing the local waters to catch human beings for food. I'll be packed off to Bethesda for psychiatric study and therapy . . ."

"Captain, if that happens, I'll be right beside you," Natalie told him.

"So will I," echoed Laura Raye.

"We saw what we saw," Zeke added.

"I know that. And thank you. But we can't let that happen," Corry reminded him. "What is needed is simple: proof."

"Sorry I blew the photographic data, Captain," Terri apologized for the twentieth time. But Corry wasn't keeping track.

"So we'll get more photo data," Corry maintained. "We must make a few assumptions. And hope we're right. I think we will be. The first assumption is that there are more than the single alien that Zeke and Norm killed."

"I saw them and I heard them," Zeke confirmed.

"I believe you did. The second assumption is that the 'fishing' is pretty good around here. So the aliens won't leave. Therefore, we can go looking for them and probably find them."

He stopped and looked around. "When we do, we can't attack them."

"Suppose they attack us like they came after Natalie?" Terri asked unnecessarily. She really knew the answer, but she wanted to ask the question anyway. She knew she'd shoot to kill if she had to. In fact, she'd try to hunt them down.

Corry knew that too. He understood his CAG.

"We'll defend ourselves. You're going to do that anyway. That's the first survival instinct. Orders won't stop you."

"Ah, yes, in spite of all the exhortations to love thy neighbor, one tries to do unto others first before they do unto you," was the comment from LT Tom Chapman, the ship's Chaplain. "Captain, while you're quite correct, we shouldn't go hunting them just because they're fishing for us. We should try to find out why they're fishing for us . . ."

"Probably because we taste good, Padre," said the ship's Medical Officer. "Which means that our DNA is close to theirs. At least, close enough so we don't poison them. They do operate biologically with different symbiotes than we do. I saw that firsthand. Maybe they're not interested in eating us. Maybe they're merely catching us for other creatures to eat. Maybe the maggotlike creatures I saw are the dominant ones in the symbiosis."

"I think what you're saying, Doctor," said the Engineer Officer, "is that we shouldn't jump to conclusions here before we get to know more about these sea monsters. That means we have to take one or more of them alive."

"That would indeed be a benefit," Laura Raye admitted.

"It would also solve our believability problem," Natalie added.

"So that's what we need to do," Zeke decided. "Catch at least one of them. And I think I know how to do it."

"XO, please educate me," Corry invited him.

"If they don't eat their prey where they catch it, they must take it somewhere. If they don't eat it in the place they take it to, they must then store it and transport it to market, so to speak." Zeke paused. "Sometimes you can catch something by waiting for it to come and take the bait. The creature wasn't doing that. It had set a trap. Like a lobster trap. It probably showed up when it did because it was making the rounds of its trap line for the day. It wasn't doing aggressive fishing, but there's nothing to keep us from doing that. We can go after them."

"How?" It was a a one-word question from the skipper of the *Shenandoah*.

"Sir," Zeke addressed him, "you command a submarine. It has an air patrol squadron fitted out for ASW work. It also mounts some of the best passive sonar available. Plus it has something no other type of submarine has and something the aliens won't suspect. It has a mass detector, and I think the masdet can spot and track an alien because we have a rough estimate of its mass. At least I do. I wrestled one in the water and up on the beach. So we don't go fishing. We go hunting, and we go looking for more of these aliens. Charlie Ames, you're our masdet officer. Since I haven't heard a peep out of you in objection to this, I assume the masdet will do what we want it to."

Zeke got the answer he wanted. "Yes, XO, it will."

15

It didn't take them long to figure out what to do and how to do it.

If Europeans had risen to be the top peoples on the planet because they were better managers than anyone else, Americans continued that trend. They even eclipsed the people of Europe because not only were they good managers but they *planned* better. This was nowhere more evident than in the U.S.S. *Shenandoah*. American naval officers just didn't set a goal and then effectively lead their crews toward its attainment. They tried to *think through* the whole plan, to consider possibilities, and to evaluate the consequences. They didn't like surprises, and they tried to plan them away.

Of course, they couldn't succeed. A "surprise-free" future can never happen. No one can predict the future with certainty. However, by working through the planning exercise, they weren't locked into "the plan," the one sure and certain way to do the job. They knew how to succeed when they had to be opportunistic. They knew what to do when it came time to be flexible.

That's why the U.S. Navy and the other American armed services had developed something they called the "Papa briefing."

The machines, the technologies, and the capabilities for unleashing death and destruction—to say nothing of killing themselves—were now too complex for any single individual to know everything. The general astride his horse atop the hill could no longer manage the battle (and, in fact, never really did). Even Horatio Nelson knew this. He'd organized his own "Papa briefing" before Trafalgar and, because of the primitive communications, had counted on "every man doing his duty."

Corry didn't see himself as another Nelson. So he just sat back and listened. He let his people work out the operations plan. Because it was *their* plan, they'd make it work. His job was to keep them focused. He was also there to advise them of what they could *not* do because of regs, policies, or diplomatic reasons. Or to suggest a way to do it that was easier, based on his own experience.

However, no one in the United States Navy had had any experience in hunting down and capturing alive an underwater extraterrestrial being.

"It's like hunting miniature submarines," LCDR Bob Lovette posed an analogous operation for them to think about. Sometimes the use of an analog made a planning breakthrough possible. Or it pointed out aspects that should be taken into account.

"Well, we'll need to move the *Shenandoah* offshore," LT Charlie Ames pointed out. As Special Sensors Officer, he knew the conditions under which the new mass detector would work best. And he realized that the situation was one in which the masdet could shine. For four years, he'd lived with the shipboard version during its development at White Oak Laboratories. More of a scientist than a seagoing officer, he'd willingly gone through what he considered the hell of submarine training in order to shepherd the masdet during its initial fleet use. "I can get some masdet readings here in Makasar harbor, of course. But I'm looking along the coastline. Hard to discriminate targets from Sulawesi itself. So it will help if we can move westward into Makasar Straits. Furthermore, I'll get better target resolution with the ship submerged. I've never tried detecting a two-hundred kilogram target before. But I shouldn't have any trouble if I know the mass, which we do."

"Okay, Charlie, so we move offshore. How far should we go?" Natalie Chase asked.

Ames was one of those men who would always be a bachelor. He was afraid of women. However, he got along very well with the women engineers and scientists at White Oak. And with the professionals in the *Shenandoah*. Chase was one of them. He could treat them as professionals without worrying about what to do around them and how to treat them. "How much shoreline do you want good resolution on?"

"How about down to the southern tip of Sulawesi?" Lovette suggested.

"That's a hundred kilometers," Chase recalled. She was looking at the charts displayed on her hand-held terminal. "Suppose we initially scan a hundred klicks north and south of Makasar . . ."

"Move out fifty klicks west of Makasar," Ames told them. "I'll get good angular resolution there. Furthermore, you won't have to move the ship very far for me to get enough stereo effect for usable ranging data."

"We can tie your masdet data in against my passive sonar data," Roger Goff remarked.

The conversation was moving quickly and sharply. Officers had their calculators out and working. Some had tied their pocket terminals into the ship's LAN and were thus linked to "Holland," the master ship mainframe.

"What do we do when we find them?" Zeke asked a typical Corry question. Corry noted that. His XO was picking up some command traits.

"Watch them," was the brief response from LTJG Ralph Strader, the Intelligence Officer. "Find out where they go. Don't move until we learn that. As Commander Lovette remarked, we're like an attack sub stalking a boomer or a carrier sub."

"No more boomers around—we think—but I'm sure we all remember how to handle them," was LCDR

Mark Walton's quip. Certainly, his Deck Department had drilled and drilled with that scenario. As he knew that LCDR Bob Lovette and the Operations Department had, too.

"Look, when you sensor people get tracks on them from a submerged position, we need to surface. Then I can launch the Black Panthers," Terri interrupted. She was having to learn how to live with the new mass detector. The Air Group was once the only long-range senses of the carrier submarine, supplementing surveillance and reconnaissance satellite data. The CAG knew her patrol squadron's ASW sensor suites and equipment couldn't match the passive sensing ability of the masdet. Furthermore, in order to launch aircraft, the ship had to surface and break its stealth. Someday, she knew, the tech-weenies would reduce the size, weight, and power requirements of the mass detector down to the point where it could become an airborne sensor. But those times hadn't arrived yet. When they did, Terri Ellison wanted to be in a position of having worked her chickens in concert with the shipboard masdet. Then she might be commander of the true long-range senses of a future submarine carrier. "I can put the Ospreys over the targets and dip passive sonar to keep close track of them. These aliens are damned noisy critters when they're talking or navigating. I heard them too."

"We'll get good sound signatures for your Ospreys to lock onto," Roger Goff promised.

"That will help, and we'll refine them from our close-in data."

"Mark, I want some of the underwater special team people to be aboard those Ospreys . . . armed," Zeke told the First Lieutenant. "Ask Rick Brookstone to assign only volunteers. We should have someone we can put in the water if necessary. And they should be prepared to encounter unfriendly AUSMs."

"Aye, aye, XO. Can do!"

"AUSMs?" Terri Ellison asked.

"We've got to call them something," Zeke pointed out. "And, in the best Navy tradition, I made up an acronym for them: Alien Underwater Sea Monsters. AUSMs."

"Awesomes?" Ray Stocker created a word out of the acronym. In the Engineering Department, he lived in a world full of acronyms. Someone once maintained that a piece of Navy technology wasn't real until it had an acronym.

"Why not?"

Natalie Chase shrugged. "Beats having to call them 'sea monsters.' Which they are. However, I've had a close encounter with one. So I'll agree that the phonetic of the acronym describes one very well indeed!"

Thus are traditions born.

"What do we tell the Chinese?" Strader brought up the fact that they were anchored near a Chinese patrol submarine.

"Just what we tell the Sulawesis, Mister Strader: nothing," Corry replied. While his officers had been working out the plan, he'd been thinking about his additional responsibility: external affairs. While the XO looks inward to the ship, the Commanding Officer looks outward while retaining full responsibility for the ship itself. "I don't want to tip our hand to *anyone* until we have solid proof of this. Otherwise, the rumors will start. Then we'll spend all our time trying to explain this to CINCPAC and Washington. At the moment, we have orders. I've convened this Papa briefing. I've laid on you the staff job of telling me what I ought to do with the ship in order to carry out those orders. So I'm not going to ask permission of anyone. If we're wrong, I'll take the flak. But forgiveness is easier to get than permission."

His officers knew the truth of that. They often used it themselves.

"We don't tell *anyone* what we're going to do or how we're going to do it. And I'll take care of the Ambassador. So we'll leave quietly at about oh-two hundred tomorrow morning without talking about it to the world. After all, we are still the 'silent service.' "

"Captain, the Chinese boat will come looking for us," Strader guessed. As the ship's Intelligence Officer, he was always suspicious of anything and everyone outside the *Shenandoah*. That was his job. He had to collect intel data, evaluate it, and work up the worst-case scenarios. He was bringing one of these to the attention of everyone now.

"Good! That will confuse the Awesomes!" Corry told him with a smile, putting his stamp of approval on the phonetic and the acronym his officer had created. "Mark, I want you to look for a deep scattering layer or a density layer when we get fifty klicks out. Natalie, what's the depth fifty klicks offshore?"

The navigator consulted her hand-held terminal that was plugged into Holland. "Two hundred meters, Captain."

"Excellent! A nice, deep channel! Mark and Bob, if you can also find a phantom bottom when we get there, so much the better. I want to hide from both the *Bei fung* and the Awesomes. I don't want to be detected until we're *ready* to be seen!"

"Captain, what's the status of the land operation now?" Major Bart Clinch asked. He'd been sitting quietly and watching the Papa briefing unfold. He sensed that it was now winding down. The naval and air sides of the crew appeared to have their act together. And he saw that the Marines weren't involved. He didn't like that. He was a Marine. He wanted to be in the thick of it. "Sir, I spent the afternoon with that dumb General Helamahera trying to work out some joint exercises. Do I toss all that work down the scuppers now?"

Corry shook his head. "No, but delay it, Major Clinch."

"Delay it? Sir, we haven't even worked out what we're going to do yet!" Clinch had been totally frustrated that afternoon. He couldn't work anything out with the Sulawesis. Helamahera hadn't been un-cooperative. The Sulawesi defense minister simply re-fused to make decisions and fobbed them off on his staff "pending a study of this."

"So much the better! I want you to continue to do so," Corry told him bluntly. Clinch was the sort of person who had to be given a specific, carefully worded, direct order. Clinch was a tactician, not a strategist, whereas Corry was the opposite. "You're going to be ashore during this mission. Base yourself and your batt at the American embassy. Continue business as usual."

Clinch really didn't like that. He didn't want to be left behind. He knew he really wasn't being left be-hind, but he didn't understand why. "Sir, won't it look strange tomorrow morning when the Sulawesis wake up and find the *Shenandoah* gone but her Marine batt still in the American embassy?"

Corry nodded and agreed. "Yes. It will confuse ev-eryone. It never hurts to be a little devious in a situa-tion like this. The Sulawesis and the Chinese both will know we're coming back because we left you and your batt . . . ostensibly for legation guard duties and to work out joint exercises with the Sulawesi Army. But now they won't be sure. First of all, they will know that we can both come and go at will without their foreknowledge."

"Captain, rumors will run rampant!"

"Let them! I am under no compulsion to explain my actions to anyone except CINCPAC and CNO once the cruise is completed," Corry said. What he didn't say—because he didn't like to criticize an officer in front of others—was that he knew Clinch was upset. The Marines hadn't been included in any aspect of the AUSM search mission. Clinch was objecting to that in his own way. However, the Marine batt com-mander had offered no input on how the batt might participate. That was because Clinch didn't know how it could. And that made him even more upset.

The Commanding Officer of the U.S.S. *Shenandoah* knew that some Marines have a tendency to believe the Corps is somehow separate from the naval establishment. It was Corry's job to remind Bart from time to time in a firm and gentle manner that the Marine batt was the land arm of the U.S.S. *Shenandoah*. It was the naval infantry contingent aboard. It was not the job of the *Shenandoah* and its crew to chauffeur the Marines around from fight to fight.

Corry wasn't angry with Clinch. He'd requested that Clinch be assigned to the ship when he'd taken command. Clinch was a gung ho aggressive Marine, just the sort of person Corry wanted as his Marine batt commander. However, occasionally Clinch did get upset with Corry. This was one of those times.

"Major, it's your job to continue to represent the U.S.S. *Shenandoah* and the United States Navy presence in Makasar while the ship goes a short distance offshore for a day or so," Corry explained clearly. "I have full confidence in your ability to do just that. Your part in this plan should be clear to you. You're to hold the fort, so to speak. So carry out your orders, sir. Make it so!"

"Yessir!" Bart Clinch didn't like it, but he was a Marine and he'd obey orders. He felt a little better, however. He'd made his point, even if he'd had to make a little fuss about it. "I'd like to take Charlie Company ashore with me to the embassy. I don't want to split my command."

"Understood and agreed. Make it so."

"Yessir! Thank you, sir!"

Corry looked around the group. "Does anyone have any additional inputs to the general mission plan at this point?"

The wardroom was silent.

"Very well! XO, prepare to raise anchor and depart Makasar harbor at oh-two-hundred hours local. All liberty parties should be recovered by twenty-four-hundred hours. Dive the ship when clear of the harbor mole once water depth permits. Make for a space point fifty kilometers west. We will remain submerged and rigged silent and stealthed. Masdet and passive sonar only. Maintain Condition Two. Be prepared to surface and launch Ospreys."

"Aye, aye, sir! Liberty parties aboard by twenty-four-hundred. Weigh anchor and depart Makasar at oh-two-hundred. Make for fifty kilometers on heading two-seven-zero true. Dive when safe to do so. Run silent and stealthed. Condition Two on departure. Stand by to surface and launch ASW patrols." Zeke repeated the order as per protocol. It was now more than an order. By repeating it back, giving the "brief-back," Zeke and the rest of the crew had essentially made a contract with Captain Corry.

The U.S.S. *Shenandoah* and her crew were going out to hunt extraterrestrials—not in outer space, but in the Planet Earth's "inner space," the oceans.

No one had ever expected it to happen this way, of course.

And no one expected it would end the way it eventually did.

16

Ships once sailed with the tide. But that was in the days when ships actually moved under sail. A twenty-first-century carrier submarine was a figurative four-hundred-kilo gorilla; it sailed anytime it wanted to.

The U.S.S. *Shenandoah* SSCV-26 got under way at 0200.

CAPT William M. Corry was at his position in the retractable conning tower. This dodger bridge was raised hydraulically 10 meters above the flat upper flight deck. It was used only for maneuvers that required the ultimate in sensors and intelligence: the human eyes and brain.

LCDR Mark Walton, the ship's First Lieutenant, was on the bridge with him along with CPO Clancy Thomas, the chief boatswain's mate.

The *Shenandoah* had been anchored with her bow seaward and a stern line to a buoy. These held her in position so she didn't swing with the tidal currents. A 390-meter ship needs space if it's allowed to swing around a single anchor chain. Makasar harbor wasn't very big. And the *Shenandoah* shared it with another large submarine.

Corry could see the two anchor lights of the *Bei fung* to port. No other ship was in the harbor then, but several small boats were anchored inshore.

He looked down at the PPI of the surface radar repeater and the display of active sonar and u-v lidar data on two other screens. Satisfied that the ship could depart in the clear, he gave the order: "Weigh anchor!"

"Aye, aye, sir, weigh anchor! . . . Anchor free of the bottom . . . Anchor coming up," Chief Thomas repeated.

"Let go aft!"

"Aye, aye, sir, let go aft." The bosun's mate then passed the order via subvocal N-fone to the deck detail on the stern. When he got a reply, he confirmed, "Lines clear aft, sir!"

"Bow thrusters ahead one third."

"Bow thrusters ahead one third," the captain's order was repeated.

The two aquajets beneath the waterline near the bow came alive. High-pressure superheated steam from the fusion boilers was valved to their slots by the Main Propulsion Officer, LT Paula Ives, from her position on the main bridge below. As the steam expanded out of the slots, its temperature dropped and it condensed. This formed a silent, low-velocity, high-flow Coanda entrapment sheath around the thruster body. It produced thrust. The ship began to move.

"Anchor lights off, running lights on," Corry snapped.

Thomas repeated the order.

Corry wanted to clear the harbor mole with plenty of room. Although the 51,000-ton *Shenandoah* had a lot of inertia and momentum, the aquajets had the necessary thrust and could be swiveled to make her lively at low speeds. "Come to a heading of two-five-five magnetic," he ordered.

"Come to two-five-five magnetic. Coming around."

Once the ship had cleared the mole and was out in the tidal current of the Makasar Straits, Corry saw that the depth-sounding display was reporting consistently increasing depth under the ship.

He looked around at the upper flight deck. "Mister Walton, have the deck crew go below. Prepare to dive."

"Aye, aye, sir! Deck crew go below. Prepare to dive!"

Once the telltales had reported all hatches secured, indicating that the deck crew was below deck, Corry snapped shut the waterproof covers on the bridge instruments and displays. "Gentlemen, let's go below ourselves."

Down in the control room that was also the main bridge of the ship, Corry went to his station. He took his N-fone from behind his right ear, set it to the main command channel, and then replaced it.

"Conning tower retracted, Captain. All seals secure," reported the bosun's mate.

The depth beneath the ship was rapidly increasing. It was already at 50 meters.

"Prepare to dive!" Corry said.

The bridge was strangely quiet. Communications took place on the subvocal N-fone channels. Corry didn't hear all the N-fone communication; he was on the exclusive comm channel reserved only for those who might need to talk to the Captain. He didn't need to hear everything that was going on, although he could have switched onto any channel he wished at any time. People were checking and double-checking their displays and readouts.

Diving a submarine is the most tense moment of submarine service. There is no room for a mistake.

The bridge of a carrier submarine was in many ways similar to the "starship" bridges depicted in science fiction adventure series on commercial television. Except that this wasn't a set. It was the real thing. The *Shenandoah* didn't operate in outer space, but in inner space. Some day, Corry hoped, real starship bridges might resemble and be operated like this one. But he didn't expect to live to see a future Space Navy operating starships. He was happy enough to be in command of the largest mobile man-made machine in existence. Some people said it was the most complicated toy a person could ever play with. However, Corry and the others in the *Shenandoah* did *not* treat her as a toy. She could kill them if they didn't treat her right.

"Sir, the ship is ready to dive," came the report from Zeke Braxton.

"All ahead two thirds, come to diving speed,"

Corry told him and gave the classical submarine commander's order, "Dive! Dive! Dive!"

"Dive! Dive! Dive!" The command came over all N-fone channels as well as the ship's PA system.

"Stop dive at thirty meters!"

"Stop dive at thirty meters!"

The deck pitched down five degrees as the two sets of General Jet aquajets, bow and stern, began to thrust and were swiveled to take the ship down. The *Shenandoah* could actually move sideways in the water, but it was far quicker and more efficient to "fly" her by using hull lift.

"Sir, the bubble is steady at thirty meters," Zeke reported. "Our ETA at our sea point is zero-three-one-five."

"Thank you, XO. You may secure the ship from diving stations. Come to Submerged Condition Three."

"Aye, aye, sir. Securing from diving stations. Submerged Condition Three," Zeke repeated. "Captain, do you wish to go silent?"

"Negative, XO. But you may secure the surveillance sonar. We'll depend on the masdet for that sort of data. Keep sounding single-pulse every minute until we reach our sea point," Corry decided.

"Aye, aye, sir. Secure surveillance sonar. Sound single pulse every minute until reaching sea point."

Now that the boat was dived, it was time for Corry to step back and consider the strategies he might be able to use. He carefully checked all the necessary displays—water-tight integrity, position, depth, forward speed, and sensors. Satisfied, he stood up. "XO, you have the con. Set the watch and maintain local time base."

Zeke nodded. "Aye, aye, sir! I have the con. Set the watch on local time."

"Very well. When reaching the sea point, let me know. I'll be in my quarters. Do not hesitate to call me." Corry's last order was unnecessary. Everyone aboard knew it was a standing order. But he gave it anyway. He always did. It was one of the responsibilities and duties of command.

He went back to the emergency cabin off the bridge but he didn't go to sleep. He stretched out on the bunk and relaxed by re-reading parts of John Keegan's *The Price of Admiralty*.

Corry relaxed too well. He fell asleep while reading. He was abruptly awakened by the OOD's N-fone voice in his head, *Captain, this is the deck. Lieutenant Brewer here.*

Corry cleared his mind and subvocalized his response, *CO here, Lieutenant.*

Sir, we have reached our sea point.

Thank you.

He got up, checked his tie, ran his hand through his thinning dark hair, and decided he didn't need a shave yet. Only when he knew he was presentable did he walk into the control room.

Zeke was already there. That was no surprise.

Corry didn't take the con. "What's our bottom?"

"Four-seven-three meters, sir." Zeke merely repeated what he saw on the display. Again, it was a redundant action. But the ship was fifty meters down. Redundancy meant safety.

"Has Goff seen a deep scattering layer yet?"

"He's looking now."

"All thrusters stop," Corry suddenly ordered. Now that the ship had reached its sea point fifty kilometers west of Makasar in the Straits, it was time to stop and take measure of the situation.

"Aye, aye, sir, all thrusters stop."

When the ship's relative forward motion through the water slowed to five knots, he gave another order. "Drop a probe. I want to get under anything that will give heartburn to the Chinese sonar or whatever sound detection system the Awesomes have."

"Aye, aye, sir. Drop a probe."

Within minutes, a deep sea temperature/pressure/salinity sensing probe fell out of its bay in the *Shenando-*

ah's hull. It went down trailing its comm and recovery cable. The probe was tethered and had a hard-wired system that could be used when the ship was under stealth-and-silent conditions. As it descended, it sent back the sort of information Corry and his Sonar Officer needed.

"We're in luck, sir!" Zeke announced happily. "Look at that inversion at one-five-three meters. And thick enough to hold us, too. And not so deep that we can't operate underneath it."

"Looks like we've found our hiding place, XO. What does Goff say?"

There was a pause while Zeke communicated subvocally with the sonar office by N-fone. "He's getting a good false bottom return from it now. He recommends we go down and check it out."

"Does masdet sense any change in density?"

"Wait one, sir." Pause. "Negatory, sir. Charlie reports that the density change is too gradual for him to see yet. He says the masdet will work through the layer without any trouble."

"Very well, XO, have the steersman make two-zero-zero on the depth gauge. Upon reaching two-zero-zero depth, go to zero bubble and have the ship put in a stealth-silent mode. Go to station-keeping with auxiliary thrusters. Then we start watching and waiting."

"Aye, aye, sir. Down to and level at two-zero-zero and come to stealth-and-silent. And we go into sentry mode." Zeke confirmed the orders and passed them along to the OOD.

"It's a waiting game now, XO. Stamina and holding power are important factors."

"Yes, sir. Well, we've had our share of excitement in the last thirty-six hours, anyway."

Corry smiled and simply said, "Yes."

However, no one had time to become bored.

The OOD called Corry at 0620. *Captain, this is the Officer of the Deck. Lieutenant Strader here, sir. Spe-*

cial Sensors Officer reports multiple masdet contacts, bearing zero-five-zero through one-two-five. Passive sonar confirms Awesome targets on the basis of sound analysis. The Awesome activity just started. It's a few minutes after sunrise up there. And something is booming south in the Straits, probably a skunk, target bearing three-five-seven, speed ten knots, no sonar signature.

The crew of the U.S.S. *Shenandoah* wasn't going to catch up on their lost sleep, the Captain decided. But blue water service wasn't a nine-to-five terminal job ashore. He recalled the adage about submarine service: "hours of boredom interrupted by moments of sheer terror."

He wasn't terrified and he didn't intend to be. Neither would he allow his crew to be. They wouldn't break anyway. They were too good, too professional, too proud.

And the carrier submarine was perfectly capable of handling anything except a nuclear mine against her side. On the surface, she could be killed by direct targeting from a high-power laser or a one-tonne hypersonic de-orbiting kinetic-kill weapon. Submerged, she was one of the safest machines ever devised. She was most vulnerable only on the surface. And that, of course, was why the Navy had almost forsaken its surface fleet for submarines. Her composite construction was stout, and her defenses were thorough. And her crew was motivated and competent.

Corry was inwardly elated at having picked up Awesome signatures and masdet returns. He didn't know what the big southbound masdet target was. If it was truly a surface vessel, he wouldn't worry about it. Many commercial freighters still used the Makasar Straits. But he'd keep a suspicious eye on the skunk until his sensor people got a better reading on it.

Thank you, Mister Strader. Keep watching those targets and recording. Let me know if anything changes.

The aliens weren't true aquatic beings like dolphins and whales, Corry decided, piecing together the data he'd just received with the other information brought back by Zeke and the beach party. They operated during daylight hours. Maybe their sound-ranging capabilities weren't good enough to permit them to operate without some visual data. Maybe their home world had a slower rotational rate, was in a multiple-star system, or had a brighter moon than Earth's. He'd read some science fiction, and he'd liked astronomy ever since he'd been introduced to the mysteries of the heavens in a celestial navigation course at the Naval Academy. (The Navy gave up old techniques with great reluctance. A line officer was required to do celestial navigation just in case all the pretty new technology quit on him. He had to get the ship home with a sextant, a compass, an ephemeris, and a copy of Bowden's.)

But Corry knew he was operating with very little data and relying on a lot of speculation. What he had to do, of course, was get hard data. Very hard data. A live Awesome would be best. But he figured that the probabilities of getting one were very low indeed.

First of all, he needed to watch the movement of the AUSMs on the west coat of Sulawesi. He wanted to learn what they were doing with their daily harvests. If they had a base somewhere, he would find it. If they were merely lone fishers, that meant doing something else.

He had to admit that this was the strangest mission he'd ever been involved with during a naval career that spanned twenty-two years in the submarine and air services.

And if it had not been for the firsthand reports of five of his most trusted officers, he would have been extremely skeptical. The whole idea of making contact with an alien creature was something that made good copy for the supermarket tabloids. It certainly wasn't the sort of thing that naval officers expected to encounter.

He knew he would have to handle this situation

very carefully. Any premature disclosure, even to his friend, former commanding officer, and Academy shipmate at CINCPAC, VADM Dick Kane, could bring an end to his command of the U.S.S. *Shenandoah* and perhaps even his naval career.

As he was mulling over these dark thoughts in his mind, his N-fone chirped. *Captain, this is the Officer of the Deck again.*

This is the Captain. G-A, Mister Strader.

Message for you just came in via teleprinter on the S-W-C from CINCPAC.

Corry sat up in his bunk. *Read it to me, Mister Strader. Then bring me the hard copy.*

Message says: "Early-morning satellite pass shows Shenandoah no longer in Makasar harbor. Respond soonest reporting present position, condition of vessel, and reason for departing Makasar." It's signed by Admiral Kane at CINCPAC.

What the hell was Kane trying to do, micromanage him?

Is there a reply, sir?

Not yet, Mister Strader. Give me the hard copy and note the time in the log, please.

Maybe Corry would be forced to tell Kane before he was ready to do so. And that might ruin everything.

17

VADM Richard Kane, CINCPAC, sat back and looked again at the hard copy of the SWC message that had just been received.

It answered the questions he'd asked in his SWC message to Corry in the *Shenandoah*. But, then again, it didn't.

"Ship and crew in excellent operational condition. Location submerged silent and stealthed, coordinates 6°5'00"S 119°0'0"E. Departed Makasar to check possibility unknown party evacuating missing people via submarine for reasons unknown. Playing hunter. Will report findings. Not to worry. SSCV-26 Corry CAPT."

He wondered what sort of wild chase Corry was running down there. Kane wasn't really worried. Corry wasn't known for crazy stunts. In fact, a more solid and reliable commanding officer probably didn't exist.

Kane's first concern had been the possibility that the Chinese submarine had somehow done something to the *Shenandoah*. The very expensive carrier submarine was a part of the Third Fleet, and Kane didn't like the idea of risking a carrier submarine *too* much. Risk was always a factor in the turbulent twenty-first-century world. However, a flag officer didn't play loosy goosy with expensive ships and hope to remain on active duty. Especially if something happened.

Kane had nearly panicked when the surveillance satellite image on Makasar harbor taken shortly after dawn had shown the *Shenandoah* to be *gone*. The Chinese sub was still there. He thanked the gods of technology for the new scalar wave communications that allowed him to talk to submerged vessels almost anywhere in the world. Actually, the SWC facility at Pearl was designed to cover the Pacific and part of the eastern Indian Ocean.

However, he felt better having the SWC message in his hand. He knew he couldn't micromanage the operation. In the first place, he knew Corry would have politely gone ahead and done it his own way anyway. And the commander of the *Shenandoah* would have done it in such a way that no one could ever say that orders had been disobeyed or that he was insubordinate.

He decided he wouldn't have to call off his golf match with three other flag officers at Pearl that afternoon.

His aide took that moment to contact him on the intercom. "Admiral, a telephone call from CNO."

Kane swallowed. Maybe something *had* come unbonded out there. He picked up the phone. "Admiral Kane here."

The CNO didn't waste time with protocol. Most flag officers, had known one another since Academy days. And they had been members of "The Secret Society" (its name was never mentioned and officially it didn't exist) at the school on the Severn. Few people who were not members made it to flag rank. "Dick, what's Bill doing with the *Shenandoah*?" ADM George Street wanted to know.

"George, he just sent me an SWC message . . ."

"I know. Dolores McCarthy brought it in just now."

Dammit! Kane knew that naval intelligence had real deep sources. And outstanding equipment. Technically, Corry's SWC message should not have reached as far as Washington.

"George, if Bill's doing as he reports in his message—and I trust he is because I know the man—then he's broken open a new lead on this matter."

"But this message is wild! Using submarines to take captured Americans off Sulawesi! What the hell? No nation in the Indonesian region has submarines! Most navies down there are coastal fleets made up of fast surface patrol boats . . ." The CNO was only mildly upset. Like Kane, he'd gotten antsy when the latest intel reports showed that an expensive carrier submarine wasn't where it was supposed to be. It had been on the surface and therefore vulnerable. To have a Chinese patrol submarine somehow nail an SSCV on the surface in a friendly harbor would cause more than ripples to run through the White House and Congress. Thus, the receipt of Corry's message caused the CNO to decide he'd better call CINCPAC and get the hot skinny.

But it was clear that CINCPAC knew nothing more than CNO and naval intelligence.

"Let's let Bill work at what we sent him down there to do, George," Kane told the four-star in the Pentagon. "He's on the spot. He knows the conditions. In spite of SWC, he might not have the time to signal me. Or he might have discovered that the Chinks can snoop on SWC. If so, that information alone is worth the risk we're running right now."

"Got any patrol submarines you could send to Makasar? Maybe he ought to have some cover or escort." CNO had never really bought off on the concept of a carrier submarine operating without escorts. The old CVs and CVNs always had a long tail of Aegis cruisers, CGNs, and DDGs to screen them. But carrier battle groups had been big, easy to track from space, and vulnerable to space-launched, air-launched, and submarine-launched guided weapons. The development of the carrier submarine had combined the stealth of the submarine with the versatility and reach of the aircraft carrier. It depended upon operating submerged and being difficult to detect.

The mass detector, if it worked well, was probably going to change that, Street knew. He had several think tanks and the Naval Postgraduate School working on what those changes might be.

"Bill Corry hasn't asked for it. And if he needed it, he'd ask," Kane reminded the nation's top naval officer. "In fact, a couple of patrol submarines might screw up what he's doing. If there's a man in the Navy who knows how to operate an SSCV, it's Bill Corry. And he doesn't like to depend on speculation. He's on to something new, and he doesn't want to appear premature by reporting it until he *knows*. If and when he learns more, he'll let us know, George."

The CNO sighed. "I guess I'm getting overly cautious in my dotage. I was once in a similar situation with one of the earlier carrier submarines. In fact, the operation is still so highly classified that I can't talk about it. And I tend to forget how isolated sea command really is. And how commanders hate it when we flag officers try to run a long-distance operation." Street paused for a moment, then decided, "Okay, I was being cautious. We gave him a loose rein and sent him out there to do an impossible job because State and the White House put the pressure on. I just quail at the thought of what it will cost to replace the *Shenandoah* if Corry loses it."

"He won't lose it, George."

CAPT William M. Corry wasn't about to. Furthermore, he was a good strategist and an even better tactician. One of these days, he had told himself, he'd like to teach history—after retirement. The academic environment might suit Cynthia better. Once the children had left home, she had grown increasingly dissatisfied with her role as a sea wife. She didn't like her husband being at sea for long periods of time now. Basically, like her husband, she realized that most of her life had passed and that the end was somewhere down the line. So she wanted as much as possible of the things she dearly loved. Her husband was one of those. When her possessive stance had had no effect upon her husband, she'd gone the way of many sea wives. The antidote for too much salt water in a naval marriage has often been alcohol. Bill Corry couldn't do too much about Cynthia's drinking problem when he was at sea.

Except worry about it.

When he had the time to do that.

Right then, he didn't.

He grabbed a sandwich for lunch and began to prowl the bridge. His restlessness didn't bother the watch. They knew Corry wasn't looking for anything that was wrong. He was fretting about the mission and trying not to show it. His crew knew him better than to believe he wasn't concerned.

At 1304, Roger Goff reported to the OOD, LT Bruce Leighton, via N-fone, *The Chinese boat is weighing anchor. Strong anchor chain sounds on passive sonar.*

Thank you, Sonar. Report any changes in other sonar targets when they occur.

Masdet signal indicates the Chinese boat is moving seaward, came the report from Charlie Ames in the Special Sensor compartment.

I can't see him. I'm on passive sonar. We're below the deep scattering layer, anyway. My sonar data would be invalid if I was pinging, Goff observed.

On all but the main command net, N-fone chatter was usually extensive. It was five times faster than verbal communication. So it didn't hog channel time. Corry had never promulgated an operational policy concerning chatter on the nets. Some skippers insisted on maintaining strict communications protocol at all times. Corry *wanted* his people to communicate with one another. So he never had his XO step in to quash N-fone chatter except on very specific occasions, most of which had a high pucker factor where utmost concentration was demanded.

"Qian is coming out," Zeke Braxton said over Corry's shoulder and took his seat on the bridge.

"As expected, Number Two." Corry sat back. Some

of the tension seemed to have left him. "Now I want to watch very carefully what happens with our Awesome targets."

Zeke nodded in understanding. The *Bei fung* wasn't trying to be quiet coming out. Captain Qian had risen that morning to find the American carrier submarine gone. Being submerged, the *Shenandoah*'s Communications Officer hadn't been able to monitor radio frequencies. Therefore, Corry wasn't privy to any exchanges between Qian and the primary Chinese naval communications facility at Zhoushan.

As the Chinese boat cleared the Makasar harbor mole, it began pinging.

"Qian is being pretty noisy and aggressive," the XO observed from the displays.

"Yes." It was a typical, cryptic Corry reply.

"I wish I could be sure he's not out for our hide. I have trouble reading those Chinese."

"They think differently, XO. That's because they speak a language with different basic roots than our Indo-European tongue."

"Yes, sir. I know. I read the Dalgliesh book on linguistic research you gave me."

"My question to you is: Did you understand it?"

"Most of it, sir. The important stuff, I think."

"Then tie that in with what you know of Chinese history. The Chinese have been xenophobic, shut-in, centrist, and lords of all their creation . . . which is eastern Asia. They never pushed westward through the Dzungarian Gate as far as Europe. The Mongols did, but only because the Chinese pushed them out of east Asian lands that the Chinese believed were theirs by divine right. Chinese are not aggressive in the same way we are. As for what's going through Qian's mind right now . . ." Corry paused and took a sip of hot coffee. Like most naval people, he ran on coffee and the stimulation of caffeine during even the most modest action.

After a moment, he went on, "He's only out looking for us. Beijing must be worried about where an American carrier submarine suddenly went to. Qian isn't worried about aggressive reaction on our part. And he isn't being aggressive himself. Otherwise, he'd be running silent. He isn't. He doesn't care if we know where he is or not."

"He's not going to find us."

"That's right! Now let's see what happens to our Awesome targets and their signals. I think they'll sense his pinging and know he's coming out. Their reaction to his Makasar departure is going to tell us a lot about how they operate." Corry had worked this out carefully that morning. He'd talked with Zeke about it, of course. He always did. Corry kept little to himself. He was fully aware that if something happened to him, Zeke was in command. Therefore, he had to keep his XO apprised at all times of his thinking and planning.

There are few secrets among the close knit teams of a submarine crew.

They watched the displays for several more minutes. Zeke was far more sanguine than Corry. He got up from his chair, paced the command ramp, and looked over the shoulders of the watch.

Corry noticed this. He handed Zeke his empty coffee mug. "XO, would you get me another cup of coffee, please? And sit down with one yourself."

That brought Zeke up short. He realized he was exhibiting his anxiety. The Captain had been very gentle with him about it. Officers had to remember that their overt actions and any display of concern, worry, or anxiety was always sensed by the crew. This had the obvious effect on others. When they saw their superior officers acting concerned or even slightly apprehensive, it became contagious.

Passive sonar signal becoming stronger, came the report from Sonar.

Corry and Zeke expected that. As the Chinese submarine closed the range, the angle at which the transmitted sound waves intercepted the scattering layer increased. Less of the wave energy was reflected by the layer. It was like the reflection of an object on a smooth sheet of glass—except that the scattering layer wasn't a sharp discontinuity like the glass surface. The reflection occurred through the depth of the layer. And the layer itself wasn't smooth or even homogeneous. So a small portion of the impinging sound waves managed to go through it. As the angle of incidence increased, more went through. A good sonar operator could almost get ranging data on passive sonar because of this. It hadn't always been that way, of course, but the sonar equipment in the *Shenandoah* was the best and the culmination of over a century of sonar and "asdic" technology development.

Masdet signal becoming stronger. He's closing.

Any range guesstimate. Charlie?

Affirmative. Given the displacement mass, I calculate range as four-three klicks and closing.

Thank you. I'll enter that data in my computer and use it to help me estimate range on passive sonar.

The masdet signal now indicates the Chinese boat is diving.

Roger, Charlie, I'm getting diving sounds now. This guy doesn't care what we hear, does he?

Right. He doesn't care. Otherwise, he'd be more careful.

Okay, the skunk coming southward through the Straits is emitting strong propeller beat sounds now. They're tending to mask the Chinese pinging. The skunk target will be passing between us and the Chinese boat in approximately seven minutes if my passive ranging estimates are right.

"The skunk sounds could affect how the Awesomes behave," Zeke remarked with unusual caution as he handed Corry a mug of coffee, wrapped his hands around his own coffee mug, and resumed his seat.

"We'll see. It will give us another datum, XO. It

may tell us something about how well the Awesomes' sounding systems work."

" 'When in total ignorance, try anything and be less ignorant,' " Zeke quoted some unknown sage.

Corry nodded in agreement. "Only if 'anything' doesn't hurt you in the process of trying it, XO."

Sonar has identified the skunk. Computer analysis matches the propeller sounds with the signature of the Australian ore carrier Iron Wallaroo *out of Port Hedland. Calculated speed indicates she's probably running empty and returning to reload down there.*

Correy was somewhat relieved. It could have been a Chinese surface warship. The People's Navy still had some. Or a Chinese submarine tender. Or an Indonesian patrol cutter. An Australian iron ore carrier was no threat. So he dismissed that possibility from his mind.

Awesome active sound signals have abated, came the sudden report from sonar.

"They must have detected the *Bei fung* coming out of Makasar," Zeke guessed.

"You're right, XO, but what caused you to come to that conclusion?" the Captain wanted to know.

"Sir, the *Iron Wallaroo* was coming down the Straits. They couldn't help but hear her. They didn't go silent because of her. They must be used to surface shipping coming through Makasar Straits," Zeke replied, going through the logic processes that had brought him to his conclusion. Typically, it took him far longer to explain what he'd done than it had taken him to do it. "They heard the *Bei fung* pinging. That told them the Chinese boat was looking for something. So they stopped making sounds themselves."

Corry asked his usual embarrassing questions. "XO, then why didn't the Awesomes stop their sounding when they first heard the *Bei fung* pinging as it came out of the harbor a few minutes ago? And why don't they know we're here?"

Zeke thought about that before he answered. "Let

me answer the latter question first. It's easier. We came out last night before the Awesomes came out at dawn. That must mean they have a base. Their base doesn't maintain a security watch because it's so well hidden they don't think it's necessary. The Awesomes do not know we're here. They have not detected us with their sounding senses. And they don't know we have the masdet or that they're being watched with it. How could they? The masdet depends on one of the basic characteristics of matter: mass."

"Very good, XO! Very good, indeed!" Corry told him with a smile. "Now, how about the answer to the first question?"

Zeke shook his head. "The answer? I don't know, sir."

"Sometimes admitting that you don't know the answer is almost as good as trying to speculate your way through the data to arrive at a solution," Corry observed. " 'I don't know' means that not enough data are yet in hand. So we continue to sit and watch, Number Two."

They didn't have to wait very long for something new to happen.

Corry and Zeke saw it on the display even as LT Charlie Ames called on the N-fone channel, *Bridge, Masdet! I have a new target. A big one! Just came around the south end of the island. Uh, Captain, its signature and behavior closely resemble those of the bogies we picked up in the Flores Sea and the one that we spotted trailing the Chinese boat down the Makasar Straits the other day!*

18

"Damn! Is that another mass detector anomaly?" Zeke wondered.

Corry studied the masdet visual display. In some ways, it was similar to the early radar displays. It showed relative bearings of the targets. The resolution of masdet wasn't as good as sonar, radar, or lidar. Therefore, the targets appeared as smudges rather than sharp pips. The intensity of the smudges gave some indication of the mass of the target.

LT Charlie Ames had conducted analyses of the targets. These had produced calculated masses. Using graviton theory, which he understood but couldn't fully explain to his shipmates, he could give the derived range. Next to each smudge, the Special Sensor Officer had posted alphanumerics showing this data.

"I cannot assume that it is, but we're going to find out," Corry said, studying the display. He toggled his N-fone. *Special Sensors, CO here. How closely does the new large target to the south resemble the anomalies we've seen before?*

Sir, computational analysis indicates a nine-five probability of a match.

"Close enough for government work," Zeke muttered. "Could it be the 'fishing trawler' the Awesomes return to with their catches?"

"Probably more likely the 'factory ship,'" Corry guessed. It wasn't a pretty simile. Human whalers used to harpoon their prey, haul it to factory ships, and then process the dead whales for their valuable ingredients.

"I wish you hadn't said that, Captain."

"I wish I hadn't thought of it, Zeke," the Captain admitted gravely. "However, if our analogy of the Awesomes as fishers for humans is valid, it's a possibility we can't ignore."

"On the other hand, it could be just a 'fishing boat.' "

"Frankly, that's my initial assumption. However, let's see what it does. It may reveal its function and purpose by its actions." Corry muttered, as he concentrated on watching the smudges move around the display.

The small ones were identified as 150- to 200-kilogram Awesome organisms. They were close to the Sulawesi shoreline. This caused the masdet smudge intensities to vary or drop out as the creatures moved around and through the rocks and corals.

The image of the *Bei fung* matched the position and range on the hydrophone display. It was a very positive sonar and masdet target. Captain Qian wasn't being cautious. He was booming out into the Makasar Straits unaware that the *Shenandoah* was tracking him. And, since the Chinese knew nothing of the Awesomes, Qian wasn't suspecting anything to be in the Straits except the American carrier submarine.

Corry shook his head in dismay. "I'm afraid that Captain Qian isn't demonstrating good tactical sense," he remarked to Braxton. "However, we may be seeing an example of Chinese submarine doctrine at work . . ."

"We're recording everything, Captain," Zeke assured him. "Naval intelligence will get its crack at our data."

"We're also going to need our data for other purposes, Mister Braxton, if it shows the presence of the Awesomes."

"Yes, sir."

The big target kept moving in azimuth from right

to left as it proceeded north along the coast. But it had no sound signal showing on the passive sonar display. It was very quiet. *Almost as quiet as the* Shenandoah, Corry thought, keeping his subvocalizing out of his N-fone. He didn't know what it was. He didn't know its intentions. It was a very tense time for the Commanding Officer of the U.S.S. *Shenandoah.*

However, he could do nothing but wait and watch right then. That made the situation even worse. Although he was a careful man, he was also a man of action.

As a result, he was almost uncontrollably tense. And he realized he shouldn't get that way. Others would see that their Commanding Officer was tense and would react accordingly. It also meant that perhaps he might unwillingly begin to stutter. So he began to chat with Zeke to relieve the tension and because there wasn't very much else he could do right then.

"My Academy classmates used to chide me because I read a lot of science fiction," Corry admitted to his XO in a conversational manner. "I maintained—and I still do—that an officer in a high-technology naval establishment has to be a little bit of a visionary. We must stay ready for the new technology that the techweenies give us. If we don't, we'll find ourselves facing an enemy who has it. So I always considered it part of my professional expertise to master the technology. The rest of professional expertise is mastering the management and leadership of people. Some of my classmates had trouble with current technology. They depended upon their rates to make technology work. But they've done well with the people side of the equation. Some of them have gone on to flag command. But I'm the only one who is commanding an SSCV."

"That says a lot, sir," Zeke told him easily.

"Well, that's not what really interests me about this situation, XO," Corry went on. "Do you realize how fantastic this is? How bizarre? Fifty years ago, the mere concept of a carrier submarine was suitable only for use in a science fiction novel. Frank Herbert was one of the few science fiction authors of the twentieth century who wrote about submarines at all. Everyone else was thinking about spaceships, not submarines."

"Who's laughing now, Captain? We're operating a second-generation carrier submarine," Zeke put in. Braxton had read science fiction too. It was apparent that the CO wanted to chat. The XO knew it was one of Corry's ways of relieving tension. Zeke was tense, too. And the situation was indeed becoming bizarre. "As I recall, another science fiction author who was a naval officer pointed out that it does not pay a prophet to be too specific."

Corry nodded as he watched the displays change. "I was thinking that we're living one of the most popular science fiction themes: contact with extraterrestrial beings."

"We're not sure yet, Captain."

"The probability is high and increasing every minute. Or didn't you kill one yesterday?"

"I'm sorry I had to," Zeke admitted. "I had to operate on the assumption that it wasn't exactly friendly. It hit Natalie. That could have meant something else to the alien. But I couldn't be sure. I had to act. I would rather have gotten to know it and learned to communicate with it. Then we could find out what it was really doing." That was a typical remark from a professional naval person. Contrary to the beliefs held by pacifists, antiwar, and antimilitary people, military and naval officers are probably the most pacifistic people in the world. They are the first ones to get shot at and probably to be killed in any armed conflict. Most of them hate war and believe their work prevents physical violence between people and states.

"Yes," Corry replied in his usual, simple way while he was formulating what he was going to say next.

"Well, Zeke, I *think* I know what the Awesomes are doing. But I could be wrong. I probably am wrong. I don't understand their psychology. I don't know their mental picture of the universe. I can only proceed on the basis of human psychology. And I know that's not the right way to do it."

"It's the only way to play the opening round, Captain," Zeke assured him.

"Agreed. But it may cause mistakes to be made that will take a lot of time for both species to forget. That means it will take us a long time to figure out what's going on. Or to really establish communications. We can't even communicate with the dolphins yet, and scientists have spent more than a century trying."

"Have they ever considered that maybe the dolphins don't want to communicate with us?" Zeke asked as the question suddenly arose in his mind.

"XO, that has occurred to me, too. And I'm concerned. Maybe these Awesomes don't want to communicate with us. We don't try to communicate with fish, although we try to think like them so we can catch them."

"And we don't try to communicate with cattle, either."

"You could have gone a long time without saying that, XO. However, I guess we've even . . ."

CO, this is Sonar, came the call.

Go ahead, Sonar.

Big new target is now working active sound ranging. Sending a ping microseconds behind the reflected Chinese signal. Very difficult to discriminate it from the returning ping. Standard countersonar ploy for us, but the Chinese may not have the equipment to detect it. The target is now ranging the Chinese boat. So it sees the Chinese boat.

We'll find out if it does, Corry responded. *Stay with it. And don't break silence.*

Aye, aye, sir.

Terri Ellison came in and sat down. "Air Group is ready, Captain," she reported. "Can I come up and sit on the front porch with you?"

"You already have, Terri. Welcome," Corry told her in a distracted, offhand manner. He was trying to concentrate on the situation now. As he saw the disposition of targets change, he also tried to formulate his own response to various threat potentials that might develop.

"We have a big bogey out there," Zeke drew her attention to the smudge on the display.

"Didn't we see something like it in the Flores Sea?" Terri recalled.

"Affirmative."

"Maybe at last we've located the fabled U.S.S. *Tuscarora.*" Terri's facetious remark referred to the imaginary modern Navy version of *The Flying Dutchman,* a fictitious naval vessel that never makes port, is never refitted or drydocked, and has been in commission since the days of World War I. Everyone in the Navy claims to have served in the *Tuscarora* or seen it. However, it has usually departed just the day before.

"We can certainly tag it that way," Zeke decided.

"I think you miss the point, XO," Corry remarked. "When the *Tuscarora* target began pinging the *Bei fung,* that told me something: It is no masdet anomaly. It's real. Since it is using countersonar techniques, it's not an unsophisticated marine animal. It's a submersible vessel." The Captain's use of the *Tuscarora* name to identify the unknown put an unofficial stamp of approval on it for use by the people of the *Shenandoah.* It was easier than referring to it as "the big unknown target."

"Has it pinged us?" Terri asked.

"Negatory," Zeke told her, then explained, "It's using a countersonar technique. It's pinging on the coattails of the *Bei fung*'s reflected ping. The Chinese may not be able to detect that. Right now, neither the *Bei fung* nor the *Tuscarora* knows where we are."

"That suits me fine," Corry said, "but I'm not one hundred percent certain of it. I don't know the performance characteristics of that sonar of theirs."

"Sir, we're underneath a deep scattering layer. From the behavior of the *Bei fung,* we know she hasn't seen us yet," the XO pointed out.

"In a situation like this with an unknown vessel having unknown capabilities, I do not assume the apparent until it becomes the obvious," Corry reminded him. "The *Tuscarora* may be going for the most aggressive and obvious target first while keeping a watch on us. We've been passive. They may or may not have seen us. If they have they may not come after us if we just lie here." He shook his head. "I do not know the thought processes of whatever is in command of the *Tuscarora.* But I'm willing to wait and see."

CO, this is Special Sensor.

This is the Captain. Go ahead, Charlie, Corry replied via N-fone. He looked at Zeke and Terri. "Got your N-fones on?"

Both nodded.

I have a computed course for the unidentified target based on delta-azimuth and delta-intensity. The target is on an intercept course with the Chinese boat.

Corry looked, picked up a light pen, and drew a line on the display between the smudge of the *Tuscarora* and the *Bei fung.* "Expand that portion of the plot, XO," he ordered Zeke and then replied, *Charlie, label the unknown target as the* Tuscarora. *How much time until intercept?*

The N-fone "voice" of LT Charles Ames, the Special Sensors Officer, came back with a touch of confusion. *The* Tuscarora, *sir? But I've been told that it doesn't exist and is only a story . . . Uh, yes, sir! I understand, sir! Computed time to intercept between the* Tuscarora *and the Chinese boat is thirteen minutes, sir.*

Corry watched. So did Zeke and Terri.

The two masdet images grew closer on the display.
The *Tuscarora* didn't waver.

Four minutes passed.

CO, Sonar reporting that the Tuscarora *sonar ping
rate has doubled.*

"Captain, that signals initiation of attack mode in
American submarine doctrine," Zeke reminded his
Commanding Officer unnecessarily. But he felt he had
to say it. Corry seemed hypnotized by the displays.

Increasing the sonar pinging rate as the range closed
was usually the precursor to attack. Increasing the
ping rate allowed more accurate range data to be
taken as the distance between the objects decreased.

"Sir, I know something about aggressive intent. I'm
seeing something here that sure as hell smacks of an
attack!" Terri spoke up strongly. She was not one to
mince words. She called it like she saw it. "I'm damned-
well convinced that bogey is going for the Chinese
boat!"

Corry nodded. He seemed deep in thought.

"Captain, do we attack the *Tuscarora* to defend the
Chinese boat? Or do we wait to see what the *Tuscarora* does?" Zeke asked.

Zeke had voiced one of the Big Questions in the
Captain's mind.

Should the *Shenandoah* defend a Chinese submarine
against an attack from a submerged unidentified
object?

Was it really an attack?

Did the *Bei fung* now see the approaching bogey?

Suppose the *Bei fung* reacted by engaging the approaching bogey first? Would that make it nearly impossible for the Captain of the U.S.S. *Shenandoah* to
carry out his orders?

Should the *Shenandoah* attack the *Bei fung* if the
Chinese boat attacked the alien?

What were the consequences of the *Shenandoah*
breaking stealth by engaging the bogey? Would the

carrier submarine herself be brought under alien attack as a result?

Captain, this is Sonar. The Tuscarora *has increased speed. Closure rate between them has increased. Merged plot in four minutes.*

Sonar, this is the Captain. Say range from here to Bei fung *at time of intercept.*

Calculated range to Bei fung *four minutes from now, assuming no change in* Bei fung *speed, is four-thousand-seven-hundred meters, sir.*

"Sir, if we're going to put a torpedo between them to show a shot across the bow, so to speak," Zeke pointed out carefully as he studied the results of a TDC run he'd just made, "or if you want to attack the *Tuscarora,* we'll have to fire within three minutes."

Corry nodded.

He didn't like to make a decision until he had enough information to make a good decision.

He didn't like to make a decision before a decision was necessary.

However, he didn't have enough data for his first option.

Therefore, it was necessary to make a decision because it *had* to be made.

Corry was a professional naval officer and the commander of one of the capital ships of the twenty-first-century United States Navy. He did what had to be done.

In his mind, the apparent became the obvious.

"XO, sound General Quarters!"

19

"All hands! General Quarters! General Quarters! Battle stations!"

There was no klaxon horn. The U.S.S. *Shenandoah* was submerged and lying silent and stealthed. A klaxon might be heard by the Chinese boat or the Awesomes' vessel, tagged the *Tuscarora*. The word went out verbally in the control room and via recorded alarm over all N-fone channels when Zeke hit the button.

Those who were not already on watch literally dropped whatever they were doing. Those in the rack awoke, quickly pulled on their poopie suits and topsiders, and raced to their battle stations.

The U.S.S. *Shenandoah* was a multidecked vessel. At least two ladders connected the decks. One was on the starboard side, the other on the port. The ancient Navy GQ traffic rules were observed. Those people who had to go forward and up to their battle stations went via the starboard side. Those whose battle stations were down and aft used the port ladders throughout the ship.

And it was done at doubletime.

The existing watch was immediately relieved to proceed to their battle stations.

Even the Air Group had battle stations submerged. Pilots went to ready rooms. Deck crews went to their positions on the hangar decks and near the lifts. Crew chiefs slipped into cockpits and prepared to power up their aircraft.

Very few in the *Shenandoah* did not have specific battle stations. Those people went to their quarters and remained quiet.

The battle crew slipped into their stations on the bridge.

Altogether, 665 people quickly moved throughout the ship and were in place within two minutes. They had drilled for this. When it happened for real, they did it a little quicker than during a drill.

Corry hedged his bets. "Target two fish at the Chinese boat and two fish at the *Tuscarora*," he snapped the order. "Report when you have a TDC solution. Aim on passive sonar data and masdet indications. Set fish for auto homing. Set fish for command destruct. Report when ready to shoot."

"Aye, aye, sir. TDC solution coming up. Do you intend to shoot at both targets, Captain?" Zeke reported and asked.

"Affirmative. I've got to get the shots off. Stand by to auto destruct any or all fish," Corry replied tersely, still studying the displays. He had temporarily disconnected his N-fone so he could concentrate without all the background chatter that would be on the net. He would now take his inputs from his XO and from the bridge displays. Then he would verbally relay his orders to Braxton. Corry had deliberately taken himself out of operational mode and placed himself strictly in the command position. That's what procedure called for. He had to be free to grasp the big picture and give general commands through a single person. That required trust and teamwork. With Braxton, he knew he had both. And that Braxton was the man who could be trusted to look inward to the ship and make it work while Corry fought it.

Braxton immediately knew what the Captain's plan was. Corry had limited time to get shots off. Therefore, he was going to fire all four fish. Then he would have a minute to command destruct them before they reached their targets. That bought him a badly needed extra minute. But it was a close call for him. He'd put off until the last moment having to make a decision. In fact, he hadn't made it yet. But he had to get the fish on their way.

"Bow tubes ready to shoot, Captain." Zeke reported as CWO "Guns" Weaver checked in via the CWO's N-fone.

"Launch fish! Fire!" Corry snapped without hesitation. "Go to active pinging. Ahead two thirds. Come to fifty meters and level the bubble."

"Aye, aye, sir. Fire fish. . . . Four tubes fired. Active pinging. All ahead two-thirds and come up to fifty meters," Zeke repeated.

"Reload and stand by to fire again. And stand by as well to surface and launch aircraft."

"Aye, aye, sir. Reloading now. We're ready to surface and launch aircraft on command, sir."

The underwater missiles were far more advanced than the ancient "torpedoes" of the last century. They were smart, semi-intelligent underwater missiles, miniature expendable submarines with warheads. Yet they were still called "fish" by submariners.

"Counting down to fish intercept with targets," came the verbal voice of CPO Thomas, the chief boatswain's mate from his position at a console in front of Corry. "Thirty seconds to intercept on first fish . . ."

"Stand by command destruct."

"Aye, aye, sir. Standing by."

"*Tuscarora* has slacked speed. *Tuscarora* is coming hard to starboard." Zeke's report was confirmed by both the masdet and sonar displays.

"Twenty seconds to intercept . . ."

"Chinese boat is beginning evasive maneuvers."

"Fifteen seconds . . ."

"Destruct all four fish! I say again: Destruct all four fish *now*!"

The four explosions were felt and heard in the control room.

"Destruct of all four fish confirmed," Zeke reported.

Corry saw where the *Tuscarora* was going. He had no sonar returns from it. Whatever it was, it was stealthy to active sonar. But it continued pinging. Therefore, Goff could continue to track it. Ames still had a masdet indication on it. And it was coming about to a southerly course.

"XO, pursue the *Tuscarora*. Come to depth for best speed. Maintain two-triple-zero range behind it. Target two fish for the *Bei fung* and stand by." Corry hadn't had time to explain in the heat of the action. Braxton didn't question the orders. It wasn't his prerogative to question battle orders from the Captain; it was his duty to carry them out.

"Aye, aye, sir. Pursue the *Tuscarora* at range two thousand and at best speed depth. Two fish are loaded and ready to launch at the Chinese boat, sir."

Corry looked at him. "I had a third option that occurred to me as we launched fish, Zeke," he explained now that there was time for explanations. "And it was worth expending four fish. The *Tuscarora* was caught by surprise."

"I think we surprised it all right, Captain. It reacted very strongly when it found out we were here. And it broke off its attack," Zeke said, nodding. He found himself soaking wet with sweat. It had been an operation with a very high pucker factor.

"Yes. We let it know that we would not abide an attack on the Chinese boat," the skipper of the *Shenandoah* went on. "And in the process, we let Captain Qian know we had him dead nuts and didn't kill him. Qian will respect us for that."

"I wouldn't depend on having gained his respect, sir," Zeke said cautiously.

"I'm not. That's why we've loaded and targeted two fish on him."

"Qian will try to follow us, Captain. He now knows about the *Tuscarora*. He found out when it began its attack pinging on him and he saw us shoot at it. In fact, it looks like he's already setting up to follow," Zeke said, indicating the displays.

"Except he can't see it and knows somehow we can," Corry pointed out and continued to explain his strategy. "We'll let him follow us. We might need his help, because we're going to follow the *Tuscarora* at a distance it knows is within our kill range. But we won't kill it. We'll passively follow. It will either counterattack or continue to run until it sees it can't lose us. It may then begin to behave in a way that might tell us it wants to parley. Above all, we have to let the commander of the *Tuscarora* know that we can't be bullied. We won't hurt it if it doesn't try to hurt us. But we can and will defend ourselves."

"Aren't we taking a big risk that it has weapons we don't know about?"

"Zeke, if it had them, we would have seen them. Look at the data," Corry urged him, indicating the past-performance display plot. "It was within a thousand meters of the *Bei fung* when we destructed those fish. I think it has no underwater weapons. It had increased its speed and was about to engage in the most ancient of naval attacks. It was going to ram the *Bei fung*. It could have broached its hull, but since its inhabitants are aquatic, it didn't have to maintain a pressure hull like we do. So it was going to ram and run."

"So it isn't a warship," Zeke decided.

"You're right. It isn't. It's a commercial fishing vessel."

"And it went after the Chinese boat because it watched Qian leave Makasar. It must know about the Awesome I killed yesterday. Its skipper probably got a report from one of the six Awesomes I spotted from the beach." Braxton paused, then guessed, "I'll bet part of its attack was motivated by revenge."

"Perhaps. That remains to be seen. The *Bei fung* was probably seen as an intruder on its fishing grounds and perhaps as a predator on the basis of the killing of one of its fisher types."

"Uh, what about all the Awesomes it left in the Sulawesi coastal waters?"

"They'll stay put. They probably figure the *Tuscarora* will come back to pick them up eventually."

"Well, Captain, that's as good a story as any we can put together from the pieces of this action," the XO agreed. He saw both SCPO Armstrong and CPO Thomas watching them and listening to their conversation. So Zeke asked, "Chief, what do you think?"

It was Armstrong, Chief of the Boat, who replied, "You'd better tell the crew, Captain. This is the wildest damned mission I've been on in my twenty-five years of service. To be honest, if I hadn't been here, I'd have a hell of a lot of trouble believing it!"

"Chief Thomas, we've shipped together for a long time," Corry addressed the other CPO. "I'd like to hear if you think we've fallen down the rabbit hole here."

The chunky chief boatswain's mate, the number two petty officer aboard, merely shook his head. He was a man who was as well-read as the Captain, and he caught the reference to *Alice in Wonderland*. Corry knew he would. He replied in his gravelly, no-nonsense voice, "Captain, I couldn't write a fiction story about this that would be believable. But I'll tell you one thing: If that damned alien boat tries to ram us like it tried to do to the Chinese boat, I'll be happy as hell to help Chief Weaver put a fish right down its goddamned fucking throat . . . on your orders, of course, sir. I don't give a damn if it's a scared alien or a friendly alien. I don't care if it understands us or not. It's got to start thinking about us as something more than a gourmet meal or we're not going to get anywhere trying to contact it and make friends with it. I don't mind eating steak, but I wouldn't eat my family dog no matter how hungry I got. I've got some respect for it."

Corry smiled. The two chiefs often accurately represented the thinking of the other petty officers and bluejackets in the ship. "Thank you, Chief. I can always count on you for the ungarbled word."

Zeke suddenly put his hand up to his ear. He heard, *Bridge, Sonar. Hydrophone and masdet agree. The* Tuscarora *is opening the distance between us. It appears to have gone to forty-five knots.*

Zeke repeated the information to Corry.

"All ahead full, Mister Braxton. Stay on its tail," Corry ordered.

"Sir, the *Bei fung* is trailing us. Do we want to let Qian know how fast the *Shenandoah* will go?" Zeke asked.

"Qian will find out only that we can outrun him, period. He won't know whether we're operating at two thirds or emergency, XO," Corry explained. "I'm not going to give up this chase because a Chinese submarine captain might learn something more about an American carrier submarine than he's already discovered. The Chinese may learn we can go fast underwater, but they don't know *how* we're doing it!"

"Aye, aye, sir. All ahead full."

Corry watched the displays. The *Shenandoah* accelerated to full speed, 48 knots. For a few minutes while he watched the masdet display, the carrier submarine began to gain on the *Tuscarora*.

Then he saw the distance begin to open again.

Before Zeke could report that the target had increased speed, Corry snapped, "Mister Braxton, all ahead emergency!"

"All ahead emergency. Aye, aye, sir!"

The aquajet thrusters were supplemented by the auxiliary thrusters to shove the *Shenandoah* to her hull design speed.

Everyone aboard could feel it when the hull began to cavitate. The whole carrier submarine shook and vibrated.

The ship had reached its maximum possible speed.

It could go faster only by the application of two to three times the amount of power aboard. And under the threat of shaking itself to pieces.

"Captain, Engineer Officer reports that we can keep this speed for only five minutes," Zeke warned.

Corry just nodded then asked, "Does Navigation Officer see anything that could indicate a density layer above or below us?"

If a layer with lower density could be found, it might be possible to get the hull cavitation to stop. That might allow the ship to maintain emergency speed longer.

After a moment while Zeke communicated by N-fone with navigation and sonar, he replied, "Sir, Navigation Officer reports a possible fifty-meter-thick low-density layer at a hundred meters depth."

"Come up to one-zero-zero meters. Steady as she goes, Mister Braxton." Corry had just bought himself some more time. It just might be enough time to allow the *Tuscarora's* commander to decide he couldn't out-run the *Shenandoah.* This underwater speed was such that any submersible with the size and mass of the *Shenandoah* would run into hull cavitation. The *Tuscarora* either had been built with more advanced hydrodynamics technology or was faced with the same basic technology limitations. Corry didn't know which, but he was going to find out.

But he knew the limits of his ship. He wouldn't unduly risk the ship and the crew. Although the blood lust of the chase was coursing through him, a zealot he wasn't.

And he wasn't going to be permitted to become one.

He saw the change in the characteristics of the masdet display smudge even as Zeke passed along the report from Charlie Ames.

"Captain, Special Sensor reports masdet return signal change. The *Tuscarora* has surfaced at fifty knots."

"He can't run on the surface at that speed," Corry

objected verbally. A submersible could always run faster submerged than it could at the water-air interface.

"Sir, he did this before in the Flores Sea."

"That he did. Let's see if he does it again."

The image of the *Tuscarora* disappeared from the masdet display.

"Sonar reports loss of sonar pinging signal from the *Tuscarora*," Zeke told him. "It's gone, sir. It isn't in the water any longer. It must be in the air."

This time, Corry wasn't under orders to be somewhere.

"All ahead one third. Surface! Surface! Surface! Prepare to launch aircraft. I want CAP plus a pie-plate Osprey up at once," Corry ordered, referring to the airborne radar version of the P-10 Osprey patrol plane with its large planar array. The Black Panthers had three of them. "And get the surveillance radar array working as quickly as possible. I want to see where that vessel goes. The *Tuscarora* might be sonar stealthed, but we're going to find out if it's radar stealthed, too."

"Captain, I'll bet it is," Zeke remarked because a couple of other pieces of the puzzle had dropped into place for him.

20

"I'll be damned!" CDR Terri Ellison exclaimed as she stepped out on the PRIFLY bridge. "Duke, I can *see* the damned thing!"

And indeed she could.

The *Tuscarora* target was about two kilometers to the southeast at an altitude of about a thousand meters.

"It's a big humper!" was the comment of her Flight Deck Officer, LT Paul Peyton. "Must be four hundred meters long!"

"Reminds me of the pictures of the old Navy blimps," Terri recalled.

"Except it's bigger. Almost as big as the ZR-1 *Shenandoah* Navy dirigible of the nineteen twenties," Peyton remarked. As a naval aviator himself, he knew the history of naval aviation. "But it isn't silver. It's camouflaged gray and blue."

"Well, the dirigible *Shenandoah* didn't have to operate underwater in a clandestine mode," the CAG told him and touched her N-fone behind her ear. *Panther Looker, this is Alley Cat,* she called, using her airborne call sign. *Do you have a photog aboard?*

Alley Cat, this is Stripper in Panther One. Negatory! the reply came from the female pilot of the EP-10. Some of the women pilots had call signs that were rougher and raunchier than those of the men. Most of them had been given their call names by their male colleagues while in training. The occasions that prompted the call names were usually embarrassing.

To get the story of a call name out of a pilot usually required an hour or more at a bar with the inquisitor buying. However, the women pilots loved their call names. A questionable and tasteless call name signified that they were "one of the boys." However, off-duty they did their best to prove they weren't.

We can see your target, Stripper. Before launch, get a photographer aboard. I want good, sharp, clear air-to-air photos of the target!

Roger that, Alley Cat! But it will delay our launch one minute.

CDR Teresa Ellison prided herself on the speed and efficiency with which her Air Group could work. She was reluctant to accept even a one-minute delay on launching the radar patrol aircraft. But she really wanted to compensate for screwing up the earlier photo documentation of the Awesome on the beach.

Do it, Stripper! We need that photo documentation! And after you're airborne, ease up to that target gently. Take pictures. Lots of pictures.

One of the major tactical advantages of the carrier submarine was stealth and surprise. It could appear and disappear quickly. The faster its crews could activate or deploy its various systems when it dived or surfaced, the more effective it was.

It did no good to have an aircraft carrier with submersible features if it took ten to thirty minutes to deploy or strike down its aircraft. Likewise, it did no good to have a submarine with aircraft carrier capabilities if it took too long to go from one operational mode to another.

LT Peyton had his topside crews trained tightly. They'd been up and readying the upper flight deck for launch even as seawater was still draining through scuppers. On the lower flight deck, the fore and aft hatches had been opened as quickly as they had freeboard. Lifts had the VTOL F/A-48 Sea Devils up and ready to launch as quickly as the upper deck was clear.

Within three minutes of surfacing, the U.S.S. *Shen-*

andoah had Sea Devils on CAP over her. One minute later, an EP-10 was catapulted off the lower deck.

And Terri had gotten another photographer with a long-focus lens beside her on deck. He was shooting photos and video of the entire operation around the big gray-and-blue target in the sky.

Stripper, this is Alley Cat. I'm having the Tigers stay well outside of you. I don't want to panic whatever is in that blimp. But if it attacks you, get the hell out of out of there and let the Tigers go to work.

Terri wasn't going to take any crap from the alien ship. Neither would she have her aircraft threaten it.

Alley Cat, Stripper here. We've got a very solid radar return from it. Same with lidar. We're pacing it now. Its airspeed is about fifty knots. We have to hang down and dirty so we don't overfly it. And it's climbing at about a hundred meters a minute.

"Why the hell isn't it stealthed?" Terri wondered. "Something that big will stand out like a black cat in a snow bank on any radar screen in the world!"

Then in a flash of insight that came from several thousand hours of piloting a P-10 Osprey, she knew.

Air Boss, this is the XO. We confirm negative stealth on the Tuscarora. *Brewer is painting it solid with the surveillance array. But if it was running silent and stealthy submerged, we can't figure out why it revealed itself when it went airborne. You got any insights on this?*

Yes! Ask Barbara Brewer! Terri fired back. She knew the Radar/Lidar Officer, a highly competent electronic engineer who really understood the magic of radar and lidar. *She'll confirm my guess about it. There may be two reasons why we're painting it. First, it may not have radar stealth. It may not have radar aboard, period. Just because the Awesomes have a combined submersible and airborne vehicle doesn't mean they have the other technologies we do. Panther Looker and Tiger Flight One report no active radar emanating from it. Second, even if the Awesomes have the technology, maybe they think they don't need it in this skirmish.*

What makes you think they don't need it, Air Boss?

Look, if I'm tooling along at four hundred knots in an Osprey and see a target moving at fifty on the radar, I'm going to ignore it. I'm going to think it's a weather balloon, Terri explained.

Weather balloon? Terri, an airborne object that big can be picked up on any air traffic or space control radar in the world!

Yes, and it will be tagged as a weather balloon because it's moving so slowly! Or ignored because it may appear to be a big blip. Radars still display anomalies just like Charlie's masdet was . . . Or that we thought his masdet was displaying. Looks like we were seeing something real and didn't know it!

Stand by, Air Boss . . . Air Boss, launch a second P-10 and Tiger flight now! Sonar reports the Chinese boat is two thousand meters off the stern and making sounds like it's surfacing! Put the patrol aircraft near it and cover it with the Tigers as a CAP! Zeke passed along the order from Corry on the bridge below.

Terri understood perfectly the reason for this order. Corry wanted to make sure the Chinese submarine captain realized he was up against more than just another submarine if his intentions were to make life difficult.

And the Captain is coming up. He wants to see the Tuscarora himself before it disappears. Zeke went on to advise her.

Terri replied using submarine protocol rather than the slightly different and less formal air communications procedures. *Aye, aye, XO. Launching patrol aircraft and additional CAP now.* She touched her N-fone to switch channels and snapped to the commander of VP-35, *Flak, this is Alley Cat. Launch a second Osprey now. Position it two thousand meters astern at a hundred meters altitude. The Chinese submarine will be surfacing at that location shortly. You will have Tiger CAP!*

Roger, Alley Cat. I'm in the left seat and we're on the cat now.

Then she fired the order off to LCDR Pat Bellinger, CO of the VA-65 "Tigers", *Bells, this is Alley Cat. Launch the second CAP flight. Your mother hen is Flak in an Osprey coming off the lower cat now.* She could see the four F/A-48 Sea Devils already position on the upper flight deck next to the retractable PRIFLY tower.

"Roger, Alley Cat. Tiger Two has kicked the tires and lit the fires. Flight leader is Rats. He's spooling up in front of you now.

The P-10 Osprey erupted into the air off the bow of the *Shenandoah.* It began its climb out and a left turn.

The upper flight deck was no longer wet. The few puddles left on it were blown dry by the air curtains of the F/A-48s as the VTOL attack fighters blasted off.

Terri checked the action and saw her chickens maneuver into their assigned positions.

"Duke, we're sitting between two hot mamas," she verbally told her Flight Deck Officer. "I don't like it. The Chink could make trouble even though he has no aircraft. And the *Tuscarora* may or may not decide to be difficult in a way we can't anticipate. So I want to put another two Tiger flights on the deck and fill the lower cats with Ospreys loaded for ASW. Can you handle it?"

"That's an affirm, Alley Cat." There was far less formal protocol between officers of different ranks in the Air Group. They *knew* they were supermen and superwomen. They believed the carrier submarine *really* existed to carry them and their aircraft around to interesting places and challenging fights. They behaved with expected respect to the other officers aboard. But among themselves, they were equals among equals. The collar tab insignia of rank merely denoted seniority and differences in pay grade. And maybe more logged hours. Yet they also knew that seniority ruled and RHIP, especially when it came to giving and following orders.

Terri Ellison was a woman, but she was treated as both an equal and first among equals in her role as CAG. That she was. Peyton still recalled the day early on when a slight professional disagreement had arisen between them. They'd met after duty alone in the gym. She took him to the mat in less than a minute and walked off untouched. His groin hurt for several days afterward. But Terri was a lady. She never mentioned it to anyone. They got along just fine from then on. In fact, he discovered he really wasn't enough of a man to stay with her. Terri was demanding in all her activities. Duke Peyton secretly envied the prowess of both Zeke Braxton and Bart Clinch.

"We'll have to move some aircraft fast if you don't scramble the ones on deck," Duke went on, checking the disposition of the Sea Devils spotted on the deck, their cockpits manned and their ground crews standing by to light the fires. "We can always launch the on-deck Devils to take care of any airbornes that need to trap because of bingo fuel. Whatever, I can hack it. I promise I won't shove any good airplanes over the side to make room . . ."

She looked askance at him, realizing that his sense of humor was at work. Caustically, but with a touch of humor in her own voice, she replied, "You do that, Duke!"

Then she saw the black sail and hull of the Chinese submarine break water behind the *Shenandoah*.

XO, Air Boss. Sail ho! The Chinese submarine has surfaced behind us. My chickens are over it now, she dutifully reported to Braxton.

She discovered Captain Corry and Chief Warren on the PRIFLY bridge beside her. She saluted. They were all on the open PRIFLY bridge and not under cover. "Welcome to PRIFLY, the next best thing to God's country, Captain!"

Corry returned her salute without comment. He was

wearing his old blue cap from his days commanding VF-43 "The World Famous Pukin' Dogs." He only glanced at the *Bei fung* and confirmed that it was being circled by a P-10 covered by four Sea Devils above it. Then he turned his attention to the *Tusca-rora* that was now three kilometers ahead of them and climbing while it slowly opened the range.

It was still a *big* object in the sky.

"Take a good look, Terri," he told her, handing her his binoculars even before he'd had a chance to use them. "And remember what you see. I wanted to come topside and see it for myself too. We're going to be interrogated by a lot of people about this. I wanted to be sure that I had actually seen what we tangled with in Makasar Straits."

"It's as real as life, Captain," Terri told him. She took a look through the binocs and decided she could see just as well without them. Thousands of flight hours had sharpened her eyes and greatly improved her ability to see distant targets. "And this time we'll get sharp, clear color photos and video of it! Thank you, sir." She handed the binoculars back.

"Is it still climbing?"

"I have no report from the Osprey to the contrary, sir."

Corry nodded and put binoculars to his eyes. He carefully watched the *Tuscarora*. "Charlie was right. He usually is. It's at least as big as the *Shenandoah*. And probably as massy. But what the hell is making it fly? What kind of propulsion system can drive a fifty-thousand ton shape like that through the water at fifty knots and then make it climb out at several hundred meters per minute?"

Terri shrugged her solid shoulders. Her short, curly blonde hair blew in the wind as she watched the big dirigiblelike object slowly climbing and growing smaller to the eye in the eastern sky. "Sir, I'd have to give you the same answer Sir Francis Drake might have given if he'd seen the *Shenandoah* and was asked what made it go. 'I don't know.' Or simply 'magic.' "

"Ever read science fiction, Terri?" Corry asked without taking his binoculars off the disappearing target.

"No, sir, in spite of the fact that Zeke has done so at your insistence."

"I've never insisted that my officers accept my likes and dislikes, Terri," Corry corrected her. "But you're right. It's Arthurian magic. 'Any sufficiently advanced technology is indistinguishable from magic.' "

"Sir, I thought Clarke said that," Duke Peyton put in. He was another closet science fiction reader. Life can get boring in a submarine. Most submarine officers are well read. In fact, they'll read anything they can get their hands on, including bread wrappers from the galley.

"He did. His first name was Arthur."

"Oh. Yes. Of course, sir."

"Well, if they can develop it and we know that it can work because they have it, we'll develop it," Corry mused, putting down the binoculars. "What's impossible to one generation of technologists is only difficult to the next and commonplace to the third."

CO, this is the XO, came the N-fone call from Zeke on the bridge below. *Signal for you from Captain Qian of the Chinese boat.*

Put it on the verbose channel to PRIFLY, XO. I'll take it via regular handset here. Corry didn't want to use N-fone with the Chinese. He didn't know if Qian had it in his boat. It was no great secret weapon, but it made communication five times faster. Corry and the United States Navy didn't believe they should simply give away something that would make the life of a potential adversary easier.

"Captain Qian, this is Captain Corry. I'm glad that thing didn't ram you, sir."

Qian's voice sounded somewhat confused. "But you shot at me, Captain Corry."

"I shot at what is in the sky to the east of us and going somewhere else. Yes, I aimed at you, too, but destructed the fish to confuse our unknown enemy,

Captain," Corry explained. "Take a good look at what's up there in the sky, sir. And if you have photographers aboard, get pictures of it."

"What is it, Captain Corry?"

"I'm not certain I know, Captain Qian." Corry wasn't lying.

"I didn't see it while I was submerged. It had no sonar return. How did you know where it was and how to follow it?"

"Captain, we have a complete sensor suite aboard. And it was in such a condition that we could see it," Corry replied, being truthful but not totally truthful.

"We are photographing it."

"Good!"

"Where is it going? How can it be a submarine and also fly?"

"I don't know, Captain Qian."

"Your actions and behavior over the last twelve hours make me doubt what you're telling me. Why did you leave Makasar harbor in the middle of the night, for example?"

"Captain, we're in the middle of an operation here. When it's over, we'll meet you in Makasar harbor and talk about this. Right now, we are at battle stations because I don't know what that airborne target will do next. It tried to ram you, and I don't know what its intentions are right now. I suggest you come to battle stations in case it decides to come after us."

"Hah! What can it do to us? We have close-in weapons systems as you do!"

"Captain Qian, I don't know what it can do. But I'm not taking chances. I am at battle stations ready to defend this ship with everything we have." That was a subtle signal from Corry to Qian. He wanted to let the Chinese Captain know that the *Shenandoah* was prepared against anything, including a preemptive attack by the *Bei fung*.

Qian didn't miss that clue. He could also see the P-10 and the F/A-48s overhead. Corry had air supremacy. Qian's only attack mode would have to be preceded by diving. "Very well, Captain, we shall . . ."

Terri touched Corry's elbow and pointed to her N-fone.

"We have things happening here, Qian. Remain on this frequency," Corry snapped, then went to N-fone. *What's going on, Terri?*

Look, sir! The Tuscarora *is now accelerating vertically at more than ten meters per second squared!*

Alley Cat, this is Stripper! The target has stopped forward motion and is accelerating vertically! I can't stay with it!

Alley Cat, this is Rats. I've got my Devil at full military power in a vertical climb, and it's pulling away from me straight up!

Corry sighed as he saw the target tagged humorously as the *Tuscarora* now quickly vanishing in the vertical. He guessed it was headed for space. His aircraft couldn't possibly follow it.

XO, this is the CO. Zeke, the Tuscarora *is headed straight up. Have Brewer maintain radar track on it as long as possible. But it's going elsewhere, someplace where our aircraft can't follow. So secure from General Quarters, but come to Condition Two. We could still catch a steel rod it might heave at us from space. As quickly as Air Boss can trap her chickens, we're going to dive for security along with the Chinese boat. Then we'll return to Makasar.*

Aye, aye, sir! I confirm that array radar shows the bogey going straight up. The angle is nearly vertical now, and it's accelerating through ten thousand meters' altitude, velocity increasing. I confirm your estimate that it's headed elsewhere.

He turned to Terri. "Well done!" he told her. "Trap your chickens and let's go back to Makasar. We've got a Marine batt waiting for us there, plus an unknown number of Awesomes that the *Tuscarora* left behind. I think. Unless there's another of their fishing trawlers hanging around . . ."

21

"Captain, I don't think we should tell the Chinese anything!" Terri stated with considerable conviction in her voice.

"We're going to have to tell them something, sir!" Zeke objected. Corry had called a Papa briefing in the main wardroom for all department heads as the U.S.S. *Shenandoah* was at anchor in Makasar harbor again.

It was now 0700 hours the following morning. Corry had deliberately not called a meeting until everyone had had a breather. The crew was exhausted after being at General Quarters or Condition Two for twenty hours the preceding day.

Furthermore, they'd had to bring the *Shenandoah* into Makasar harbor on the surface in the dark using radar, lidar, sonar, and visual conning. The harbor channels were not well marked with lighted buoys. In fact, except for a few shore establishments that catered to visiting sailors, the whole town of Makasar shut down at night.

The *Bei fung* had elected to remain two kilometers off shore. Captain Qian had apparently decided not to carry out a difficult and hazardous night harbor entry.

That told the officers of the *Shenandoah* something about the sensor suite in the Chinese boat.

Corry wanted to get the day started early. He hadn't reported to CINCPAC yet. He would do so after the meeting. Kane would see the *Shenandoah* back in Makasar harbor, and thus CINCPAC wouldn't worry.

The meeting had been called for immediately after breakfast. Corry commanded with the philosophy that good operations couldn't be planned when people were fatigued. When tired, people make mistakes. Furthermore, on this mission they'd already made too many mistakes—although the problems hadn't involved the ship. Mistakes can't be tolerated in a submarine.

All the department heads were wondering now, "What next?" The situation had a lot of unknowns in it, perhaps even more now than two days before.

"We don't have to tell them anything! They followed us after we shot at the *Tuscarora,* and they saw it in the air!" Terri continued.

"And they haven't the foggiest damned notion what it was," Zeke replied.

"Neither do we! So let them figure it out for themselves!"

Corry sat back and listened. It was his usual way of exercising command. When required, he was a decisive man who acted on the information he had at the moment. But when it came to planning, he didn't depend on a formal staff. His operating officers were his staff.

The officers and the crew of the *Shenandoah* knew this. Corry's technique contributed to the high state of morale. When it came to action that could be planned in advance, everyone aboard knew that the department heads had reached a consensus and Corry had bought off on it. Thus, any orders from the Captain weren't spurious. In emergencies, however, the orders didn't come from planning sessions but from the endless drills that left no time for worrying.

No one had to be invited to participate in the give-and-take. Papa briefs weren't run by Robert's Rules of Order. If the discussion got out of hand, Corry would step in. That rarely happened.

"Agreed, but we know the *Tuscarora* was real," Operations Officer Bob Lovette put in. He ticked his points off on his fingers. "One, we took airborne and surface visual data when it went airborne. Two, we got good radar *and* lidar data then too. Three, we recorded active sonar signals from it when it was submerged; its ping rate increased as its range closed with the Chinese boat. And, four, we have masdet data that correlate with the visual and electronic data." He spread his hands. "So it was real!"

"And it damned near outran us underwater," the Engineer Officer added darkly. He was upset. Until yesterday, the *Shenandoah* had been the fastest known underwater vessel. He had more than a little pride involved with being Engineer Officer in it. "Furthermore, it *outflew* us! And I don't have a clue about what sort of propulsion system it used to do that!"

"It was certainly real, but we still don't know what it was," Natalie Chase pointed out. "We don't really *know* if it's connected to the Awesome that trapped me off the beach."

"And we can only *speculate* about its purpose!" Mark Walton reminded them.

"Speculation don't feed the bulldog," growled Major Bart Clinch who had been flown aboard from the Embassy at dawn. Zeke had given him a thorough background briefing on what had happened offshore yesterday.

Clinch had been upset about that. He'd spent the day haggling with General Helamahera about what they were going to do in the way of joint exercises camouflaged as search-and-find missions. He knew he'd been in charge of what was ostensibly a holding campaign on that front. He didn't really like it. He liked action. But an order was an order.

"And the bulldog is going to be asking questions if it hasn't already started to do so," Engineer Officer Stocker added.

"Whether or not we tell the Chinese is a moot

point," Lovette remarked. "As you reminded us, Natalie, the Captain is going to have to report to CINCPAC. That report is far more important." He turned and asked Corry, "Sir, do you intend to ask CINCPAC about the advisability of informing the Chinese?"

Corry shook his head. "No, Bob, I don't. I know what the answer will be, so I don't need to ask the question. I'm going to make a cold, rational, specific report to CINCPAC that includes all the data. I will *not* attempt to analyze or interpret the data. Nor will I suggest what CINCPAC, CNO, and higher authority should do with it. That's not my worry and not my responsibility. If Admiral Kane asks for my opinion about what's going on, I will give it to him with many caveats. But I will not include speculation as part of my report. We really *didn't* know what we were chasing, did we?"

The Commanding Officer of the U.S.S. *Shenandoah* paused. No one interrupted him. They were interested in what he had to say. Then he went on, "It's not proper for me to report speculation. My objective in reporting only what we know is *not* to mislead CINCPAC or CNO. After all, among ourselves we've spun a science fiction tale that has no proof. I'm not going to mention that. The Navy doesn't run on science fiction. And I'm not ready for retirement yet."

"So what's the next step, Captain?" Terri asked. "Are you going to request supplementary orders to cover the new situation?"

Corry shook his head. He took a sip of hot coffee, then said, "I don't believe it's a new situation. We were given orders to come here and find out what was going on. So I'll report that we intend to continue to carry out our orders. We really *haven't* learned what happened to those hundred missing Americans, have we?"

He paused, then said, "As for the Chinese, I've told Captain Qian all that I can. I don't intend to share our data with him. I'm not authorized to do that. But

I invited him to take his own photographs. Lieutenant Brewer reported that the *Bei fung* was painting the airborne *Tuscarora* with its own radars, so they've got multisensor data themselves."

Corry looked around the table. "That, ladies and gentlemen, has put Captain Qian and his crew in the same position with their high command as we enjoy with ours at this moment. Qian may think differently than we do, but he's not going to report that he helped an American carrier submarine chase a blue-and-gray UFO."

"And the Sulawesis aren't going to believe it either, Captain," Clinch added. "In fact, even with the data and the personal reports of the alien attack on Natalie, Zeke, and Norm, I have trouble believing it."

"Believe it, Bart," Zeke told him.

"I said I was having trouble believing it, not that I disbelieved it," Clinch replied curtly.

"Captain, I'll report what the crew is thinking: Do we sit here and watch for another appearance of the *Tuscarora* or one of its kind?" Chief of the Boat Carl Armstrong was the one who cut through the fuzz of discussion to ask the important question of the day. "Or do we follow our hunch and go fishing ourselves?"

"We weren't sent here to anchor in Makasar harbor and go on liberty," Corry reminded them all. Then he asked his usual question, "What do you recommend be done, ladies and gentlemen?"

"Let's go fishing, Captain," Zeke spoke up.

"An Awesome caught me," Natalie pointed out. "If we're as smart as an Awesome, we ought to be able to catch one ourselves."

"Dead or alive?" CDR Laura Raye Moore put in.

"Which would you prefer, Doctor?" Zeke asked, aware that the physician and her biotechnologists would be the ones who would have to take care of it alive or store it dead.

"Preferably dead," she told everyone. "I don't

know what an Awesome eats except maybe people, and I don't expect to get any volunteers for that. So I might have some trouble keeping it alive. I don't have anything that would hold a creature that large, and I don't know how strong the enclosure would have to be. I certainly don't want to bring a live Awesome aboard and then have it get loose."

"Can we get a dead one into some sort of storage before it's eaten by its own parasites like the last one?" Terri asked.

"If we're prepared to do it, I think we can," the Medical Officer said. She explained, "If Awesomes eat us, their DNA can't be that much different. They get nourishment from the breakdown of our proteins, carbohydrates, and such. That gives me a clue to proceed with. If I pickle it fast enough in alcohol or form-aldehyde, I can probably pickle the parasites, too. However, I don't have about two hundred liters of either alcohol or formaldehyde. So we'll have to quick-freeze it."

She turned to the Supply Department head. "Fran, how much space does Ken Keyes have in the cold storage lockers right now?"

"How much space do you need? And will you need a special, isolated freezer compartment for this creature?" LT Frances Allen responded.

"How about an empty meat locker? Something that will hold about two hundred kilos?"

"I'll check. If it's not empty, Ken can move some stores around to free it up."

"Please do that."

"Consider it done, Doctor."

"Okay, we find one and kill it. Then we get it back to the ship fast and deep-freeze it before it eats itself," Terri broke in. "I can arrange a fast airlift using a cargo sling to get it to the ship. Now let me ask the next question: How do we catch an Awesome?"

The idea of deliberately killing a creature because of their ignorance so they could get a close look at it wasn't something that the department heads of the U.S.S. *Shenandoah* really wanted to do. If the Awesomes were indeed extraterrestrial aliens, that would be one hell of a way to start a relationship. It could very well lead to the first interplanetary war with the Awesomes being on the offensive using unknown weaponry and unfathomable doctrines, strategies, and tactics that humans didn't understand.

The tension in the room could almost be felt.

Zeke didn't want to kill an intelligent being. He didn't like the fact that every year dolphins and whales were killed, deliberately or accidentally. But he forced himself to think like his fisherman forebears from Maine. "We go about catching Awesomes the same way we figure out how to catch fish."

"I'm not a fisherman. How do we figure out how to catch fish?" Lovette asked.

"You have to think like a fish," Zeke explained.

"Is that why the virgin sturgeon has never been caught?" Lovette suddenly inquired.

The explosion of laughter rocked the wardroom as the officers released their tension at this bit of humor deliberately introduced by the Operations Officer for just that purpose.

Major Bart Clinch leaned forward and put his green-khaki clad arms on the felt-covered wardroom table. "All right, everyone, this is a job for the Marines! So listen up, because here's how the Marine batt is going to catch an alien for you!"

"Why the Marines?" Mark Walton asked. "Do you think more like fish than we do?"

"No, but we're experts in close, personal, hand-to-hand combat. With all due respects, the rest of you are super systems managers. That includes the Air Group." He held up one of his hands. "Now, don't get your hackles up! We've got a job to do! Now, here's what I'm going to do, so the rest of you figure out how to do your thing along with it . . ."

Clinch didn't give anyone time to react. He launched right into a detailed operational plan.

Zeke knew the Marine major had been sitting quietly there, watching and listening, putting all the pieces together, and formulating his plan in his mind without the help of computers and data bases. It was the Clinch way of doing things.

Bart Clinch knew how to use computers, but he didn't depend on them. Once he told Zeke, "When you're taking incoming, it's no time for the fucking batteries to go dead! So I teach my Marines not to hang their asses on high tech always working for them! At some point, you're going to have to fall back to being a real Marine with sand in your shorts and nothing between you and the enemy but what you've got. And you'll never have enough of that, either!"

So Bart Clinch announced, "My boys can fight on land, on sea, and in the air, just like the Marine Hymn says. Except more so. We can also fight underwater! I'm taking Alpha Company out onto the beach where you first tangled with that alien. We'll be in scuba gear. And we'll carry spearguns and high explosives. We'll borrow some of Rick Brookstone's underwater N-fone units from his underwater special team. That way, we can communicate with one another and with you. The *Shenandoah* should stand by on the surface offshore with the masdet running to give us data on where these monsters are. I'll need a Sea Dragon standing by spooled up on the beach with a cargo sling under it so we can get the critter out of there fast. If we can pull this off before the *Tuscarora* comes back, it might mean those monsters it left behind are getting hungry. If they are, they may not be so picky about their catch. They won't be wary. And they probably still have their traps out there. So we'll beat them at their own game. We'll go out on those rocks and nail one of those bastards for you. To do that, we'll put out our own trap and bait it for them!"

A moment of silence followed this rapid-fire announcement of the aggressive Marine plan.

"Bart," Zeke asked, "what kind of trap are you going to use and how are you going to bait it?"

"Our trap isn't physical. Our bait will get caught in *their* trap, just like Natalie did!"

"Who's the bait, Bart?" Zeke persisted.

"Me."

"I thought so! Dammit, a commander doesn't risk his own hide, Bart!" Zeke objected. "A platoon or company officer is expected to, but not the unit commander! Who takes over if you buy it? Did you think of that?"

"Yeah. I always do. I don't intend to buy the farm. And I won't ask any of my Marines to do anything I won't do."

"That doesn't mean you have to do it! And I'm not sure the Captain will approve of you putting yourself at risk!"

"What do you mean, at risk? What risk?" Clinch exploded in retaliation. "Hell, Braxton, I'll have comm with Captain Pres O'Bannon and my top kicks. And with you. And I'll be armed! It's not like Natalie being caught down there and not expecting it. Risk, my ass! We Marines are trained to take far more risk than you Navy types! Now I know you've got to sit around and hold these long planning meetings because that's the way you do things. You've got a complicated ship to run and a damned near impossible set of orders to follow. But we Marines operate on a much simpler level."

Zeke knew better than to argue with Major Bart Clinch. The XO could overrule the Marine battalion commander, but he didn't want to do it. So he asked, "When do you want to do this, Bart?"

"Today. No latter than early this afternoon. As fast as we can get all our ducks lined up."

Zeke turned to Captain Corry. "Sir?"

Corry looked around the table at each of his department heads. He was searching to see if any of them objected to the Clinch plan or had any additions to it. Each of them looked back at him impassively. They told him by their expressions and lack of reaction that Clinch had consensus, but only by tacit consent.

No one really liked the idea of Major Bart Clinch or anyone else volunteering to be the bait.

But someone had to do it.

Clinch wanted to.

Corry leaned back. "Let's do it."

22

"Rex, it's six o'clock in the morning! I haven't even had breakfast yet!" the President complained.

"Sir, I've just gotten the report from Makasar. It's the most fantastic thing I've ever seen!" replied General Rex Hill, USAF (Ret.) over the telephone. The wan light of dawn was in the eastern sky. Washington was just coming awake after another night of diplomatic dinners, embassy parties, lobbying, turf protecting, posturing, liaisons, and affairs other than foreign and domestic.

"JCS and their staff have been up since oh-two-hundred studying this and trying to figure out what to do," Hill went on, his words tumbling over one another so fast that it was difficult to discriminate them. "The Outer Ring is in a flap. They're scared this is going to leak before the morning is over. If it does, we have to be ready for it. The more time you have to prepare a position, the better. That's why I contacted you as soon as I thought you might be awake. You need to see this report from Makasar soonest."

"Slow down, Rex! What report from Makasar?" The President still wasn't fully awake.

"Don't you remember, sir? You authorized sending a carrier submarine to Makasar to carry out some power projection, Mister President."

"Yes, but as I recall, the overt reason was to help in the search for a bunch of missing American tourists and business people. I didn't much want to do it in the first place," the chief executive remembered, trying to sweep the fog of sleep out of his mind.

"They ended up getting some of the very best UFO data I've ever seen, Mister President. This looks real as hell! And the skipper of the *Shenandoah* also filed a very straightforward report that five of the ship's officers were attacked by something in the water. They had to kill it. The photos they got of the creature are out of focus. But even if they weren't, I still can't figure out what the hell it was."

"Oh, boy!" the President breathed. "On top of all my other problems right now, I'm going to have to stand up and try to explain away a flying saucer sighting! Who's the idiot that reported this?"

"Captain William Corry of the *Shenandoah,* sir. It's got CNO baffled. I'm told Corry is one of the best submarine commanders we've got. He was being groomed for flag rank . . ."

"We'll see about that! What does Captain Corry allege?"

"Nothing, Mister President. He just reported it like he'd report completion of a training exercise. Just his report and the data. He drew no conclusions and made no speculations."

"Why the hell was he chasing UFOs? He was sent there to do something else!"

"Sir, this turned out to be part of his mission."

"Well, let me get some breakfast and then I'll come down to the Oval Office. Draft a possible statement for release if we have to. We'll deny the encounter ever took place. And have CNO figure out a way to keep Corry quiet!"

The National Security Advisor hesitated before he dropped the next one on his boss. "Mister President, a Chinese submarine was there, too. The Chinese crew saw it. We don't know if they'll release their data from Beijing or not. Or when. And I don't have the authority to contact their embassy here!"

"Oh, boy!" the President breathed again, more fervently this time. This was going to be a bad day all around, he decided. "Rex, get the National Security Council together for a seven o'clock meeting . . ."

"Sir, that's less than an hour from now."

"So bring them in by air to the south lawn if traffic might delay them. Get them here! And get the Joint Chiefs over from the Pentagon, too! Have Jill and Mike reschedule my morning appointments. Sounds like doing damage control on this incident is going to take some time I haven't got. But it also sounds necessary in order to head off a worldwide panic. I'll get dressed, grab a bite of breakfast, and see you and the NSC in the conference room at seven."

The President had made himself a promise. He'd seen how the pressures of the office had aged his predecessors. Therefore, he followed a strict regimen. He didn't rush *any* of his meals, and he didn't miss any, either. And he always had a good breakfast before taking on Congress and the world, usually in that order.

The Director of the CIA had been in his office ever since the first satellite transmission of Corry's report from the *Shenandoah* had been intercepted along with all the other Department of Defense communications.

Alan Dekker had to admit that it was probably the best photographic and video coverage he'd ever seen of what the CIA termed an "anomalous encounter." The CIA "crazy" files were full of other data of a similar nature. Some of the data were more than a century old. Some were of very poor quality and highly questionable authenticity. Other data were bizarre and inexplicable. None of it showed any repeatability or correlation except for those smudgy photos of pie plates that revealed poor modeling techniques. He recalled seeing globs of glue and paintbrush marks on some "interplanetary spaceships" in various photos.

A search of the CIA data base indicated two reports of a similar nature showing a similar craft. However, there were thousands upon thousands of reports of objects accelerating vertically at high rates, thousands more of large objects entering Earth's atmosphere and impacting the ocean at low velocities, and thousands of "weather balloons" where no weather balloons should have been at the time.

The data were worldwide in extent but showed no pattern.

When faced with the *Shenandoah* data, however, Dekker was forced to admit to himself something that had nagged at his mind for years. His experts probably would see no pattern in radar tracks of aircraft arriving and departing a place like Casper, Wyoming, on a given day.

Or the spaceport at Ajo, Arizona.

In company with the FAA, the Department of Defense, and other federal agencies involved in aviation, the CIA simply filed away the random data that posed no air traffic problem, had been determined no security threat, or didn't look like a drug runner.

Well, he was ready for an alien invasion. Or an alien contact. It didn't change his reality structure. And he knew that most Americans would simply yawn and say it was about time, what had they waited for? The news media would have a feeding frenzy, and many experts would be called in to view with alarm the fact that the sky was falling. It would have little impact on the average person going about a daily struggle to live. He didn't even pity those whose religions would be severely affected. Religions would bend and adapt. They always had in the past. But it would take time and perhaps create some instability in the process. That's where his job made a difference.

When Dekker received the call about the NSC meeting, he was glad he'd spent the night getting his ducks lined up. He had a fat dossier of similar "anomalous encounters" he could present to the President. He knew the President would ask for it, and he wanted to be Johnny-on-the-spot. It would make him look good. It would help the appropriations for the

CIA which was now often perceived as a drain on the tax base.

In the Outer Ring of the Pentagon, the situation wasn't being handled with such calm and couth. General Tony Lundberg, CJCS, had gone ballistic. Foreign intelligence officers at Wright-Patterson Air Force Base had been rousted out and sent to their offices; they'd been there all night, viewing the *Shenandoah* data with amazement and incredulity. None of them thought about doing what Dekker had done at CIA, and they were sitting right on top of one of the main archives. However, those who had known of the archives or even suspected that they existed had long ago departed.

ADM George L. Street, CNO, was taking it with a large degree of pride. He'd spotted Corry years ago as a comer. The man had not disappointed him. The Corry report was a model of a dispassionate, accurate, facts-only, no-nonsense document. Street would have no trouble protecting the Navy or Corry. Otherwise, he'd keep his mouth shut and let Lundberg take the heat from the news media or Congress, if any came. He suspected the White House would either clamp a lid on it at once or try to explain it away. The White House would thus be the focal point. In any event, the Navy was clean. The documentation was clean. The paperwork was clean. The White House had no real leverage on the Navy on this one.

In fact, Navy had an ally. RADM Dolores McCarthy in naval intelligence had quietly supplemented Dekker's CIA documentation by providing some quick-and-dirty computer cleanup of the Ellison film. A blurred image is still a blurred image. Not much can be done to correct it "in the sink."

But McCarthy had made her mark in the Navy by developing new fuzzy programs that would ask, "Suppose, just suppose, the color/contrast/object edge is here; what will the resulting image look like?" It took a lot of computer power, but naval intelligence had it.

One of the main naval computer complexes, Decatur, had run several hours that night cleaning up Ellison's out-of-focus photographs. The results were startling.

ADM Street had copies. And others had found their way upriver to Langley. Dekker was not a Navy person, but a warm fuzzy existed between CNO and CIA because of such "cooperation."

Such was the situation when the National Security Council convened in the West Wing of the White House at 0700 EST.

There were a lot of coffee cups around the table at that hour of the morning.

The agenda kicked off with a briefing on the *Shenandoah* mission by the Secretary of Defense. John D. Long. Then everyone had the opportunity to see data Corry had sent from the *Shenandoah*.

It began with the display data from the masdet and sonar displays accompanied by the N-fone conversations.

Although it had occurred hours before halfway around the world, the firing of the fish by the *Shenandoah* still had a high pucker factor.

Then they saw the gee-whiz part, the raw video data taken from an EP-10 Osprey that flew around and around the object, plus other video taken with a long lens from the upper deck of the *Shenandoah*. The visual data concluded with the radar displays of the target disappearing vertically.

The President had to admit that this was no ordinary UFO contact. The data were too good.

Everyone in the room had come to that conclusion. The President allowed the buzz of excited conversation to go on for about a minute before he rapped on the polished tabletop. "Thank you, John," he said. "Now, the first question in my mind is the one that should be uppermost in the mind of every member of the NSC here today. It's simple: *Does this incident constitute a threat to the security of this nation?* First in line: John?" He directed the question toward the SECDEF.

"No, sir!" the Secretary replied at once. "The only aggressive intent I saw was the intercept course the object held against the Chinese submarine . . . until the fish from the *Shenandoah* caused it to break off. Then it ran . . . fast. I saw it fire no weapons. Ergo, it is not a threat."

"John, how can you say that?" was the immediate comment from the Secretary of State, Henry W. Foster. "If its inhabitants identified the *Shenandoah* by its size and shape, they could retaliate against the United States proper. And we'd never know it until they began their attack!"

"I think that highly unlikely, Henry," was the calm response from the SECDEF. "I've ordered the space defense facilities to full alert. Nothing is going to get inside the orbit of the Moon without our sensors picking it up."

He had more faith in space defenses than the Chairman of the Joint Chiefs did. But General Tony Lundberg kept his mouth shut. He'd been the champion for the systems presently deployed. He knew their strengths and their shortcomings. he knew how and under what conditions something could get through them. He wasn't about to let this incident reveal what he'd covered up in order to get support and funding to put them there. He didn't feel badly about doing that. A partial defense was better than none. And potential enemies on Earth didn't know those shortcomings. It's difficult to explain to those who don't understand such matters that the purpose of a defense is not to create impregnability. An adequate but incomplete defense is viable if it causes an enemy to look at you every morning and decide, "No, not today."

"I'm more concerned," the Secretary of Defense went on, "about the release of this data."

"Do you think it will cause panic, John?" the President asked.

"No, not at all," Long replied in his gruff but no-

nonsense way. "However, the fact that the *Shenandoah* could see this thing and the Chinese sub couldn't implies that we've got a sensor system they don't have. Well, as you all know, we do indeed have such a thing. It's the White Oak Labs' mass detector. The *Shenandoah* is one of the first vessels in which it's been installed. Actually, the Mark One version is so damned big that the River class carrier submarines are the only naval vessels that can accommodate it. We should be able to put the Mark Two in a very large satellite, which we're planning to do to supplement space defense. However, the fact that our big submarines can cruise silently without transmitting anything and detect another silent-running submarine . . . Well, that could change the whole twenty-first-century sea power equation, ladies and gentlemen."

"And we depend on the sea," added the Secretary of the Navy, H.W. Gilmore. He was in the Cabinet seat he'd longed and worked for as a naval reservist and dedicated scion of an old Massachusetts seafaring family. "We're a sea power. We always have been. Most of our trade goes by commercial merchant marine. *That* is really why we have a Navy. Our sea commerce needs protection. Then to make sure the pirates of the world understand that we can and will crush them, we use our Navy for power projection." He didn't go into the full lecture he liked to use before congressional committees; in it, he reminded them of the problems the fledgling United States of America had had with Algerian pirates and the British before the authorization of the United States Navy in 1797. In his mind, the state of the world hadn't changed very much, although the names and faces of the players had.

"Mister President," said Admiral Street, "we see no objection to the public release of this visual imagery taken from the Osprey in flight. But the computer reconstruction of the color still photographs of the alien monster not only look hokey, they could reveal some of our new computer enhancement techniques. Furthermore, the data must be selectively culled and the story properly recast so that no hint of the mass detector is revealed."

"You're not afraid of the negative image of the Navy that might result from one of your crews sighting a UFO, George?" was the question from Rex Hill.

"No, not at all. I think Captain Corry did an excellent job of accurately and scientifically reporting the incident."

"The question I've put before the Council this morning has nothing to do with public release of this information," the President interrupted. "Do we or do we not face a national security threat as a result of these findings?"

"Mister President, the Joint Chiefs of Staff believe it poses no national security threat," Lundberg intoned.

"I agree," said the SECDEF.

"Al?" the President asked his CIA Director.

"This 'anomalous encounter'? No, sir. But perhaps its consequences may."

"That is one of the most weasel-worded replies I've ever heard you give, Al."

"What can I tell you, sir? We know nothing about these creatures. I think the *Shenandoah* ought to stick around and see what its people can find out. Maybe they can bag an alien."

"That may anger the aliens," Secretary of State Foster said quickly.

"So you think we may have angered them?" the President asked.

"I do," said Foster. "I don't know what these aliens can or will do about it. That's John's department. But from my point of view, this incident causes me some trouble with the Chinese. The *Shenandoah* shot at them."

"Henry, it's your job to smooth that over."

"Mister President, I probably can't do it if the news media start to run with this story," Foster admitted.

"What do you recommend?"

"Back off. Get the *Shenandoah* out of there. Bring her back to Pearl Harbor. Let our Earl Abbott handle damage control with the Sulawesis. And sit tight on this data. All of it. I've got a lot of work to do to prepare other nations for this. Then we can work toward properly orchestrating how we're going to tell the people." The Secretary of State wasn't a wimp. He was an Ivy League Brahmin, an elitist who believed that he and others like him could and should run the country and tell the rest of the people only what was good for them to know.

The President wasn't going to buck his Secretary of State on this one. The foreign policy situation was too flaky, and too many international affairs were at stake. On the other hand, no one was sabre-rattling around the world either, so the Defense Department was doing its job.

The Commander in Chief turned to his Secretary of Defense. "Sit on this stuff, John. Sit on it hard. Henry will work the Chinese side. And get the *Shenandoah* back to Pearl Harbor. I want her out of Sulawesi right now!"

23

It was 1300 hours Makasar time on a bright, sunny afternoon with puffy cumulus clouds dotting the sky. The beach was long, curving, and beautiful. A short distance offshore, the flood tide left only the tops of a group of rocks above water. The rocks served to protect the beach from the light surf that swept on-shore from the Makasar Straits.

The scene might have been one suitable as a photo advertisement for an exotic tropical beach resort.

In fact, the location had once been an exotic tropi-cal beach resort. The old hotel was crumbling to ruins as the tropical vegetation slowly took over again.

On that particular afternoon, however, it resembled a twenty-first-century version of Omaha Beach.

A C-26 Sea Dragon VTOL cargo plane sat on the beach. Reefed underneath its fuselage was a cargo sling.

Four F/A-48 Sea Devil aircraft rested on the beach nearby. Another four were airborne and hovering a kilometer offshore.

Further out in the Straits was the long black hull of the carrier submarine U.S.S. *Shenandoah,* riding on the surface. Other Sea Devils were poised on her upper flight deck.

Thirteen men and one woman in scuba gear were poised on the offshore rocks. They were armed. On the beach, six other people in scuba gear waited.

You're sure you want to do this, Natalie?

Affirmative, Bart! I'm not afraid of these things now.

We're armed, and we know we can kill them. Somebody has to show you what a trap looks like.

I ought to be able to find one from your description.

Want to take the chance? A lot is riding on this operation.

No, I don't want to take any unnecessary chances. I never do. And I want to make damned sure you'll surface and get on a rock as soon as the Awesome trap is sprung.

I'll do that. Don't worry.

The conversation went on via a special underwater model of the standard Navy Mark XI N-fone. LT Rick Brookstone, commander of the Special Underwater Team of the *Shenandoah*, had provided the special N-fones that his unit wore for underwater communications. On the shore, Brookstone stood by with a repeater, acting as a relay station for both types of N-fones. It picked up the UW N-fone transmissions, sent standard ship N-fone transmissions to the UW units, and was linked to the *Shenandoah* offshore.

Communications are a key element in any military or naval operation. During the previous encounter with the Awesome in this spot, the group had had no underwater comm. Now the participants were closely linked by comm gear.

The plan was in place and ready to go.

In the PRIFLY of the *Shenandoah*, Corry stood with Captain Dao Lin Qian on one side of him, General Achin Helamahera on the other, and Ambassador Earl Abbott with LCDR Herb Hewitt behind them.

About 0900 that morning, Corry had informed Abbott of the operation because it was technically in Sulawesi territory. The *Shenandoah* was in Sulawesi's territorial waters as well. The Ambassador had quietly gone ballistic in his own way when Lowden Manwaring informed him that the Sulawesi authorities had to be notified. And Hewitt had pointed out that if the Chinese submarine captain wasn't briefed, a lot of trouble could come from that quarter.

As a result of pressures from the American embassy, Corry had to back down a bit from his position of not telling anyone anything.

So he put it to General Helamahera and Captain Qian this way in his invitation to them:

"Yesterday, we chased an unknown submersible. We learned of this because one of our officers was caught in an underwater trap while scuba diving inshore north of Makasar. She was then threatened by an unknown underwater creature. This creature was an aquatic life form we had never seen before. Correlation and analysis of our sensor data indicated that the creature was operating in conjunction with the unknown submersible vessel. Although we pursued the unknown submersible, we could not catch it and attempt to communicate with it. We know from our sensor data that a number of creatures were left behind when the submersible vessel departed. We believe these creatures may be fishing in the Sulawesi offshore waters. They may or may not be involved in the disappearance of our people. However, we want to find out. There is the possibility that some or all of the missing Americans and Chinese may have been trapped by them. Therefore, we're going to attempt to detain one of these creatures and communicate with it. That is all we know. It may be a spurious path that leads nowhere. But it's the best lead we have at the moment. On the basis of our experience thus far, we have planned an operation to find and detain a creature so we can learn more about it. It will be a delicate operation. I do not believe we'll need help from either the Sulawesi military or the Chinese submarine. In fact, their presence may make the operation impossible. However, in a spirit of cooperation, I invite you to join me on the bridge of the *Shenandoah* during this activity so you can see exactly what happens when it happens."

Helamahera and Qian accepted because they could do nothing other than make an issue of high-handed

American treatment that they might have called "bullying." But that would delay the operation. In their position, the best deal they could get was the one Corry offered: come, look, and learn. Because they had no idea of what to do about this matter themselves, they were glad to get what they got, which they thought was a ringside seat.

This didn't mean that they left their forces sitting around idly. But Qian agreed to leave the *Bei fung* in Makasar harbor when Corry pointed out that two large submarines in the vicinity of the activity might be too many.

Corry didn't like inviting these people to his ship for the operation. It meant he couldn't be directly involved. He'd have to shepherd the VIPs. Zeke would have to run the show while Corry communicated silently with him via N-fone.

Nor did Corry use the main dodger bridge as a VIP viewing position. He used PRIFLY. The dodger bridge had all the masdet, sonar, radar, infrared, and lidar displays. PRIFLY had only the display screens for the air defense and traffic control radars. From PRIFLY, the visitors would not see the sensitive technology that had allowed the *Shenandoah* to find and track the *Tuscarora*.

The loss of her PRIFLY bothered Terri Ellison because she had to transfer her flight ops control to the dodger bridge.

Corry had brought the *Shenandoah* to General Quarters for this operation. The whole ship and the entire crew were involved.

And the Marine batt commander was deliberately putting himself at risk.

Even Zeke—who thought Bart was often too aggressive for his own good—was impressed by the man's guts.

Okay, final checklist. Clinch?

Clinch ready.

Marine unit?

*Marine rock detail ready. Marine beach detail ready.
Navigator?*

Navigator ready. Natalie's nominal call sign had not
been altered for this operation. She would navigate
Bart to an Awesome trap.

Underwater Special Team?

Brookstone's Boomers ready. Although the Marine
batt was qualified for underwater ops, the ship's frogmen were ready on the beach and in an orbiting Sea
Dragon, ready to get into the water if needed. They
were also armed.

CAG?

CAG ready.

Tikki One?

LCDR Virginia "Tikki" Geiger, commander of VC-
50, was at the controls of the C-26 Sea Dragon on the
beach. She was ready to pick up the captured Awesome in the cargo sling and speed it back to the ship.
Tikki ready.

Tigers?

Bells is ready.

Sick bay?

We're ready in sick bay.

Sensors?

Radar go.

Sonar go.

Lidar go.

Infrared go.

Masdet ready.

Deck?

*Ship is at General Quarters. Zip guns are armed and
ready. Fish loaded and ready. Damage control parties
standing by. Engineering has steam.* Walton and Guns
Weaver were on top of it, although they were more
than a kilometer from the action center around the
rocks. No one knew if the *Tuscarora* or its compatriots
had come back. No unknowns had shown up on masdet yet.

The *Shenandoah* was more than just the place to

bring the Awesome when it was captured or killed. The carrier submarine was covering the operation from the sea. Its crew was using its facilities to check minus-x.

CO, the operation is ready to commence, Zeke reported to Corry.

The Captain subvocalized his reply, *This is the Captain. Proceed. Go!*

Then he said aloud to the VIPs on the PRIFLY deck, "The operation is getting under way."

"You run an unusual command, Captain Corry," Captain Qian remarked. "I have not heard you give an order."

"I have a well-trained crew, Captain," Corry replied carefully.

"How do you do all this without communication?" General Helamahera asked.

Corry decided that he should put the N-fone command channel on the PRIFLY audio. *XO, this is CO! Have Atwater patch the N-fone command channel into the PRIFLY audio system here on my verbose command via PRIFLY telephone. But tell him to eliminate the channels from Sonar, Special Sensor, and Lidar.*

Aye, aye, sir."

Corry remarked casually to his guests, "My apologies. I didn't want to bore you with the routine check lists. I'll have my Communications Officer patch the audio up here for you." He picked up the PRIFLY telephone handset and ordered, "XO, this is the Captain. Pipe the verbose command channel into PRIFLY, please."

"Aye, aye, sir," Zeke came back on the loudspeaker.

That seemed to keep Helamahera and Qian happy.

They heard the exchange going on in the rocks.

Bart, you're sure the Awesomes didn't see us being airlifted to the rocks?

No, I'm not. But from the chase reports, there was no radar from the Tuscarora. *They can't see us above the surface.*

*You're right! Not beyond the angle of refraction.
And I remember they had to surface and look around
during that first incident. They didn't know where we'd
taken their buddy. Okay, I believe you.*

Bart had his mask on and had checked Natalie's.
Okay, we're going in the water . . .

Right with you, Bart.

The instant both of them were in the water, they
heard it.

It sounded like a series of high-pitched, keening
calls.

Awesome sonar, Natalie explained. *They're here, all
right. Stay on the alert! I don't think they'll come after
us until one of us is caught in a trap.*

Clinch kept his head on swivel as they went down
about three meters. *O'Bannon, you got a visual on
me?*

*Affirmative, Major! Water is pretty clear! Sergeant
Wren sees you.*

Does anyone see any of those monsters?

Negatory! But lots of stuff moving down there!

The two of them swam together, their spear guns
loaded, cocked, and held at the ready. *Stay close to
the rocks, Bart. The traps are glued to them somehow.
Look for something bright and shiny. Something that
would attract attention.*

*Lots of things down here to attract attention . . . ex-
cept those beasts that want to hide . . .*

It's all deception, Bart.

So is warfare.

*Okay, okay! There's a trap! See it? Over on the
right! On the slope of that rock among all the fronds
waving in the flow?*

Yeah. I see something! Let's get a little closer . . .

*Don't get too close. I don't know if it can reach out
and grab. The one that caught me didn't latch on until
my hand and arm were on the bauble.*

Okay, yeah, I see it now! Nice looking bait! Looks

like a length of pearl necklace and some damned big gold pieces.

Which was what led me to believe later that these traps were deliberately designed to catch human beings. What else around her would reach for something that looked like pirate treasure?

All right, Commander, head for the surface. Now!

On my way! Natalie kicked and rose quickly to the surface. Two Marines pulled her out of the water onto the rock.

We've still got a visual on you, Major. Sergeant Quinn sees you.

I'm going to trigger the trap now. Let's hope that it likes leg of lamb as much as I do. It was the closest thing I could get to something the size and general shape of a human arm. Clinch had "borrowed" a frozen leg of lamb from Mess Officer LTJG Calvin Baker. He'd thawed it and brought it as close as possible to human body temperature before diving with it. He wasn't about to stick his good pistol arm into one of those Awesome traps.

The instant the tip of the leg of lamb touched the bait, the trap sprang.

It was the same sort that had grabbed Natalie. Except this one closed around something that had been planned for next Sunday's dinner in the *Shenandoah's* officers' mess.

I swear that damned trap sent out a sonar signal when it tripped! Clinch exclaimed.

Roger, that, Major, we just got confirmation on that signal from the ship. The sounds from the Awesomes have changed, too.

I'm moving away to get a better field of fire. Still see me?

Affirmative.

Major, this is McIvers. We've got several big, hulking, hard-to-see shapes moving through the rocks now. Too many to track. You sure you want to stay down

*there? Must be at least six of those monsters heading
toward you.*

Why so many? Clinch wondered.

*If they've been here since we chased their mother
ship away, they're probably a little hungry,* was the
guess from Battalion Sergeant Major Joe McIvers,
who didn't mince words.

You see where I am?

We know where you are, Major.

*When those things close on me, dive! Get in behind
them as we planned!*

Roger. We're ready.

We've got a ten count on them now.

*Okay, stand by. Put every Alpha Company man in
the water now. And have Bravo stand by. We may
need all the help we can get if these Awesomes show
up and go into a feeding frenzy!*

Roger that, sir. We're diving. Everyone in!

Then Bart Clinch saw his first Awesome. It came
at him fast. He saw the huge bulk, two big eyes, the
central nostril, and the central mouth orifice. But he
didn't fixate on the eyes as most people would have
if they'd been surprised by something this strange
underwater.

He saw the pistollike weapon it held in one of its
four-fingered hands.

Just as the Awesome began to emit a dark cloud to
make the water murky, Clinch aimed and fired.

Major Bart Clinch held the Expert Marksman
Medal with so many bars on it that he couldn't wear
them all. Zeke had told him to aim for the central
nostril. Bart did. The range was only two meters when
the spear hit the Awesome. It went right up its nose
and into its brain.

But not before it fired something from the pistol it
held in one of its "hands."

It apparently hadn't qualified for even a Sharp-
shooter's Medal. Something went past Bart's ear. He
didn't see it. But he heard it hit the rock behind him.

Major Bart Clinch was also an excitable man in combat. *I got it! I got it! It shot at me and missed! Look out, men, these beasts are carrying some sort of pistol that shoots something! Standing orders are changed. Don't wait for one to shoot at you. Shoot first! We'll apologize later!*

Water is cloudier. Hard to see, Joe McIvers reported. He was in the water and swimming toward Clinch when something hit him hard. It forced the air out of his lungs, but he recovered quickly. Then he shot. He didn't have an incoming target. He had to shoot at one going away. The spear hit the fluked tail of the Awesome, but it penetrated. The sergeant major didn't try to reel that one in. He severed the lanyard, cocked the spear gun, and got ready to fire again. *Just shot and missed. One caught me from behind and tried to knock me against the rocks. Be careful! Watch your minus-x, everyone!*

They can't shoot for shit! was the exclamation from First Sergeant Sol Wren of Alpha Company. *One just missed me. It's firing some sort of dart!*

Carmick here! I'm hit! I'm hit! Dart in the leg! Hurts like hell! Christ, I can't move my leg!

Come on, Lieutenant, we're getting you out of the water!

Major, best I can estimate, there's a dozen or so of these things down here! was the quick report from Lieutenant Archie Henderson. *And they act mad as hell!*

Maybe they're just hungry as hell.

Maybe. But they're communicating. Can't you hear them? And they're working together. Four of us in a rock grotto here, and three of them trying to get at us!

Bravo Company, this is Clinch! Into the water! McIvers is hit! He's gone unconscious on me! Solly, take him to the surface fast! Jesus, two more of them! God, they're fast! Oh, no you don't, you bastard! You're not pulling me out of here by yanking on my

*spear lanyard! See how you like a spear up your nose,
you son of a bitch!*

*Major, Bravo is in the water and deployed! Damn,
those things are hard to see in this cloudy water!*

*Christ, the bastard bit me as it went past! I'm
bleeding!*

*Got it! Got it! Hey, guys, it's got an asshole! I just
put one up its ass end! Took care of its hemorrhoids!*

*That's no asshole! That's its jet exhaust! When it
didn't hit me with its tail, it tried to blow me away with
a water jet! Damned near made me lose my spear gun!*

Major, Carmick and Casey need help!

*I can't give you any! I'm up to my asshole in Awe-
somes here!*

The underwater skirmish was quickly going to slime.
Any listener could tell that from the rapidity of the
N-fone messages and the rapid delivery.

*Brookstone, this is Major Clinch! Get your frogmen
in the water and out to the rocks fast! We need help
now! These goddamned things are mad as hell and
whupping our ass! Get out here now before we all become supper for them!*

24

The C-26 Sea Dragon moved in over the rocks and hovered a meter above them. Six frogmen of Brookstone's team dropped out of the belly hatch to the rocks. It would have been dangerous to drop into the water between the rocks. They didn't know the depths there.

They can see us better with their sonar in this cloudy water. But we can maneuver faster than they can! Use that! Bart Clinch advised his Marines and the new frogmen reinforcements.

And we can leave the water! They can't! Head for the surface if your furball is too tight! Lieutenant Archie Henderson advised.

And don't tangle hand-to-hand with them! They're too strong! And too heavy, even underwater! said Carmick's first sergeant, Solomon Wren.

Their hands are armored. Sort of a bony carapace. They can't be cut there if you've had to go to your knife, was the additional advice from Captain John Gamble, who had just entered the water with his Bravo Company.

This was combat information, valuable intelligence about how to fight these creatures. Because of good communications, all the N-fone conversation was heard by everyone underwater. And it was recorded on the U.S.S. *Shenandoah.*

Bart had his hands full. Three Awesomes were hassling him and trying to get from him the Awesome he'd speared through the nostril.

He was an experienced combat officer. He could think fast. And he was doing it then. All his men and all the reserves were in the water. Thus far, the fight had not swung to the advantage of the humans. The Awesomes were fighting in their environment.

But he quickly realized what his fighting advantages were: mobility in the water and the ability to get above the surface of the water for movement in safety.

He had an Awesome on the end of his lanyard. He had what they'd come for. No need to prolong the fight for the sake of the fight.

Marine unit and frogmen! This is Clinch! If you've got an Awesome on your lanyard, head for the surface with it now! The rest of you provide cover! Let's go!

Tikki is coming in over you and deploying the cargo sling!

Can you evac our wounded, too?

That's an affirmative! Jewels will move in with another Dragon as soon as Tikki clears. Jewels can pick up your wounded.

Marine Captain O'Bannon of Alpha Company bitched, *Dammit, I don't like to retreat!*

Captain, this is no retreat! We came out here to do a job. I got one Awesome and I'm coming to the surface with it! You're doing an outstanding job covering me! Look out! Over on your right! Get it! Get it!

Got it! Right under the mouth! But it busted off the spear shaft!

Never mind! You discouraged it! No fight left in it!

Clinch surfaced and was glad to see blue sky again. Natalie was guiding the cargo sling hanging down from Tikki's Dragon. *Bart, haul that Awesome to your left! There's a shallow tidal pool in the rock about two meters away. Enough water to float it into the pool. We can get the sling under it there without worrying about being hassled by live and nasty Awesomes!*

You get the hell out of here and up into that Dragon! This is no place for a woman! Clinch berated her.

Major, you don't outrank me, and this is an equal

opportunity fight! So you're going to tell Annie, the Dragon's cargomaster, to stay up in the ship too while you mess with the sling? Look, the two of us are here. We can help if you and your machos will keep the nasties away. Now stop arguing with me and let's finish the job!

Clinch was momentarily surprised. LCDR Natalie Chase had never acted in an aggressive manner before when she was around him. That was only one of the surprises of the day. He didn't acknowledge her N-fone call. Instead, he clambered up the rock and proceeded to haul the dead Awesome through the narrow channel into the little tidal pool.

As he was doing so, he looked around. Men in scuba gear where climbing out of the water onto the rocks around him.

Companies, report when you've got your men out of the water! he snapped via N-fone as he helped Natalie and Annie Miller rig the cargo net around the dead Awesome.

Alpha is out of the water! reported First Sergeant Solomon Wren. *Lieutenant Carmick has taken a dart in the leg. He's paralyzed on his left side from his hip down. Sergeant Major McIvers is on this rock with me. Casey is with him. McIvers is unconscious with a dart in his right side.*

Bravo just came out. Lieutenant Gale has a bite of some sort on his left upper arm. It's bleeding. Captain John Gamble was on top of things in his company.

Wait for Tikki to clear, then Jewels will come in to evac the wounded. How many Awesomes did we bag? I heard N-fone reports of several hits.

Alpha Company got two. We're beaching them on the rocks.

Stand by to get them out of here. Okay, Tikki, we've got the sling around your cargo.

Tikki, this is Annie. All secure. Ready for lift.

Grab that rope ladder and get aboard. Tikki is not leaving you here, Annie. Or you, Commander.

Yes, ma'am.

Happy to oblige you, Tikki. Navigator complying!

Okay, Tikki lifting off. Alley Cat in PRIFLY, Tikki is airborne with a load, making direct for the ship.

Alley Cat here. Cleared for approach and touch down. Medical team is waiting.

Major Clinch, this is Mister Brookstone. Are all your men out of the water?

Affirmative? Yours?

Coming out in a minute. We're going to get rid of the rest of these monsters real fast. Couple of kilos of Comp D should do the job. We're placing charges now.

For Christ's sake, get out of the water before you blow them!

Sir, we've done this before. Not to worry. Okay, surfacing!

Six more divers broke the surface and scrambled up on the rocks.

The rocks themselves suddenly shook with the concussion of six explosions.

Six geysers of seawater erupted skyward.

That should worry them for a little bit, Major.

Thank you, Mister Brookstone. Well done! XO, this is Clinch. We've got two more Awesomes on the rocks here. How about airlift?

Stand by, let me check, Zeke replied. He was working CIC off the dodger bridge with Terri, so he said to her, "We need two more Dragons with slings."

"Got only one. It was backup for Tikki or Jewels. But it developed turbine trouble. We had to strike it below," Terri reported. "It will take a few minutes to rig slings on two more Dragons, position them for cat shots, and get them in the air. Ah . . . ten minutes best time for two of them."

"I don't want to leave the Marines and the frogmen on those rocks," Zeke told her. "The froggies may have delayed any immediate assaults the Awesomes might have had in mind. We don't know if they can attack our men above the water on the rocks. So I want to get them off there."

"They'll have to swim to the beach."

"The Awesomes may come after them."

"We did it without a problem."

"We saw only one Awesome and we killed it. There must be nine or ten around the rocks this time. And Clinch reported they acted mad as hell."

"Then Clinch and Brookstone had better get their men ashore towing the other two Awesomes . . . and do it now! And hope the live Awesomes were stunned by the explosions." Zeke was about to make an N-fone broadcast to that effect when an incoming message sounded in his head.

XO, this is Ops. Masdet reports ten targets departing the rock region of the beach and heading north along the coast.

Thank you, Bob. How about sonar? The Awesomes still sounding?

No, sir, and neither are we. We're not even listening. Those ten explosions weren't expected. We've got to reset the safety trips on all our passive gear. Give us three minutes on that.

Masdet okay?

Affirmative! Charlie Ames got some interesting data on what explosions look like on a mass detector, too. He's kind of excited about that.

He would be! Zeke knew that Ames was the ultimate techie. *Clinch, this is the XO. Sensors report ten objects leaving the rock area. They are submerged and proceeding north along the coast. Looks like you're clear to swim your detail to the beach safely. Tow the two Awesomes to the beach with you. We'll have another Sea Dragon there for Awesome pickup in about ten minutes.*

Aye, aye, will do! Frankly, XO, I'd like to put these carcasses back in the water. They're starting to stink.

I know what you mean, Bart. I know what you

mean. Put your scuba masks back on and breathe your bottled air, Zeke advised him.

Okay, we'll be in the water anyway. We'll head for the beach now. McIvers, Carmick, and Gale are being evacced by another Sea Dragon right now, so we're all getting the hell out of here!

Overhead, Tikki Geiger brought her C-26 Sea Dragon to a hover over the upper flight deck. The blue-and-gray Awesome swung in the cargo sling below it. Duke Peyton talked Tikki down slowly as Laura Raye Moore and her biotech detail helped the deck crew position an ordnance lift truck under the airborne sling. The carpenter mates had rigged a wooden table on the truck to hold the Awesome's carcass. When the Awesome was on the truck, Moore didn't even bother removing the cargo sling. Tikki dropped it. The ship's doctor wasted no time. She knew that parasites might already be consuming the alien. She had to stop that right away. Her crew tossed the ropes over the body. Quickly, they moved to the aft lift. Within seconds, the Awesome was on its way down to the deep freeze.

Corry had watched this from PRIFLY with Ambassador Abbott, Captain Qian, General Helamahera, and Hewitt.

Qian wished he'd brought his camera. But he'd suspected he wouldn't be allowed aboard the *Shenandoah* with it. He wouldn't have allowed Corry aboard the *Bei fung* with one.

Actually, Corry would not have objected. Qian wasn't going to be taken near any classified or sensitive equipment. Photos of carrier submarines had appeared in popular magazines as well as naval publications. Hobby models were in retail stores. He knew Qian had seen all these items. So had Qian's superiors in Beijing.

"Well, there we have it, gentlemen," Corry remarked as the deck lift disappeared with the Awesome's body. "We'll have that one in deep freeze within minutes. And we have two more on the beach."

Helamahera shook his head in disbelief. "I have no idea what that monster is. And I know something of the sea life around Sulawesi. Our coastal patrol ships often detect dolphins and whales on their sonars and radars. We train our crews well using the aquarium in Makasar. What is that thing?"

"A dragon. A seagoing dragon," Qian muttered. "Right out of legends. But the legends were just stories. This was real."

"Captain," Helamahera asked with hesitation, "do you believe these monsters may have come from . . . somewhere else?"

"What do you mean, General?" Corry knew what the Sulawesi general meant.

"Another world?"

"I don't know."

"If a connection exists between these sea monsters and the large object we followed yesterday—and watched as it disappeared into the sky—I would certainly be led to that conclusion," Qian put in.

"General, Captain, we are military and naval personnel. We are not free to speculate. That will have to be left to others," Corry reminded them.

He wasn't sure they operated under the same restraints.

Qian didn't answer Corry directly. Instead, he said, "I look forward to receiving copies of your photographs and video, Captain."

"And tissue samples," Helamahera added.

Corry simply looked at them and said, "Please arrange that through your diplomatic channels, gentlemen. I have no authority to release any samples or documentation. I invited both of you to be here today to observe as my guests—because the operation took place in Sulawesi waters and because you, Captain Qian, were involved and cooperative yesterday."

"Captain Corry is right, gentlemen," Ambassador

Abbott put in quickly. "I'm sure there won't be a problem. General, I'll forward your request as quickly as I get it. I'll even tell the State Department to expect it."

Captain Qian suddenly looked very Mongolian— mean and nasty. But he maintained his composure as he said, "Captain Corry, it would eliminate a lot of trouble if you would pre-release the data as soon as you can in the next few hours."

General Helamahera wasn't so polite and mannered. "Captain, you're in Sulawesi waters! You have taken something out of Sulawesi territory and placed it in your ship! You do not have a valid commercial fishing permit or license! You have no clearance from our customs officials to export this material from Sulawesi!"

"Ah, General, I'm sure we can arrange that," Abbott hastily said as he tried diplomatically to handle this sudden conflict. "We'll apply for the necessary government formalities . . ."

"I will block their issuance on grounds of national security, Mister Ambassador! Before we allow this material to be taken from Sulawesi, we must obtain information that helps us determine the nature and purpose of these creatures in our waters! It is an issue of security for us! If these creatures are in our waters and are causing the disappearance of our citizens, we must know what do to about them!" The General was now very adamant.

And he had publicly admitted that Sulawesi citizens had disappeared.

Qian made no such admission. He remained silent and inscrutable.

And Corry said nothing. He'd said all he could say. It was up to Abbott, if the Ambassador would take the job.

He did.

"Gentlemen, gentlemen," Ambassador Abbott said in soothing tones. He suddenly saw his role in this situation. It could make points for him in Washington if he resolved it amicably. "Let us return to Makasar and talk about this. There is nothing more to see here. And Captain Corry is correct in telling you that he doesn't have the authority to release the information or turn over to you any parts of the carcasses."

The loudspeaker on the PRIFLY bridge announced in Zeke's voice, "Captain, Major Clinch has just reported all his men and our frogmen are on the beach along with the two dead Awesomes they towed ashore. He also reports that several hundred Sulawesi soldiers and a dozen armored vehicles have appeared out of the vegetation inland of the beach."

There was a slight pause as if Zeke had been interrupted by another message. Then his voice went on, "An additional report: Our radar and passive sonar reports that the Chinese submarine *Bei fung* is under way and departing Makasar harbor . . . Wait one . . . Sir, I have a report that a very large underwater object is approaching to the north of us on a southbound course through the Straits. It has the sensor response characteristics of the vessel we pursued yesterday . . ."

25

This was one of those times when Corry had to think fast as well as act fast.

He had four hot potatoes to juggle at once.

Number One was the Sulawesi Army troops on the beach possibly confronting the two companies of the Marine batt.

The second was the Chinese submarine *Bei fung* coming out of Makasar harbor. When Qian had accepted Corry's invitation to come aboard the *Shenandoah* to observe the Awesome trapping operation, the Chinese commander had said that the *Bei fung* would remain in the harbor.

The third one had a very high pucker factor. An unknown masdet target showing characteristics similar to the flying *Tuscarora* was coming southward through Makasar Straits submerged at forty knots. Corry assumed from the reports that it was a *Tuscarora* object. He had no inkling of the intentions of this incoming target, but he knew he could see it and therefore could hit it with a fish. If it was another *Tuscarora,* its occupants probably didn't know that the *Shenandoah* could see it with her masdet.

And the fourth and final hot potato was the presence of the Chinese and Sulawesi commanders in his ship along with the United States Ambassador and the Naval Attaché.

The Commanding Officer of the U.S.S. *Shenandoah* was in a position no commander likes to find himself. The ship could be targeted with unknown weapons, perhaps artillery, by the Sulawesi Army ashore. Corry knew the Sulawesi Army had some 155mm guns. The two-thousand-meter range was almost point-blank. Or the carrier submarine could become the target of the Chinese submarine and be whanged by a Chinese fish if Corry didn't dive in time. Then there was the on-coming *Tuscarora* . . .

Such a multifaceted attack situation was extremely hard to handle. The Naval War College simulation episodes never went beyond presenting two simultane-ous threats. A submarine commander wasn't expected to be stupid enough to get himself and his command into more than a dual-threat situation.

Corry didn't feel stupid. Instead, he felt he'd come off on the short end of the odds.

He had to do something and he didn't have time to think about it. He had to act.

First he to get these VIPs out of the way. They prevented him from exercising full command.

"Gentlemen," he told them, "The ship is at General Quarters. We may come under attack. I cannot expose you to risk. I'll have my quartermaster escort you below. You will be quartered comfortably until the threat is gone. Ambassador Abbott, will you and Commander Hewitt please take charge of our two guests?"

"Captain, do you consider my ship a threat?" Qian suddenly asked.

"Yes," Corry told him bluntly.

"May I ask why?"

"Can you explain why it's leaving Makasar harbor when you told me it w-w-w-wouldn't?" Corry fired back at once with irritation in his voice. He was has-sled and didn't want to show it. However, his inadver-tent stutter gave him away to those who knew.

"I gave a standing order to my Executive Officer to sail the *Bei fung* to your aid if evidence of fighting was detected," Qian explained, somewhat put out by the sudden change in Corry. "The explosions set off by your frogmen activated my standing order."

"Very well then, sir. If that's the case, what do the rest of your orders say? What are your intentions, sir?" Corry demanded to know.

"My orders to my Executive Officer are to position my ship on the surface on your seaward side at a range of two kilometers and stand by the standard ship-to-ship radiotelephone frequencies to offer assistance," Qian said.

Corry believed him, up to a point. It was quite improbable that the *Bei fung* would submerge and threaten the *Shenandoah*. The Chinese submarine's captain was aboard the carrier submarine. However, the Commanding Officer of the U.S.S. *Shenandoah* wasn't about to place full trust in the Chinese officer. They had a bond between them because they were both submariners, and that counted for something. Every submariner knows that the first enemy is the sea. After that, human enemies are considered. But Corry wasn't about to place his command in danger by placing too much credence in that intangible.

"Captain Qian, I want you to verbally reconfirm that order to your Executive Officer on our ship-to-ship radiotelephone," Corry told him.

"I will do that, sir."

"Very well, I'll arrange it with my Communications Officer who speaks Chinese. However, at this time and under these conditions, for your personal safety I want you and the General to go below with the Ambassador and Commander Hewitt," Corry insisted. This was taking too long! The situation was ripening by the minute, and he wasn't in immediate command!

General Helamahera planted himself firmly on the deck of PRIFLY with his legs apart and his hands on his hips. Pompously, he huffed, "You're holding me prisoner, Captain! I demand to be released and sent ashore!"

Corry just looked at him. "General, if you wish, I'll

send you ashore right now. But you'll be in one of our aircraft. Are you willing to risk the chance that one of your soldiers on the beach may get a little nervous and shoot at you with something more than an assault rifle? Maybe a shoulder SAM? Even if we broadcast that you're coming? You know there's always someone who doesn't get the word!"

Helamahera backed off as gracefully as he could. And fast. Corry knew what he was doing with Helamahera. It wasn't that some soldier might not get the word. The General had political enemies. He hadn't been able to purge all of them from the Army, much less the government. Some officer might decide this was the time for an "accident" to happen. "I protest this treatment! I shall have my government lodge an official protest through diplomatic channels . . ."

"Sir, I think you might want to talk to Ambassador Abbott about the perceptions of the United States of America at this point!" Corry snapped with growing irritation and frustration. He was eager to get these VIPs below and out of the way. He needed to get back in the direct command loop as quickly as he could.

At that moment with all the stress bearing down on him, Corry got as angry as any of the crew had ever seen him, and many of them were watching him in PRIFLY. His face turned red and he clenched and unclenched his fists. But he kept his voice under control and didn't stutter again.

"We came here because the Sulawesi government could tell us nothing about our citizens disappearing. We offered to help you find out. You were reluctant to act with our help. We were open and friendly toward you. We reported our activities yesterday when we believed we'd found one possible solution. We told you of our operation today and invited you as an observer; hence, you gave your tacit consent to it! Now you've deployed your troops against us. The United States might have been willing to share everything with your government because of a cooperative attitude. But now you've invoked regulations that would allow you to take what we risked our lives to get. I don't know what the United States government will do about it, but I am here with my ship and I will take whatever action is required to protect it and carry out my orders! You are in my ship, which is United States territory. True, you're my guest, and I shall continue to treat you as my guest. And for your safety as my guest, I ask that you go below. When we've reduced the threat, we can talk about this. But for now, I've talked too long and too much! I must resume my duties! Ambassador Abbott and Commander Hewitt, please take charge of these guests. Mister Berger will be here in a moment. He'll see to your wellbeing. Follow him to the main wardroom. You'll be comfortable there!"

The determined but courteous attitude of Captain Corry wasn't lost on Captain Qian. The Chinese commander decided that Corry would be a formidable adversary if provoked. He wasn't sure he wanted to provoke a man who controlled the sort of death and destruction that could be meted out by a carrier submarine and her crew.

Corry turned, walked quickly and purposefully off PRIFLY, descended the ladder to the upper flight deck and entered the lift that would take him to his battle station on the bridge buried in the massive black hull. He erased the VIP party from his mind. Abbott would handle the protocol, and the naval attaché knew where to find Corry if necessary. Corry shifted his attention to the mess he was in.

It hadn't improved while he was laying down the law to Qian and Helamahera.

On the beach, the four F/A-48s had scrambled, spooled up, and lifted off when the Sulawesi troops became visible. They didn't wait for orders from Alley Cat or Bells. The Tiger flight knew they were dead meat on the ground. So they jumped into flight and headed out over the rocks fifty meters offshore. This put them just beyond point-blank range for the Golden BB but close enough to be able to move in fast with their genius ordnance.

Bells, scramble Tiger Flight Two. Terri ordered. Attack aircraft on the flight deck were of no use to the Marines ashore. *Proceed to the beach. Stand by to support the Marines.*

Roger that, Alley Cat. Flight Two is spooling for flight and spoiling for a fight. Rips is leading.

Roger that. Terri keyed the information into the flight commander terminal that listed all the flights aloft and their leaders' call names.

Flak, Alley Cat. Launch two more Ospreys. Put them near the Chinese boat. Be ready to lay some ordnance if the boat starts to get nasty. But look out; it has teeth that can reach out and bite you!

Terri knew the Chinese submarine had a version of the four zip-gun close-in weapons systems mounted on the *Shenandoah.* However, according to both *Jane's* and naval intelligence, that Chinese submarine class mounted only one such gun. That's why Terri wanted two Ospreys over there watching the *Bei fung* as it cleared the harbor and came north. The pilots of the two patrol craft knew what to do to keep the gunner on the Chinese ship confused if necessary. Sometimes a target-rich environment causes you to make choices and assign priorities: If you can't take out every threat in the first mad minute, will the stuff you couldn't kill get you instead?

Roger, Alley Cat. Tigger is the lead. She's the ship with the airborne Herky gun, too.

On the beach itself, Bart had retrieved his M33 assault carbine and ammo harness from the corporal who'd been left in charge of the gear. He didn't have time to slip back into cammies. The Sulawesi troops were all along the beach where the vegetation met the sand. He'd just have to endure the harness chafing the hell out of his shoulders and back. That was the least of his worries right then. He and his batt were on that beach without body armor and their asses bared to the breeze.

But the seventy-five men of the ship's Marine batt were ready. Even in swim trunks they looked mean. They were. Major Bart Clinch ran a clean but mean outfit. His gun apes were socially housebroken; otherwise they couldn't have served in the confines of a carrier submarine. But when it came to fighting, they were men who liked to fight. They were more than warriors.

Some men like to fight. They'll go out of their way to find a fight. They like the high that comes from violence. It had taken Americans a long time to acknowledge this quirk of human nature in some people. It had taken even longer to realize it had to be used, not suppressed. It couldn't be suppressed. However, it could be harnessed by offering a socially acceptable outlet for it. This existed in those parts of the armed services where it wasn't necessary to be a space scientist but only to be capable of controlled, disciplined violence. The Marine Corps was one of those places. And the Corps was proud of it.

Clinch didn't like to count on fancy tech when it came to one-on-one combat. He kept his N-fone behind his ear but bellowed in his parade-ground voice, "We're going to protect our fishing catch! If you can't stand the stink, keep your scuba masks on and breathe your bottled air! The stink may actually keep these Sulawesis at a distance. Alpha, take the right! Bravo, take the left! If fired upon, return fire! If they close with you, shoot their balls off!" His verbal commands were picked up by his N-fone and relayed back to the ship. "Where's our air support? Okay, I see it! You airplane drivers, listen up! I want one flight of you on the north along the beach, the other on the south. I want you on their flanks! Who's up there? Give me call codes!"

Bells will be on the north! Rips is on the south! What

do you need, Black Bart? The Tigers squadron commander had used the Marine major's standard call code.

Corry heard them and said nothing. Bart was doing his job. So was Bells and his squadron. Until the Sulawesis initiated a fight, neither Corry nor Bart wanted to start it.

"Clear the beach, Americans!" came an amplified voice from a portable PA system. "Those fish are being confiscated by the Sulawesi government! We're here to take possession of them! It is against Sulawesi law to resist such action by the Army!"

"Go piss up a rope!" Bart shouted back. "We caught them. We killed them. They're ours!"

"They are hazardous to the health and security of the people of Sulawesi! We have been ordered to confiscate all creatures caught!"

"Semper fi, Mac! Screw you! You want it? Try to take it!"

Some Sulawesi soldier heard that. He, too, was a fighter, and he didn't like what he heard. In his anger, he squeezed off a shot from his Singapore SAR 88. The man was a lousy shot. The 5.56mm jacketed bullet snapped past Clinch.

The man didn't have the chance to get off a second shot.

The Marines dropped to the beach. A three-round M33 burst cut down the Sulawesi who'd shot at the Marine commander.

Combat soldiers know it as the "mad minute." It's the opening moments of any fire fight. Every gun in the whole world seems to be shooting at you.

The Marines were prepared. Each was armed with either an M33 5.56mm high-velocity, laser-ranged, semiautomatic rifle firing caseless ammunition or with a Browning M100 Ripsaw light machine gun firing the same ammo. Together, the small arms of the Marine batt on the beach could launch a hail of 500,000 rounds per minute.

They did.

Bells, we need you! Bart told his air support boss via N-fone. *Carpet-hose the line where the bushes meet the beach! These Sulawesi bastards have worn out their welcome!*

Roger! Rolling in from the north! Want some AP?

Negatory! I want you to tear up the beach between us and the Sulawesis! That may make them think twice about attacking! Then have your south side boys stand by for possible AP if the Sulawesis are stupid and decide to attack!

Every F/A-48 Sea Devil carries a pair of high-rate 25mm cannon firing caseless ammo. The firing rate is so high that the shell clears the gun muzzle by less than a meter before the next round is fired. Because of Bart's request, the four Sea Devils fired stupid ground-impact explosive shells. The other flight selected intelligent people-seeking air-burst rounds in case they had to come in from the south and take out a Sulawesi assault.

That turned out to be unnecessary.

The high-speed low-level gunnery passes by the four Sea Devils literally blew a trench along the beach about a meter out from the vegetation.

"Way to go! Way to go!" Clinch yelled exuberantly. His words were carried by N-fone back to the ship. "That ought to discourage the shit out of them if it didn't scare it out!"

Down in CIC on the bridge, Corry and Zeke watched the action via long-focus video from the upper deck and relayed video from the Sea Devils.

"Bart isn't going to have any trouble holding off the Sulawesis unless they've got armor behind them," Zeke observed.

"They don't," Corry remarked. He'd studied the TO&E of the Sulawesi armed forces as part of his homework on the cruise to Makasar. "They've got about six APVs based in Makasar and a like number up in Manado. Parade vehicles mostly. When they're running. The guns on the Sea Devils will penetrate their armor."

"The guys have never had to fight a high-tech war, have they?" Zeke decided.

Corry nodded. "All they need are motorized infantry out in the boonies plus urban infantry units to maintain the government in the two main cities. Their air force consists of counter-insurgency attack aircraft . . . and there they come, off Makasar International Airport!"

Air Boss and Marine Boss, this is XO. Zeke got on the command net right away, seeing the radar blips of about six aircraft take to the air. *Aircraft departing Makasar airport in formation. Appears to be six in the flight.*

I see them! Terri shot back. *They're only old Hardarto Harahap Fours with dumb-blind combat directors. No match for Sea Devils. The CAP can take care of them. That's why I put the CAP up there.*

"As I said, they've never had to fight a high-tech war," Zeke muttered.

Corry nodded. "Agreed. I hate to have to order Terri to run a hot intercept on them. They're dead already if they attack."

"I'm more concerned about how long Bart can hold out on the beach," Zeke confessed "We might have to lay some serious ordnance on the Sulawesi Army so we can get VC-50 in with Dragons to pick them up. Otherwise, the Dragons will be prime targets for Golden BBs . . ."

However, before Corry could evaluate that situation further and come to a decision, two other matters were simultaneously brought to his attention.

XO, Special Sensors reporting. New data.

Almost simultaneously, the call came in from LTJG Fred Berger, *CO, Quartermaster here. Captain Qian has sent his message to his ship. But General Helamahera wants to speak with you. He says he's got a proposition for you.*

26

The external threat was Priority Number One. Zeke knew that, too. *Special Sensors, this is the XO. What have you got, Mister Ames?*

The small targets that are Awesomes from the rock area were heading north along the coast until a few seconds ago. Now they have turned southward. The Tuscarora *has turned toward them,* the Special Sensors Officer reported.

Corry and Zeke both saw that on the repeater.

"I thought the Awesomes were running for their mother ship," Zeke commented, scratching his head in bewilderment. "Now it looks like they're running *from* it!"

"You presuppose it's their mother ship, Zeke. It could be something else." Corry said.

"Why would they suddenly act like they're afraid of it?"

"Suppose it's the game warden . . ."

"Uh . . . Yeah . . . Suppose it is!" Zeke exclaimed in sudden recognition that the Captain's speculation might be true. "Captain, this points up our basic problem with the Awesomes. We don't know a damned thing about them! Nothing! If they're truly extraterrestrial, they're also truly alien. Alien in the way they think. Alien in the way they approach problems. Alien in their responses."

"I know," Corry agreed glumly. "That has worried the hell out of me, Zeke. And it's going to worry me until we find out more about them. Right now, the possibility of doing that isn't very good. They attacked us twice that we know of. Their mother ship attacked the *Bei fung* and ran from us when we defended the Chinese submarine." Corry held up his hand to make a point. "*That* much we know. We've only speculated about the rest. And speculation isn't going to make our mission report believable!"

"Yes, I know that! But, Captain, if they are 'fishing' for humans for some reason, they've hit us very deep in our psychological makeup," Zeke reminded him. He looked back at the masdet visual repeater. "This new behavior of theirs sure doesn't make any sense without your hypothesis about the game warden showing up. Maybe they aren't supposed to be fishing for us. Maybe it's part of some nonintervention policy they have."

Corry remembered something he'd read that had its roots in the twentieth century. "Maybe we've encountered their renegades, Zeke. Maybe their civilization—and I'm making an assumption that they have one that we'd recognize—maybe their civilization follows something that resembles metalaw."

"Sir?"

"I'll explain later," Corry promised. *Special Sensors, this is the CO. Do you have a projected south-bound course for the* Tuscarora *at this time?*

No, sir! It's just changed course to south-southeast. It's trying to close with the Awesomes.

Continue to track it, Charlie!

Aye, aye, sir!

XO, this is Bart! The Sulawesis got sort of discouraged after the Sea Devils made their pass. They've withdrawn into the bush and gone silent. Our i-r sensors show they're still there. I think we can cover pickup of the Awesomes by Dragons if we continue to get such outstanding air support. Can we get the airlifters in here, sir? These carcasses are beginning to stink to beat hell! The smell has made two of my Marines sick to their stomachs. With Marine chow the way it is, any-

thing that will make a Marine throw up has gotta be pretty bad!

"Captain, an Awesome carcass begins to decompose in a short period of time with that terrible odor," Zeke told his Commanding Officer. He recalled with distaste his own experience on the beach with the first Awesome. "It's probably too late to get those two back to the ship."

Stand by, Major. I've got several problems hitting me at once here.

Roger, CO. Your Marine batt won't go anywhere but here.

CO, this is Quartermaster, LTJG Fred Berger repeated his call.

Corry hadn't forgotten him, but the *Tuscarora* had occupied his attention. *This is the CO. Go ahead, Mister Berger.*

Ambassador Abbott has cut a deal with both Captain Qian and General Helamahera. He said since the United States already has its alien aboard in deep freeze, he'd let the Sulawesis have one of those on the beach in exchange for allowing us to get our Marines off the beach. And the Chinese could take the other one in exchange for not filing a formal protest for being fired on by us.

Wait one, Mister Berger. Let me check something, Corry told him. Corry suddenly realized that Ambassador Abbott was more than just another ambassador who'd bought his diplomatic post by campaign contributions. The Good Ol' Boy was a smart Good Ol' Boy.

Sick bay, this is the Captain. Ship's doctor, please.

Doctor Moore speaking, Captain.

Doctor, what's the condition of our Awesome carcass?

Johnnie Reb is all tucked away in an isolated deep freeze locker at minus forty Celsius, Captain. Turned the heat way down so it would get frozen absolutely solid. We got it before the parasites really went to work.

Now I'll have the chance to do some real studies on its biochemistry!

Johnnie Reb? Why did it get that nickname?

Its fabriclike covering is blue and gray, sir. We couldn't think of a better nickname!

Corry had to smile at that. He had an outstanding crew. As the Captain, he had to remain somewhat aloof, but he enjoyed the sense of humor that pervaded the ship. *Nor can I, Doctor!*

And, Captain, please tell Bart that he's as good a shot as Zeke. I expected Zeke to put a shot right down its throat; he's a submariner. Bart did the same thing. Right to the brain, by the way.

Thank you, Doctor, Corry told her and switched channels, saying to Zeke as he did so, "I think we can afford to let Qian and Helamahera have their aliens, don't you, Number Two?"

Zeke nodded with a smile. "As far as I'm concerned, Captain, it's cash and carry. They can take what they want from what's left on the beach!"

"Yes, but we'll get our Marines and frogmen off the beach first," Corry said, suddenly serious again. *Quartermaster, this is the Captain. Tell Qian and Helamahera that I accept their offer. Take the General to Communications. Have him pass the word to his troops ashore. Tikki and her chickens must be allowed to operate unmolested to get our Marines and frogmen back to the ship. Make sure General Helamahera knows that some of the pilots are women.*

Corry was aware that some Muslim sects carried on the Arab tradition of chivalry. A Muslim warrior isn't ensured entry to paradise by killing women.

And as soon as we've recovered our Marines and frogmen, Captain Qian can bring the Bei fung *close inshore to pick up his alien,* Corry went on.

"If the Chinese and Sulawesi can stand it," Zeke muttered. "Those Awesome ought to be pretty ripe by then. If they haven't been devoured by the parasites, that is."

Captain, they thank you for your helpful and cooperative attitude. We're on our way to the comm shack now so they can pass the word to their people. Then I'll escort them to the upper flight deck, Berger reported.

"XO, tell Terri to get the Sea Dragons up for beach party recovery," Corry said verbally to Braxton, as he became engrossed in the masdet plot. The big problems had gone away almost as if they'd solved themselves. Corry knew that many problems solved themselves. The *real* problems were the ones that didn't and thus required action.

He wanted to make sure the *Tuscarora* wasn't one that required action.

He didn't know what action he'd take. The *Shenandoah* could dive and fight submerged, but it couldn't catch the *Tuscarora*. At least, it hadn't been able to catch the first one. Maybe this was a different kind.

The swimming Awesomes from the beach battle apparently knew it was different. Their masdet images showed they were evading it. As Corry watched, two of the Awesome images merged with the *Tuscarora* plot.

For the next thirty minutes, the Captain of the *Shenandoah* watched what he guessed was an undersea battle between the Awesomes and the new *Tuscarora* target.

It *had* to be a battle! Corry was a submarine officer. He saw these alien targets using the same submarine warfare tactics and techniques that he'd been taught and had fought.

When some of the Awesomes couldn't get away, their mass images merged with the coastline.

New small images split off from the big target. Were other Awesomes pursuing the first ones into the rocks? "Hand-to-hand" underwater combat among those strange aquatic creatures? He didn't know. But he was fascinated. He was watching something no one had seen before.

The passive sonar signals were a mélange of sounds,

a cacophony of screeches and yelps and whines and piping toots. No one in the *Shenandoah* knew what these strange sounds meant. But they were being recorded. Maybe marine biologists and psychologists would be able to make some sense out of them later.

"Captain, Communications reports a priority cipher has arrived via SWC for you," Zeke suddenly reported.

Corry broke away from studying the masdet display. "Have it delivered to my cabin," he said, rising to his feet. "You have the con, Mister Braxton!"

"Aye, aye, sir. I have the con!"

In his quarters, Corry took the message cube from Atwater and signed for it. When he was alone, he slipped it into the handheld decryption terminal he removed from his safe.

In one way, he was pleased with the message. In another way, he wasn't. But it was an order:

Cancel Execute Order 53-A-04. Cease present operation. Return Pearl soonest. Ref SECDEF order 53-A-04.1 issued 1500Z. Kane ADM CINCPAC.

The brevity of the message wasn't due solely to the shortcomings of the scalar wave communications system. Nor was it caused by the complexity of the multi-level encryption code that Corry's hand-held had taken two minutes to decipher. Corry knew Kane. He knew that CINCPAC didn't like to have operations micromanaged by Washington. Like Corry, Kane was a "can-do" person who was trained to carry out an order without a lot of detailed instruction from above.

Kane hadn't forwarded the SECDEF order itself. This detail told Corry that the Admiral was upset about it. In fact, Kane had probably delayed forwarding the order. He'd probably been on the horn to the Pentagon most of the day.

Corry did a quick time calculation. It was nearing 1500 hours, Sulawesi time. That was 0200 EST. Kane had sat on it for eight hours. He had put his flag on the line for Corry. Kane knew the general terms of the beach operation because Corry had informed him that morning. Corry hadn't tried to justify it, but he knew Kane would realize he was trying to carry out the mission and get the most convincing data of all.

Kane apparently was giving him an opportunity to save his career by bringing in a captured alien. Corry didn't know that for certain. However, he knew he'd find out why when he saw the Admiral in Pearl.

The most important clue was the wording of the SWC message. Kane had not set a time. Corry had no deadline to work against. He only had to comply "soonest." That was a loosy-goosy word in any order.

Therefore, Corry had some latitude.

He needed it.

So he decided to finish the operation before departing the Makasar Straits. He really couldn't do anything else without exposing the *Shenandoah* to possible danger.

He slipped the printout into his shirt pocket and buttoned the flap over it. He then yielded to his compulsion for appearance and checked his image in the mirror before returning to the bridge. He decided that this Makasar mission had indeed taken its toll on him. He noticed that he looked tired.

But it wasn't over yet, and it was up to him to finish the job and comply with orders. He'd take a little leave when he got back to Pearl. Maybe a few days on Maui with Cynthia might help if she was feeling up to it.

When he slipped into his chair on the bridge, he told his XO, "I have the con, Mister Braxton!"

"Aye, aye, sir! You have the con." Then Zeke reported to him, "Captain, the Marine battalion and our frogmen are back in the ship."

Corry looked at the time. "Well done! Have a Dragon stand by to take the General ashore and another one to lift Captain Qian to his ship. Tell Berger I'll meet the party upstairs to bid them farewell." As he got up, he suddenly remembered something. "And have a third airlifter take the Ambassador and Commander Hewitt back to the embassy. Now that I have the opportunity to get them off the ship, I want to do so. I have no idea what the intentions of the *Tuscarora* are. And I don't want the Ambassador aboard if we have to take action against it."

"Aye, aye, sir! I know we're at General Quarters, but do you want to man the gangway and pipe them over the side?"

Corry shook his head. "No. Frankly, it's only custom that compels me to be present up there. Someday, Zeke, you'll wish you were still an Executive Officer. A Commanding Officer has compulsory duties that require him to be polite and gracious to visitors, some of whom he may not like or even trust." He paused, then added, "And, Zeke, watch the *Tuscarora* closely while I'm getting rid of the VIPs. We may have to take action if that phantom materializes into a threat. So keep everyone at General Quarters and keep the steam up." Corry touched his ear to switch his N-fone to a discrete channel so Zeke could reach him if necessary. "Do not hesitate to call me. You have the ship!" He didn't reveal the CINCPAC message at that point. It wasn't urgent that he do so. First things first.

"Aye, aye, Captain. I have the ship."

On the flight deck above, Corry met the visitors as Brewer brought them up the PRIFLY personnel lift. He saluted Helamahera and told him curtly, "General, that aircraft on the left will take you to the beach."

"Captain, you're a man of your word," the Sulawesi defense minister complimented him as he returned the salute. "You withdrew your Marines and frogmen without attempting to take the carcasses."

"We made an agreement, General," Corry reminded him. "You and I are both officers, and our word is our bond."

"When I'm dealing with politicians, that isn't the

case," the Sulawesi general remarked. "Captain Qian and I have also made an agreement. I will allow him to take the other carcass. I have no desire to cause an international incident. I have enough troubles of my own with our internal security."

Corry said nothing but knew that the Sulawesis really didn't want to upset either of the two superpowers. The TO&E of the Sulawesi armed forces was available for all to study, and the Sulawesis didn't have the resources to handle an international situation. That probably was why Helamahera had been so blustery and defensive at first.

Corry knew all too well the truth of the nameless first sergeant's remark to the young Subaltern John Hackett, "Remember, sir, it is all a matter of bluff, sir. Really." In his own career, Corry had learned that too.

"Yes," Corry gave the man his usual brief response. Turning to the Chinese submarine skipper, he said, "Captain, the middle aircraft will lift you to your ship; I trust you don't mind climbing down a rope ladder to board your vessel. We can't land you on the *Bei fung*."

Qian didn't comment on that. Instead, he offered his hand. "Thank you, Captain. And thank you for making it possible for me to recover one of the carcasses."

Corry shook his hand. He didn't mention that the *Shenandoah* would withdraw, allow the *Bei fung* to come closer inshore, and then attempt to cover the Chinese rear. He wanted to be outside the *Bei fung* in the channel so he could depart quickly. "Don't thank me. Ambassador Abbott cut the deal, I understand. Good luck, Captain!" he returned the Chinese commander's salute, then said to Abbott, "Mister Ambassador, thank you for your help. The Sea Dragon on the right will return you and Commander Hewitt to the embassy."

"Will you and your department heads join me at the embassy for dinner tonight?"

"I'll contact you later, Mister Ambassador. I am really under the gun at the moment. I apologize for the informality of your departure, but the press of events requires me to return to the bridge at once . . ."

And he didn't add that the orders in his pocket required him to return to Pearl Harbor as soon as he was gracefully clear of this situation.

Provided the incoming *Tuscarora* didn't have something else in mind.

27

Corry didn't dive the *Shenandoah*. Terri still had her chickens out. So he moved the carrier submarine farther out in Makasar Straits. This allowed Qian to bring the *Bei fung* in to his former position two kilometers off the beach.

Then the Commanding Officer of the U.S.S. *Shenandoah* showed his XO the hard copy of the CINC-PAC message.

Zeke read it and nodded knowingly as he muttered, "Okay. They want us home. So home we go. I don't know anyone aboard who can object to that. Or would." He folded it and handed it back to the Captain. "Now I know why you got the Ambassador off the ship in such a big hurry."

Corry wanted to get his Executive Officer's unbiased opinion. It wasn't that Corry didn't trust his own judgment calls, but he preferred to have inputs from several sources. "What do you think, XO?"

"About the recall order? Sounds to me like someone back in Playland on the Potomac forgot to put on their woolen socks after they looked at the data we sent back."

"Who do you think got cold feet, Zeke?"

"Sir, an Execute Order officially comes from SEC-DEF, but SECDEF can't issue an Execute Order without approval of The Man. And the Commander in Chief doesn't act without consulting his National Security Advisor and the National Security Council," Zeke ventured to say. He recalled the gates through which an Execute Order had to pass before it ended up in the hands of the commander on the spot. "Someone is scared. And I'm not sure who."

Corry thought he knew. However, he didn't say so aloud. And neither did Zeke Braxton.

All the officers in the U.S.S. *Shenandoah* operated within the tradition that American military officers are not free to openly criticize their superiors, especially their civilian ones. And even more specifically the elected ones. Freedom of speech in the armed services isn't any more restricted than in a civilian corporation. Someone in uniform has no personal opinion as long as that person wears the uniform. Someone receiving a paycheck doesn't bite the hand that signs it. Freedom still exists: anyone is free to quit and take another job.

So Corry was careful as he replied to his Executive Officer. "I'm not sure it's that simple. I don't doubt that someone is scared as a result of what we've found. If we're right, the whole world is suddenly in a new ball game. This caught Washington even more off guard than we were. We had to accept what we found because it was right in our laps. They don't. So no one really knows what to do at this point."

"For God's sake, why, Captain? they must have kicked this around in planning sessions for the last hundred years or so!"

"Not at the top. At best, the subject of possible contact with extraterrestrial beings has been a rather detached academic exercise or a science fiction plot device far removed from everyday actions in the political mud wrestling ring," Corry pointed out. "I think we have to be careful. We'd better not get zealous about trying to make contact with the Awesomes. My reward would be commanding the Podunk Naval Ordnance Station in East Chitlin Switch, Kansas. You'd end up going back to Maine and fishing for lobsters."

"Captain, we've got perhaps the most important

data since the invention of the wheel! Do you mean we can't do anything about it?"

"We can. We will. And we will follow orders," Corry went on. He paused. "That CINCPAC order has no 'drop-dead' time. I know Admiral Kane. He's given us a reasonable amount of time to comply. Not much, but a little. As things stand right now," he said, indicating the masdet display, "we can't just make for Pearl. We're in a potential threat situation. Our first priority is to get out of that situation."

"Yes, sir. I understand perfectly, sir." Zeke knew his CO.

And Corry knew his XO.

In company with Zeke, he watched the position of the unknown submersible on the mass detector display.

"In addition, if we left right now, we'd probably get a reprimand for departing without getting additional data, given these circumstances . . ."

"We're damned if we do and damned if we don't," Zeke muttered.

"Not at all, XO! The Navy has always been interested in exploration. If we do this right, we won't be damned but praised. We've got to orchestrate it that way. This mission has just started!"

"I'd sure feel a whole hell of a lot better if I knew the intentions of the *Tuscarora*," Zeke muttered. "This has a very high pucker factor."

Corry tried not to show the strain. "Look at it this way, Number Two. We know where it is. All of the masdet data we've taken is recorded. It will later be analyzed so damned thoroughly by experts that we won't believe what they've been able to extract from it. In the meantime, if we're as smart as we think we are, we may learn something more about it by watching it. If it doesn't shoot."

Zeke nodded, but added, "Mark reports that Guns Weaver is ready. Eight fish are in the tubes. One of them is carrying a nuke if you want to use it."

"I wish I could. However, any authority I might

have to pop a nuke is gone because of that recall order from CINCPAC."

"Except under extenuating circumstances, Captain."

"The circumstances aren't extenuating yet, Mister Braxton."

"Let's hope they don't get that way."

Corry didn't reply. He studied the masdet display, wishing the *Tuscarora* also had a good sonar or lidar return with which to confirm the masdet data. The only other sensor data available were passive sonar. The different sounds made by the Awesomes and the numbers of different sound sources out there made it difficult for Roger Goff to merge his data with Charlie Ames's outputs. "What do you think it's doing now, Zeke?"

Zeke shook his head. "Frankly, sir, I don't know."

"Speculate."

"Very well. Looks like a mopping-up activity to me. I've lost count, but I think the *Tuscarora* and its small entities have either killed or captured all of the Awesomes they were chasing."

"Two great minds with but a single speculation. We're either brilliant or equally noncreative," Corry said, trying to lighten up because he could feel the strain now. He wasn't being very successful at that. He was more successful in comparing the *Tuscarora* activities with the Navy's own submarine warfare tactics and doctrine.

Bridge, this is CAG, Terri Ellison's voice sounded in the N-fones. *I've recovered my Sea Dragons and struck them below. I've recovered all but the four CAP Sea Devils and the Ospreys. They can be trapped and struck below in five minutes to make the flight deck ready for dive.*

CAG, this is XO. How are their fuel states?

One hour on the Devils; they just relieved. Seven-zero minutes on the Ospreys.

Corry looked at the masdet display. Something new was going on up north in the Straits. The small smudges were heading for the mother ship and merging with its smudge. The *Tuscarora* was recovering its own "birds." He remarked to Zeke, "Have Terri stand by. The *Tuscarora* has completed the mop-up. If it heads this way, I'm going to put a couple of Ospreys over it and keep the CAP orbiting us. I don't believe it can see the Ospreys through the air-water interface."

"The P-10s can't see it more than fifty meters down, either," Zeke replied.

"They can if we feed them our masdet position data," Corry said. "I want the Ospreys over it as an additional counterattack tactic. I want to be in a position where I have several options."

"I'll take care of the data stream reply, sir."

CAG, this is the CO. Put the CAP over us ready for ASW vectors, explosives on missiles set for depth initiation. But be prepared either to trap them fast or go to Makasar International Airport under emergency fuel status if I have to dive. Same for the Ospreys, but I want the Ospreys over the Tuscarora *with ash cans ready to drop. XO is arranging data stream feed to them now.*

How much advance warning can you give me before you dive, sir?

Only enough time to secure the flight decks.

I should have known better than to ask that. Sorry, Captain, it was a stupid question! Very well, that means three minutes' warning. If my chickens get caught aloft, they'll go bingo fuel and head for Makasar. I hope they aren't impounded by the Sulawesis.

They might and they might not. But I won't leave Sulawesi without them.

Captain, I can get a Sea Dragon tanker up if I've got ten minutes to fuel and launch it. That might alleviate the problem. It would give us another two hours on the aircraft.

Make it so, Terri.

Aye, aye, sir! It was the first time he'd heard her use that phrase from PRIFLY.

"Captain, do we have ten minutes? Look at what the *Tuscarora* is doing now," Zeke called his attention to the displays.

The huge target had changed course. It was now heading south-southwest. This would take it out into the Makasar Straits and deep water.

And on that course, it was now closing.

"What is the computed closing rate, XO?"

"Ten knots, sir."

"If course and speed do not change, what is the computed time to intercept us?"

"Nineteen minutes, sir."

CAG, this is CO. You have seven minutes to launch the tanker.

We can do it in five, sir!

Report when it's clear, then rig the flight deck for dive.

Sir, we'll pre-rig for dive by securing the lower flight deck now and launching the tanker from the upper deck. Can you put the bow into the wind and give me thirty knots? We might get it off without a catapult that way.

Corry shook his head. He was a naval aviator himself. To attempt launching a Sea Dragon loaded with fuel without a catapult was a sure way to put a Sea Dragon into the water. *Negative, CAG. I say again, negative! Secure the upper flight deck now! Shoot from the center cat on the lower deck. Partially secure the lower deck by closing the aft doors now.*

"Captain, that's going to be close if you want to dive this ship before the *Tuscarora* closes within two thousand klicks," Zeke warned him.

But Corry knew what he was doing. "XO, I do not intend to dive, nor do I intend to get under way. But I want to be prepared to do so in the shortest possible time if I'm forced to do either one. My intentions are to sit here on the surface dead in the water and let the *Tuscarora* approach."

"Sir!"

"Zeke, if it can only ram me, I can maneuver. If this is a different vessel than before and it mounts some sort of weapons system, I can't call the shots at all except to shoot six fish down its throat if I can after it fires on us. And if it shoots, the ASW Osprey will pinpoint it with ash cans. But at this time I will not make any overt move that could even be remotely considered by it as a threat."

Bridge, this is Communications. Call on the TBS for Captain Corry from Captain Qian. That was the first time the Chinese boat had used the international ship-to-ship radiotelephone system.

Put it on the verbose handset, Mister Atwater.

Aye, aye, sir. Go ahead.

Corry picked up the handset. "Captain Corry here, Go ahead, Captain Qian."

"Captain, our shore parties are about to reach the beach. But we have passive sonar that indicates a large target in the Straits is approaching you."

"Captain Qian, I am tracking that target. I will protect you as agreed. But I must ask that you do not take any aggressive action against the target. I do not know what it is, and I am going to try to find out by being passive. However, if it attacks me, I will counterattack. And I would appreciate your assistance if that happens."

"Please keep me advised, Captain. I have instructed my Communications Officer to keep this TBS channel open."

"I will, sir." Corry put the handset back in its cradle and directed his full attention again to the displays.

"Still closing, Captain, but dead slow at less than two knots now," Zeke reported.

"It slowed down. It sees us now. It's curious," Corry muttered.

"Sir?"

"It wants to look at us, XO. I'm going to let it do so as long as it doesn't attack. Because I'm looking at it too."

"Captain, isn't that a bit risky?"

"Yes, it is. It's risky every time we dive the ship. But without risk, we don't get anywhere or anything. If we're not ready to take risks, we'd all better leave the submarine service and go back to sit on shore." Corry paused, knowing that he was risking more than six hundred lives as well as the ship itself. The lives were more important than the ship. So he remarked, "I know the limit of risk I'll accept. We haven't gotten there yet."

Long, sweat-soaked minutes passed.

CO, this is CAG! Terri's voice announced in his head. *Tanker is launched . . . Forward doors coming closed . . . Flight decks secure to dive. I'm going to give that flight deck crew a pile of medals for this!*

Thank you, Terri. Well done! Corry didn't take his eyes off the displays. In a loud and firm voice full of confidence, he announced so that everyone on the bridge could hear, "Steady as she goes, Mister Braxton! Steady as she goes!"

"Range five thousand meters," Zeke announced. "Well within fish range. We have a solution on the TDC. We can put six fish right down its throat . . ."

"Steady as she goes, Mister Braxton."

"*Tuscarora* has gone to active pinging," Zeke reported. "Roger Goff reports it's a different signal and rep rate than before. Lots more overtones. Very much like the complex signals we use to get sonar signatures."

"It's looking us over, Mister Braxton. Is the ship ready to dive?"

"Aye, aye, sir. The ship is ready to dive."

"Steady as she goes, Mister Braxton," Corry repeated for the fourth time.

He was as ready as he could ever be for whatever was going to take place.

Right then, it was like a watery game of chicken. It was evolving into an eyeball-to-eyeball confrontation.

Corry did not intend to be the first to blink.

But it took all the guts he had not to do it.

"One thousand meters. Closing rate zero. I repeat, closing rate zero," Zeke almost whispered. Yet the bridge was so quiet that everyone heard him.

"Sir, Flak reports visual on the target. It's at an estimated thirty meters depth. Flak is recording as well as transmitting video from his Osprey," Zeke said slowly in a louder voice this time. "Shape is similar to the previous *Tuscarora* but with less beam and greater length. Its color is not silver. He can't identify a color at this time."

"Image on screen!" Corry snapped.

The full-color frame in high-definition mode appeared on the bridge master display screen. It showed something big and streamlined under water.

"Enhance that, Mister Braxton. Have Atwater and Strader take out the water signal."

The powerful image enhancement computer in the Operations Department took out that portion of the video signal that was the random and constantly changing air-water interface.

The shape that appeared on the screen looked like it was floating in the vacuum of space.

"Holy shit!" someone breathed, and then quickly shut up.

It was longer than the *Shenandoah* and almost shiny smooth. Strange protuberances extended from the front and back ends. It had no markings on it.

Slowly, it began to turn.

"Flak reports the target is rotating in yaw. It's presenting its broadside to us," Zeke reported.

Corry knew he'd won.

"It's looked us over. Now it's inviting us to look it over," the Captain of the *Shenandoah* said. "Helmsman, rotate the ship in yaw at ten degrees per second and come broadside to the target. We'll give it a better look in exchange!"

CO, this is Communications. Signal for you on the TBS, sir.

Corry picked up the handset. "Captain, what is that ship?" Qian's voice asked.

"I don't know, but it is not attacking. I repeat, it is not attacking," Corry told him. "Do not ping it!"

"What is it, Captain Corry?" Qian repeated. "We are receiving the video transmission from your patrol aircraft."

Qian's statement didn't surprise him. That data link was straightforward commercial technology available from Japan and Singapore, as well as Senegal. Even if Qian was picking up the Osprey video signal, Corry knew that the Chinese didn't have the computer power to enhance the image. They were seeing the *Tuscarora* as an indistinct, very large underwater shape. And that suited Corry fine. That was just the story he hoped Qian would take back to Beijing. "Captain Qian, I don't know what it is," Corry replied honestly.

Bridge, this is Special Sensors. Target has started accelerating westward, course two-seven-zero.

Bridge, this is Sonar. We confirm Special Sensors' report.

We see it! Zeke told them.

"Captain Qian, the target is now moving westward and away from us. I believe you are now clear to complete your activity. Therefore, we will depart. We have received new orders. My best wishes to you."

"And I wish you long life and prosperity, Captain Corry. Until we meet again, and I hope it is under such friendly circumstances," the Chinese Captain replied.

Corry put away the handset. The *Tuscarora*'s image smudge on the masdet display showed it was now five klicks to the west and opening the range at twenty knots. Its speed was increasing. Its acceleration was surprising. However, Corry told himself he should expect nothing less if the ship—and it was a ship—was also capable of leaving the water and accelerating into space.

"Mister Braxton, secure from General Quarters. Come to Condition Two. Set the watch. Activate the flight decks and trap all presently airborne aircraft. Upon recovery of aircraft, rig for dive and inform me when ready to do so. Have the Navigator give a course for Pearl Harbor," Corry said with relief in his voice for the first time in days. He had no urge to stutter uncontrollably now. The tension had dissipated. "I'll be in my quarters. After we dive and set course for Pearl, would you and the division officers join me in the wardroom for a sandwich and a cup of coffee, please? I think it's time we relaxed and had a chat."

28

Captain William M. Corry passed the hard copy of his message around the wardroom table for all to see.

Receipt of order canceling Execute Order 53-A-04 and activating Execute Order 53-A-04.1 acknowledged. Returning soonest Pearl. ETA 5d. Believe mission accomplished. Data and sample aboard. SSCV-26, Corry, CAPT.

"Captain, I note that you haven't transmitted the last Makasar Straits encounter data yet," LCDR Bob Lovette noted. As the Operations Department head, he'd been waiting for the transmit order to come to Ed Atwater. But it hadn't.

"If I receive a request from CINCPAC, it will be transmitted, Mister Lovette," Corry told him, picking up the second half of his tuna salad sandwich. "The order from Admiral Kane only told us to return to Pearl."

"I'll bet the request comes, Captain," Natalie Chase guessed. Then she snickered. "And I like your comment about the data and sample. That should cause someone to go hyperbolic . . ."

"Spoken like a mathematician," growled Bart Clinch.

"Do you have something against mathematicians who can steer you around?" she fired back at him.

"Only if they don't steer me wrong." He looked at Natalie with a little more appreciation now. She wasn't just another brilliant Navy woman techie. Nor was she a superwoman with iron ovaries. He saw a pert, attractive, and very female two-and-a-half-striper who'd had the guts to accompany him into dangerous water when she didn't have to. Furthermore, she'd done it willingly and chewed him out mildly for being oversolicitous of her. He wanted to get to know her better.

Corry noted it too. And he noted Bart's look.

"Well, I did lead you into a trap. You haven't forgiven me for that yet," Natalie reminded him.

"And you haven't apologized," was Bart's reply.

"That can be arranged," she told him.

"And the 'sample' is doing very well," Doctor Laura Raye Moore put in. "I'm treating it as our frozen asset. If we didn't have Johnnie Reb all tucked away, we'd have a hell of a time explaining what we did and why we did it."

"We're going to have a hell of a time in any event," Terri Ellison put in. "Who the hell is going to believe me when I tell them I went scuba diving with an alien?"

"Well, don't put that in your report, Terri," Mark Walton told her. "Leave that to Bart and Zeke. They both scored kills. Let them explain it."

"I'm not going to explain anything. I can't," Zeke admitted. "I'll just report it, telling it like it happened. And that's something I need to remind you. Make sure your rough logs are finalized before we get to Pearl. I suspect they'll be impounded and classified the instant we tie up to the dock."

"I've always got my private log," Terri remarked.

The ships's Personnel and Legal Officer, LCDR Darlene Kerr, spoke up, "Terri, don't admit you've kept one. They can confiscate it too."

"Darlene, that's my *private* log and it contains information of a *private* nature as well as comments about official activities," Terri snapped. "Naval intelligence will have to pry that out of my cold, dead hands first!"

"We'll keep your secret, Terri," Zeke promised her, then added the caveat, "provided you share some of the juicy parts of it with us. I've run out of things to read. It's a long five days to Pearl."

"So come by and I might let you look. And flatter me. Flattery may get you everything . . . or almost everything . . ."

Corry listened and watched. He wanted to let his crew unwind as rapidly as possible and as soon as possible. He wanted to kick back and relax too. At least to the extent he was able as the Commanding Officer. The last several days had been incredibly tense. If he didn't loosen up the crew, he'd have a lot of cases of channel fever four days hence as they approached Pearl Harbor.

But he also wanted to talk to them as soon as the ship was under way and while events were still fresh in their minds.

He finished his sandwich and washed it down with a swig of hot coffee. He'd deliberately ordered a tuna salad sandwich. It tasted good. It had been days since food had tasted good to him. He'd taken meals on the run when he could get them, catching snacks whenever possible. That wasn't the way to live to become a flag officer. Not that Bill Corry really believed an admiral's job could be any better than the one he had. Commanding a terminal desk ashore would come all too soon if it came. And if he didn't retire first. In spite of a wife who kept bringing up the subject of retirement, that wasn't in Corry's immediate plans.

However, those plans might be shot to hell as of now.

Corry was concerned over what would or could happen when they docked at Pearl.

And that was really why he wanted to talk to his officers early.

So he put his napkin on the table, sat back, looked around, and said, "Don't plan on being bored on the way to Pearl, Terri."

"I don't plan to be, sir."

Corry knew the Dolphin Club would be open during

the next five days. He saw no reason to be a hard-nosed Captain Bly about it.

"Although we'll be standing regular watches, you and your subordinates are going to be very busy working on your finalized logs," he went on. "And I'd like everyone aboard to prepare a detailed and separate report of personal recollections and impressions based on the data in those logs. Those should be dictated or written as soon as possible."

The silence in the wardroom spoke loudly. It was the first time Corry had ever requested such documentation. These were career line officers who knew how to write a report but preferred action to writing. This would be a chore for most of them. Some wanted to forget as much of it as possible. Corry couldn't let them do that.

"I'm not trying to be a martinet. I couldn't if I wanted to," he went on to explain, although he didn't have to. Technically, he wasn't required to explain an order. Or a request, which was the same as an order. However, Bill Corry didn't command people; he led them as a commander. "And I want to remind you that you will be referring to those logs and reports a lot after we tie up at Pearl. Ladies and gentlemen, we can look forward to being interrogated by anyone and everyone who can possibly fake up a good excuse to do so."

"The old UFO syndrome," Zeke muttered. "We can't duck it even if we wanted to. It was part of an official mission of a ship of the United States Navy. It's in the logs."

"And we have solid data," Natalie added.

"And a sample," Laura Raye finished.

"Damned hard to deny what happened to us!" Bart put in.

"Oh, no one will deny anything. They'll just classify it!" Terri exploded. She wasn't used to limits other than those imposed by the physical universe, the Uniform Code of Military Justice, and Navy customs and traditions.

"And don't even consider leaking it," Darlene Kerr warned. "Naval prisons are not known for their graceful living conditions."

"Captain, what do you foresee as a result of this? Will the CNO break up the crew?" Ray Stocker was a submarine engineer in his guts. He lived, breathed, ate, and slept submarine technology. While this single-mindedness often dismayed some of the ladies—Ray was a handsome man—everyone was glad that he was so dedicated. Technology and expertise with it were the only things between them and the enemy sea. A dedicated engineer was a highly prized person to have in a submarine.

And Ray had put his finger on one of the hidden fears of everyone in the wardroom. The crew of the U.S.S. *Shenandoah* was a team. They were "family." In fact, the crew was the only family most of them had ever had. Many people in the ship were orphans or came from single-parent families. Some had never had a father. Some came from broken or violent homes. The idea of breaking up the crew bothered them at a very basic human level.

The Navy had long ago realized the value of cama-raderie as a result of the old Blue and Gold crews in the boomers, the ballistic missile submarines. Thus, many people served in the same ship for many years as part of a team that was never really broken up. They would serve a hitch together at sea, then a hitch ashore in training, educational, or staff assignments intended to make them better at their jobs.

To break up a crew in the twenty-first-century Navy meant that the crew was no damned good. Even if a person had outstanding fitness reports, the stigma of having served on a disbanded crew was something no one wanted to live with. Personnel from disbanded crews usually resigned very soon after it happened.

Crews evolved over the years as people came and

went. But when you went back to sea, you found yourself with most of the people you knew and had worked with before. New people either fit in or went elsewhere. Crews were almost as long-lived as the ships in which they served.

"No, the Navy won't break up the crew," Corry told them with confidence in his voice. "I'm reasonably certain of that. We may all end up being classified Cosmic Top Secret, Destroy Before Ready and Suicide Afterward. But they won't break up the crew."

"I wish I could be as sure of it as you are, Captain," Mark Walton said with a sigh.

"If they break us up," Terri Ellison stated forcefully, her fists clenched on the green felt of the wardroom table, "I've half a mind to make a damned nuisance of myself at Fort Fumble." She could, too. She came from an old Navy family with over a century of outstanding service. She not only knew the Old Salts Network, but she ranked high in the equally unofficial Brown Shoe Navy Club.

"They may make you resign your commission," the ship's Legal Officer pointed out.

"Scroom!" Terri exclaimed. "If they break up this crew and try to put a lid on the data we have, it would go against the Navy's exploration tradition. If the Navy hasn't been on the forefront of science and technology, it's been among the first users of it."

"Ladies and gentlemen, I don't know what our superiors are going to do with the data," Corry interrupted. He had an ace up his sleeve. It was time for him to reveal it for the benefit of his people. "Politicians—and even officers, I'm sad to say—have tried to sit on data in the past. It can't be done. Our government functions through a network of calibrated leaks. Some bureaucrats and politicians use leaks to gain power. Few real secrets remain secrets for more than five years. Sometimes, they can be kept for twenty-five years. However, as time passes, it becomes more and more difficult to preserve security.

"In this situation, no one in Washington will be able to keep a lid on this for very long at all. And we are not going to be the ones to be crucified," he confided in them. "In the past, a reported UFO sighting has often ruined careers. It could be hushed up. The observer's credibility could be attacked. It won't happen this time."

He smiled and told them, "We are not alone."

Zeke thought the Captain was making a joke at their expense until he realized that Corry had put a new spin on that old cliché.

"The Chinese and the Sulawesis," Zeke said.

"And a separate report will come through the State Department as well," Terri realized. "You're right, Captain! The others that were involved in this are going to save our buns. And we'll save theirs."

"Precisely."

"But why won't they keep it quiet?" Lovette asked.

"Because we got the better data. They know it. And they'll want it," Natalie guessed.

"And because we have a frozen specimen. They ended up with two rotten, stinking lumps of nothing," Laura Raye put in.

"I'll bet the Chinese are mad as hell about that," Terri said with a smile.

"So are the Sulawesis!" Bart Clinch put in. "I tangled assholes with Helamahera for more than a day trying to set up a joint exercise. He's a mean sonofabitch, almost as mean as I am. I'll make book on what both nations are going to do. They're going to go public, raise hell, and demand that the United States share the data and samples of the carcass." Clinch was smiling for the first time in days. He understood now what a master strategist Corry was.

"You won't get me to take your bet, Bart. I don't want to lose my money," Zeke told him lightly.

"So," Corry told his department heads, "let's get to work on those logs and reports."

"Captain, do you intend to talk to the crew about

all this?" Chief of the Boat Carl Armstrong never said much in these department head meetings, although he was present because he was the direct link with the rates.

"Certainly. Department heads, work with Mister Berger and set up a schedule for me to come around and speak personally to everyone about this."

The Captain of the U.S.S. *Shenandoah* knew that things could still get flushed down the scuppers. Nothing was certain. But he felt that they were in a good position. "All of you can start to pass the word. When we get to Pearl, we treat this like an ordinary cruise. Business as usual. We'll let others classify the information, and we'll comply. We'll also let them fight the ensuing battle. And they'll be forced to fight it, whether they want to or not. There will be a huge flap for several weeks. No one will know what to do. But we'll play it very professional, very calm, very cool."

"What's next, Captain?" Terri felt better about it, but like other naval aviators—including Corry and Zeke—she always tried to stay ahead of the situation. Get behind the power curve and you were either dead or in the water. Terri planned ahead and worked like hell to make her plans become reality. And she had plans for what she was going to do after the meeting. And for the next four days while the ship was submerged and there would be no air activity.

Bart had the same thoughts, and he wanted to develop a new relationship.

"That's not for us to say. CINCPAC isn't upset. So I suspect we'll lay up at Pearl for a couple of weeks. We may not get any leave, but I'll grant liberty. Then I'm anticipating that CINCPAC will forward some interesting orders, because right now the U.S.S. *Shenandoah* is the only ship with a masdet and a crew that's used it."

Captain William M Corry paused. "I believe we'll be ordered to go fishing."

APPENDIX I

SSCV-26 U.S.S. *SHENANDOAH*
Crew Roster

Commanding Officer: CAPT William M. Corry

Ship Staff
Executive Officer: CDR Arthur E. "Zeke" Braxton
Personnel & Legal Officer: LCDR Darlene H. Kerr
Quartermaster & Ship's Secretary: LTJG Frederick G.
  Berger
Chaplain: LT Thomas H. Chapman
Chief of the Boat: SCPO Carl G. Armstrong
Chief Staff Petty Officer: CPO Alfred K. Warren

Ship Division
Operations Department
Operations Officer: LCDR Robert A. Lovette
Communications Officer: LT Edward B. Atwater
Sonar Officer: LT Roger M. Goff
Special Sensor Officer: LT Charles B. Ames
Radar/Lidar Officer: LTJG Barbara S. Brewer
Intelligence Officer: LTJG Ralph M. Strader

Deck Department
First Lieutenant: LCDR Mark W. Walton
Gunnery Officer: CWO Joseph Z. Weaver
Cargo Officer: LTJG Olivia P. Kilmer
Steering & Damage Control Officer: LT Donald G.
  Morse
Underwater Special Team: LT Richard S. Brookstone
Chief Boatswain's Mate: CPO Clancy Thomas

Navigation Department
Navigator: LCDR Natalie B. Chase
Assistant Navigator: LT Bruce G. Leighton
Assistant Navigator: LT Marcella A. Zar

Engineering Department
Engineer Officer: CDR Raymond M. Stocker
Assistant Engineer Officer: LCDR Norman E. Merrill
Main Propulsion Officer: LT Paula F. Ives
Damage Control Officer: LTJG Robert P. Benedetti
Electrical Officer: LT Richard Fitzsimmons
Electronic Repair Officer: LTJG Myra A. Hofer

Supply Department
Supply Officer: LT Frances G. Allen
Disbursing Officer: LTJG Harriett B. Gordon
Stores Officer: LT Kenneth P. Keyes
Mess Officer: LTJG Calvin S. Baker

Medical Department
Medical Officer: CDR Laura Raye Moore, M.D.
Dental Officer: LT Fred S. Rue
Chief Pharmacist Mate: CPO Nathan C. Post, P.N.

Air Group
Commander Air Group: CDR Teresa B. Ellison
  (Alley Cat)
Flight Deck Officer: LT Paul J. Peyton (Duke)
Aircraft Maintenance Officer: LT Willard L. Ireland
Squadron Commanders:
  VA-65 "Tigers" AttackRon: LCDR Patrick N.
    Bellinger (Bells)
  VP-35 "Black Panthers" PatrolRon: LCDR Meryl
    P. Delano (Flak)
  VC-50 TransportRon: LCDR Virginia S. Geiger (Tikki)

Marine Battalion
Marine Officer: Major Bartholomew C. Clinch
      Battalion Sergeant Major Joseph McIvers

Marine Company A: Captain Presley N. O'Bannon
    First Sergeant Solomon Wren
    First Lieutenant Daniel Carmick
    First Lieutenant Archibald Henderson
Marine Company B: Captain John M. Gamble
    First Sergeant Luke Quinn
    First Lieutenant George H. Terrett
    Second Lieutenant Anthony Gale
Marine Company C: Captain Samuel Miller
    First Sergeant Jeff Mackie
    First Lieutenant Alvin Edson
    Second Lieutenant Chester G. McCawley

Other Characters

The President of the United States of America

Rex C. Hill, Gen USAF (Ret.), National Security Advisor

Alan M. Dekker, Director, CIA, Langley, Virginia

The Honorable Henry W. Foster, U.S. Secretary of State

The Honorable John D. Long, U.S. Secretary of Defense

The Honorable H. W. Gilmore, U.S. Secretary of the Navy

General Tony R. Lundberg, USAF, Chairman, Joint Chiefs of Staff

ADM George L. Street, USN, Chief of Naval Operations

RADM Dolores T. McCarthy, USN, Chief of Naval Intelligence

VADM Admiral Richard H. Kane, USN, CINCPAC, Pearl Harbor, Hawaii

The Honorable Robertson Earl Abbott III, U.S. Ambassador to Republik Sulawesi

Lowden Manwaring, Chargé d'affaires, U.S. Embassy, Makasar, Republik Sulawesi

LCDR Herbert K. Hewitt, USN, Military and Naval Attaché, U.S. Embassy, Makasar, Republik Sulawesi

The Honorable Kertanargara Vijaya, Foreign Minister, Republik Sulawesi

General Achin Helamahera, Defense Minister, Republik Sulawesi

Abdul Haras Subandrio, Portmaster, Makasar, Republik Sulawesi

CAPT Dao Ling Qian, NPRC, Commanding Officer, Patrol Submarine S.49 *Bei fung,* Navy of the People's Republic of China

APPENDIX II

The Ship
SSCV-26 U.S.S. *Shenandoah*
A Rivers Class Fusion-powered
Aircraft Carrier Submarine

Specifications:
Length: 390 meters
Beam: 35 meters
Draft: 12 meters
Displacement: 51,000 tons standard, 58,700 tons dived
Members of Class: SSCV-26 U.S.S. *Shenandoah*
                    SSCV-27 U.S.S. *Sacramento*
                    SSCV-28 U.S.S. *Sabine*
                    SSCV-29 U.S.S. *Susquehanna*
                    SSCV-30 U.S.S. *Savannah*

Complement:
   Ship: 31 officers + 410 ratings
   Air Division: 52 officers + 172 ratings (3 squadrons)
   Marine Battalion: 13 officers + 72 enlisted men

Propulsion:
   Two Deseret Energy Corporation Type PF9N fusion
generators producing 280,000 kW delivering steam to
four sets of General Jet Corporation Coanda aquajets
and position thrusters

Performance:
   Maximum speed 48 knots submerged; diving depth
400 meters operational, 600 meters maximum

Armament:
Eight 500-millimeter amidships tubes for 24 anti-submarine, anti-ship, and submarine-to-surface missiles. Four 50-millimeter multipurpose rapid-fire deck guns

Electronics:
One SPY-48 multipurpose phased array search and track radar; two BQQ-54 multipurpose sonars; one LDR-7 long-range wide-angle sweeping laser range finder; various satellite and long-wave communications equipment; one WSS-1 mass detector; one BRC-98 scalar wave communications system

Remarks:
The Rivers class boats are the US Navy's new large carrier submarines replacing or complimenting the smaller Admiral class SSCVs. The boats of the Rivers class incorporate two larger flight decks, improved hangar deck facilities, and a new hull designed with advanced computational fluid dynamics and built with high-strength nonmetallic composite materials. This nonmetallic hull aids in evading the usual ASW sensors designed to locate metal boat hulls. The advanced design permits shallow surface running draft, allowing the boats to utilize most harbors. The propulsion system is extremely quiet because of the convection-type steam generators and the collapsing-condensing steam-fed aquajets, but also offers extremely low thermal signature when running submerged. While the Rivers class boats do not have the sprint speed of the Chinese Bravo Delta or Han boats, their underwater stealth characteristics coupled with an outstanding sensor fit and Mark 16 artificial intelligence equipment allow them to operate over extremely long ranges with minimum escort and logistic support. The primary mission of the Rivers class boats is naval power projection with the capability of self-defense combined with hard-hitting offensive power from attack air squadrons and Marine battalions.

APPENDIX III:

Glossary of Terms and Acronyms

(*Note*: A = Air Group term
M = Marine unit term
S = Ship term
G = General military/naval term

ALO: (G) Active Level of Operation readiness. Every unit has one. Usually it varies according to the whims of the high brass and how badly CNO and JCS want to assign a tough mission to an exhausted, depleted ship or outfit.

Anchor watch: (S) Personnel available for night work. When not standing watch, eating, sleeping, or recreating, naval personnel work on professional advancement, maintenance, repairs, sweepdown, and other tasks that must get done because no one else is available to do them. Some personnel standing day watches thus become available for night work.

AOG: (A) Aircraft on the ground. A grounded aircraft that is damaged or needs unavailable parts. An expensive naval aircraft is worthless unless it is either flying or flight-capable. "AOG" therefore is a super-emergency get-it-fixed-quick term applied equally to aircraft or any other air division equipment.

AP: (M) Anti-personnel. Applied to ammo, bombs, mines, or the first sergeant's latest set of work detail assignments.

APV: (M) Armored Personnel Vehicle. A small, lightly armored, fast vanlike vehicle intended to give Marines the false sense of security that they're safe from incoming while inside.

ARD: (S) A floating dry dock. Sometimes an SSCV or SSF must undergo hull repairs. The Navy maintains a few floating dry dock ships that can go to a damaged SS and repair it.

ARS: (S) A submarine salvage vessel. The sort of ship submariners greatly dislike. They hope they never have to call for one.

Artificial Intelligence or AI: (G) Very fast computer modules with large memories which can simulate some functions of human thought and decision-making processes by bringing together many apparently disconnected pieces of data, making simple evaluations of the priority of each, and making simple decisions concerning what to do, how to do it, when to do it, and what to report to the human being in control.

ASAP: (G) As soon as possible.

ASW: (G) Anti-submarine warfare. Engaged in between submarines and sometimes between surface vessels and submarines. Often undeclared. Submariners believe in only two types of ships: submarines and targets.

AT: (M) Anti-tank. Refers to ammo, guns, missiles, or mines. Few main battle tanks are left in the twenty-first-century world because of the effectiveness of shoulder-launched and air-launched AT weapons.

Bag: (A) Flight suit. So named because the standard-issue full-length coverall-type flight suit is extremely baggy. Naval aviators, both male and female, have to be in outstanding physical condition and therefore arrange for smartly and tautly tailored bags. Some have opted for the tight-fitting combination flight suits and g-suits. A non-flying naval type can always be spotted on the flight deck by the baggy, non-tailored issue flight suit.

Bingo: (A) Minimum fuel for a comfortable and safe return. When you hit bingo fuel, you'd better either have the carrier in sight or have picked out a suitable "bingo field" to land on because you will shortly descend.

Binnacle: (S) The stand or enclosure for a compass. Not often used in SSCVs because of sophisticated space-borne and other electronic navigational systems. A magnetic compass is still carried "just in case" the electronics suffer a nervous breakdown, something the earth's magnetic field has never been known to do.

Blue U: (G) The United States Aerospace Force Academy at Colorado Springs, Colorado. A term usually spoken with varying degrees of derision because the Aerospace Force stole blue as a service uniform color back in the days of the "wild blue yonder." The Navy, whose uniforms have been blue for much longer, has never really forgiven the Aerospace Force for stealing the Navy's color.

Blue water ops: (G) SSCV operations beyond the reach of land bases that can be reached by CAG aircraft or Marine unit boats. This is what the SSCVs were designed for. A submarine in a harbor or coastal waters is like a gazelle in a pen.

Bohemian Brigade: (G) War correspondents or a news media television crew. Highly disciplined military and naval personnel often dislike the sloppy appearance, sloppy dress, and sloppy discipline of news media people. The Navy assigns officers to cater to the news media in hopes that the media people will leave the rest of the real Navy types alone to do what they're paid for.

Bolter: (A) An aircraft landing attempt aboard a carrier that is aborted, forcing the pilot to take the aircraft around again, thus screwing up the whole recovery flight pattern. Once was more common when the Navy pilots landed jets on CVs and CVNs, an operation that involved crashing onto the deck under full military jet power. With VSTOL aircraft on SSCVs, a bolter usually occurs because of a screw-up in approach control, a damaged aircraft, an injured pilot, or bad weather.

Boomer: (G) A nuclear-powered ballistic missile submarine. Some of these are still in commission in the U.S. Navy, more in the navies of other nations. In a world where it doesn't pay to use thermonuclear area weapons, the dominant role of the SSBN diminished in favor of SSCVs and other sea control ships capable of dealing more effectively with brush fire and regional conflicts.

Braceland: (G) Naval slang referring to the United States Military Academy at West Point, New York. The Naval Academy operates with a far more sophisticated plebe disciplinary system involving more psychological pressure than physical abuse.

Briefback: (A) (M) (S) A highly detailed discussion of the intended mission in which all commanders participating take part. Some of the plan is in the computers, but not all of it because technology has been known to fail when most urgently needed. Therefore, the operational plan is always presented then briefed-back to ensure that it has been committed to human memory as well as computer memory.

Bug juice: (S) Fruit punch available from the galley at any time. The Navy still runs on coffee day and night, but fruit juices contain roughage and vitamins that coffee doesn't.

Burdened vessel: (S) The vessel required to take action to avoid collision. The burden of maneuver is on the vessel that must alter its course. In twenty-first-century submarine jargon, a burdened vessel is the one that makes contact first and upon which the burden of initiating attack rests. The submarine captain is the one who actually bears the burden of decision making under these conditions.

CAG: Commander Air Group, the SSCV's chief pilot. Or "carrier air group," the SSCV's aircraft complement.

CAP: (A) Combat Air Patrol, one or more flights of fighter or fighter-attack aircraft put aloft over a carrier submarine to protect the ship against attack from the air.

Cat's paw: (S) A puff of wind.

CP: (G) Command Post.

Channel fever: (S) A predictable behavior pattern

of the crew after a long submerged patrol as the ship approaches its base or a tender.

Check minus-x: (G) Look behind you. In terms of coordinates, plus-x is ahead, minus-x is behind, plus-y is to the right, minus-y is left, plus-z is up, and minus-z is down.

CIC: (G) Combat Information Center. May be different from a command post. On an SSCV, it is usually located in the control room which is the brainlike nerve center of the ship.

CINC: (G) Commander In Chief.

CJSC: (G) Chairman of the Joint Chief of Staff.

Class 6 supplies: (G) Alcoholic beverages of high ethanol content procured through nonregulation channels; officially, only five classes of supplies exist.

CNO: (G) Chief of Naval Operations.

CO: (G) Commanding Officer.

COD: (A) Carrier Onboard Delivery aircraft used to transfer personnel and cargo to and from the SSCV.

Column of ducks: (M) A convoy proceeding through terrain where it is likely to draw fire. Has also been applied by submarine officers to the juicy torpedo target of a convoy proceeding in line astern.

Comber: (S) A deep-water wave.

Confused sea: (S) A rough sea without a pattern.

Conshelf: (S) The continental shelf.

Crabtown: The city of Annapolis, Maryland, so-called by U.S. Naval Academy midshipmen because of the famed seafood of the area.

CRAF: (G) Civil Reserve Air Fleet. Nonmilitary commercial aircraft of all designations and sizes that the government has paid to have militarized or navalized. All or part of the CRAF can be called up in an emergency to provide airlift support for the Department of Defense at taxpayers' expense. However, the concept of the CRAF means that the government doesn't have to buy large numbers of aircraft and maintain them for use only in emergencies.

Creamed: (G) Greased, beaten, conquered, overwhelmed.

Crush depth: (S) The depth at which the water pressure causes the pressure hull of a submarine to implode. The "never exceed" depth of a ship, numbers that are deeply engraved in the memories of the ship's officers and operating crew.

CTAF: (A) Common Traffic Advisory Frequency. A radio communications frequency set aside for use by all aircraft where ground control frequencies and facilities such as airport control towers don't exist. These are normally in the VHF frequency spectrum and can be monitored and used by any radio-equipped aircraft.

CYA: (G) Cover Your Ass. In polite company, "Cover Your Anatomy."

Dead reckoning: (S) (A) A method of navigation using direction and amount of progress from the last well-determined position to a new position. Not a widely used or desirable navigational method in the twenty-first century, but a method still taught for use in an emergency. Most officers reckon that if they have to use it, there's a high probability they'll be dead soon after. Actually, derived from the term "deduced reckoning."

Dead water: (S) A thin layer of fresher water over a deeper layer of more saline water. Dead water causes problems with sonar if you're looking for a target. On the other hand, dead water can be turned to an advantage if you're trying to avoid contact.

Deep scattering layer: (S) An ocean layer that scatters sounds of echoes vertically. Some submarines can dive deep enough to make use of this phenomenon nearly everywhere. If you can get into a deep scattering layer, enemy sonar can be confused and even lose track of you. When the enemy uses this ploy, it becomes more than frustrating.

Degaussing: (S) Reducing the magnetic field of a ship to protect against magnetic mines. With the twenty-first-century naval vessels using titanium and composite hulls, degaussing has become less of a requirement. Modern SSCVs and SSFs cause practically zero magnetic anomaly.

Density layer: (S) A layer of water in which density changes sufficiently to increase buoyancy. This can raise hell with a commanding officer's planned operation by causing the ship to inadvertently change its running depth. A density layer can also cause sonar anomalies. Apparently the new masdets aren't immune to this, either.

Dodger: (S) Once a term applied to a canvas windshield on an exposed bridge. Since the topside surface bridge on an SSCV is on the retractable tower, this term has been applied to it.

Dog: (S) A metal fitting used to close ports and hatches.

Dolphin Club: (S) That portion of an naval vessel unofficially set aside exclusively for privacy between male and female crew members. Like the U.S.S. *Tuscarora*, it doesn't officially exist. However, no captain who is concerned about the physical and mental health of his mixed crew prohibits the establishment of the Dolphin Club on his ship. It is closed temporarily only during Condition Two and General Quarters. Or for longer periods of time if members of the crew abuse the privilege.

Double nuts or coconuts: (A) The CAG's aircraft usually has a ship's operational or squadron number ending in 00. This has been corrupted, in the usual bad taste of hot pilots, in the term "double nuts" if the CAG is male or "coconuts" if the CAG is female. However, the ladies who fly and otherwise occupy combat positions look upon such tasteless slang as indicating that they are "one of the boys"; they have been accepted. Some personal pilot call names are even more tasteless.

ECM: (G) Electronic countermeasures.

ELINT: (G) Electronic intelligence gathering.

FCC: (G) Federal Communications Commission.

FEBA: (M) Forward Edge of the Battle Area.

FIDO: (A) (M) Acronym for "Fuck it; drive on!" Overcome your obstacle or problem and get on with the operation.

FIG: (G) Foreign Internal Guardian mission, the sort of assignment American military units draw to protect American interests in selected locations around the world. Also known as "saving the free world for greed and lechery."

Following sea: (S) Waves moving in the same general direction as the ship. Therefore, they break over the ship with less force.

Fort Fumble: (M) Any headquarters, but especially the Pentagon when not otherwise specified. Some naval officers call the Pentagon the "Potomac Interim Training Station." More often, they use the acronym for that.

Fox one (two, three, or four): (A) A radio call signifying that a specific type of attack is about to be or has been initiated. The meanings have changed over the years as new weapons have entered service. Fox One is the simplest sort of attack, usually with guns. Fox Four is an attack with complex weapons such as missiles.

Fracture zone: (S) An area of breaks in underwater rocks such as sea mounts, ridges, and troughs. Nice places to hide if you're pinned down and want to become invisible to sonar.

Freshet: (S) An area of fresh water at the mouth of a stream flowing into the sea. Can change the water density, which in turn changes the buoyancy of a submarine. Something that navigators try to warn submarine commanders about well in advance.

Frogmen: (S) Underwater demolition personnel, crazy people who don scuba and flippers and then go out to play with high explosives having a high probability of going bang while they're working with them.

Furball: (G) A complex, confused fight, battle, or operation.

GA: (G) "Go ahead!"

Galley yarn: (G) A shipboard rumor. Much the same as "scuttlebutt." Usually clears through the nebulous Rumor Control Department.

Gig: (S) The ship's boat for the use of the commanding officer.

Glory hole: (G) The chief petty officer's quarters aboard ship.

Golden BB: (A) (M) A small-caliber bullet that hits where least expected and most damaging, thus creating large problems.

Greased: (A) (M) Beaten, conquered, overwhelmed, creamed.

Hangfire: (G) The delayed detonation of an explosive charge.

Horsewhip: (S) The ship's commissioning pennant, rarely flown from a submarine. Refers to English Admiral William Blake's gesture of hoisting a horsewhip to his masthead to indicate his intention to chastise the enemy.

Hull down: (S) A ship slightly visible on the horizon.

Humper: (G) Any device whose actual name can't be recalled at the moment. Also "hummer" or "puppy."

ID or i-d: (G) Identification.

IFR: (A) Instrument flight rules, permitting relatively safe operation in conditions of limited visibility. Usually conducted through clouds that contain rocks ("cumulo granite").

Intelligence: (G) Generally considered to exist in four categories—animal, human, machine, and military.

Internal wave: (S) A wave that occurs within a fluid whose density changes with depth.

"I've lost the bubble": (S) "I'm confused and in trouble."

IX: (S) Designation for an unclassified miscellaneous vessel or target.

JCS: (G) Joint Chiefs of Staff.

JIC.: (G) Just In Case.

KE: (G) Kinetic energy as applied to KE-kill weapons. Missiles that kill or destroy by virtue of their impact energy.

Kedge: (S) To move a ship by means of a line attached to a small anchor—also called a kedge—dropped at the desired position.

"Keep the bubble": (S) Maintain exactly the angle of incline or decline called for. Also maintain a level head, a cool stool, and a hot pot at General Quarters.

Klick: (G) A kilometer, a measure of distance.

Lighter: (S) A bargelike vessel used to load or unload a ship. Usually welcomed by SSCV and SSF crews who have been on long patrols and are beginning to run out of such essentials as ice cream and toilet paper.

Log bird: (A) A logistics or supply aircraft. For an SSCV, as welcome as a lighter. (See above.)

Mad minute: (G) The first intense, chaotic, wild, frenzied period of a fire fight when it seems every gun in the world is being shot at you.

"The Man": (G) Term used to designate the President of the United States, the Commander in Chief.

Masdet: (S) The highly classified mass detector sensor system used on a submarine. Has replaced passive sonar (which is nevertheless still carried). A trained masdet operator (masdetter) can determine bearing, depth, and (if the displacement of the target is known) range of an underwater object. Masdet will not work across the sea surface interface.

Midrats: (S) The fourth daily meal served in a submarine, usually at midnight, ship's time.

Mike-mike: (M) Marine shorthand for "millimeter."

MRE: (M) Officially, Meal Ready to Eat; Marines claim it means "Meal Rarely Edible."

NCO: (M) Noncommissioned officer.

No joy: (A) (M) Failure to make visual or other contact.

Non-qual: (S) A person fresh from submarine school who is being taught firsthand how a submarine operates by on-the-job training, usually under the watchful eye of a petty officer.

NSC: (G) National Security Council.

OOD: (S) The Officer of the Desk, the officer in charge who represents the Captain.

Order of battle: (S) The disposition of ships as they ready for combat. Or the personnel roster of a Marine or Army unit.

Oscar briefing: (G) An orders briefing, a meeting where commanders give final orders to their subordinates.

Our chickens: (S) Term originating from the World War II submarine service, where it referred to friendly aircraft detailed to escort submarines engaged in rescuing downed pilots. Has been appropriated by SSCV crews to describe the aircraft based aboard their ships.

Papa briefing: (G) A planning briefing, a meeting during which operational plans are developed.

Phantom bottom: (S) A false sea bottom registered by electronic depth finders.

Playland on the Severn: (G) Derogatory term applied to the United States Naval Academy by those who never attended same. Not used in the presence of an Academy graduate without suffering the consequences.

Poopie suit: (S) Navy blue coveralls worn in a submarine.

PRIFLY: (A) The primary flight control bridge of a carrier submarine where the CAG and others can direct air operations.

Pucker factor: (G) The detrimental effect on the human body that results from an extremely hazardous situation, such as being shot at.

Q-ship: (S) A disguised man-of-war used to decoy enemy submarines. Submariners don't give any quarter to such deception on the part of the enemy, the only good Q-ship being one that's permanently on the bottom.

Rack: (S) A submariner's bed or bunk.

Red jacket: (S) A steward in the officer's wardroom/mess.

Reg Twenty-twenty: (A) (M) (S) Slang reference to Naval Regulation 2020, which prohibits physical contact between male and female personnel when on duty except for that required in the conduct of official business.

Rigged for red: (S) The control room lighting set for night operations. Was once deep-red lighting. Term remains in use meaning ready to operate under Condition Red or general quarters.

Rips: (S) A turbulent agitation of water, generally caused by interaction of currents and winds. If this occurs deep, it can tear a submarine hull apart by simultaneously stressing it in many directions at once. A large submarine hull that will handle rips above a certain level of turbulent activity cannot be designed and built.

Rough log: (S) The original draft version of a log. The rough log is later loaded into the ship's computer memory where it becomes the final log. The rough log can be corrected before becoming the final log.

Rules of Engagement or ROE: (G) Official restrictions on the freedom of action of a commander or soldier in his confrontation with an opponent that act to increase the probability that said commander or soldier will lose the combat, all other things being equal.

SADARM: (M) Search-and-destroy armor, a kind of warhead. Navy types do not like this warhead because it can wreak havoc against the exposed portion of a ship on the surface.

Salinity: (S) The quantity of dissolved salts in seawater. The degree of salinity affects the density and thus the buoyancy of the water, an important operational factor to a submarine.

Scroom!: (A) (M) Abbreviation for "Screw 'em!" Rarely if ever used by line naval officers; however, some CPOs and petty officers have been heard voicing it.

Scuppers: (S) Fittings on weather decks that allow water to drain overboard.

SECDEF: (G) Secretary of Defense.

Sheep screw: (G) A disorganized, embarrassing, graceless, chaotic fuck-up.

Sierra Hotel: (A) What pilots say when they can't say, "Shit hot!"

Simple servant: (G) A play on "civil servant" who is an employee of the "silly service."

Simulator or sim: (A) A device that can simulate the sensations perceived by a human being and the results of the human's responses. A simple toy computer or video game simulating the flight of an aircraft or the driving of a race car is an example of a primitive simulator.

Sit-guess: (M) Slang for "estimate of the situation," an educated guess about your predicament. Rarely used by submariners, who eschew such contractions for fear they could be misunderstood.

Sit-rep: (M) Short for "situation report" to notify your superior officer about the sheep screw you're in at the moment. Rarely used by submariners. (See above.)

Sked: (G) Shorthand term for "schedule."

Skimmer: (S) A submariner's term for a surface ship.

Skunk: (S) An unidentified surface ship contact.

Snivel: (A) (M) To complain about the injustice being done you.

SP: (G) Shore Patrol, the unit put ashore during liberty to maintain law and order among the ship's crew. SP works closely with local law enforcement authorities.

Spook: (G) Slang term for either a spy or a military

intelligence specialist. Also used as a verb relating to reconnaissance.

Staff stooge: (G) Derogatory term referring to a staff officer. Also "staff weenie."

SS: (G) U.S. Navy designation for a submarine.

SSCV: (G) Aircraft carrier submarine.

SSF (G) Fusion-powered fast attack submarine.

SSN: (G) Nuclear-powered fast attack submarine.

Strakes: (S) Continuous lines of fore and aft planking or a raised thin rib or fluid dynamic fence running lengthwise along the outer hull.

Submariner: (S) A person who serves or has served in a submarine and is qualified to wear the Double Dolphins. Always pronounced "sub-mareener" because "sub-mariner" implies a less than qualified seaman.

SWC: (S) Scalar wave communications, a highly classified communications system that allows a submerged submarine to communicate with other submarines and shore facilities.

TAB-V: (A) Theater Air Base Vulnerability shelter. Naval aviators consider all Air Force bases to be vulnerable. Air Force pilots feel the same way about SSCVs.

TACAMO!: (G) "Take Charge And Move Out!" Also a radio and scalar wave communications relay aircraft stationed at critical points for the purposes of communications integrity.

Tango Sierra: (G) Tough shit.

Target bearing: (S) The compass direction of a target from a firing ship.

TBS: (G) Talk Between Ships. A short-range communications system. Originally a World War II short-range radio set. The submarine service now uses a scalar wave communications set designed especially for this service with a range of about a hundred klicks.

TDC: (S) Target data computer. Originally "torpedo data computer." However, the tendency of the traditionalists to hang on to acronyms resulted in this one's being held over and converted for use with any of the many weapons systems on an SSCV.

TDU: (S) Trash disposal unit. The garbage dump on a submarine. A vertical tube that ejects packaged garbage which is weighted to sink to the bottom.

Tech-weenie: (G) The derogatory term applied by military people to the scientists, engineers, and technicians who complicate a warrior's life by insisting that the armed services have gadgetry that is the newest, fastest, most powerful, most accurate, and usually the most unreliable products of their fertile techie imaginations.

Tender: (S) A logistics support and repair ship. Like lighters and log birds, SSCV crews—who have been long at sea and are running short of everything—love to see these. Not much good for liberty, but a chance to go topside for sunshine and fresh air while the ship is tied up alongside.

Three-Dolphin Rating: (S) A humorous reference applied to a submariner who has paid a visit to the Dolphin Club. Refers to the fact that three dolphins are required for two of them to mate underwater. The "Two-Dolphin Rating" is the right of a person to wear the two-dolphin badge of a qualified submariner.

Tiger error: (A) What happens when an eager pilot tries too hard.

TO&E: (G) Table of Organization and Equipment.

Topsiders: (S) Rubber-soled cloth shoes worn in a submarine and when going topside on a surfaced submarine. Also known as "Jesus creepers" because someone wearing them can move with almost total silence.

TRACON: (A) A civilian Terminal Radar Control facility at an airport.

Trick: (S) A helmsman's watch at the wheel.

Umpteen hundred: (G) Some time in the distant, undetermined future.

U.S.S. Tuscarora: (S) An imaginary ship that has been in commission in the United States Navy since

World War I. Somehow, it never makes port when any other ship is there and is never refitted or dry-docked. Yet it always seems to have officers and a crew. Every seagoing naval person claims either to have served aboard the ship or to have actually seen the ship in some far off port of call. However, usually it has departed just the day before.

VLF: (G) Very Low Frequency radio wavelength. Rarely used by the Navy in its submarine service in the twenty-first century.

VTOL: (A) A vertical take off and landing aircraft type utilizing surface blowing or Coanda Effect to achieve lift at zero forward airspeed.

XO: (G) Executive Officer, the Number Two officer in a ship, air unit, or Marine unit.

Yaw: (S) The port-starboard rotation of a ship around her vertical axis.

ZI: (G) Zone of the Interior, the continental United States.

Zip gun: (S) The retractable radar-directed high-rate fully automatic 50-millimeter gun that is deployed topside by an SSCV when necessary to take care of approaching close-in unfriendlies or targets. Progeny of the twentieth-century Phoenix CWIS or the Goalkeeper system. Zip guns can also detect and handle incoming targets directly overhead, thus providing defense against space-launched anti-ship KE weapons that can go right through a submarine from deck to keel. Zip guns can't penetrate the armor of some surface ships, but can make life difficult for anyone topside on such a ship. Zip guns all have the 1775 Navy Jack painted on them, the flag with the thirteen red and white stripes, the rattlesnake, and the legend "Don't tread on me." And for good reason.